Cartledge Creek

ISBN: 978-1-7353545-2-1 (Paperback)
ISBN: 978-1-7353545-3-8 (e-book)

BISAC Subject Headings:
FIC002000 FICTION / Action & Adventure
FIC014060 FICTION / Historical / Civil War Era
FIC032000 FICTION / War & Military

Address all correspondence to:
Fireship Press, LLC
P.O. Box 68412
Tucson, AZ 85737

Visit our website at:
www.fireshippress.com

Praise for *Cartledge Creek*

Through its intimate focus on one plantation-owning family, *Cartledge Creek* illuminates the irreconcilable human conflicts that caused and ended the Civil War. Sam McGee's gifted storytelling connects us to and makes us care deeply about his complex characters as they live these conflicts: the blindness to the stark inhumanity of slavery, and the tension between southerners who welcomed the war that secession destined and those—like patriarch Alfred Dockery—who opposed secession and warned of the bloodbath and ruin it would bring.

With almost photographic accuracy, McGee captures episode after episode of battlefield courage, making us near-participants in the grim brutality of the face to face combat that inevitably brought horrendous suffering to a generation of young men who fought for or against a lost, wrong cause. McGee paints searingly the pain of a lost limb or a lost brother, but, in young Jim Dockery, he demonstrates the power of human resilience born of the hope for reconnection with family and with a possible soulmate.

—**Jonathan E. Buchan, Jr.**, Author of *Code of the Forest*

Cartledge Creek is a vivid journey into the heart and heat of the Civil War, both a moving family saga and an arresting story of defeat and lost time. Sam McGee spreads it out before us in well-crafted prose, a complex and intricate plot, and unforgettable characters. Battle, cold, disease, death, sometimes even hope and joy—McGee takes us into the smell and feel of it. We march along with the people and the indomitable spirit that carries them through. This novel is a good read, but more than that, it's a deep and meaningful look at the past.

—**Walter Bennett**, Author of *The Lawyer's Myth* and *Leaving Tuscaloosa*

I found *Cartledge Creek* a refreshing and touching look at some very contradictory issues in southern history. Sam McGee is a born storyteller, perhaps something he inherited from the oral tradition of his ancestors. He has created a vibrant new chapter in stories of the South ... Jim's journey from battle to imprisonment to home and beyond is a testament to the power of the human spirit to overcome all odds set to mar one's path ... I was swept away by this powerful family drama.

—**5-Star Review, Readers' Favorite**

Dedication

In loving memory of my grandmother, Lib Covington. She heard these stories on the front porch from her grandmother, who lived them. Then, on the same porch, she told them to me.

Preface

My late mother, Hannah Covington McGee, was the most devoted reader of every never-to-be-published scribble I ever wrote. She told me she loved them all. When my wife Marci came along, it didn't take me long to realize that every word I wrote, I wrote for her. When our children Hannah Cole McGee and Brooks Covington McGee entered our lives, I truly understood the importance of passing along the story of our family, without deleting the ugly parts. Few people on Earth get to live in a home with as much love in it as ours.

Perhaps my biggest challenge in writing this novel about the real story of my actual family, was how to deal with the complexity of my ancestors. How could some of them have done so many valuable things with their lives, but been so squarely on the wrong side of history? Over the last several years, the Brick House has been visited by several descendants of Alfred Dockery's slaves. One Easter a few years ago, I found myself standing in the Dockery family cemetery struggling out loud to figure out how to present the whole truth about General

Dockery, and asking the advice of the great-granddaughter of one of his slaves. That conversation helped me decide how to address the issue. Many thanks to Holly Carr.

I have had several dedicated readers/editors of various drafts of this book. My father and brother (Jerry and Ryan McGee) —both fine authors themselves — each gave excellent suggestions. Bob Inman, another excellent writer, gave me way more of his time and attention than I warranted, and provided invaluable advice. Thanks also to Christian Bohmfalk, John Gresham and Kris Lawton for reading drafts. Kris read each chapter as they rolled out, and has read the completed manuscript at least three times. Mike Burgess, a fine student of the Civil War, gave the final manuscript a read for historical checks.

Before any of this could happen, I had to believe I could write. I have two teachers to thank for that. One of them may not even remember me. Mrs. Ribelin was my seventh grade English teacher, and the first person to convince me I could one day be a decent writer. I had JoAnn Clanton for English in the ninth and eleventh grades, and she encouraged my writing as much as anyone I have ever known. One college professor stands out as well. Ralph Wood gave me both the highest praise and the harshest criticism I ever received for my writing. I deserved at least one of the two.

This book took a great deal of research. Although there were too many sources to mention, my best source was the family oral tradition as conveyed by Grandma. After that, I learned a lot from the writings of Michael Horigan, Rod Gragg, James I. "Bud" Robertson, Jr., Shelby Foote, Richard Triebe, Irving Long and John Hutchinson. And I was inspired by Ambrose Bierce, Stephen Crane and Michael Shaara.

Although the oral tradition as passed down to me from Lib Covington was my primary guiding star, I spent a great deal of time and effort comparing and connecting these stories to the historical record. Sometimes there was a perfect fit, sometimes there was not. At times I found myself looking at conflicting accounts, challenging timelines, or simple differences of opinion. Hopefully my family will forgive me for having to make some choices, sometimes based on historical fit, others to stay true to a story as I first heard it, and others because they helped me present the story in the best way I could. At the end of the day, some details or personality traits have been lost to history, and I did my best to fill the gaps. Most of what you see in this book really happened, but it is necessarily still a work of historical fiction.

Thanks to Susan Reid for raising Marci, and for being the splendid caretaker of the Brick House. Suzy, you are a human ball of energy.

Finally, thanks to Mary Lou Monahan, Jacquie Cook, and everyone at Fireship Press. I needed a chance, and they gave me one.

Cartledge Creek

SAM MCGEE

FIRESHIP
PRESS

PART I

Prologue

Elmira, NY
January, 1865

A lone frail figure stood in the middle of the frozen pond, shivering. He had not always been alone. There had been friends, close ones. Fellow soldiers stripped of their cause. Left with the sole common cause of survival. All dead now, or sent home to die out of sight.

A fresh layer of snow covered the camp. There were no footprints to be seen along the hill that sloped down from the tents and barracks to the pond. The pale morning light revealed only a smooth blanket of white. Even Jim's footprints, made moments ago, were already gone. If he fell through the ice, there would be no evidence he had been there at all.

A biting wind rolled down from the distant mountains and over the prison wall. A dust of snow lifted from the edge of the pond and skipped across the surface at Jim's feet. A chill spread up through his frozen legs, the wind finding every rip and tear in his ragged gray uniform. The shaking in his knees became so violent he could barely stand.

The tattered pant-legs flapped loosely in the wind, brushing against what remained of his legs. The waist had been rolled up several rolls to prevent them from falling to his ankles. Now the pant bottoms stopped mid-calf, revealing emaciated legs, one with a poorly healed, round scar the size of a musket ball. The shirt that had fit snugly when issued just two years prior hung so loose it gave no indication of his form. His cheeks were sunken, his eyes hollow. The hair withered and brittle like that of an old man. An old man of twenty years.

Jim stared intently at the white-frozen pond beneath him. The freeze could not erase the memory of the pond in summer. Both bathhouse and latrine to the thousands of condemned souls crammed within the walls of the stockade. The stench in the summer heat a constant reminder of the specter of disease hovering above the pond, descending upon every prisoner at its own pace.

Somehow he had escaped illness since his arrival in summer. Overcome near certain death on a daily basis. But he could not escape starvation. He was dying now. After all he had survived. All he had done to stay alive. Willfully keeping death at bay. Finally dying this time. An insidious death. Wasting away. Soon when the Death Wagon made its daily morning rounds, he too would be carried around the pond to the Dead House.

He had walked on ice once as a boy. The swimming hole in Cartledge Creek had frozen just once during an extended cold snap. Jim, his brothers, and his cousin Ben Covington had gotten running starts and slid across the creek on their bellies with their arms outstretched. Screaming and laughing from the joyous novelty of the frozen creek. There was one spot near the steep bank where the water bubbled from underneath the sheet of ice and ran unfrozen around the bend and out of sight. The moving water thinned the ice in an arc that spread out toward the solid top of the swimming hole. The older brothers warned the younger to steer clear of the spot for fear the ice would give way. Some of the Dockery boys ventured recklessly close to the thinner ice. Not Jim. The thought of crashing into the icy water below kept him well away. He could handle anything but bitter cold. Otherwise the boys' greatest fear was the scolding they would receive from Anna, the head house servant, if they tracked snow onto the fine rugs scattered about the heart of pine floors of their father's mansion.

There was no such weakness in the ice of Foster's Pond. Of that Jim was certain. He had searched. That's why he had come out into the frozen darkness. To find a weakness in the ice where he could break through and disappear. Starvation be damned.

A small black spot appeared in his vision. It had happened before, in the months since his last good meal. He rubbed his eyes, hoping it would go away. It did not. He tried everything he could. Snapped his head from left to right, looked at objects near and far. The spot followed. Closing his eyes tightly and opening them wide again did not help. Two more spots formed. They began to grow and merge together, threatening to block out the entire frozen landscape. Peering desperately through the growing darkness he focused on the ice beneath him again. The raw, broken lips parted slightly. A sound escaped, barely audible even to himself.

"Crack open, ice … crack open and take me in."

Another dusting of snow flew low over the ice, each tiny flake dancing across the surface until settling and freezing immediately into its new home.

"Take me in, dammit! … please?"

Foster's Pond would not comply. The ice remained solid. The ever-expanding black spots merged together and Jim could see the ice no more.

Blind, he turned back in what he believed to be the direction of his barracks, and began sliding his feet in tiny steps across the ice.

To his left Jim felt a presence. One he had felt before, seen before. On the observation towers built by local businessmen eager to charge a modest fee for well-dressed townspeople to take in the horrid sight of the captured enemy. She had come to him there before, whether real or imagined. The long yellow dress. The perfect ringlets of brown hair dancing about her shoulders. The lively green eyes. Her presence known only to him, her gaze singling him out amongst the mass of dying men. Speaking words of encouragement only to his ears. "Home is waiting, and death can wait."

He stood ankle deep in snow and turned himself toward the presence. Even in the darkness that now held him, he saw her as he had seen her before. Heard her words again. Felt something stir down inside. The broken lips parted and he spoke aloud once more.

"Death *can* wait."

And so, yet again, Jim Dockery decided that it was not his day to die. He turned back to his original path and headed up the hill. Yet as he walked, he became less certain of the way. The snow at his feet kept him from feeling the road. No warmth from the sun could divide east from west. No fellow prisoners were there to guide him. He zigzagged aimlessly with his arms extended before his face, blocking unknown obstacles from his path. He grew even less certain, his pulse quickening. Having just decided to live, Jim now faced death again alone in the snow.

But there was a sound. One he had heard so many times before. One he heard each morning in his bunk as he fought to regain sleep alongside three other dying men. There was a wagon approaching.

One

Jim Dockery
February, 1861
Rockingham, NC

Jim sat alone on the wide front porch. There was a cool breeze that crept across the wooden planks. He closed his eyes and leaned back in the rocking chair and felt the sun on his face. It felt good to be outside under the sun, even if spring had yet to arrive.

The house was a fortress of red bricks, all made on site. The front porch was covered to shield the dark green rockers from the summer sun. But on this day Jim had pulled a rocker to the edge of the porch where the sunlight sliced its way into the shade. The grand front door was trimmed in white, as was the identical door that opened to a balcony just above. Rising from the porch to the roof were two massive white columns. Richmond County, like most in the state, was a collection of farms and plantations, all dotted with white farm houses. The handmade brick, white trim and federal detail set Alfred Dockery's house apart. Anywhere in the county it was known as simply, the Brick House.

At seventeen, Jim was fully grown, though not yet fully filled out. He was still a good deal thinner than his older brothers. His shoulders were square and strong from long days in his father's fields, but there was little spare meat on his bones. The hair was dark and cut short. The face solid, if unexceptional, with a dimple appearing on one side when he smiled, which was often. He was handsome in the way young men can be handsome when they finally shake off the awkwardness of their early teens. The face was calm and straight, but there was an excitement underneath that revealed itself through his eyes. Somewhere behind those serious, thoughtful eyes was a boy, and that boy was excited to see his father, and that father would be able to see it, whether the son wanted him to or not. As usual there was a book in his hand, unless of course there was a girl on his arm. There was always one or the other.

Two hounds burst from the thicket below the long lane to the house, signaling the arrival of their owner, General Alfred Dockery. They raced one another down the lane and headed left onto the Cartledge Creek Road until they reached the approaching wagon. Above the lane there were few trees, the fields visible to the horizon. Across the sprawling acres were horses and wagons and groupings of dark figures moving about amongst the winter wheat.

As the wagon turned in from the Cartledge Creek Road, Jim could make out the shapes of two large men sitting up front. They traveled down the slope of the lane and back up again, passing through the shadows of towering oaks.

Solomon worked the reins. He was a massive man. Even taller than the General, and at least as wide. As always, he was in formal attire. Whether accompanying General Dockery to the Legislature in Raleigh or helping Miss Anna in the house, he insisted on dressing to match his master's formality and status. He was insulted by suggestions this was not necessary. Thus, whenever the General's clothes began to show the slightest bit of wear, his wife Sally would sneak them out of the wardrobe to Miss Anna, who would alter them a bit and give them to Solomon. General Dockery noticed, but never said a word.

Most men as wealthy as the General rode in fine carriages, or at least in the backs of their wagons out of the weather. Alfred Dockery preferred to sit out front with his driver, taking in God's creation as he traveled. So up to the house they came. Two giants atop a plain wagon, nearly as big as the horses that strained to pull them. Both in formal attire. Solomon with his jet-black skin and head shaved clean, his master sitting beside him with his white skin and dramatically brushed back silver hair. One man wearing the hand-me-downs of the other.

Solomon stopped the wagon right at the front door. Through the door behind Jim appeared Miss Anna, the quiet yet unquestioned dictator of the Brick House. She had no doubt been busying herself in anticipation of the General's arrival home from the Legislature. Her hair was pulled tightly into its ever-present bun. Her small thick body hidden behind the ever-present white apron. She scowled at Jim for camping out on the porch waiting for his father, but said nothing. Jim smiled back at her knowingly as he stepped to the wagon and offered his father a hand. Alfred looked down from the wagon, the great man in formal dress with his striking hair and hawkish eyes. As he descended from the wagon his face softened, and he laughed at his son and his house servant alike.

"So what shall it be immediately upon my arrival home? The history lesson with my eager young son, or a survey of all the work that has been done in my absence from my dear drill sergeant, Miss Anna?"

Anna and Jim cut their eyes to one another. Anna smiled and took a step back.

"Mister Alfred, sir, I will be in the warming kitchen when you are ready. And, yes, I would love to show you all the work that's been done since you were here last. But I'll wait my turn. That boy's been waiting for you all afternoon."

Anna was gone as quickly as she had arrived. Solomon worked the horses back into motion, heading for the stables. Alfred stepped through the door and removed his coat, taking a deep breath and releasing the tension from his journey.

The two-story foyer was dominated by a grand staircase that rose to a landing, then curled around to the second floor. From floor to ceiling, the walls were covered in a formal, green wallpaper that depicted a fishing scene from a time when fishing was still done in formal dress. The floors were heart of pine planks nearly a foot wide, with single planks that ran the entire length of the room. Father and son turned right and passed into the parlor. The doorway to the parlor was sixteen inches thick, constructed of brick and then covered in wood panels painted a pale, cooling green.

Alfred and Solomon had become such efficient brick makers that the entire house was framed from bricks shaped by Alfred and fired by Solomon in a low-set brick-makers' shed that sat alongside the lane to the house. Every wall in the house was of the same formidable thickness and strength. In the formal parlor the brick walls were covered in plaster and painted a light cream, with fine moldings and trim of the same green as the doorway. The ceiling above was adorned with an ornately crafted plaster medallion made by a free black craftsman who had traveled down from Maryland at the risk of his own freedom. A well-tended fire burned in the fireplace, and light shone in from windows along the outside walls. There were two small settees facing one another. Jim and his father sat and looked each other in the eye, as they had done so many times before. After so many votes in Raleigh, so many books. Jim waited for his father to speak first.

"Did you finish it, Jim, the book?"

"Yes, sir."

"Very good. So what have we learned from Napoleon's attack on Russia?"

"Defensive tactics, of course."

"And?"

"Logistics. Keeping your army clothed, fed and armed."

"Tell me more, son."

"Russia was too big. They just kept retreating, burning things up and making sure the French army could not live off the land. Scorched earth, they called it. So Napoleon, he had no way to feed his army, or to keep them warm during a cold Russian winter. But he just kept coming anyway. Stubborn, I guess."

"The result?"

"The Russians defeated the greatest army on Earth. They killed 380,000 of them, most without firing a shot. The Russian winter got them."

"And the lesson?"

"You can't win a war without bullets, food and coats?"

"Well, that's easy enough. What else?"

"Don't go charging into a war you're not prepared to fight?"

"There we go, son. Excellent."

"So are we, Dad? About to charge into a war we aren't ready to fight?"

"Not yet, son. Not yet."

"Well, what happened in Raleigh? What was the result of the vote?"

The General stood, and his son did the same.

"Let's take a walk son, and I will tell you all about it."

Two

Alfred Dockery
January, 1861
Raleigh, NC

The Senate Chamber was alive. Reporters hounding senators about their votes. Young men waiting for messages to be written, then dashing off to deliver them. Others running into the room, handing folded papers to senators, then standing silently to one side, awaiting the written response. Here and there groups of men gathered and spoke. Arms gesturing. Little bursts of last-minute oratory vibrating from the arches, the balconies and the half-domed ceiling high above. Smoke always rising from each group.

General Alfred Dockery sat alone in a wooden chair looking out a window down onto the Capitol grounds. Hundreds stood bundled in the gray cold awaiting the result of the vote. Men in hats and long coats. Entire families huddled together, moving about slightly to fight the chill. Several North Carolina flags waved by young, enthusiastic supporters of the cause. A few United States flags out along the edge of the grounds. Police officers standing prominently among them. Straight-faced, ready to stop trouble before it started.

Dockery looked away from the window across the chamber. The neat rows of dark desks, angling toward the podium at the front of the room. One wide aisle passing between the rows. The dark red carpet lined with large gold stars. Two fireplaces were burning, one on each side of the podium, pushing back the cold that passed through the windows and slipped in the doors each time they opened to allow another messenger to pass. The pale blue walls trimmed with white, bringing color to the dark chamber. Some of his best days had been here. His best service to God, and man. Spanning four different decades. His success obtaining a charter for Wake Forest College, achieved only with the tie-breaking vote of the president of the Senate. His resolution which brought to life a system of public schools for North Carolina. But there were other days as well. His repeated failure to obtain the vote for blacks. And, of course, today.

He looked back out the window again. *They will not understand. Some will, of course. Some will. But most will not. History will not stop for them. Nor will they move for it.* He looked out over their heads across the City of Raleigh and imagined a day to come. A day of an educated North Carolina citizenry. Of commerce and industry, not just farming. Of black freedom and suffrage. The dreams of an uneducated man. A farmer. A slaveholder.

"General Dockery."

The General turned to look. There were five of them there. He knew why. Had been expecting them. He remained seated.

"Yes, Gentlemen. What can I do for you?"

The man in the middle spoke first. He was short and round, with a bright red face. The little hair remaining was brushed across the top of his head in unconnected stands.

"You know damned well what you can do, Senator!"

The time for politeness or gentle persuasion had passed. It had all been said before.

"You can change your futile position on this matter and vote with *us.* This motion *will* pass. The matter of secession *will* be put to the people. We need as strong of a statement from this chamber as possible. The vote here may very well affect the vote across the state."

"I can only hope you are correct, sir. I know I will not win this vote today. But I hope the people see my vote, and that they hesitate to accept the reckless course you, sir, are laying out before them."

Another of the men stepped forward. He was tall and thin and young, but had a long trim beard and round glasses, giving him the look of an older man, a professor perhaps.

"South Carolina. Mississippi. Florida. Alabama. Georgia. Already seceded. Louisiana and Texas are likely to follow within the week. Surely, sir, you do not believe that *you* can stem this tide."

"With all due respect, gentlemen, it is *you* who are camped out about *me*, telling *me* how important *my* vote is. Tell me, gentlemen, how do you think the Negroes would vote on the topic, had all five of you not voted against giving them the vote?"

The red-faced man stepped forward, now standing right over Dockery and talking down into this face.

"The niggers voting on secession? You damned fool! You hypocrite! You own as many slaves as any man in this chamber. And you of all people talk this nonsense. Should you wonder, gentlemen, where General Dockery conjures this garbage that he bids us all to suffer, he does so sitting on his grand plantation, in his massive brick house."

The General smiled and held his large ruddy hands out in front of him.

"Yes, gentlemen. And it was these old yaller hands of mine that built all of it."

"Those and a few dozen black hands, maybe. This is no use. How can one reason with a slaveholding unionist? General, your entire political career is some silly effort to prove you are someone that you are not."

"No, sir." Calmly. Still sitting. "My entire political career is an acknowledgment that who I am is not who my children will be. That the world I live in is not the world they will inherit."

The red-faced man still hovered above the general. More lines appearing in his face.

"History will make a fool of you for what you do today."

"One word before you go, gentlemen. Because you are leaving now, right George? Do you know what are you asking for? How do you think this will end? Peacefully? Do you think Lincoln will just let half the country leave? I am not raising my sons to be soldiers."

"So that's it. You fear war. You're a coward. You fear your sons will be cowards as well."

Finally Dockery stood. At six feet he towered above most of the other men. Even now in his sixties he was an imposing sight. His broad chest swelled under his gray suit. Now he was looking down on the red-faced man, close enough to feel his breath. He had a bird's eye view of the man's failed efforts to cover his bald scalp. The General's broad face was calm, but his deep-set eyes and thick graying brow still combined with his size to shadow the smaller, more agitated man. Even the General's hair, the thick gray brushed dramatically back across his head and over each ear, gave the sense of a sleeping giant awaiting his moment. When he spoke it was plain and soft, barely above a whisper, but the words brought authority down on the man below.

"A man that goes to battle for the right reason is brave. A man who goes to battle for the wrong reason is a fool. A man who goes to war for fear of being called a coward by the likes of you, well, he proves himself the biggest coward of them all. Good afternoon, gentlemen. I believe we are done here."

As the men moved on, the General sat down slowly. Back in the chair, he was an old man again. No longer the giant that had loomed above his adversaries and stared them down. Not a state senator for a moment. Just a man. A father. The crowd on the grounds was growing. More flags appeared. Little pockets of argument broke out amongst the mob. The policemen easing over, making themselves seen. Alfred looked out over the city and imagined a future again. Not the same future. An independent South. Agrarian. Uneducated. Starved for resources. Swindled by richer neighbors to the north and opportunistic traders from across the Atlantic. Not a solitary government this time that taxed from abroad as before, but thousands of independent commercial powers, each happy for markets for their goods. More than willing to carry home shiploads of cotton acquired at depressed prices. Slaves still providing the labor for the farm economy, while citizens drew good wages for industrial jobs in the free North. The Southern future sacrificed for an illusion that one moment could last forever.

Even worse, he imagined the horrors that would be endured to secure the flawed dream. *Right down there, on these grounds.* With the masses below the window surrounding the seat of government, it was easy to imagine them armed and in a battle to protect the Capitol. He rested his eyes for a moment, but the image stayed with him. Thousands of professional soldiers uniformed in blue, storming the grounds from all directions. Cannons firing from Fayetteville Street, blasting holes in the Capitol itself. Shattering the windows of the Senate Chamber. Smoke pouring from the shattered glass. Down in the grass, men and young boys in ragtag outfits hiding behind makeshift barricades built in part from the broken desks of senators. Fewer guns with fewer bullets. Fewer cannons. Fewer men. In the vision he saw a group of boys fighting well together. Solid men, working together as if connected at the mind, despite a wide difference in their ages. Loading, firing and reloading. Three of them manning a small field cannon. Shells bursting around them. Bullets tearing a flag with its pole wedged into the barricade. Their faces smeared with soot and blood, partially obscured by the cloud of battle.

One commanded the others. A thick, handsome gentleman, standing out through the smoke. A round, proud face and smart moustache. The General recognized him. It was his second oldest son. Oliver Hart Dockery. Already almost as prominent as his father. Natural for command. Pointing and yelling coolly to the others amidst the din of battle. Having recognized Oliver, the other faces came into focus. The soldiers were his sons. All of them. Close at Oliver's side were Benjamin and the General's namesake, Alfred, who let out a bloodcurdling yell as he fired into the approaching wave of blue. In command at the cannon was his oldest, Thomas, the strong, quiet image of his mother. John Morehead Dockery calmly loaded the cannon, as Jim determined the shots path, eyes both pensive and passionate. Even young Henry, just a child, stood tall beside his brothers. The blue wall was closing in. From above the outcome was certain, but the boys fought on. *What is their cause? Their motivation? Why do they fight so well, with so little hope?*

They were not alone. Two others stood with them. Alfred strained to recognize the faces, knowing they were creations of his own imagination. The faces were familiar, intimately so, yet somehow purely imagined. He knew them as one knows characters in a dream, as true to the dreamer as they are fictitious to all others. The features of the faces called out to him, from other imagined futures in days intentionally forced into places his mind knew not to travel. A line of Southern troops gave way and blue uniforms rushed forward toward his sons. The two unnamed boys charged forward. There was no hesitation. They yelled and ran with bayonets into certain death. As they disappeared into the smoke of the muskets guaranteed to kill them, the General suddenly knew who they were. James Turner Dockery, dead as an infant. Puss Dockery, dead at the age of four. He recognized them as men only as they died again in his imagination. Though the vision was his own, he could not call them back. Tried to. But events were in motion he could not reverse.

He thought back to the days of their deaths. Sally disappearing into darkened corners of the house, unable to face her survival of her own children. His failed efforts to comfort her. The lingering distance that the deaths brought between husband and wife. Yet Sally always emerged. Powerful, if hardened. Damaged, but never broken. Always a miracle in his eyes was her ability to find the strength to continue.

In the image now was nothing but smoke. The Northern cannons ripped the walls of the Capitol, sending gray stone collapsing down onto the Dockery boys in an explosion of dust that would not clear. A fate he could not handle. That not even Sally could handle.

The rap of the gavel from the podium jolted him back to awareness. His eyes opened and snapped eagerly to the window. The gray walls of the Capitol still stood. No smoke filled the grounds but that from scattered pipes or cigars. The citizens still waited quietly to learn to what nation they would belong.

General Dockery made his way back to his desk, feeling the eyes of fellow senators on him as he moved. The question of whether to submit the issue of secession to popular referendum was called. The Chair made his way through the role. "Aye." "Aye." "Aye." General Dockery sat at his desk and rested his eyes again, listening to the affirmative votes called, one after the other. Many of those votes cast by men caught up in a foolish fervor, or terrified of accusations of cowardice.

He opened his eyes and glanced across the chamber. The red-faced man was staring back across at him. Grinning, but with fierce eyes. The scattered strands of hair had slid down his face, now dangling at his eyebrows. He brushed them back and stayed focused on the General. A "nay" vote was cast. The man winced, but did not look away. Another "aye" was called.

"Mr. Dockery?"

He stood slowly. Took a deep breath, the only sound in the otherwise silent chamber. His shoulders and chest grew. He was imposing once again.

"Nay!"

Three

Jim Dockery
April, 1861
Rockingham, NC

Four horses exploded from the narrow, wooded path into the open road. They climbed a slight rise, then rolled down a gentle slope toward a bridge where the creek crossed. At the bottom the trees gave way to vast planted fields that spread in all directions. Wildflowers swayed in the breeze along the creek bed. The growth that followed the creek cut a green path through the fields, dotted by dogwood saplings, their buds just beginning to open white against the stripe of green. With the trees behind them, the sunlight swept down across the valley, painting brighter each color of the spring landscape that lay before the Dockery boys and their horses.

As they passed over the bridge and sped across the valley, the specks of dust kicked up by the horses caught the light of the sun and glinted as they rose and drifted back in a pale, fading tail. Workers in the fields straightened their backs and watched as the horses passed. Dark figures in light clothing, faces peering out from heads wrapped in cloths to ward off the sun.

Young Jim Dockery pushed his horse to draw even with the leader, Oliver. The older eyes were filled with purpose, focused on the road ahead. Then, seeming to sense Jim's eyes upon him, Oliver turned to the right to face his little brother. His look was one of total confidence. Of joy. A slight smirk appeared beneath his carefully groomed mustache. He winked knowingly at Jim, then turned back to the road, the fierceness returning to his eyes. Thomas, the oldest, had already moved to Mississippi, taking John with him, in search of an independent fortune in the cotton trade. Oliver had slid effortlessly into the role of oldest brother. Unlike Thomas, Oliver had been content to stay close to home, building his fortune alongside their powerful father. Not only was he already the owner of his own grand plantation, he and his father owned a piece of the Richmond Manufacturing Company, the largest and finest textile mill in the county.

On the opposite side of Oliver rode Alfred and Benjamin. Young Alfred, not yet twenty, was the fierier and more dashing of the two, a younger version of Oliver. Like his older brother, he seemed to feel Jim's eyes and looked back in his direction. He smiled widely and let out a holler as he worked the horse and sped out in front of his brothers.

Benjamin, though only two years Alfred's senior, was far older in his carriage. The large, solid head, fixed on broad, powerful shoulders. Whatever magic had caused Oliver and Alfred to look up and meet Jim's gaze had no effect on Benjamin. His face remained ever forward, undistracted, unflinching.

Alfred and Benjamin would join Oliver in his new company of Confederate soldiers. The Brave Richmond Boys, he was calling them. As soon as he could gather the volunteers and get them equipped, Oliver would ride off to war with two of his brothers at his side. Jim, not yet eighteen, would be left at home. Farming. Studying. Chasing girls. But mostly dreaming of his chance to get into the action.

It isn't fair. Alfred and Benjamin are barely older than I am. And I know more about war than either one of them. I'm a better shot, too.

The unfairness welled up from some place inside of him each day. Seeing the newspapers with their talk of imminent secession. Hearing Oliver give speeches to anyone who would stand still long enough to hear. Watching his father give instruction to the older brothers that they would soon need in the fields of battle. Everything brought thoughts of war, which brought thoughts of the coming day his brothers would leave him behind.

He shook the thought from his head. *Not today. I am not left behind today.* It had meant so much to him when Oliver had asked him to ride with him. "Private Dockery," he had called him. Jim had felt a deep gratitude. His brother Oliver was making him a part of the war effort.

A crowd was gathered in the center of the tiny town. Crowds as were gathering in the center of most all towns throughout the county. At one end of the square was a large stump with no one on it. The townspeople stared forward as if expecting something. An audience ready to be addressed. Oliver winked at Jim as they pulled their horses to the front. He dismounted dramatically before his horse was even stopped, then jumped upon the stump with a flourish.

"To arms, to arms, to arms, fellow citizens, our rights and liberties are invaded by the tyrant Lincoln. As freemen knowing these rights you should dare maintain them. I mean to raise a company to go immediately into the service. Who will join with me?"

"Why should we join you? You're a Union man, just like your daddy!"

The shout came from the back of the crowd. They had spilled out of the square and up onto the sidewalk under the signs of the offices and stores that made up the little downtown. There was an office door open, with a smartly dressed man smiling a devious smile, one foot in the door and one out. A white sign hung from above his head, "Attorney at Law."

Oliver smiled down at the man, though Jim could see a flicker of irritation in his eyes. Oliver took a deep breath, calming himself. Knowing to let the matter settle before his retort.

"It is a fair question, sir. Yes, I was hesitant to embrace secession. Yes, my father voted against it. But if you, sir, are critical of these sentiments, if you would have had us secede and fight before now, you above all should be ready to go into battle. You should join regardless of who leads you. Whether your company be mine or that of someone else. To you, sir, I suppose I should be, as they say, preaching to the choir."

There was a chuckle from the crowd. The man blushed and eased back ever so slightly into his office.

"But to many others of you, those who shared my hesitation to divide the nation. To you I should be the perfect example of the need for your service. Perhaps, should you humbly so choose, I would be a company commander well-suited to your service. The tyrant the Yankees have elected in the stolen election has proven to be worse than even his biggest enemies had suspected. With the fall of Fort Sumter in South Carolina, he has now called upon North Carolina and other Southern states to send 75,000 soldiers to join the federal army, to fight and kill our brethren from South Carolina, Georgia, and all the other states which have seceded. To force men to belong to a country from which they choose as free men to separate, much as the colonies chose to separate from the King of England. Secession will happen now. There is no doubt. North Carolina will go to war, and it will go to war along with the rest of the South. Make no mistake about it, Mr. Lincoln's army is an invasion army, sent here to force you to surrender to a government not of your own choosing. There is no more a question as to whether this war will occur. There is only the question to each able-bodied man in this town as to whether *he* will go to war, whether *he* will do his part, whether *he* is a man, or a coward. I urge you to join us. To do your duty. If not, the last one hundred years of our history have been wasted. So much blood and toil and effort only to trade a king in England with a crown, for a king in Washington in a silly tall hat."

There was an enthusiastic cheer from the crowd. Still some faces remained hardened. Others angered. Many saddened. A handful of men in dark suits conspicuously moved through the crowd back toward the office of the heckling lawyer. They leaned in close to each other and whispered in a huddle, then drifted into the law office and shut the door.

As Oliver stepped down off of the stump, he looked away from the crowd and down at the ground. Jim spied him smiling to himself with momentary exhilaration. He then composed himself and turned to stand beside the stump and look back over the crowd, his face stern and stately.

Young Alfred hopped onto the stump and raised a hand to his heart.

"When the first shot is fired, I will be there. When the last shot is fired, I will be there, or I will have died trying to get there. Choose what company you will. What officers you will. Just make sure you join and fight. That you not use politics as an excuse not to join this company or that, to not serve under this officer or that, until the entire war passes you by. As for me, I have chosen. When the Brave Richmond Boys leave for war, I will leave with them. And as for my leader, my commanding officer, I will follow Captain Dockery to Hell if necessary."

"You rich boys make a good speech, but I have 5 children and a store to keep open. Who will keep my family together should I go to war?"

Young Alfred's head snapped to his left and locked in on the man who had spoken. His hawkish eyes betrayed excitement.

"You, sir, come here. Let me speak with you directly."

The man looked back up at Alfred uncertainly. The Southern patriots around him began to shout encouragement. Some pushing him slightly toward the front. He tried to wave them off. Laughed a nervous laugh. Looked again up at the much younger man who had thrust him into this situation. Walked uneasily toward the stump. Alfred never broke his stare. His eyes exuded total certainty of conviction. Finally, the man was at the stump, standing below Alfred on one side, with Oliver on the other.

"Citizens. This man has shared with us his hesitancy to join up and fight. Over concern for his family. First of all, sir, I assure you, if you sacrifice for this community, this community will sacrifice for you. Am I right?"

A loud cheer. The crowd was near frenzy now.

"Second of all, sir, should you choose not to fight, I have a gift for you, purchased in Raleigh at a fine store."

He reached down into his jacket, pulled out a black and pink corset and held it high above his head to the delight of the crowd.

"You can come to war with us, be a man, and wear our uniform … or you can stay at home, be a woman, and wear one of these!"

As the crowd erupted in laughter, Benjamin looked over to Jim and they rolled their eyes in unison. The younger brothers set themselves up behind two wide tables, each with a stack of papers before him. Oliver moved about the crowd, slapping backs and giving encouragement. The men of the town formed into lines before the young Dockery boys, signing their papers to become instant soldiers.

Alfred Dockery
Rockingham, NC

General Dockery walked out to the stables alone. He walked along the dirt path in the moonlight under the long arm of an oak that reached out over the path. One of his cats meowed at him from above, then hopped down from the tree branch and landed at Alfred's feet, rubbing against each leg with his tail raised in the night air. As he reached the stables, the General looked down across the orchard as it sloped slightly toward the pines. The eyes of three does peeked back at him from the trees. He looked up at the half-moon, which lit distant clouds that drifted by slowly.

The stable was dark and quiet. The horses had all been brushed and fed for the night. At the far end one lantern was burning, giving off a faint glow that captured a small, lonely figure in a ladderback chair. Before he could see her, he knew it was his bride, Sarah Lilly Turner Dockery … Sally.

He had been looking for her. She had disappeared from the house earlier and no one seemed to know where she was. Once he found her, General Dockery knew what came next. She sat between the four horse stalls left empty by the recruiters when they set off on their wild ride.

It wasn't the first time a lady from Sally's line had faced the horror of her children going off to war. Her great grandmother, Kerenhappuch

Turner, had been at home in Virginia when her son and seven grandsons fought the British 350 miles away at Guilford Courthouse in North Carolina. Her name, Kerenhappuch, was that of the youngest and fairest daughter of the great Biblical sufferer Job. When word of her son's severe injuries came to her, she could not sit at home and suffer idly. Instead, Kerenhappuch mounted her horse and rode to Guilford to nurse him back to health. Old enough to have grandsons as fighting men, Kerenhappuch was still bearing children of her own. The youngest, a baby, was strapped to her side and nursed during the several days ride. The baby died *en route*. Kerenhappuch climbed down off her horse, buried the child beside the road, and continued her ride.

When she arrived in North Carolina, she fashioned her own makeshift hospital in a shabby log cabin near a creek known as Bloody Run. She hung wash tubs from the ceiling with holes punched in the bottoms, and constantly shuttled between creek and cabin to keep them full. The continuous drip of cool water onto the wounds was a revolution in wound care, and she soon saw her son well enough to pick up his musket and fight again.

So as a mother of soldiers, Sally came from good stock. Sitting in the stable, she did not notice her husband's approach. He watched her a moment more, delaying the inevitable confrontation. He took a deep breath and stepped out from the shadows.

Sally stood and faced her husband. She was small and showed her age, but there was still beauty there. Her hair was pulled back tightly behind her head, and the dim light failed to reveal the wrinkles around her mouth and eyes. Her piercing eyes. Over the decades he had seen in them great joy and great suffering, but there was always strength. And knowledge. Alfred had often suspected she was smarter than him, and knew it was silly to believe any secret could be kept from her, at least for long. He smiled at her, using the lack of light to see her face as it had once been. Her eyes returned the love, briefly, but she did not return the smile.

"You have let them go. My boys, you have let them go."

She was standing between the four empty stalls, motioning to them as she spoke.

"Only for today. A recruiting trip. Oliver is forming his own company to go off to war."

"He didn't stay a unionist for long."

"Well, you know how I feel. Everybody does, I suppose. But it's hard not to get caught up in it all. The fervor, the patriotism. And when Lincoln asked North Carolina for troops, well that was the straw that broke the camel's back. You know Oliver, as much as he may not want this war, he isn't going to let someone else go off and be the leader. Or the hero for that matter. If you can't beat them, lead them."

"He's done this on purpose hasn't he? Lincoln. He asked for troops to force us to choose sides. To force men like Oliver, and *you*, to choose sides."

"You've been around politics too long, Sally. You are starting to think like a politician."

He stepped closer to his wife, gingerly. She was much more difficult to handle than the needle-nosed legislators that troubled him in Raleigh. He smiled at her, hoped to calm her. Awaited her reaction. Seeing none, he continued talking.

"One thing for sure about Lincoln, he's always thinking five steps down the road. Makes him seem a bit odd, I guess. People talk to him and he seems like he's talking about something completely different. Truth is, he's already thought through what they were talking about and moved onto the next thing."

"You've met him. Is he the tyrant they all say he is?"

"It was a funny meeting. In a little tavern in Washington. Back in '47. I was giving up my seat in Congress to come home and he was just showing up to take his. Some of the other Whigs thought we needed to meet for some reason. He was sitting at a table holding court, with other fellows sitting around listening to his stories. He stood up to shake my hand and studied me real seriously. He was a tall fellow. Lean, but strong. Firm handshake. Of course, you know how I looked back then, so we were two pretty big fellows standing there. Country fellows at that. He smiles at me and says, 'Nice to meet you Congressman. Would you like to fight?' I just stood there looking at him for a second waiting on him to smile or laugh, but he didn't. I decided I had better come up with something clever to say. All I could come up with was, 'I better not Congressman. I'm afraid I might break those skinny arms of yours.' Well, he busted out laughing. He was still holding onto my hand and he grabbed my shoulder with the other hand and gave me a little shake as he stood there laughing and looking at the other men around the table. We sat back down, and it seemed like he took a liking to me from the start. I told him I was hearing that some of these fellows thought he would be president one day. He rocked way back in his chair and told me this story:

Once upon a time Jesus was walking through the wilderness. He came up on a poor young man sitting by the road just crying and screaming. Jesus looked down and said, "Son, what's the matter?" The man didn't look up, but said, "I've been struck blind. I can't see a thing and I've lost my way." Jesus puts his hand on the man's head and said, "Open your eyes and see, my son." The young man opened his eyes and saw the Lord standing before him.

Jesus walked on and a little while later he came upon an older gentleman sitting on a stump crying and moaning. "My son, what's the matter?" "I've grown old and feeble and I can no longer walk. I fear I'll be stuck here on this stump for the rest of my days." Jesus reached down and laid his hands on the old man's shoulder and said, "Arise my son, and walk." The old man stood and walked like he was young again.

A little while later Jesus came upon a middle-aged man sitting on a large rock, weeping softly. "My son, what is the matter? What can I do to help?" The man said, "I am the President of the United States." Jesus sat down on the rock beside the man, hung his head, and wept with him.

"Alfred? You're smiling? We are talking about the man that is about to send our sons off to war and you are smiling? Do you *like* this man?"

The General looked back at his wife, realized he had gone astray with Lincoln's story. That his expression was not appropriate for the occasion of his sons heading out to recruit an army for a great war. She was standing in the middle of the stables, hands on hips, unimpressed. He was fumbling, somehow lacking the finesse and power he showed elsewhere.

"Yes, Sally. Yes, I do like him. It can be rather hard not to."

"This is the man that asked North Carolina for troops for his invasion army. The man who would take all we have and give it away. And you *like* this man!"

"He's no tyrant. A bit too strident perhaps, too ambitious. But I have a son that way whom I adore. No, Lincoln is just another man trying to do what he believes is right. No different than the rest of us really. Just a difference of opinion about the issue that happens to be on the table right now. I may send my sons to fight a war against him, but I cannot hate him."

Finally, she cracked a smile. A knowing smile. One that said this was her husband and he drove her crazy but she loved him anyway. She plopped back down into the chair, shaking her head slightly.

"OK, Alfred. OK. I get it. I am not sure I will understand how you do that. Look at the bigger picture. Be the bigger man. Understand your enemies. Whatever you want to call it. But I can't do it. I'm looking at the small picture. *My* family. *My* home. So you don't hate him. You even like him. Fine. But do this for me. Just let *me* hate him. Don't take that away from me. Don't tell me stories designed to make me like the man that is tearing my family apart. Maybe I *need* to hate him. At least give me that."

He grabbed another ladderback chair and sat it across from Sally's. He sat down and faced her as they talked.

"OK. I can do that. I promise. And I suspect you are right, anyway. That he called for troops to force us to get off the fence. What kind of war would this be with Maryland, Virginia, Tennessee and North Carolina all trying to be neutral? How would the armies know who was who, whether they were on friendly or hostile ground? If all the border states were neutral, would the whole war be fought in neutral territory, destroying the farms and homes of those who proclaim to have no dog in the fight? What would become of the slaves in the slave states that did not secede if the North won? What a mess it would all be. No, you are right, dear. He wants clear battle lines, so he is forcing the rest of us to draw them."

"And you agree with that?"

"No. Not at all. But I understand it."

"Is there anything we can do? Any way this can be stopped?"

"Not now. The Legislature passed the bill for a secession convention last time, and secession was narrowly defeated by the people. But now, after this call for troops, the votes will not be close. North Carolina will secede. We will be a part of a new country that will be invaded from the North."

"And all we have is here. Our family, our home, our land, our church. All we know and love."

"Yes. And we cannot go against our home."

"So the sons of Alfred Dockery, the great anti-secessionist, the great unionist, will secede and go to war against the Union."

"Yes, Sally, I suppose they will."

"But not Jim. And not Henry. You must promise me you will not let them go. At least not until they turn eighteen, like we said, and even then only when I say so. Don't you dare let them talk you into anything else. Especially that Jim. He's a persuasive little cuss."

"Yes, dear. I promise."

Alfred Dockery
May, 1861
Raleigh, NC

Dockery was back in the Senate Chamber. The atmosphere was different than it had been at his last visit. There was an air of self-congratulation. Constant chatter not about a secession convention vote, but about war. Some discussed the companies they were forming with themselves as commanding officers, others the certainty of rapid victory. The chamber was called to order and the clerk read the journal from the prior day. The Legislature had convened on May 1st, but General Dockery was held up on business and unable to attend the opening session. On the matter of whether to again submit the question of secession to convention, the hurried vote had been unanimous. He rubbed his eyes and looked down at his desk. A runner handed him a note.

"The early bird gets the war."

General Dockery looked up from his seat and saw the snarling arrogant sneer of the little bald, red-faced man that had harassed him over the last secession vote. The General then rose from his chair and took a deep breath. Felt his broad shoulders sag as he exhaled. Suddenly felt very, very old.

"Mr. Chairman, may I be heard on a motion."

"The Chair recognizes the gentleman from Richmond County."

"I move to amend yesterday's record to cast my vote."

"Your motion will be allowed."

"I vote in favor, Mr. Chairman. Had I been present yesterday ... I would have certainly voted to submit the action of the convention to the people for ratification."

"The record is so amended."

He sat heavily back into his seat, held his head in his hands and closed his eyes. Once again he saw the vision of his sons, firing with bravery and futility into the endless waves of blue charging the Capitol grounds.

Four

Thomas Covington Dockery
October, 1861
Mississippi

The whole world was the curve of the cloth wagon top and the battle sounds beyond. The cloth fluttered in the wind and jostled with the motion of the wagon. The sun was setting outside, and the fading light gave the cloth an almost orange glow, broken by flashes of brighter light. Shells whistled over the wagon, followed by the violent shaking of the ground beneath. Amongst the distant firing of cannons and the nearby explosions, Captain Thomas Dockery heard broken shouts from the driver, pushing the horses, racing for safer territory. As the wagon bounced over uneven ground, the shoulder erupted with new pain. He longed for something to bite with each jolt of pain as the wagon wheels navigated the rutted-out path below. He gritted his teeth and tried to hold in his pain. Knowing the staff had heard enough complaining, that they needed to believe their officers capable of tolerating the suffering that might one day strike them. With the harder jolts he failed, and his pain poured out audibly.

"Slow it down driver. You must slow it down. You're killing me. How do I return to my boys if you kill me?"

"We have to get out of here, Captain. Yankee guns are on us."

"I didn't say stop, young man. I said slow down."

"Yes sir, Captain."

The wagon slowed its pace slightly. There were still rips of pain from the shoulder down the arm and through his body. They were less frequent now, and Captain Dockery succeeded more often in remaining quiet. His eyelids fluttered and narrowed, the cloth above blurring to a pale glow before him. When the eyes finally closed, he forced them back open, fearing he would travel into the light for good. When the wheels bounced and pain shot through him again, his eyes would pop open wide and he would regain full understanding of his situation. The jolts kept him awake, and he began to rely on them, to desire them to come despite the pain, just to stay awake a moment more.

Strangely, the wagon came to a stop within range of the exploding cannon shells. Between the blasts he heard a new voice. Then a horse *behind* the wagon. Men were discussing his wound, and the fact that he would not let them travel to the rear with sufficient haste. The face of a surgeon appeared. Looking down at the wound. Calm, business-like eyes. The surgeon tore away at the crusted bandage on Thomas's shoulder, then poured water onto it from his canteen. The water crept its way down into the gash and sent new pain deeper down into the arm. The man moved calmly, but efficiently, cleaning the wound as best he could, pressing a wet bandage upon it firmly.

He's trying to save my arm, Captain Dockery thought to himself. *He thinks he can save my arm. If he is thinking of the arm, he believes I will live.*

Thomas smiled through the pain. But the explosions grew closer. A shell whistled just above the wagon, so close Thomas thought he saw the shadow of the shell black against the glow above.

"Doctor, we will all be killed here."

The surgeon said nothing. Continued with his work.

Then there was an impact that seemed to travel below the wagon. The mules shrieked and raised up on their heels. The wagon lifted from the front, listed slightly to one side, then crashed back to the ground below. When it landed Captain Dockery let out a shout, but the surgeon continued about his business. Eyes focused. Wrapping the arm tightly to the body to stabilize its position. The explosion was just beyond the wagon, as if the shell itself had skipped beneath the mules before it burst. Smoke poured into the wagon from the seams where the fabric was tied down to the wood. It filled Thomas's eyes and nose, and he could barely see the surgeon above him, still working as if nothing had happened.

"I tell you doctor, we will all be killed here."

"I had just as soon be killed fixing up a wounded man as at any other time, but driver you let those mules go, and get away from here."

The wagon lurched back into motion. Thomas groaned, but embraced the thought of escape. The surgeon continued to wrap the arm tighter and tighter to his body. With the wagon back at full speed, the ride brought pain to Thomas repeatedly. He fought the urge to yell out, failed often, but never again asked the driver to slow down. The tightly wrapped arm moved less now and the pain was less intense. The whistle of shells above and the roar of their impact continued, but began to fade. As they rode the sounds changed. No longer were the blasts all around, but only behind the wagon, with safety ahead. The sounds of more wagons came to his ears. The gallop of mules, the calmer speech of drivers, the moans of other wounded men. It was a train of ambulance wagons.

The pace of the wagons slowed. The battle sounds were almost gone. Thomas wondered who moaned from the backs of other wagons. How many were his boys? How many had been lost? He thought of his young brother John, who had been with him on the field. Was he in one of these wagons, or worse? It was a foolish attack and he had known it. Many officers had known it. All but the commanding officer, it seemed. Into well-built enemy breastworks, into a superior force, within sight of well-placed enemy guns. But he was duty-bound to accelerate the failure, to charge into certain defeat with boys that yelled and charged because he told them to. Because they believed he would lead them to victory. Something he did not believe himself. Not that day. The shell had exploded to his left, right in the midst of the men following him. Six had died instantly. He stopped momentarily, looking at their torn bodies on the ground. Knew their names, their parents. Had sat alongside them in the church pew. Had even encouraged some of them to join when Mississippi was quick to secede. Had seen the enthusiasm in their eyes, the absolute faith in the righteousness of their cause and the certainty of their victory. Even in the skill of their leader.

His duty came back to his mind. He had to continue the ill-fated charge. It was only then he realized he was on the ground. The pain suddenly announced itself. He looked down to his shoulder and saw the massive gash, with a wedge of broken shell still protruding from it. The singed flesh surrounding the still-hot metal. He grabbed it with the other hand, and jerked with all his might. His palm burned against the metal. The shell fragment slid painfully from the wound and he fell unconscious amongst the dead and dying.

Now the wagon rolled slowly and more gently on flatter ground. The cloth above was gray, little light still illuminating it from above. He fought his eyelids again, but with less desperation. He believed now he would live. Would maybe even keep the arm. That there was sleep other than death. With his eyes closed and in the relative quiet, the sounds of the gurgling brook along the path came to his ears. In his mind he tried to picture the stream. Shallow riffs over rows of rocks. Plunging into deep clear pools. His mind traveled back before the battle. To Cartledge Creek, that ran through his father's land back in the old North State. The cool feeling of the creek water against his skin, beneath the hot sun. His brothers at the creek with him, dreaming of bright futures.

Benjamin Dockery
Near Raleigh, NC

Benjamin Dockery stood guard while the company slept. In his hand he held one of the only Confederate-issued rifles in camp. On his back were the same clothes he wore the day he left home. That first recruiting trip was ancient history, but the Brave Richmond Boys were still yet to be equipped for battle. But they could march. Oh, how they could march. Not at first, of course, but after months of nothing but marching and drilling, drilling and marching. They had marched through rain, marched in the sun, drilled in the mud and shot targets at dusk. With a few wagonloads of uniforms, they could have been the pride of any parade. Yet none of them had fired a hostile shot.

Benjamin shivered at his post. Like most of the men, he had left home with no winter coat, expecting to be home soon. The camp was the flat bottom of a massive bowl of earth. The only trees stood up on the ridges of the bowl, so the wind rushed down across the floor and made standing guard near unbearable. The tents flapped audibly in the wind. The ashes of spent fires spun off in tiny funnels and disappeared into the night.

The enemy was far away. Up in Virginia or Maryland, depending on which rumor you chose to believe. They had coats. They had guns, uniforms. Good shoes. Better food, even. But from the rumors that constantly danced about the camp, they did not yet have the heart to win a fight. Richmond had proven elusive, and the Rebel army a much worthier opponent than any Yankee had predicted.

Yet here were the Boys. Still in North Carolina. Not yet in the fight. And with the enemy hundreds of miles away, Benjamin's job was not to keep the Yankees out, but to keep his fellow soldiers in. More than a few had already bolted as more and more weeks passed with no signs of battle. One night a fellow from Hamlet had been standing guard at one end of camp. The next morning his post was empty, save for the musket he had left in plain sight to be recovered in his absence. Standing over the rifle with Benjamin and young Alfred, Oliver had shrugged off the unexpected departure. "Well, ol' Bobby may be a coward, but at least he isn't a thief."

Since then Oliver had taken to assigning guard only to the men he knew best and trusted most. That meant Alfred and Benjamin stood guard most every night. The nights were long, cold and painfully boring. For a week or two Benjamin had occupied his mind with thoughts of glory to be won on distant fields of fire. Images all the men relished, and still believed were soon to be theirs. Over time, the images began to dim. The battlefields more distant, the glory less certain. With future glory disappearing as an aid to stand dutifully all night, and no present threat of genuine hostilities, Benjamin turned to the one image that never faded: Betty Ann Covington.

He had known Betty his entire life, but truly took notice on a spring Sunday afternoon at a dinner on the grounds at Cartledge Creek Baptist Church. Spring was already hot in the Sandhills region of North Carolina, so the long tables were set up end-to-end in the shade of the pines behind the church. The men stood to one side, sweating in their suits, only a few taking off their jackets and vests. The older gentlemen puffed on pipes and talked business or politics. The younger men stood close. They scratched their chins, wore pensive looks, but added little to the conversation. There was always a dog or two about, as anxious as the men for the dinner to be spread out across the tables. Pacing back and forth, tails wagging, waiting for table scraps. Ladies buzzed about the long tables. Some spread thin tablecloths that would slide off in the breeze if not covered promptly with heaping dishes. A couple of old ladies beyond their ability to scamper about the table sat in chairs pulled up by their daughters and barked out instructions to the younger girls.

Soon the long tables were filled from one end to the other. Stacks of plates stood at one end, followed by baskets of cornbread and biscuits wrapped in flowered towels. Bowls of homemade butter and jam covered with napkins to protect them from the heat. Beyond the bread were vegetables of every variety, most seasoned with large chunks of ham. String beans, field peas, butter beans. All cooked until soft, then piled into large bowls. At least half a dozen dishes of fried chicken, each with a child standing nearby saying "This is my Mom's and it's the best in the world." Each time a child or an anxious daddy got too close, there was a mom or a grandma ready to shoo them away, telling them to wait until grace was said. After the chicken was country ham, cured since winter and now bursting with flavor. Calling out to be sliced and placed in the biscuits at the front of the table. Finally, there were the desserts. Chocolate pies, pecan pies, tall cakes with homemade frosting.

Wide dishes of peach cobbler topped with a thin, golden crust.

Children were scattered all over the place. Chasing one another about. Arguing for a moment about nothing, getting over it quickly, then playing on. A few daring boys standing deeper in the pines behind the tables, venturing dangerously close to the strangely dark cemetery. Hand-scraped headstones with dates nearly a hundred years old. Not too close to the adults were little pockets of teenagers, less scattered than their younger church mates. Divided by gender and age. Whispering scandalously, then cutting their eyes at the boys or girls standing in little groups just a few steps away.

He had seen her a thousand times. In the church pew. At Sunday school. On days such as this. She lived just around the bend behind the church. Across the creek and up the hill on the other side. Her brother Ben — strong, devout and silent — was often down at the swimming hole when Benjamin and the other Dockery boys snuck off for a dip. But this day she was different. It was as if she had suddenly grown up, or Benjamin had just grown up enough to care. Finally, he saw the beauty that had been right before him all along.

Though no more than fifteen, she stood with some of the older ladies by the food. Doing most of the talking. Animated. The curly black hair, cut short and bobbing playfully about her neck as she spoke. The shining eyes, ever unintimidated by any company, female or male. The uneven little smile, always saying "I know something you don't." Benjamin knew the ladies she was with. Knew their stern, Baptist manner. Their hardness, wrought from hard lives. As Betty stood and talked to them, they transformed. Came to life. Laughing. Smiling. Hearkening back to former selves. Before cold winters and sweltering summers. Before bearing and raising a dozen children, losing some of them in infancy. Before stretching food supplies through harsh winters after poor farming years. Before seeing mulatto children born to their young slaves, knowing only their husbands could have fathered them. Back to days when they were young girls in white linen dresses, whispering at church luncheons about the cute boys a few steps away that would one day be their husbands.

When the preacher stepped to the table, the congregation gathered.

Grew quiet. Hungry young boys began to circle the plates at the end of the table. Their mothers moved to block them. "Wait on your elders," they said. The old, sober gentleman held up his hand to signal the prayer's beginning. "Every head bowed, every eye closed." He began his prayer, thanking the Lord for the day, the nourishment, those that prepared it, "may it strengthen our bodies that we might better serve you." Benjamin had closed his eyes dutifully. Prayed along with the preacher. Yet his mind drifted. She was still standing right there. He imagined her bowed reverently, the big, lively eyes quieted for the moment. Just a peek, he thought. He opened his eyes, narrowly. There she was. Head not bowed. Eyes not closed. She was looking right back at him. Their eyes locked, and there was the smile.

Things moved slowly at first. Glances across the sanctuary or the Sunday School classroom. Short meaningless conversations, conjured excuses to speak even if just for a moment. Then long walks after church with their parents watching nearby, beginning to get the idea. Finally, one summer Sunday morning, the congregation was standing about outside the church doors waiting for Mr. Kelly, a deacon, to pull the rope that hung down from the ceiling to ring the bell and let everyone know it was time to come in. Betty strode up to Benjamin, grabbed his hand and led him quickly behind the church. As they turned the corner, she backed up to the wall, pulling him along, grabbed his head with both hands and kissed him in a manner he had not before experienced. He wrapped his arms around her, felt the line of her shoulder blades with his hands, then ran his hands down her back until they were resting on her hips. She pulled back from him slowly. Looked him deeply in the eyes for a moment, then looked away and smiled. Benjamin's hands reached back out for her hips. He wanted to kiss her again. The church bell began to ring. Betty smiled back up at him again, grabbed his hand and headed back around the building. When they reached the front door she dragged him into the church behind her. She pulled him right past his family and down the pew where her family sat. As Benjamin sat down amongst the Covingtons, he looked back over his shoulder to his own family. Jim gave him a wink. Sally did not look at him, but locked arms with the General and smiled. Now sitting beside Betty,

Benjamin noticed that the Covingtons were studying him curiously. He smiled awkwardly and looked up toward the pulpit waiting for the service to start. The preacher rose from his chair and asked that his congregation bow their heads in prayer. Once every eye was closed, Betty shifted herself ever so slightly closer to Benjamin. He felt her leg press up against his and lost track of the preacher's words. His mind was behind the church in a kiss, with no worries about family coming around the corner to see.

Suddenly there was a sound nearby. His daydream interrupted. Benjamin was back on the frozen ground standing guard over soldiers who had never fought a battle. He heard the sound again. A soft, sliding sound. It blended to nothing when the wind blew, but he heard it between gusts. The softness seemed intentional. Whatever made the sound meant to be quiet. Benjamin looked but saw nothing. His eyes weren't much good in the light, much less the dark, so he listened and tried to let his eyes follow his ears. Finally, he shouldered his rifle and walked casually as if making a regular patrol. There was a sound for a second, then nothing. But now he had a bead on it. Knew it was close by. Continued along his path as if innocently surveying the ground. As he drew closer, there was a voice.

"Aw, shit," the voice said. Then a silhouette emerged from the dark ground and began to run. Benjamin broke into a sprint. Had the angle on the deserter. The man tried to turn sharply to the left, but Benjamin leapt and pushed him to the ground with the stock of the rifle. After that the man only gave token resistance. Benjamin was the bigger man, and pinned the offender to the ground with his rifle across the smaller man's chest. Only then did the man speak again.

"Benjamin Dockery, you jackass. Can you just let a fellow go?"

He knew the voice. Was finally focusing in on the face.

"Jimmy Pillar? What in the world are you doing?"

"Same as every damn body else in this chickenshit outfit, I reckon. I don't know about rich boys like you, Dockery, but some of us has got shit to do back home."

"Oh, come on, Pillar. What have you got to do other than drink liquor and give people a hard time? I guess you can do that here as well as you can at home. What you want to run for?"

"Same as everybody else. I came here to kill Yankees. To run'em back home. To protect my r…well, wait a damn minute, Dock, if we're gonna have a damn conversation will you at least get that fire stick off my chest."

"Only if you promise not to run … and if you stop talking so loud. You'll wake everybody up and then you'll get punished for trying to run."

"Fine. Fine. Just let me up."

Benjamin pulled the rifle from Pillar's chest and crawled off of him. He sat beside him with the gun across his lap. Pillar sat up and looked at Benjamin with a disgusted look on his face. He was a sorry looking sight. Always had been. Red, pitted out face of an alcoholic. Scraggly beard that hadn't been shaved in months, still with patches of bare skin peeking through.

"What the hell you want to knock me down for?"

"For running off, you drunk. What you want to run for?"

Pillar dusted himself off. Pawed at his beard for a moment.

"I ain't no coward. I want to kill Yankees more than any of you bastards. I'd be pretty damn good at it too. You know I would. Seen me shoot. Hell, Dock, you're the worst damn shot in this company. I can shoot a yellow jacket in the left nut from 100 yards."

"I can't shoot what I can't see. And I can't see much. Not far away, anyway. But if you want to fight so bad, why were you sneaking off?"

"I was running off to find another unit. One that would get to go north and fight for a change. Hell, that fast-talking brother of yours promised me I'd see some real shit near a year ago. We didn't even leave Rockingham for seven or eight months on account of his politics. I know what the hell happened. Democrats took control of everything once we knew the war was coming. Wouldn't give no bullets and guns and uniforms to no yellow-bellied, unionist Whig asshole to go fight. Hell, they probably figgered he'd turn coat and start shooting at'em when the shit jumped off. Same shit happening now. Finally let us get trained up but won't use us none. Still cause of that damn brother of yours. Like that company song … "we'll follow bold Dockery wherever he leads." Only place he led me was up here to freeze my ass off on nothing but a camping trip. Couple of boys done already froze up or died of camp fever and we ain't seen one blue suit. So yeah, I decided to go find me a fighting man's unit."

Benjamin sat quiet for a minute. He didn't always have a quick comeback like Oliver, Alfred or Jim. He'd accidentally learned over the years that silence worked just as well anyway.

"Now, I bet you're gonna go tell your brother I said all that shit, aren't you?"

Benjamin was still quiet. Smiled. Finally knew what say.

"I'm sorry private, did you request permission to speak freely?"

Pillar grinned back at him, his scattered teeth reflecting the moonlight. He spit between his teeth through one of the gaps without opening his mouth.

"Shit, boy. You're a-ight, I guess."

"Fact is Pillar I think you'd be a good man to have around in a scrap. Just hang tight, bud. We'll get our chance. Now go on back to your tent and get some sleep. What Oliver doesn't know won't hurt him."

Pillar jumped up on his feet, pulled his shoulders back in mock attention and saluted.

"Excuse me, sir. You mean what Lieutenant Colonel Dockery don't know won't hurt him, don't you, sir?"

Benjamin smiled again. Slapped Pillar on the back.

"Get your sorry ass to bed, Jimmy."

As the would-be deserter strolled back toward the tents, Benjamin resumed his post, and his thoughts. Soon he was kissing her again. Up against the church wall. His hands sliding down the sides of her legs.

Five

Jim Dockery
June, 1862
Rockingham, NC

The summer heat bore down on the Dockery place. The house had been strangely quiet all morning. Jim paced about the big empty house. Uneasy. Anxious. There weren't even any slaves about. Henry and the girls had ridden off somewhere with Sally and the General, so Jim was left alone. Normally on a Monday he would have work to do on the farm. Not this day. Later that night there would be another feast, just like others before. Toasts. Tears, maybe. But today, during the day, they were giving him space.

He walked out the front door of the Brick House and looked out between the oaks lining the long driveway. The sprawling oaks shaded the path, but out beyond in either direction were vast pools of sunlight. The ground in either direction seemed to bake as each sloped gently away from the driveway. Beyond the oaks the road shone in the unchecked sun.

Jim took a moment to consider the ground. His father had taught him about the study of ground. How the choice of ground for a fight often determined the result. Jim had read everything he could get his hands on about the topic, and all other topics of military significance. To the right the ground sloped more sharply until disappearing into a dense thicket. Beyond, he knew the ground was low and wet. In the thicket it sloped off even more, rolling over hills gradually lower and lower to the creek. To the left of the driveway, the ground sloped a bit before climbing to higher solid ground. The high ground swept along the road in a gentle bend that looked down on a bowl of lower ground below.

That would be the place to make a fight.

The swimming hole on Cartledge Creek was a half mile down the road from the entrance to the Brick House. Jim looked again at the heavy sunlight, then chose the longer, shaded path through the trees behind the house.

Jim slipped into the woods directly behind the house and walked along the dry creek bed of a rainy day tributary of Cartledge Creek. It was a thin stretch of woods, a little valley cut from days when the tributary was something more. Up the steep hill from the creek bed, the fields opened up and sprawled in all directions. He kept close to the bed, hopping over stumps, downed trees and the giant roots of long-since fallen oaks. Even in the heat of the summer there was a coolness about the valley. A constant dampness that followed the empty creek bed. A darkness amongst the mature trees where their darkened trunks absorbed the moisture from the ground below as their branches blocked the sun from above.

He had once walked this valley with a girl he wished to impress. She had been spooked almost instantly, and tucked herself up against him as they walked. He had wrapped his arm around her, providing the security she sought. It had been a good plan.

But for Jim there was nothing uneasy about this little valley. There was a comfort, a belonging. He thought of it often when trying to fall asleep at night. About days of playing war with his brothers. When the creek bed became a trench, any stick of respectable length a musket, and the saplings up above on the hill became mysterious unknown enemies stalking them through the dark woods. Oliver would give the command, and they would all charge up the hill into the approaching enemy, clubbing them with their make-believe muskets, rushing to the hilltop and spilling out into the open fields, embracing their inevitable victory.

Jim had been knee-high to Oliver back then, but he was part of the game. The game of an imaginary war against an unknown enemy, for an unknown cause which somehow, despite not being fully imagined, still commanded the honor of complete bravery and unquestioned loyalty. After all, it was his brothers' war, fought on his own land. How could they be wrong?

Jim returned to awareness and realized he had covered much more ground than he had noticed. His eyes and feet had carried him along despite the absence of his mind. He came to a familiar crossing of the creek. A vine hung down from high at the top of the forest. It dangled well out of reach as he stood atop the sharp drop off of the creek bed. Though the bed was dry, he thought back to days past again. His brothers daring him to leap and swing across. Now alone in the woods he could still hear their jeers. He looked from left to right, as if someone had followed him into the woods. He shrugged his shoulders, backed up a few steps, got a running start and leapt. Still on the rise, he caught the vine and carried across. His eyes caught a patch of sand a yard over the far edge, a soft landing spot. As the momentum carried him across, Jim pulled up on the vine and launched himself. Overshooting his mark, he landed feet-first in a mound of mossy earth. His feet sank deep into the moss and he flopped backwards on his back into the sand. There he sat, alone in the woods, feet buried in the earth, with his head pressed down into a patch of wet sand. He looked from left to right again, laughing out loud only when he knew he was alone.

Soon he arrived at the swimming hole. It was a deep, slow pool in an otherwise shallow creek. Arriving through the woods, Jim stood high above the water on a cut bank carved by years of high storm water. Most folks arrived from the road, and thus could wade in gradually from the shallow, sandy side of the creek. The deep end required a more abrupt entry.

Across the river, sitting on a large rock on the sandy bank with a Bible in his hand, was Jim's cousin, Ben Covington. His hair was wet and matted down to his head. His round, cherubic face was bowed down as if in prayer. He had not yet noticed Jim.

Jim smiled at his devout cousin, tossed his shirt onto a bush, and backed up into the woods several feet. With a running start, he jumped as high and as far as he could out over the swimming hole, tucking both feet under him and wrapping his arms around his knees to maximize the splash. He came down hard into the pool, feeling the rush of the water all around him, imagining the rising column of water he could not see from underneath. When he rose back to the surface, Jim turned over on his back and floated with his head at the surface, propelling himself across the pool with his feet. Once over on the shallow side, he crawled up out of the water and sat down on another large rock near Ben, who was smiling his rosy-cheeked smile.

"Hey there, Jim."

"Hey, Ben."

"Nice day for a dip, huh?"

"Absolutely."

"Of course, you didn't have to go and scare me half to death."

"Sorry, cousin. Couldn't resist."

They sat for a few minutes watching the creek roll by. Ben pulled out a sandwich of thick sliced ham on a soft roll. He unfolded a pocket knife and sliced off a piece and handed it to Jim, who smiled and nodded his gratitude.

"Say, Jim. Didn't you turn eighteen a few months back?"

"Yep. But here I sit. How about you?"

"Not quite. Soon as I do, though, I'm shipping out."

"Yeah, that's what I used to think. I've been eighteen for over seven months now, fighting with mom and dad about joining up every day."

"Leaving any time soon?"

"Finally. I head out tomorrow. I'm joining the North Carolina 33rd Infantry. They're up near Richmond somewhere, been fighting about every day."

"You ever been?"

"To Virginia? Nope. Been to Raleigh with my dad. Been down to South Carolina a bunch. That's about it, really. How about you?"

"Shoot. I've been about as far west as Wadesboro and as far north as Ellerbe. I can't even spell Virginia."

Both men smiled and snacked on the sandwich. Jim heard the buzzing flutter of grasshoppers' wings in the summer heat. He spotted one as it rose and fell in the high grass along the steep bank. Another came into view from his right, sputtering about on the surface of the creek, trying to shake off its wet wings and take flight again. Exhausted, it stopped fluttering and floated along in the current without resistance. In an eddy in the middle it swirled around in two large circles before traveling on down the creek. Small popping sounds and quick splashes emerged around it as tiny bream came from beneath and tried to slurp it off the surface. The hopper began to kick again. Desperation outweighing exhaustion. The wings were too heavy to fly, but the bream were too tiny to eat the large hopper. Jim watched until it was almost out of sight, as if escaping his line of sight somehow meant the little creature would survive. Suddenly there was a large rolling swirl and a gulping sound from beneath. The hopper was gone. A bigger fish had finally found it.

"Ben, do you ever think about what it will really be like?"

"I think about what it will be like if the war ends and I miss it. What it will be like years down the road when men talk about how they whipped the Yankees, and all I can say I did during the war was fished and hunted and took dips in a swimming hole."

"I think about that, too. Especially with five brothers off at war. I envision a charge into the enemy, seeing them break and run. And I do think we will win. I hope for my share of the glory too. But that's not what I'm talking about right now. I'm talking about the war itself. The battles. The bullets and cannon balls flying. Smoke and explosions everywhere. Running full speed right at the people that are shooting at you, making it easier for them to hit you. Stabbing at people with bayonets. Killing people. Maybe being killed. Maybe biting on a stick while some field doctor saws off my leg. I mean that kind of stuff. What war will really be like."

"No. I can't say I've thought much about it."

"Why not? It's all I think about."

"Well, cousin, I know you well enough to know that you spend a good deal of time thinking about girls."

Jim smiled for just a second but didn't take the bait to change the topic of conversation.

"Don't you wonder about it, worry about it?"

"Nah. I figure it like this. War is supposed to be hell, right? Well, I don't plan on seeing the real hell. Whether I see a bit of hell on Earth is up to God. Reckon if I do it will make me more grateful for heaven. Of course, I don't know what heaven will be like either. So why worry about it. Out of my hands. I can't spend my life worrying about things that I can't change. I just put my trust in God and put one foot in front of the other and things will work out alright."

Jim looked from left to right as he had done back in the woods. He studied the face of his cousin, wondering if he could tell him what he knew he could not say at home, at church, anywhere. Certainly not amongst soldiers at war.

"I worry about heaven and hell all the time, Ben. What they're like. Whether they're even there at all. I doubt heaven and it makes me fear hell. I doubt both and it makes me fear death. I've prayed to have faith like you do, Ben. Most of the time I do. But not always. And when I think of war I think of death, and that starts me thinking about heaven and hell and nothingness. Nothingness. I think that would be hell to me."

Ben got up and walked over to Jim. He put his hand on his shoulder and looked him in the eyes.

"Don't you go feeling guilty about any of that. No man goes through life without doubts. About all kinds of stuff. Himself. God. Whatever. Especially a fella who's about to go off to war. It'd be unnatural if he didn't think about this stuff."

"You don't."

Ben smiled his cherubic smile again.

"Maybe I'm unnatural. You just remember this. Any of us may get killed out there. But it ain't for nothing. There's a cause. A reason. Something worth dying for. Isn't there?"

"There is. But not what they say it is. Let's not get started on the cause. My daddy didn't want this war. Everybody knows that. But there are things I'd die for. I'd die for my family. I'd die for my brothers away at war. I'd die for my home. That's why I can't wait to head out tomorrow, fear be damned."

"That ain't all you'd die for, Jim."

"What else?"

"I'm pretty sure you'd die for that curly-haired Jenkins girl that sings in the choir on Sunday morning."

Jim laughed. He was looking back across the creek.

"Well, she's sure killing me just sitting there and she doesn't even know it."

* * *

Jim's belly was full. They had killed a hog for the occasion and cooked it over a fire in the backyard. Miss Anna had pulled the long strips of pork from the hog, and piled the strands of soft, piping hot meat in a massive dish to be passed around the dining room table. The cobs of corn had dripped with butter, and the sugary glaze over the pecan pie had shimmered in the candlelight from above. Guests had been invited to fill the seats left vacant by brothers at war. As with each farewell dinner for a departing soldier, there were cheers for the cause, and for victory, with guests cheerful and unthinking. Still around the table Jim found thoughtful eyes. His father Alfred, the anti-secessionist sending a sixth son to fight for the Confederacy. His mother Sally, with eyes at once hard but loving, soon to have only one son remaining at home. Little brother Henry. Eager, left out, more anxious for war now than anyone. His zeal further breaking his mother's heart. As glasses were raised and hoorahs sounded out for the cause, Sally excused herself quietly, in search of a quiet room in which to cry. Alfred followed shortly thereafter. Henry stayed put, not wanting to miss anything. Finally, Jim himself slipped out through the side door of the warming kitchen.

The evening air, though a bit cooler, was still heavy with heat. Jim walked out into the grass between the house and the cemetery that sat amongst the pines. He laid himself down in the thick grass and stared up at a crescent moon. The dining room windows were open to catch the evening breeze, such that the laughs and cheers from the table drifted out to him, muffled in the background.

He thought of the faith of ol' Ben Covington. He pretended to have Ben's faith for a moment, looking to the moon and stars, and for a moment knowing … knowing … that God was with him. He thought of those charges in the darkened woods, older brothers at his sides, the feeling of importance charging beside them as one unbreakable unit. Now the sapling enemies would have faces. They would have rifles. They too would have a cause they held dear. Jim would not charge shoulder to shoulder with his brothers, but they would still charge together, no matter how many miles separated them. They would be united in their efforts for home and family. He had watched them become men, become more like their father, and leave home. He had envied their age, their manhood. Manhood which he finally now possessed. Now he lie in the grass listening to the whispers of celebration of his coming of age drifting low across the grass. There was a pride that filled him and pushed out all else. He was a man like his brothers now. Even if he had to be killed to prove it. With that thought he felt a fear begin to threaten the welling pride. He pushed it down. No more thoughts of war. There will be plenty of time for that. He thought of the girl from town he held tight in the wooded valley. He thought of the curly-haired girl in the choir, who turned shyly to the side each time he looked her way. *Yes, I would die for them too. They are a part of home as well.*

Six

Benjamin Dockery
June 26, 1862
Mechanicsville, VA

With a Rebel yell, the Richmond Boys were suddenly in the mix. They charged rapidly downhill toward Beaver Dam Creek, away from the Virginia summer sun that lay low in the sky at their backs. No more endless drilling without guidance from Richmond. No more days with pneumonia or fever as their biggest threat. No more skirmishes turned momentous in their rookie minds. No more romantic notions of the glory they would claim on distant fields. Richmond was threatened. The Union Army was just across the creek.

Benjamin Dockery kept pace with the fastest of the Richmond Boys. Perhaps they would stop the first bullets, but he would risk it to stick close by his colonel, Oliver. Around him on all sides were cousins and friends. Many he had known his whole life. Even at the edge of his vision their forms were familiar from months of marching and drilling.

His brother Alfred among them, coming and going from sight. Always just ahead was Oliver, striking in his tailor-made uniform, turning occasionally to survey the charge behind him. The Boys were tight together, Benjamin always making sure others were near him on all sides so he would not lose them in the chaos.

Big guns began to rumble nearby. The sound rattled from the hills and up from the river bottom, seeming to come from both above and below. Benjamin could not tell where the guns were but they were ahead, and they were close. The charge was much broader than the Richmond Boys. As the cannons roared the men crowded even closer together to cross the river. Men from other units began to merge into and between the Boys. Into Benjamin's peripheral vision came strange figures and faces, weaving in and out of the friends and family, concealing or replacing them. First, he lost Alfred in the sprinting mob. Then, as men came from the left and right and cut him off, his speed slowed and Oliver pulled away.

Between the dusty shoulders and hats of strange men, through their rifles and bouncing canteens, Benjamin strained to focus on his brother. Just a few yards ahead, Oliver slipped into the haze that surrounded Benjamin at all times in whatever direction he cast his eyes. No longer focused nearby on the comforting silhouettes of his comrades, searching instead to the limits of his vision, he was forced to look beyond where his eyes could see. His poor eyesight had never been more than a minor inconvenience, a source of jokes from his brothers. But now in battle, it was all that seemed to matter.

Once broken from the nearby focus, he could not regain it. He quickened his pace to bring Oliver into view but the varying paths of other men made it impossible. Now his fellow soldiers crossed his path at a dizzying pace. Blurred figures emerged from the cloud around him. They eased in as vague shadows, then either faded back or began to take form, depending on their movement. Some darted into focus, and then out again, fading back to ill-defined shadows. As new figures entered his narrow field of vision, his mind imagined them blue for a moment before they came into focus as gray. As flags waved through, there was red, white, blue and stars but his eyes could not make out their configuration. Cannons roared louder and the ground exploded to the sky at random around him. Men fell, downward into the blur with each explosion. Small arms volleys peppered the afternoon sky between the cannon blasts. At first they sounded together in a blast, followed by the falling of men around him. As he ran and the creek water splashed up his pant legs and ran down into his shoes, the musket blasts grew rapid, random and constant.

The men around Benjamin stopped and fired. Sometimes left. Sometimes right. Sometimes straight ahead. Not every man fired in the same direction. They were firing everywhere at all times. Others stopped to fire outside of the bubble of his vision, and he could not tell in what direction. He only assumed they were stopping to fire, unable to see for certain. Smoke from the rifles began to fill the air around him, the bubble of vision shrinking around him with every shot fired. He loaded and fired his own musket in the same direction as the man closest to him. He knew neither the location of his enemy nor the contour of the land in front of him. He learned it one step at a time as his feet felt the land rise or fall through mud and over rock. When he fired, he looked ahead for Oliver, finding him sometimes, others not.

The sounds were no longer distinct. The cannons, the singing of approaching shells, the explosions all around him, the yells, the muskets both friendly and hostile, all merged into one roaring scream that rattled him to his core. He tried to force his ears to distinguish sounds, not for safety but for sanity. His ears failed him and his eyes added nothing. His field of vision tightened like a noose in the smoky field. There was nothing but blur. Both eyes and ears useless, he was alone amidst the charging army. Unsure what lay in any direction, where to go, where to fire his gun, in what direction safety might hide. Each time he stopped to fire now, he faked it. He went through the motions, pretended to load and fire, then ran on when the men closest to him ran. He never really loaded or fired. Not knowing who was where, friend or foe, he was as likely to kill one as the other. The fear of killing one of his fellows was too much, and the ruse was not worth the waste of precious ammunition. Irrationally, he wondered if any of his comrades were able to tell that his shots were fakes. Though he himself had no hope of seeing the details of his comrades' actions, he assumed them all professionals. Calmer, more aware, more prepared than he. Their shots into the dark always assumed to hit a blue target off in the invisible distance.

The only cause to his charge now was completion. To the army it still held purpose, but Benjamin's blindness prevented any contribution. Was he running in the same direction as before? Was the river still behind him? Was the enemy to the left, the right, ahead, or simply everywhere? His charge was confined and directed by the bouncing gray shoulders nearest him. Had they run straight toward an object of military significance, straight to the enemy, or were they as lost as he was? Still he ran on. There was nothing left to do but run.

There is a moment in battle where unknown factors combine to create an unlikely monster of war, that speed a mission free of hesitation into almost certain death. Whether it is anger, fear, comradery, insanity, or merely the overwhelming of a human being to a temporary breaking point, it causes one to yell from his gut and throw himself into the impossible as if he cares nothing for the consequences. No matter what the real cause may be, soldiers refer to this as courage.

Without senses to guide him, Benjamin screamed and shook his musket before him and doubled his speed. His mind no longer raced. All analysis ceased. There was only a charge. Feet springing off of uneven ground, one after the other. But then a vision. Oliver, lost in the smoke and blur and din some moments earlier. His fancy uniform, his broad-brimmed hat with tassels. Benjamin focused on the back of his brother's head. His mind returned. He slowed his pace just to that of Oliver's before him. His single focus was a spot on his brother's neck just below the brim of his hat. Everything else came and went in a haze. The sound faded. The entire world was that tiny little spot, a mole just below the line of Oliver's closely-cropped hair. And it was in that spot that the neck suddenly opened, bloodied. The head snapped back and the hat was tossed in the air. The hands were thrown upward as if surrendering a moment too late. All sounds vanished under a single explosion. All sights went white. Benjamin felt himself rising, then tumbling blindly forward. He crashed into an object in front of him. His eyes opened and he squinted and turned his head to one side, trying to focus. Slowly the object beneath him came together before his eyes. There was a dark spot, from which the darkness flowed outward in every direction. Then a shape around the spot, round but ragged. Then a face. A face with grotesquely open eyes and mouth. Short hair appeared, with a broad-brimmed hat inches away. The dark spot was a hole in the neck. And the man was dead. But it was not Oliver. It was someone's brother. Perhaps someone else's protector and point of focus in this charge, but not Benjamin's. He clamored to his feet and continued forward.

Running now faster than ever, Benjamin abandoned any hope of finding his brothers. Another shadow came gradually into his vision. Frustrated by his eyes' deception again, Benjamin doubted it could really be approaching from directly in front of him. But then a face—not the back of a head—formed from the blur of the shadow before him. The face was broad, grimy and determined. There was an impact that hurled Benjamin again onto the ground amongst fallen bodies. He raised his head and looked what he believed to be forward. More shadows, appeared, grew faces, and disappeared to his right or left. Had they run directly into the charging Yankee army? As his eyes focused, he saw that the men were not in blue, but butternut and gray. The retreat had begun. Still, he crawled forward over arms and legs and abandoned weapons, just beyond the smoke from muskets fired in retreat. He was at the front. No figures passed from in front or behind. Balls whizzed by seeming to come from everywhere. Benjamin fought to focus on what lay across the field. Vague flashes of red came and went from all directions. They curved around him as if targeting him from every angle. For the first time Benjamin understood he had been in a crossfire.

He turned and ran backwards in what he hoped was the direction from which he had come. Neither vision nor memory could tell him where to run. Instead his path was guided by the fallen. As long as he was within the path cut by those either dead or wounded, he must be headed in the right direction. And he was headed there fast. In his mind minie balls were chasing him and he was fast enough to outrun them.

No one else was running nearby. He was behind the entirety of the retreating army. With no brother to search for ahead, no fellow soldiers running by his side, he focused his eyes on the ground before him. The ground, and those upon it, were close enough that his eyes could focus. Even still the eyes were slow to adjust to his rapid movement, and clouds of gun smoke passed in and out of the bubble around him, smearing large tracks through his field of vision.

Individual images molded into focus for fleeting seconds, then melted back to shadows and disappeared behind him. An open-mouthed boy propped up against a faceless body, gurgling his last breaths. A man with a long beard shaking an empty canteen above his mouth. Crawling men, pulling themselves over the bodies of others, back in the direction of the creek. A disoriented soldier staring back in the direction of the failed charge, cussing and gesturing toward the Yankees firing at him from all directions, oblivious to the musket fire around him. Then suddenly, there was the river. The whirring of minie balls was gone, as was the thud as they entered already fallen bodies. The big guns still rumbled behind him, but the explosions were fewer and more scattered. He caught up to limping men, and those being carried back to camp. Across the river he could see a moving mass of gray, with little squares of color floating above.

* * *

The day approached from across the field he had charged the previous afternoon. For once Benjamin Dockery was thankful for his limited vision. The path of bodies that led down the hill and into Yankee crossfire was beyond the reach of his eyes. There was merely a pasture that fell to a creek, then rose on the other side toward a line of trees illuminated by the rising sun. His eyes saw only smudges of misplaced gray, but he knew what they were. His ears, however, worked all too well. There was still wailing and moaning that came from across the river, where now some of the men walked unthreatened to assist.

Standing on a large rock outcropping looking down over the destruction was a man in an impossibly clean dress uniform, doubtless changed from that worn in the charge the evening before. The man looked through field glasses and scanned the trees across the creek. He pulled the glasses down and removed his hat to wipe his brow. His dark hair was short on the sides and back, but longer where swept across the front. His face was very large and round, with a neatly trimmed mustache, but no beard. The eyes were bright, set beneath prominent eyebrows. He smiled as his brother approached him.

"Good morning, Benjamin."

"Morning, Oliver."

"And a fine morning it is."

"How's that?"

"He's gone."

"Who's gone?"

"That Yankee coward, General McClellan."

"How can that be? He laid a whipping on us yesterday."

"Surely he did, but apparently we know that better than he does. I heard it from some of the other officers, and didn't believe it myself. I've been looking through these glasses for thirty minutes and see no sign of him. Care to have a look."

"Yeah, you're funny Oliver. I'd have a better chance of seeing a fly on mule's ass from a hundred miles away. But what in the world do you think he's doing running off with the high ground?"

"I guess ol' granny scared him off. I almost feel bad for him. He has no idea he has us outnumbered. No idea that Richmond is almost bare as we attack him here. All this attacking from General Lee has him convinced we have the superior force."

"What do you think we will do today?"

"Chase him. Keep up the myth of our superiority. As long as Lee takes the fight to him he can't take it to Richmond. We'll be headed out any minute."

"Where's little Alfred? Should I wake him?"

"Oh no. He's awake. He's down there going from tent to tent getting the boys fired up for the attack."

"You have to admire his energy."

"Agreed."

The two men stood and looked off thoughtfully in the distance, one discerning little from his distant gaze, wishing he had the vision of the other.

"Oliver?"

"Yes, brother."

"I was completely blind out there. I didn't know who was us and who was them. I had no idea where I was shooting, so I stopped shooting altogether. I was just running around under enemy fire with no hope of inflicting a wound on a single Yankee."

"You need to get out of here, Benjamin. Get home to Betty. Get married. Start a family. Figure out what you plan to do with your life. Stay alive, for goodness sakes!"

The younger brother glared back at the man up on his perch.

"I'm no coward, Oliver. I'm no shirker."

The big brother laughed, eyes still on the horizon.

"Obviously not. I can't imagine many men would keep charging headlong into the enemy with no way to see him and no way even to hurt him. Running into musket balls and cannon fire coming from all directions, unable to tell who is who and what is what? There may be a lot of words for that brother, but cowardice is not one of them."

"I'll be called a coward and you know it."

"Any man who calls you a coward knows nothing of what you just did. And any man who does so is probably holed up behind a desk thumping his chest and imagining what a great soldier he would be, if only he were ever to be one."

"What about the cause?"

"The cause? When you were charging into that maelstrom yesterday were you thinking about the cause? Well I wasn't, but I *was* thinking. And I have been thinking looking over this field with our friends dead and dying out there. With those Yankee boys across the field dying. What are we doing here, Benjamin? What is this cause?"

"This is Virginia, brother. This is the South. We are fighting them because they are down here. We are fighting them because they won't let us decide for ourselves what we want to do!"

"To do what exactly? What is it we want to do? Govern ourselves? Of course I believe we should. But nobody started talking about cannons and muskets until they threatened to take our slaves. Father understood that, and he didn't want this. He never wanted North Carolina to secede. He told us all what would happen. What this would look like. But off we all went. Caught in the fervor that all men our ages must have felt. Swept up in the feeling of being a part of something. A cause."

"You're talking nonsense, Oliver. Father owns slaves. You own slaves of your own. There's more to this than that."

"I suppose there is. I suppose they should have left us alone. But now here it is before us. We are killing each other. Less than a hundred years ago we ran out the British because we wanted to be free. Now we are killing each other over our right to deprive others of the very freedom we fought for."

"So you are an abolitionist, now?"

"No. I guess I'm not. If we could end this war and I could keep my slaves, I suppose I would do just that. Maybe if we end the war fast enough I still can. But this war is a mistake. And we may just be on the wrong side of history. You need to go home because you'll be killed for nothing charging blind into bullets. I need to go home and try to talk some sense into those that haven't seen what we have just seen. The offices and streets and churches back home are filled with those who have never seen the likes of the horror we have just seen. God willing they never will. They haven't even imagined it. If they had, they would not be for it."

"What are you saying, Oliver? Are you going to quit this war?"

"Maybe not today, but yes. Yes, I believe I will. Men make mistakes every day. Then we make more mistakes because we're too stubborn to admit we have ever been wrong in the first place. We dig a hole deeper and deeper, making mistakes in service of our previous mistakes. Not me, brother. This war is a mistake. And I'll be damned if I will insist on the death of tens of thousands more just because I am too damn stubborn to admit I was wrong in the first place. And you think *you* will be called a coward? Imagine what they will say about me. But let them say it. Right is right and wrong is wrong. What we saw out there yesterday, what we did, cannot be right."

Seven

Jim Dockery
July, 1862
Virginia

All Jim knew was that he was in Virginia. Surely Richmond was nearby. This was all about defending Richmond, or so he had been told. Yet he had no idea in what direction it lay. Wherever it was, galas were still held, attended by ladies in elaborate gowns and men in top hats. More celebrated still were the men in gray uniforms passing through the city with stories from the front lines. Surely those men commanded the attention of the ladies in their dresses as much as they did the men in butternut and gray in the camps and on the battlefields. The townspeople would all be aware of the threats to the city, to their way of life. They would hear rumors of troop movements, of attacks, of bold defenses by their emerging hero, an aging soldier with a neat, white beard. Some had fled of course, but most refused. Their way of life was not to be disturbed by the war being fought to preserve it. To do so, in their minds, would be to let the Yankee aggressors win.

Jim didn't know the men around him. Somewhere Oliver, Benjamin and young Alfred fought shoulder to shoulder. He knew they were nearby, also defending Richmond, but again was uncertain as to the details. In the West, Thomas and John fought together as well. The only Dockery boys left alone were Jim here in the Virginia woods and Henry left at home to dream of future glory. Jim stood behind a battle line of his new comrades in a dark forest of ancient hardwoods. Waiting. Having been told the enemy would come. Many of the men around him had already seen action in a dozen engagements. Their clothes were torn, their faces hardened. Some had wounds that had failed to take them out of service. Others had disappeared to hospitals or to Yankee prisons, only to find their way back to fight again. There must have been a time not long ago when their faces seemed younger, more eager. When they arrived in camp as part of a new army, ready to deliver prompt victory to the cause they held dear. Leaving behind fields or shipyards or turpentine mills for something more meaningful. Above all, perhaps, something different. A heroic interlude in lives otherwise unexceptional. But then the realities of war had set in. A year had passed. Lined up in the woods waiting once again for those who would kill them, the rosy cheeks and bright eyes of eager young men had gone. Their faces now wore the haggard stare of worn off novelty.

They had seen more than Jim. Knew more of the truth of war. His only knowledge came from books or his father's lectures delivered in safety at the Brick House. Yet they had put stripes on his shoulder, and the eighteen-year-old boy who had never faced a hostile bullet was a sergeant, in theory a step above the privates who wore their experience on their faces. How would they respond when he gave an order? Dutifully? Defiantly? How long would it take him to prove himself to them? That he deserved the rank that was likely awarded based upon his last name.

He searched the faces for any that might know less than he did. There were always new arrivals. Boys like Jim, whitewashed and innocent, dropped amongst hardened veterans. Boys who were deprived of the excitement of arriving all together in a wholly new army, back when the ignorance of each individual had been shielded by the ignorance of the group. Jim's eyes kept returning to the same place. Just in front of him, waiting anxiously for the fight to begin, was a boy that had just arrived in camp the day before. He was a child, really. To Jim, the child appeared to be no more than thirteen or fourteen. He wondered how he had gotten here. Was he older than he looked? Had he run away from home when his parents would not let him fight? Did he have any parents to hold him back? The child was barely five feet tall, and could scarcely have weighed a hundred pounds. He had arrived in a crisp, new gray suit that must have been made by some relative. Certainly it was made from less cloth than any other uniform in the army. Yet still it hung loosely. Whatever mother or aunt or sister had sewn it had thought to allow for his growth, a sign perhaps that his family lacked the optimism of many that the war would be short-lived, though they clung to the optimism that he would live to grow into it. His large floppy hat sunk down over his ears and concealed half his face. His scared green eyes barely peeked out from under the broad brim of the hat. He had made a rather comical appearance upon arrival, like a rosy-cheeked child playing dress-up in his father's wardrobe. Though Jim feared for the child, he welcomed his presence. There needed to be someone more ignorant than Jim under his command.

Beside the child and directly in front of Jim was a tall, wiry man that seemed to do all the smiling for the entire regiment. Jim had seen him in camp the night before, holding court telling stories to a circle of faces looking back at him from around the fire. He had apparently been a bailiff back home, and his stories arose from the courtroom.

"So the lawyer jumps up to give his closing argument. He says, 'We've been in here three days but there's one simple fact and one fact only that you have to think about when you go back in there and decide whether it was these two boys stole those horses. You heard it yourself. Everybody who saw it says it was two mulatto boys. Half breeds of some kind. Light-skinned Negroes. Well just look at these two boys. Look at them! They are as black as a pot of coal in a cave at midnight. They were just as black the day those horses were stolen as they are today. Looky here, this doesn't rub off.' And so he reached down and wiped his hand right across one of their cheeks and held his hand proudly up before the jury. You should've seen the silly smile on his face. When all the fellas on the jury started laughing he had no idea why. Starts laughing with them. Reckon he figures they think he's funny. Thinks he's got'em in his pocket. Then finally he looks at the daggum fingers he's holding up and sure enough there's blackface smeared all over his fingers. The fellas had done gone and darkened up their faces to beat the charge and hadn't told their lawyer about it. He pulls his handkerchief out to wipe it off his hands. White handkerchief. Well the more he rubs at the stuff the more it seems to spread. Next thing you know the whole daggumed white handkerchief is about plum black, and the spot on his fingers is no smaller than when he started. The jury gets to laughing so hard that the judge starts wailing away with his gavel yelling 'Order in the Court, Order in the Court!' He hits the thing so hard the head of the gavel snaps off and goes rolling right up to the feet of the lawyer. He picks it up and walks it over to the bench and the whole courtroom can see that now the gavel head has big black smudges all over it. The whole courtroom gets to laughing so hard the judge has to call a recess and send everybody to an early lunch."

Now the wiry bailiff was standing beside the child, who had been one of the faces smiling and laughing at the stories the night before. The child wasn't smiling or laughing anymore. His tiny body seemed to sway back and forth slightly. Jim wondered if he was going to pass out. The bailiff reached out and grabbed the child by the shoulder, steadying him. The child found his legs, and turned to his new mentor. He leaned his head way back to look up and smile at the tall man from under the brim of the hat. The bailiff patted the child on the shoulder and smiled back down at him.

A single shot sounded in the distance, its sound rattling through the trees. Jim felt a thud on his chest. It took his breath for a moment, but felt different than he had expected. Less painful. Less dramatic. Though his body ached and he stumbled backwards a step, he felt nothing of the hot piercing of his flesh he had imagined so many times. He stood stunned, waiting to fall. Slowly, the bailiff crumbled to his knees. He reached both hands up to his neck. Blood poured through his fingers as he slumped to the ground at Jim's feet. The child dropped to his knees over the bailiff. He cradled the man's head in his tiny hands. The bailiff was motionless. His eyes already lifeless and empty. The child's chest heaved and his eyes closed tight. Just when he appeared to give in to the tears forming in his eyes, he clinched his teeth visibly and fought every child-like instinct within him. Shadowy figures were beginning to appear through the trees. A tight line of darkly clad soldiers moving in orderly fashion. The child's face instantly hardened. He gathered up his rifle and stood stone-like above the dead body of his newfound friend.

Jim was still standing. He looked at his chest and saw no wound, no torn uniform. There was a smudge of blood where the pain throbbed, but he knew it was not his own. Scanning the ground at his feet, he saw the ball. The small, round projectile lay right between his feet, smeared with the bailiff's blood. He understood what had happened. The ball had passed through the bailiff's neck, and continued on to hit Jim without the speed to do serious damage.

The shadows through the trees paused their motion, seemed to be readying themselves to fire. Jim heard orders shouted along his lines by others with stripes on their shoulders to match his own. He followed their lead. "Ready ... aim ... Fire!"

Murderous volleys were exchanged in both directions. The shadows fired their muskets, then moved forward. Coming into focus as men in blue. Rough men with beards and scars and hardened faces. Men not unlike those firing back at them. Loading their weapons as they moved ahead. Jim's boys reloaded furiously, the child no slower than the men around him. Both sides fired again. Men dropped at random through the ranks, their comrades not pausing to acknowledge them. Jim thought back to his father's lessons. The orderly portion of the battle would not last long. Organized volleys would give way to "Fire at will," followed by hand-to-hand combat. For now, he knew what to yell and when. But when the range of battle became close it was less clear what the stripes on his shoulder would require of him, other than to kill and not be killed like the battle-scarred privates he supposedly led.

There was an insane energy in his comrades. They had been marched hard to get here, wherever here was, with but little to eat and little time to sleep when they arrived. And these were men who had fought almost daily in recent weeks. Yet they seemed anxious for the close-range fighting to begin. Seemed to sense that they fought with more fury than their enemy, and could beat them in a scrap where one soldier's task was simply to whip the man in front of him.

As the men in blue inched forward, Jim sensed movement to their rear. Behind them were more shadows, not inching closer in orderly fashion but darting quickly behind the advancing column as if to reinforce their flank. He looked to his left. No more than twenty men were standing between him and the end of the line. No higher officers were to be seen. No more men. There was no need to reinforce the Yankee flank because there was no one to attack it. No, that wasn't it. It was an attack. *He* was being flanked. Soldiers in blue were rushing around the end of his line to crush him from the side or from behind. He did not know how many. Nor did he know how in God's name he had been put in this position in his first fight. In the grand scheme of things it may be but a skirmish, but if he was swept from the side the entire line would collapse.

Before him the child was firing and reloading efficiently. It would be nothing more than seconds before the order to charge would be made from both sides. Jim grabbed the child by the shoulder of his new uniform and jerked him out of line.

"Run beside me!"

The child attempted resistance, but came off the ground as Jim pulled him.

"I ain't no coward, Sergeant! I ain't running!"

"You're missing the point kid. We're being flanked. Run your ass off down this line and tell every officer you see. The more bars on their shoulders the louder you yell. Tell them we'll be dead in five minutes if they don't reinforce the flank."

The eager green eyes showed understanding. The child lowered his head and ran wildly with his arms flailing as he went. Jim, still running himself, watched as the child grabbed officers by the jacket, yelled and kept running. His youth itself seemed to draw attention to him as he approached. Before it could occur to the officers that they were moving on the word of a toddler, they were already doing so. Jim expected to hear a bugler. Expected at least to find one. When he finally did, he was lying dead behind the line, his bugle still in his hands. Jim had run past more than two hundred men, most well outside his authority to control, but it was no time for protocol. He sprinted back down the line letting his hand bounce off the back of each man, yelling for them to double the spacing between them. He extended the line further toward the left where the new assault was expected. As he ran, a soldier pulled up even with him and passed without looking. Jim was stunned by the man's speed. He stopped momentarily and turned to look behind him. More soldiers were coming. The child's urgent plea was working. From all down the line officers were sparing whomever they could, and the men were running wildly toward the flank. Soon Jim found himself leading a small army that flew past the original flank and immediately erupted into a sound Jim had only imagined. A bone-chilling screech not from the throat, but from elsewhere. A sound one could not consciously make. That could come only from an absolute release of all control or care. Knowing you are about to die, and embracing it. The last gasp of a collective departing soul. The Rebel yell.

The forming mass drove itself directly toward the blue shadow slowly appearing before it. The shadow itself seemed to falter. Even before the men had faces, they seemed surprised. It occurred to Jim he had never given the order to charge. Everyone knew what had to be done.

The shadows grew faces. They were aiming and readying to fire, but something was different now. Once visible, their faces showed fear. Once under attack, their self-assured movements gave way to unsteady feet. Their aim wavered. Men fell when their volley was fired, but most of the balls seemed to fly over the heads of the rapidly approaching Rebels. The pace of the charge was stunning. A full sprint. There was no chance for the Yankees to reload. Some broke and ran before the impact. Most of the rest died instantly thereafter.

From the menu of faces before him, Jim's mind selected one at random. He was a young man with a smart face. He possessed some quality different than the hardened men nearby. Perhaps education or wealth. The face was rugged, but distinguished. Jim was still running at full speed when his bayonet hit the man's gut. The force of the impact was so severe that much of the barrel of the rifle was buried. The man never moved. He had just finished loading his musket, a second too late. Unable to dislodge his own gun, Jim grabbed the dying man's freshly loaded musket and fired into the rapidly retreating column. Few shots were fired from men in blue. Those who managed to load and fire before meeting the bayonet fired in panic. Some hand-to-hand combat occurred up and down the line, but the retreat left the few Yankees outnumbered. Jim spotted one soldier in gray trying to fight his way from beneath a much larger man. A huge man. Jim loaded the rifle and took one knee. The Yankee was straddling the Confederate and taking wild swings at his face. Somehow the nimble Confederate dodged most of the blows, the Yankee's fists crashing into the dirt below. Jim steadied his gun and tried to time his shot at the flailing Yankee. The larger man lunged forward to finish off his enemy, but when he did the smaller man dodged again, then came forward with a small knife that slashed expertly across the Yankee's throat. Exhausted, mortally wounded, the man flopped face down upon his adversary. Jim jumped up and ran to the scene. It took him and another man to roll the giant off of the young Rebel soldier. When they rolled him away, Jim saw the battered face of the child.

He reached down a hand and helped the boy up. By now, the surging troops had doubled back and were charging back into what was now hand-to-hand combat along the original line. Jim smiled down at the boy.

"Run with me again!"

The two young men sprinted back into the fray. Flanking the original attackers. The speed and the fury of the counterattack continued. The Rebel yell erupted yet again. Before the charging Rebels reached their target, the men in blue disappeared in full retreat.

Eight

Solomon Dockery
November, 1862
Rockingham, NC

"Mr. Alfred, sir? Will you be needing anything else this evening, sir?"

The General looked up from the candlelight at his desk in the study. Held the paper he was reading well out in front of him and glanced toward the door.

"No, Solomon. That will be it for today. Have a good evening."

"You too, sir. Thank you, sir."

Solomon turned and looked back across to the door of the warming kitchen. In the evening quiet of the house he could hear Miss Anna's soft voice coming from inside.

"Will there be anything else tonight, Miss Sally?"

"No, Anna. Thank you. And Anna … the chocolate pies were delicious."

"Thank you, ma'am. Have a good evening, ma'am."

Solomon's eyes met Anna's as each stepped out of a doorway towards the another. They walked across the ground between the back wings of the house, and Solomon opened the gate and allowed Anna to exit ahead of him. He followed and shut the gate behind.

"It's gotten dark, Miss Anna. Would you like that I walk you home?"

"Thank you, Solomon."

The two of them walked slowly from the house down along the tree line, back toward the little village of cabins that sat along the western stretch of the dry run creek bed that ran behind the house. Before they got there, they parted with the tree line and walked uphill across the field. A small stand of young pines concealed their movement from any eyes about the house. As the most prominent slaves on the plantation, no slave driver would dare follow them.

They came to a split rail fence along the Cartledge Creek Road. Solomon scooped Miss Anna from the ground and cradled her in his massive arms. With ease he lifted her over the fence and placed her gently on the far side. Then he placed one foot on the bottom rail and bounded himself over. They smiled at each other in the full moon light and continued walking slowly along the road.

The road climbed gradually up a long hill before curving to the left. Without a word, he knelt down in front of Anna and felt her wrap herself around his shoulders. He stood with effort and continued up the hill with Anna on his back. The big man felt an ache in each knee as he plodded along, but never staggered or slowed. He counted steps in his mind to pass the climb more quickly, not looking to the crest of the hill above. When they finally reached the top, he knelt down again and felt the weight leave his shoulders. Anna walked around beside him as he caught his breath on his knees. Before rising, he took one of her well-worn hands, and gave it a formal kiss. They both giggled quietly, the first sound either had made since leaving the Brick House. Solomon enveloped Anna's hand in his massive bear paw, and continued walking along the trees that ran beside the road.

At last they came to the clearing. Up on the ridge was a vast swath of treeless land that spilled down on both sides of the road and swept dramatically into the valley below. The blue light from above colored the night sky down to the dark shadows of the trees that reappeared far below and continued for miles unknown. The road itself was a pale stripe that curved steeply down the clear hillside, traversed the valley and then curled to the south toward Rockingham. Down in the bottom of the valley was a fork in the road. A narrow path that veered north, then disappeared once more into trees.

Solomon and Anna sat down at the top of a tiny slope above the road that provided a good view. They each slipped off their tight, formal shoes and felt the grass with their toes. Solomon took a long look at Anna. The graying hair pulled up in a bun, tied with a blue ribbon. The thoughtful crow's feet around her tiny, black eyes. The last vestiges of beauty clinging to her face with the same dogged determination that had brought her this far in a slave's life. Both of them were getting old. He felt it in his knees and back. Saw it in her eyes. But over that fence she grew younger. In the moonlight, with her shoes kicked away, everything changed. The pensive eyes came to life. Became childlike in a way that half-filled the void he felt inside. He reached over and took her hand again. She smiled.

"Where will it take us, Solomon?"

"Don't know. Never made that turn. Always traveled the main roads with Mr. Alfred."

"No, I don't mean it like that. In your head. When you sit and look at it at night. Where does it take you?"

Solomon took a deep breath. Paused for a moment, and said simply, "Away."

They sat quiet again. Both looking down across the valley toward the road.

"We got it better than some, I reckon. They been pretty good to us."

"Yes'm they have. But they got a piece of paper says I ain't a man. Another one that says you ain't a woman. Paid good money for them papers, too."

Anna smiled and pulled herself closer to Solomon. He felt the warmth of her against him, and looked out into the darkness of the trees to the north. Wondering how the little road wound its way far away. Dreaming of what it would bring.

"Don't you move, you stupid niggers!"

Solomon looked up. The silhouette of a slender man on horseback approached. A small red circle flared and faded under the bill of a hat. The smell of cigar smoke followed. Then a familiar metal sound. The cocking of a gun.

"Let's see … what have we here?"

He rode up close and inspected Solomon and Anna, both now on their feet. Smiled deviously through a scraggly beard. Made a show of blowing cigar smoke in Anna's face. Solomon's arms flinched ever so slightly and Anna grabbed his right arm to hold it still.

"I know who y'all is. Looks like I done hit gold! Y'all'r the house niggers from down at the Dockery place, aren't you?"

It was Solomon who responded.

"We work in the Dockery house, yessir."

"Work … right. And how does he pay you?"

No response.

"I said how does he pay you, nigger?"

Now the barrel of the pistol was in Solomon's eyes.

"We are who you think we are."

The man laughed out a cloud of smoke.

"That's what I thought. Old as hell, too. So we got us an old Uncle and an old Aunt done run away together. Heading north I guess?"

"We ain't running nowhere, sir."

"Well here you are at night not on the Dockery property, traveling the highway alone. If you ain't running, I ain't riding."

"Look at us, sir. We're both too old to try to run anyplace?"

"Shut up, boy! I know plenty of stupid old people don't know what they can and can't do."

"Excuse me, sir. We need to be going now. Mr. Dockery will be missing us."

The pistol shot erupted near Solomon's head. The sound rifled down the hill into the valley and disappeared into the trees as if it had followed the road. The bullet passed so close he could feel it brush by his ear. Anna squeezed his arm. He felt her pulse quicken against his forearm while his own raced in his chest.

"*You* were running! *I* caught you! You see, there's a reward for these things. It's up to him whether he whips you or kills you. But it's up to me and the law whether I get paid for dragging your runaway asses back home. So turn your big ass around and start walking. Let's go down there to that big house and get a fella paid."

Solomon looked up at the man and did not turn to walk as ordered. He felt Anna's grip on his arm tighten even more. The pistol was back in his face again. Still Solomon did not move.

"You listen to me, nigger. I can kill you right now in this road. Won't nobody ever say nothing."

Solomon stared at the barrel of the pistol. He imagined the flash. The sound. Wondered if he would even know the shot had been fired. If he would see the flash or hear the blast. Would there be any time for pain? He imagined a darkness. A nothingness. Alternatively he thought of an escape to a better place. A place with no papers. *And the last shall be first.* Either way he would be … away. Beyond the judgment that he was less than a man. But then there was Anna. She was all there was left. His wife was murdered in Georgia. He and his children had stood together in the market in Charleston. Learned of their different fates. Both girls sold down to Mississippi. His one and only son to Arkansas. Never to see each other again. Still there was Anna. And what would become of her if this was how he got "away."

Finally he turned. Following orders again. From a man he could crush in a fair fight in a different place and time. Anna turned with him, her pulse still pounding against his arm. When they turned he saw a man on horseback approaching. Solomon smiled. Just from the silhouette he knew who had arrived.

"Is there a problem here?"

"No problem at all. Just found me these two runaways and need to take them over to the Dockery place."

"Runaways? Is that right?"

"Shore is. That biggun there was about to get what was coming to him too if he didn't finally listen to orders."

"Well, I'll tell you what, sir. How about you holster that weapon. I don't like you pointing it at the head of my house servants."

"Yours?"

"That's right."

"General Dockery?"

"Yes, sir."

"Well … I guess you and me has got a small matter of business to discuss. See, I done prevented these here from running away. Reckon I'll need to be collecting a reward."

"Very well. I hereby allow you to leave and go back where you came from without being arrested."

"You no good sonofa, well, … you better not stiff me."

"Perhaps you can explain this to me, young man. Why are they barefooted?"

"What?"

"Barefooted. And I bet they were sitting in the grass when you came up on them."

The man holstered his pistol and said nothing.

"Holding hands, right? Looking down into the valley. Tell me I'm wrong."

Again, no response.

"So you see, young man, these two young lovebirds committed the awful sin of sneaking out here to get their feet in the grass and hold hands and enjoy the moonlight. In fact, they do so about every time we have a full moon. Or did you think I didn't know that? Did you think I just didn't pay any attention at all to what was going on around my place? Respond, young man … say something clever you shit-kicking smart-ass … nothing? You got nothing to say anymore. OK then, son, just ride along and we'll call it even."

The man turned his horse away sheepishly and melted back into the darkness. Alfred, Solomon and Anna all began their slow return to the plantation. The walk down the hill was much easier. Alfred rode slowly beside them as they walked. Anna clasped Solomon's hand firmly. He felt the sweatiness of her palm. Knew he had pushed it too close. That the only escape worth making was one made with her in his arms.

"Solomon. Anna. You two be careful coming out here. These are strange times. The war may not be in our front yard, at least not yet, but things are different. There's lots of uncouth characters riding the roads out here that ordinarily wouldn't be. Like that fellow we just saw there. He could be off fighting this war. Or at this shade of night he could be at home taking care of his family. Instead he's riding up and down the road looking for trouble. Trying to make a dollar by making you two out to be runaways. Can you imagine that?"

"Seems you're right about the road, Mr. Dockery, sir. I think there's somebody coming right now."

They all stopped on the side of the road and stared into the darkness ahead. Whomever approached carried no light. No one could be seen at all. Solomon heard the faint sound of steps approaching.

"Sounds like two men and an animal of some kind, Mr. Dockery. Donkey maybe"

The General looked down at Solomon from the horse. Said nothing. Held one finger to his lips. They all stood silent, waiting. Solomon wondered if the men ahead were cohorts of the man who had pointed the pistol at his head. Whether that man, whom the General had shamed, could be circling back around behind them. Still the only sound ahead was of footsteps on the road, and the plodding steps of some beast of burden. Anna squeezed his hand harder still, her pulse quickening again. They waited in silence until the steps almost reached them. Not even shadows appeared on the road.

"Who is that there?"

The footsteps stopped. For a moment there was no sound at all.

"Uncle Alfred, is that you?"

"Ben? Ben Covington?"

"Yessir, it's me. And I sure am glad it's you."

"Step a little closer here so I can see you."

The General hopped down from his horse as Ben approached. Solomon could barely see the young man in the darkness. His round, child-like face with a few days growth of beard. Beside him was a tall, broad chested black man holding a rope attached to a stout old donkey. Alfred looked at Solomon and chuckled.

"Solomon, how in the world did you know it was two men and donkey?"

"Jest one of those things you know, sir."

Alfred shook his head and smiled, then reached out his hand and grabbed the shoulder of his young nephew.

"Uncle Alfred, I believe you know Amos."

"Of course, I do. Amos, good evening to you."

"Evening, sir."

"Yeah, Ben, I've been trying to get Amos away from your daddy and over here to work for me for a long time."

"Never happen, Uncle. My Dad would never part with Amos. And if he did my sister Betty would never let him live it down."

Amos bowed slightly to Miss Anna. He and Solomon nodded at each other. They had met, of course, but never really spoken. They drove the families to church in the wagons on Sundays and sat near each other in the back during services. They had once cooked a pig together behind the church building on July 4th, a holiday no longer celebrated in the South. There was often an awkwardness in the encounters of slaves of different masters. A brotherhood from a shared struggle perhaps, but there was a distance that was felt but never spoken. They were like strangers deserted on neighboring islands, neither able to swim across to help the other.

"Ben, what in the world are you doing out here in the pitch back dark?"

"Finally headed to war, Uncle. I'm headed east to catch up with the 36th. It took a lot to convince Mom and Dad. So they're sending Amos to make sure I get there OK and to keep an eye on me, I guess."

Alfred grabbed both of Ben's shoulders and pulled him close. "Son, is this really what you want to do?"

"Yessir. Of course it is, sir."

The General's shoulders sagged. He looked at the ground for a moment, then re-engaged with Ben. "You're a grown man. Do what you must, but do be careful, son. And be careful traveling this road. There's unsavory characters out here. They would kill you for less than the price of a good man and a good donkey."

"Yes sir. I understand, sir."

Alfred reached out his hand to Amos and grabbed his shoulder as well.

"This is a good boy here, Amos. All the Covingtons are good folks. You take good care of him. Bring him home to his family when this is all done."

"Yessir, Mr. Dockery."

"Evening, Miss Anna," Amos bowed to her again. He and Solomon traded a knowing glance, and then the boy, his donkey and his slave walked off into the darkness toward the war that awaited them. Solomon turned to watch them go, but the darkness had already swallowed them. The General was back on his horse, ready to get off the road. Having no need to hop the fence this time, they entered through the main gate and walked down the lane between the oaks. They headed to the right where the path split before the house, and helped the General stable his horse for the evening. He smiled at Solomon and patted him on the shoulder before turning to go.

"Mr. Alfred, sir?"

Alfred stopped walking and looked back at Solomon and Anna.

"Yes, Solomon?"

"We was scared, sir. Both of us got split up from our families in the slave market. They didn't want us together. We thought if you knew how things were between us you might keep us apart."

"I'm not mad, Solomon. I understand. But I can't do without you and Sally can't do without Miss Anna. We'd never let either one of you get taken away from here for any reason."

"One more thing Mr. Alfred, sir. How long have you known about me and Miss Anna?"

"About six years, Solomon."

Anna and Solomon looked back at the grinning General in disbelief. All their sneaking around for all these years. He had known all along.

"Thank you, sir."

"Have a good evening, you two."

Alfred headed to the house and the aging couple headed for the cabins, both quiet for a while.

"You so sure you need to be dreaming all the time about getting away, Solomon? That's a good master right there."

"If there was any such thing in the world he'd be it, Anna. But there just ain't no such thing ... there ain't no such thing."

Nine

Jim Dockery
July 4, 1863
Gettysburg, PA

He could not run anymore. He had run all over Virginia for months, then around the Pennsylvania countryside for the last several days. Chasing Yankees. Then being chased. Marching to a fight. Fighting. Marching again. All with little information imparted as to where they were going and why. Just keep killing the man in front of you. With fewer bullets than he has. Less food. Less sleep.

Now Jim walked slowly away, the enemy at his back. Chants from taunting Yankees carried from behind the stone wall and across the field to his ears. Perhaps they would stop chanting and charge. Perhaps they would shoot him in the back, or swarm around him and demand he drop his weapon. Still he could not run. A starving soldier must sometimes access energy hidden from all others. Must somehow charge when others would fall. Must fight when a normal body would fail. Jim already had done all that. Every drop of energy he possessed had been poured into that charge across the open field and toward an enemy entrenched on the high ground. Into the fight that awaited him when he arrived. Now there was no energy left to run away. The soldier can find an energy to attack that he cannot find to retreat. Maybe they would come. Maybe they would not. But he could not run from them.

Nor could the others. Across the vast field was a scattered mass of men with slumped shoulders, walking achingly back across the grass they had charged through moments before. Echoes of the Rebel yell still reverberated through the field as they retread their steps in reverse. No officers guided them. No bugles sounded. Most of their leaders had led them into the enemy, and would not be walking back. Jim was unable to focus on the sights around him. The dead were everywhere, in every configuration and state of demise. Craters from explosions with bodies scattered about. Officers and men laying side by side. Flags on the ground, having been carried by several fallen soldiers in succession. Horses struggling with broken limbs. Others running about the field, searching for their fallen riders. Some men trying to call out for help. Yelling for water. Crawling back to the trees from which they had emerged in a long glorious line. There were too many of them. Thousands of them. The luckiest among them could still walk, though too slowly to avoid the chase that may come.

Random musket blasts sounded from the hill above. The occasional ball whizzed by. Even an artillery blast from an eager gunman wanting one more taste of blood. Jim's exhaustion was so extreme he could not have run from a shell he knew to be heading right for him. As he walked he began to feel a pain. One he had not felt before. Though both legs resisted each step, he soon found he was dragging the left foot behind. Most of his left pant leg was torn away. There was blood from his ankle down into his shoe. Stopping for a moment and pulling up the shredded garment, he saw the neat hole in the front of his leg. The bullet had entered in the meat of the leg, just to the inside of the bone. At the back of the leg was a wider, more uneven hole, with lose flesh dangling. An exit wound. He stared at the wound for a moment as if looking at someone else. One of the men laying on the ground around him perhaps. He then dropped the pant leg back down, partially concealing the wound, and continued walking slowly back up the hill.

The mighty army that had defended Richmond against superior forces with superior supplies, that had pushed itself north seeking an end to the war, now limped its way back to Dixie, for the first time considering that it might not win the war.

Hagerstown, MD
July, 1863

Jim awakened to the sound of gunshots. He instinctively sprung to his feet. When the left leg hit the ground the pain rushed up through his body and he fell back to the bed. He heard himself groan, then quickly stopped so no one else would hear. There were more gunshots. Random, quick bursts of fire. Not sustained shooting. As the fog lifted, he tried to remember where he was and how he got there. Was surprised to be in a bed. The first bed he had felt in a year.

He looked around. Someone was coming toward him. A woman. A nurse he guessed, but not dressed like a nurse. The shots continued. He wanted to go to the window. To look out and see what was happening. But he knew the leg would not allow it. The shots ceased and he sunk back into the bed, studying his surroundings. He was not where he expected to be. It was a long, dark hallway. The beds seemed crammed into place and the ceiling was low. The hospitals he had seen were open and white and cold. This hall was dark and narrow and he felt sweat across his forehead. The woman was standing over him now, checking his bloodied bandages.

The sight of her struck him like a lightning bolt. For a moment he forgot himself. Forgot he was injured, in an unknown location, with muskets firing sporadically in the streets outside. Her hair was pulled up tight to a bun in the back of her head. There was a pencil stuck through the bun. She wore glasses, and a very serious look. Her clothes were those for church, not work. A long black skirt and matching short-sleeved jacket. She lacked only a broad hat of being fully decked out for Sunday morning. The severe look in her eyes was cut by the flawlessness of her white skin. The brightness of her light blue eyes.

Even her delicate hands that Jim noticed as she worked.

"Ma'am, what's with the shooting?"

"Haven't you heard? There's a war."

"I mean what's with the shooting *right here*?"

"It's been going on for two days. Off and on like that all the time. Just more silly boys trying to kill each other."

She continued about her work, not looking him in the eye.

"This isn't a hospital."

"No. It isn't. Not normally anyway. It's a seminary … for women."

"You aren't a nurse."

"No. Not normally."

Still, she refused to look at him. It seemed intentional to Jim. The message loud and clear, "I have work to do. Don't try to talk to me!"

"So why are you here?"

Finally she looked at him. Hand on hip. Blues eyes suspicious.

"A little early for that isn't it. You've only just woken up."

"I beg your pardon, ma'am?"

"Oh, a Southern gentleman. Do you really think you have something to say that all your friends here haven't already tried on me?"

"Well, you're mighty presumptuous, aren't you?"

"Am I wrong? Were you not about to make small talk, biding your time until the opportunity for a flattering comment came along."

Jim smiled mischievously. There was something different about her. A sharpness. An intelligence. To go along with her obvious beauty. No matter how much he wanted to find out if they were going to chop off his leg, it could wait a few more minutes.

"Yes, you are wrong. I am sorry to disappoint you, but I simply do not think you are a very pretty young lady. I would have kept these thoughts to myself — out of politeness, of course, being a Southern gentleman and all — but I feel you have forced me to say something."

At long last, a smile. Though a reluctant one.

"Then stop looking at me like that."

"Like what? Seriously, I am not interested. You would know if I was. I am incredibly good at talking to girls. There is no telling what sort of witty things I may have said by now if I was pursuing you, even in my sedated state, which I now suspect you have induced to weaken my defenses to your advances."

"My advances? Is that the way it is?"

"Of course. Had I been interested you might have gone down the hall and grabbed one of the preachers to come marry us by now."

"I am so sorry to have been presumptuous."

She smiled again and turned to walk away.

"So why is it you are here, Madame Non-Nurse?"

She stopped and turned to him. He had no idea why he was playing this game now, here. Just couldn't stop himself.

"I am a student here. My mother was a nurse, so I know enough to help. But really, I am here because Southern soldiers do stupid things like walk all the way from Gettysburg to Hagerstown with a giant hole in their legs, and then pass out in the middle of town from loss of blood."

"So … about the leg?"

"You're going to keep it. At least I think you are. I'm not even a nurse, remember? But you're lucky to be alive. Had you not passed out in the middle of the street you probably would have gone on fighting with a hole in your leg until it became infected and killed you."

"I have no doubt you are right about that."

"Why are you smiling at me again? I am telling you that you almost died, that you are lucky you collapsed in the street, and you are smiling at me?"

"Can't help it. You're getting all worked up and fussing at me and it makes you even prettier than you were before."

"So there it is. You know, you really aren't as good at this as you say you are."

"Yes I am. Come on, it's working a little bit. Isn't it? You're still standing here, right?"

"Just doing my duty," with a glance back at his name written by the bedside, "*Sergeant* Dockery."

"Hey, no fair. You know my name and I don't know yours."

"How about we keep it that way?"

"Oh come on! I need a name to give the preacher. There's

paperwork required. You know, for the wedding. Otherwise I'll have to make up a name for you. How about … Gertrude. Gertrude Ruth Ann McGillicutty."

"That's awful."

"It's what's going on your marriage certificate if you don't tell me otherwise."

"OK, fine. It's Emily. Emily Williamston."

She was smiling openly now. The severe façade cracked. Then she caught herself. Turned serious again. She looked from left to right, pulled a little wooden chair up to his bedside and sat down. She leaned in closer and whispered.

"What do you think is going to happen here, Jim? It is Jim, right? Do you think I'm just going to hop up in that bed with you and your shot-up leg? Do you think I am going to be — what was it one of your oh-so-classy colleagues asked me to be yesterday — a horizontal refreshment?"

"I know that's not who you are."

"Then just what are you after? We know how this will go. In a few days, God willing, your leg will be well enough for you to travel. You could go home, but you won't. You'll keep fighting, and you'll end up in some mass grave with a hundred others, and I will never even hear about it."

"You're probably right. But what if I live?"

"If you live you'll go home and marry some belle. If you remember me at all, I'll be the girl you tell your buddies about. The enchanted moment that came and went and left you wondering what could have been."

"That's not so bad is it? Fella lying here all shot-up sees a girl walking towards him. Sees something different in her. Sees she's worn out with being flirted with by shot-up boys. Gets smitten with her right off the bat. Sure, she's pretty. Beautiful actually, but that's not what gets him. She's smart, a bit sassy perhaps, just different somehow. Fella doesn't think it all through or wonder how it might come out in the end, but in that moment he just can't help but try to talk to her. When she starts to walk away, has to try to make her stay even for just a minute more.

And when she criticizes him, he can't help but defend himself because for some reason he already deeply cares what she thinks of him. So the fact is I have no idea what I am doing or what I am *after* as you keep saying, but I know this. I like you. And you're probably right I'll never see you again. But I sure wish I would. Makes a fella wish he had more than one life somehow. Anyway … this is the longest conversation I've had with a girl in over a year. And the only time in my life I've ever had a conversation with anybody like you. So I am sorry if it seems like I'm some sort of raging bull, but sometimes a fella can't help himself. Even if he doesn't know what he's *after*."

She looked at him for a while, neither of them speaking. Her face had softened again. For the first time in the entire encounter, Jim was not looking in her eyes.

"One more thing, ma'am." He was coming back down from his rant and he was smiling at her again. "If you're not ever going to be anything other than a wistful memory, just one kiss would sure help."

Emily smiled but did not reply. She reached out and squeezed his arm with a delicate hand, then left it resting there for a moment. Jim stared at the hand on his arm, then back at Emily's eyes again. There were no gunshots in the street. No sounds inside the seminary. For the moment he was quite content to look at her. Nothing more. Finally, Emily broke the silence.

"That little kid that brought you in here sure was right about you."

Jim's eyes snapped open wide.

"Little kid?"

"Looked like a kid to me. A kid in uniform with a rifle on his shoulder."

"You mean Willy? Private Crane? He's alive? Thank goodness. I hadn't seen him since we stepped out of the woods for that Godforsaken charge. I assumed he was dead. So many hardened men died out there. He's so young. I just assumed."

"That's right. Crane. That's how he introduced himself. I'm surprised you didn't know. He brought you in. Said you were together when you collapsed. He told me the whole story."

"I don't remember much. Not a thing from the moment we crossed into Maryland. I guess I was sort of passed out on my feet."

"Well, you're lucky. And you're lucky you had him with you. When I say he told me the whole story, I mean the *whole* story. Back to the day he joined the army. How the two of you saved the day in your first battle."

"Oh, no. He didn't try to flirt with you too, did he?"

"That child? Goodness no. He was more likely to crawl up in my lap and ask me to read him a bedtime story. But you should have heard the way he talked about you. Spreading the lines to stop a flanking maneuver, whatever that means. Charging a makeshift army into a superior enemy. He went on and on. Called you a 'gentleman warrior.' Said you'd be a general someday."

Jim's eyes glazed over, distracted for the moment by thoughts of battle.

"Well. What did you think of all that? I guess I should hope you were impressed."

"I don't know." She was blushing. Vulnerable at last. "I'm embarrassed, but ... I was anxious for you to wake up. I was curious."

"Really? The ice queen herself wanted to meet me?"

"Don't let it go to your head too much, Sergeant. I was curious. And besides, you're really quite a disappointment. Just another hillbilly shooting at people and flirting with girls because you have nothing better to do."

"My goodness, Miss Emily. Is that a sense of humor that I detect?"

She smiled, then shyly turned away. A weakened voice from down the line called out the word "nurse."

"Duty calls," she smiled, and walked back down the hall.

July 12, 1863

Jim jolted awake. Emily was coming towards him in a rush. She carried a bundle of something in her hands. There were no gunshots outside. She looked different. Better somehow. It seemed as though she had jumped from her bed and run to the seminary. She wore the same formal attire, but it seemed she had dressed in a hurry. Her hair was straight down and un-brushed. It was much longer than he expected.

Her face was flush and she moved with purpose. Despite her frantic movement, there was something about seeing her in an un-fixed state that made her completely irresistible to him. He could feel his heart pounding in his chest like the moment before a battle. His legs felt like jelly. His mind started traveling places he had not let it go when it tried the day before. She grabbed his arm and he looked up at her in a trance.

"Snap out of it Jim! You have to go. Now!"

"What? I don't ... the leg, you said several more days."

"You'll just have to limp. Like you did to get here. Look, I brought you clothes. They're my brother's. He's close to your size."

"What in the world are we talking about right now?"

"The Rebels ... your army, they're gone. They left in a hurry apparently. A lot more Union soldiers have arrived. Your army must have found out they were coming somehow and slipped away. I'm afraid you've been left behind."

"Do the Yankees know we are here, in this seminary?"

"I am sure they do. They will come here for you, for all of you. Put on these clothes and get out of here."

"Where is your house?"

"What?"

"Your house. Where is it? I will come there tonight to get you."

"That's insane. It's impossible. It's too ... how could I ..."

"Please don't tell me 'no,' Emily. Not right now. We can discuss it tonight. At your home. Just don't tell me 'no.' "

She stared back at him, silent. The long, dark hair hung down wildly to her waist. Her normally white face was flush with the excitement of the morning. The blue eyes conveyed shock. At something. At what Jim was proposing. Or perhaps what she was thinking in response. Her lips parted to speak. The doors of the hall burst open. A red-headed officer and a dozen men with rifles blasted into the hallway. The officer strutted over toward the first bed in the hall, Jim's. His eyes climbed up and down Emily as she stared back at him in horror. The soldiers spread out down the hall, covering all of the Confederate patients with their rifles. The officer spoke first in a thick Irish brogue.

"You are all now prisoners of the United States of America, except for you young lady, though we'd be happy to take you along with us as well."

The officer was now standing directly across Jim's bed from Emily. At the foot of the bed a young man not much older than the child stood awkwardly holding up a rifle seemingly too heavy for him. Nonetheless, he was strong enough to pull a trigger, and the barrel was pointed between Jim's eyes.

Emily's hand was on his arm again. He turned from the barrel of the rifle to look at her one last time. She was looking at the officer with rage. When she turned back to Jim her eyes changed. The fierceness was still there, but there was something different. She leaned down over him, cradled his head in her hands and kissed him deeply. By instinct, Jim's eyes closed and the two of them were alone, elsewhere, in some other life, where this was not the only kiss they would ever share.

"Enough!"

The officer kicked the bed and scowled down at Jim.

"That had better hold you boy-o. There won't be much of that where you're headed."

Emily was still pulled close to him. She pressed her cheek to his and whispered into his ear.

"Never forget what could have been."

Ten

Jim Dockery
August, 1863
Point Lookout Prison
Point Lookout, MD

Jim bobbed in the slow roll of the surf of the Chesapeake Bay. The salt water washed against the still-open injury to his leg. He grew used to the sting of the moving water licking his wound. Knew it was doing him good. Pain or not, the warm water washing in from the sea beyond and the sun shining down on his head and shoulders revived him. Provided refuge from what lay just behind him. Point Lookout Prison. The tainted scraps of meat served in thin broth that reeked of filth. The foul-smelling water he drank to survive. The constantly prodding bayonets of the guards, many in the hands of recently freed slaves, some kind to the prisoners, but others anxious to exact revenge for the injustices done to them down South.

Commercial ships passed slowly further out to sea, adding to the calming effect. The gentle green water rolled out in both directions and formed a peaceful arc, a far horizon that stretched infinitely away from confinement. A fiction preserved only if Jim kept his focus out to sea, away from the other haggard prisoners bobbing around him, each trying to do the same. And, of course, if he did not look back to the prison behind.

He imagined himself aboard one of the ships. Knew the work would be hard, that to the crewmen the freedom of the sea may become the confinement of the ship. Yet still he longed to be on board, *en route* to some exotic locale, where a few days' liberty in port would bring knowledge and experience never to be found in Rockingham, North Carolina.

The wheels of commerce had not been slowed in territory controlled by the North. Smoke still rose daily from the stacks of manufacturing plants. Newly made bullets and cannonballs still flowed steadily to the front lines. So did uniforms, shoes, socks and food. The troops in blue had coats to stay warm, minie balls to fill their guns, and hardtack to fill their bellies. The ships that cruised by carried the Union soldiers all they needed to win.

Jim thought of the ports of the South. Long rows of ships that did not move. Blockade ships, choking the lines of commerce which could have provided the South with all those things it could not produce for itself. The sun rising and setting over inviting inlets and passages that saw not one ship come or go. The only activity under cover of darkness, when sleek blockade runners tried to dart between the bulky blockade ships and equip the Confederacy one small cargo load at a time.

Is that why we did it? Is that why we charged up a hill over open ground into certain defeat? Because they have more men, more guns, more cannons? Is this why we made the foolish mistake the Yankees made at Fredericksburg?

It was a convenient thought. One that preserved both his belief in the superiority of the Southern fighting man and a loyalty to Southern officers who had, until now, proven their superiority to their counterparts to the north. But it was one he did not truly believe. Not that the basic premise wasn't true. It was. His brief time as a captive had proven that to him. His captors, though battle torn and weary, were better fed, better clothed, better equipped. Yet somehow their morale seemed lacking when compared to the Confederate soldier. The Northern soldier suffered from a well-fed weariness, contrasted by his opponent's gaunt-eyed determination. Over the Yankee camps had existed a constant expectation of doom. Even after the massive defeat at Gettysburg, the Southern soldier still maintained an undying faith in General Lee, in victory and in the cause.

Nonetheless, the fact was that the longer the war, the more certain a Union victory. The soldiers did not seem to realize this. The officers did. Perhaps the Confederate officers were too aware. In too big of a hurry. Though it was true they needed a decisive victory before their resources ran dry, the situation was not yet so imminent, so desperate that the high ground had to be sacrificed so easily. At least Jim did not believe so. But no one had bothered to ask the opinion of a teenage sergeant. It had been just as his father had taught him using the contours of the Brick House lawn. Whenever two great armies meet on a vast field of battle, each entrenched on ground of their choosing, there should be no battle at all.

If only the generals had learned from the General, Jim thought. So the distraction had failed. Even the calm of the sea, the dream of nothing but horizon in all directions, exotic ports offering experiences not yet imagined. Somehow it all led back to reality. To the war. To the disastrous direction it had suddenly taken. To his confinement, his inability to do a single thing about it.

His empty stomach rumbled under the surface of the Chesapeake. Jim pushed himself deeper out into the Bay. He kicked himself under and plowed through the dark water with wide strokes of his arms. He surfaced again. Wiped the salty water from his eyes. Paddled his feet to keep his head above the now deeper water. With a deep breath he lunged upwards and then dove straight down toward the bottom. He felt his way along the marshy bottom, letting tiny bubbles of air escape from the corners of his mouth. His blind fingers brushed against something sharp and ridged. He kicked his legs again to fight the body's desire to return to the surface. With both hands he pulled at the clump he had discovered until it pulled free from the mud and rose more easily. With awkward effort, he kicked himself across the surface to one of the several posts rising slightly above the water. The guards had driven the posts deep into the ground below. They rose above the surface, the water always lapping against them, forming a "dead line" the prisoners knew not to cross. At lower tides they could be found sitting atop the stumps like so many pelicans, knowing the rifles of anxious guards were trained coolly upon them. Some of the guards, Jim expected, thirsted for a bloody break from the monotony of guard life. It was rumored that more than few prisoners had ventured across the line. Most times a single rifle shot and a splash near the head of the offender was enough to trigger a quick retreat to the safer side of the line. Others, Jim had heard, drifted lifeless out to sea.

Jim hefted his clump of oysters up onto one of the posts, then crawled himself up onto the next. He sat looking at the oysters blankly, feeling the gentle lapping of the warm salt water at his ankles. The wound to his leg was in the air again, and a different pain pulsed from the scar up through the leg.

"Hello there, friend. Use this."

The man was sitting on top of the next post over. His face was a leathery red, with deep groves pressed into the skin around his eyes. His blondish hair and beard had dried stiff in the salt air and he seemed accustomed to the sea. He tossed a smooth stone the size of a belt buckle to Jim. It slid through his hands and threatened to fall into the sea, but Jim folded his arms up against his chest and trapped it before it fell. He looked back at the other fellow who nodded at him, and made a hammering motion with his hand so as to instruct Jim on opening the oysters.

Jim broke one of the oysters from the small clump, the sharp edge of one of the oysters slicing his finger slightly in the process. He looked down at the finger, licked away the thin line of blood and looked back at the man who had just tossed him the stone. The man chuckled and smiled back at Jim. He held up an already opened oyster. The gray mass was still stuck to one side of the shell. The man popped the meat lose with his thumb, raised the shell to his mouth and sucked the oyster in. He chewed it for a second, wincing slightly like an experienced whiskey man sipping the night's first taste of sour mash, then smiled and winked at Jim again.

Jim bashed the oyster with the smooth stone. He bungled it. Tiny shards of shell dug into the meat. He meticulously picked away the shell, then tried to imitate his new friend's trained style of oyster eating. The oyster came loose of the shell with some difficulty, then Jim popped it into his mouth. It was his first oyster. The brininess and the texture were a shock. He didn't know whether it the worst or best thing he had ever eaten. No parallel could be drawn to anything else he had ever tasted. When he heard the chuckle of his new friend on the post beside him, he knew his face must have shown his confusion.

"Reckon that's the first one of those you've ever had there, friend."

The accent was unmistakable. The oyster eater was a High Tider, the name given to natives of the Outer Banks, those peculiar strips of land separating mainland North Carolina from the abyss. Though clearly Southern, certain vowels were oddly elongated, as if a Maine Yankee was taught to speak in New Orleans.

"Reckon so. Seems like you may have had one before."

"Reckon I have. Had about a dozen today. Be better with a little sauce and a cracker but a fella takes what he can get under such conditions as he may find."

Jim smiled quietly at first. He didn't want to talk. Wanted to fill his belly in peace. To look back out over the sea again and search once more for the daydream that could deliver him for a moment from sad reality. Still, he felt compelled to speak. Knew the man was from North Carolina. That he could perhaps shed light on how to survive in such a place as this. Finally, he gave in.

"You from Down East in the Old North State?"

The High Tider smiled at Jim again. Popped another oyster into his mouth with a flourish.

"Whatever could it have been that gave me away?"

"It was your hair."

"Ha! That's pretty good, there, massuh."

"Massuh?"

"Yes, massuh, would you like me to empty your chamber pot for you, massuh? How'd you like a spot of damn tea, massuh? Would you like me to warm your sheets with one of them do-dads that holds a few coals from the fire down at the foot of the bed?"

Jim was beginning to regret he had spoken.

"Got you, don't I, massuh? What you got, a thousand acres? 50 slaves?"

"Something like that."

"Ha! I knew it. Us boys down east ain't the only ones whose voices give them away. It ain't just no thousand acres though is it? If it was less you'd a told me."

"OK, OK. You got me alright? Congratulations. And thank you for the stone. But to tell you the truth they just threw me in this jail and I'm not in much of a mood to be made fun of."

"Don't reckon I ever encountered nobody that *was* in a mood to get made fun of."

Jim cracked a smile.

"Yeah, I guess not."

Both men sat quiet for a while. Jim laughed to himself about the High Tider's annoying slaveholder imitation. *If it was directed at someone else*, he thought, *I would have found it pretty funny.*

He resolved to talk to the man about life on the coast. There was no telling how long they would be confined. Jim didn't know whether his war was over, or whether he would fight again. He watched the High Tider, looking so at home perched on a post in the sea. The sunburned skin, the lean frame, the sun-bleached hair. He looked out at the ships passing by and muttered to himself in a voice Jim could not hear. The laughing eyes suddenly showed a deep pain. Something out there in the sea he had lost somehow. He reached both hands down into salt water and splashed it across his face. With his back turned to Jim, the man splashed his hands in the water repeatedly and brought them up to his face.

"Say there, friend. We might be in here for a while. Other than eating oysters, what can you tell a farmer like me to help me get by out here?"

The High Tider turned back to Jim. Something had gone in his eyes.

"You mean a planter, right?"

"Excuse me?"

"I said you a planter, you ain't no farmer."

"Yeah, fine. That's right."

Jim smiled, referring back to the joke. The High Tider wasn't smiling anymore.

"Ain't shit I can tell you, massuh. There's no such thing as staying all winter. Cold wind blows off the sea. You stay here you dead. That's what they say about this place. Good place to stay in the summer. Good place to die in the winter."

The man's eyes were dead. Jim was shocked how much they had changed so quickly. The man reached his hands down to the water again. This time Jim could see. He was cupping the saltwater in his hands and drinking it.

"Good God, man! You can't do that! You of all people should know this. It's poison, man. You'll lose your mind."

The High Tider looked back at Jim, blankly. He reached both hands into the water, scooped as much as he could and made a show of drinking it.

"What the hell you know about it? Don't make a damn no how, massuh. Been drinking that shit all day."

"Listen, buddy, we've got to get you out of this water. Let's get you to the medic in there. Or get you to throw that stuff up."

"I was supposed to be in the navy, massuh. We ain't got much of a damn navy in this here outfit. I was a good man too. A good boat man. Not supposed to run through no damn grass with those damn fools shooting cannons at me. Supposed to be in a boat with those damn fools shooting cannons at me."

He smiled again, but not like before. Like a drunk trying to act sober. Trying to play off his drunkenness, having no idea how obvious it was to all around him. As if he could howl at the moon all night and then suddenly feign normalcy for a few seconds and fool everyone in the bar. Jim moved toward the High Tider as if to make good on his promise to help him ashore. Before he could get there, the High Tider jumped up onto the post with both feet, one on top of the other.

"Guards! Hey guards! Massuh here says he's gonna make a swim for it! Says he thinks he can get all the way out to one of them ships!"

Jim watched as the muskets trained themselves on him. He settled back down onto the post and didn't dare move again. In the water, the other bobbing prisoners were beginning to make their way slowly back up onto the beach.

"Come on now, fella. You're liable to get both of us shot. You been drinking too much salt water and you're not thinking right. Come on down off of there and let me help you back into shore before something goes haywire."

"It's already goddamn haywire!"

He was responding to Jim but was yelling up at the guards on their stands. His face seemed drawn in and even redder than before.

"I said I was supposed to be in the damn navy. This ain't no navy. I ain't meant to be on the dirt all the time. You see them ships out there. I could swim all the way out there. I sure could. I got three lungs, like Blackbeard. I might even have gills!"

"Come on now, buddy. Things are about to get messy. I know you can swim it, but those guards, they'll shoot you."

"You can't shoot me you dumb sonofabitch guards! I'll flop to the bottom and swim on my belly like a flounder. I'm a flounder, you bastards!"

Jim looked out to sea at the ships. There were two passing each other well out into the Bay. He guessed they were a mile away.

"I'm sure you can. I'm sure of it. But those are Yankee ships out there. When you get there, they'll bring you right back in here. Then the guards can shoot you up close."

"That red ship is the one I'll swim to, you sorry yellow jackals. That great big red one. Looks French to me. They'll be happy to have a man like me on board. They won't bring me back to you good-for-nothing blue-coated half-asses."

Every word he spoke was hollered at the top of his lungs. Despite his sickness, his balance on the post was remarkable. His face grew darker, with more lines. His voice grew louder. Gesturing at the guards with every word. His chest was bare, and he wore shredded rags for shorts, held in place by knots tied in the dangling threads. His hands were worn from work and appeared to belong to a man twice his age. Jim scanned the horizon. The two ships eased past one another. The distance between them beginning to grow. Both appeared dark in the afternoon sun. Neither was red.

A flash and a jolt came from one of the sentry posts. The water splashed at the High Tider's feet and up onto his legs. He burst into hysterical laughter.

"Wooooeee! You sorry bastards. Time for a swim."

He reached down to his waist and tore away the rags. There before Jim on a post in the Chesapeake stood the bare naked High Tider, laughing hysterically and dancing mockingly, flaunting his naked body to the guards. Somehow he turned himself around on the post and bent over, showing his white hind end to them as well.

"Take you a good gander at my white underside, you crabs. I told you I'm a flounder. And a flounder's gotta swim!"

He looked at Jim. Suddenly more soberly.

"You know, there, fella. I've done about had it with this shit."

With that he pointed himself out to sea, toward the imaginary red ship, shook out his arms by his sides as if loosening up, and executed a lovely dive into the Bay. Shots rang out from the sentry posts. Small eruptions tore the surface near where the High Tider had entered the water. As each guard paused to reload, the water cleared from the splash of his entry. By the time the muskets were raised, the surface was glassy again. Seconds passed. One of the bathers now gathered on the beach broke the silence.

"Keep swimming, Johnny Reb! Keep swimming!"

The others joined in and soon the beach was alive with the cheers and taunts of the soaked prisoners. Finally, well beyond where the last shots were fired, the High Tider emerged for a breath. As he did the guards all fired again, their bullets ripping the surface in the immediate vicinity of the swimmer's momentary reappearance. Again the surface smoothed, the guards reloaded and the prisoners cheered. A minute went by and nothing happened. All eyes scanned the surface out beyond where he had last surfaced. Another minute passed. Still nothing. Eventually the guards propped their muskets against the wall by their posts. The bathers gradually eased back into the water. Jim took the stone the High Tider had given him and opened another oyster.

Temptation

He rode horseback down the hill behind the big house, alone. The trees cleared where the creek flowed, and the horse instinctively increased its trot and easily cleared the thin flow of water. With a few slight lunges of its head and neck, the horse dipped from its vast well of strength and climbed the hill to the clearing above.

At the top was a vast field of cotton. On the east end, a slave driver sat on his horse with arms crossed. He was a tremendous, thick man. His pants were haggard and barely reached his ankles. A whip was coiled in his belt. His shirt was thin, faded red and unbuttoned, exposing a broad, muscular chest. His sleeves were rolled up and there were rows of muscle that rippled as the fingers of each hand drummed habitually against the biceps of the opposite arm. He nodded at the approaching man, and pointed silently to the patch of cotton being picked by a dozen of his fellow slaves.

The man rode his horse around the corner of the field where the driver had motioned. Each slave was crouched down between the rows pulling the thick balls of cotton from the plants. Before them were plants laden with full bunches of cotton clinging to the branches like snowballs. Behind them were lines of reddish-brown branches with just traces of white remaining. Each picker had a large woven basket filling up fast as they picked. One older woman walked with a basket on her head toward a wagon parked along a dirt lane.

The sun, high in the sky, beat down on the dark-skinned pickers. In the air above the field, its rays illuminated tiny strands of cotton that floated in the windless sky and then settled back to the Earth below.

Amongst the pickers, he saw her. She was young, maybe nineteen or twenty. Unlike the older women around her, she wore a thin cotton dress. It was oversized and meant to hang loosely, but clung to her sweating body in the stifling heat. She worked steadily, mechanically, without acknowledging anyone or anything. Her hands snatched the balls of cotton rapidly and dropped them in the basket at her feet. Her eyes were always forward, never on the basket below. Clearing a bush in seconds, she would shift to her right and start again.

Her cheekbones were high and smooth, and her skin shone brightly in the sun. She had oversized brown eyes that betrayed nothing but concentration on her work. Her ears were small, and above them was a blue rag tied to protect her from the sun. Her lips were full, and appeared puckered slightly as she worked. After filling her basket again, she stood and stretched her arms above her head. When she did, her dress pulled back tightly against her ample chest, and climbed ever so slightly up her long, lean thighs.

"God help me," the man whispered to himself.

He pulled the reigns and turned his horse back toward the woods from where he came. Only then did she look in his direction.

PART II

Eleven

Alfred Dockery
July 28, 1864
Rockingham, NC

Alfred Dockery sat alone at the head of the dining room table again. Where he had sat so many times before. Where his children sat for years, eating together in relative calm and happiness. Where, as the years passed, he saw the number of his surviving sons still at home dwindle from seven all the way down to one when Jim finally won his protracted battle with Sally and gained his freedom to join the Confederate army. That had left only Henry, who fought daily for permission to enlist. It was a fight he was not to win. Sally would not see this table emptied of her sons.

It was around this table they had celebrated every milestone, every success of every child. From childhood birthdays to graduations, marriages to the births of grandchildren. Easters, Christmases, Thanksgivings. It was here also where friends gathered when tragedy struck. Where they would line up dishes of home-cooked food from one end of the table to the other, expressing their condolences in their uniquely Southern way. Though his study was his escape, where he read under low light and considered the questions of the day, it was around this table that Alfred held court, receiving whatever dignitaries and politicians may come.

No seats had ever been assigned for family meals. Yet each child assumed ownership over their own. Now with many children grown and gone, it always seemed that visiting friends and neighbors had to fill their seats. In the empty chairs he could see the faces of tiny girls with ribbons in their hair, then eager young women, now mothers with tables of their own. In Jim's chair he saw the platinum blonde hair of his youth, the easiness of his manner, but the quiet depth in his eyes. It seemed to Alfred his whole life had been lived around this table, and that by sitting here he could see details of his past not visible anywhere else.

It was an odd day years earlier when the much-anticipated table was delivered. The craftsman himself—charged with making the grandest table for the grandest home in Richmond County—had personally delivered it. All morning Sally had fretted about how such a table would ever make it through the doors of the house, and then negotiate the tight left turn from the front door into the dining room. She and Anna and Solomon had discussed the matter at length while Alfred stood by and smiled to himself. She had gone so far as to have Solomon bring a timber of the table's anticipated length, just to see how best to make the turn without damaging the freshly painted walls. They had tried every angle without success. The curvature of the staircase limited the room to maneuver in the foyer. As the hours passed and the table did not arrive, Sally grew more and more distressed over how it would ever be squeezed into the dining room without first being sawed in two.

When the wagon pulled up, the chipper craftsman hopped down, wearing a mischievous smile under his thin-rimmed glasses. He asked for no help. Just casually disappeared behind the wagon and reappeared with a simple round, mahogany table. He barely strained under its weight as he carried it to the door. While Sally and friends watched curiously, he slowed to maneuver the table's legs through the front door and then continued into the dining room and sat the tiny table in the middle of the giant room. Sally's mouth was hanging wide open now, and the carpenter seemed to be deriving great joy from her dismay. He motioned to Solomon, who followed him to the wagon. Soon they both returned, each carrying four wide planks of beautiful mahogany. Anna, Alfred and Sally all followed the two men into the dining room. Solomon and the carpenter stood on opposite side of the little round table and pulled gently. The two semi-circles separated, revealing between and beneath them a network of sliding wooden frames, each the width of a mahogany plank. With each pull the table grew longer, and the craftsman placed another plank. Soon all eight planks had been placed, and the little round table had grown to a full twelve feet, every bit the grand table Alfred and Sally had envisioned. As they admired their new table, Solomon and the carpenter struggled under the weight of the massive matching sideboard, to be placed along the inside wall of the dining room. Alfred stood back and looked at the beautiful dining room, now finally furnished. At his glowing wife busily tucking away their finery. Years earlier he had been a mere wagon boy, toiling in the sun with blistered hands. What he had accomplished and accumulated in the years between seemed impossible. Things he had never expected of himself. Only Sally never seemed surprised by his success. She saw in him things he did not. To her his prominence had been entirely expected.

But that had been long ago. A smaller table would do now, though he and Sally never discussed removing even a single plank leaf. Sitting alone looking at the empty chairs, kept company only by memories, he looked into Jim's chair and saw him as a child. A child who had been reduced to a frail shadow in a Yankee prison, to then be paroled in a prisoner exchange. Who fought his way back to health only to return to fight again. A child now at war in an unknown battlefield, tempting death yet again to win a war his father had never wanted.

Jim Dockery
Gravel Hill, VA

A line of trees split two wide fields of green. It curved to a sharp point beside a long field that rose to a simple house. Along the ground were Union skirmish lines, with a jumbled mess of cavalry behind. The cavalrymen were scattered. Disorganized. The opportunistic Confederates charged. Shots began before Jim reached the field. The instinctive yell rang out once more.

The gray-clad army split in two at the point of trees, quickly overwhelming the skirmishers in each field and chasing the cavalry yet to find its way into position. Jim and Willy Crane, the child, fired their muskets at the backs of blue uniforms as the Yankees struggled to reach the trees beyond the long slope of green, the only cover in sight. Jim ran with Willy at his side and thought of their glorious first day of battle, now being replicated on nearby ground, chasing more Yankees away from Richmond.

Spirits are never higher than when you are sweeping an enemy from a field. You're running through green grass under the summer sun. You feel the enemy breaking, then see it before your eyes. Men struggling to mount their horses, not to attack, but to flee as fast and as far as possible. Retreating soldiers fumbling with their muskets, trying to fire a random shot back at you. As if firing that one shot somehow would mean that running wasn't really running.

"Chase the bastards back to New York!"

"Push them back into the river!"

"Kill every damn one of them!"

The whole army was in a sprint. Firing. Giving chase. Some of the boys scattered a cannon crew and seized the cannon. The gray and butternut swarmed over the modest peaks and valleys of the field. Jim could not see what was happening across the line of trees, on the neighboring field. He heard the Rebel yell tracking alongside him as he ran. Knew the rout was underway over there as well. Everywhere the Yankees were running. Everywhere the chase was underway. Maybe this would be the day they really did chase them all the way to New York.

Alfred Dockery
Rockingham, NC

Sitting at the empty table, it was hard for Alfred to believe how recently they had been there. Four of his sons, reunited again. Oliver and Benjamin home from war for good, having left young Alfred brotherless with the Brave Richmond Boys. Henry kept at home in his parent's protection, and Jim being nursed back to health by his mother. When Henry was the lone son remaining, Alfred feared he would never see any of his other sons at this table again. But then Oliver came to realize what many others were coming to realize as well, that the war had been a mistake. Benjamin returned home as well, unable to shoot an enemy he could not see, ready to marry a woman he could not see himself without. And then suddenly Jim was home. His appearance was shocking when he arrived. So thin and frail. So much age in the gaunt face. One of the young girls from church had showed up the day after he arrived, all too anxious to be the first to greet him. Alfred had seen the look in her eyes when she first saw him, sitting in his chair trying to eat. His mother lifting his spoon and wiping his chin. Politeness dictated the young lady not turn and run away immediately, but she found an excuse to take her leave at the first opportunity. It was weeks before he began to seem himself again. Only then did he begin talking of his return to war. Alfred had known this was coming. He had not said a word to Sally, whom he knew thought her son was home to stay. But then Jim told her himself. Alfred, at her urging, had invited Oliver and Benjamin to dinner to talk some sense into him.

"Jim, you've done your share. You've already fought in as many battles as any man in Richmond County. You've sat there rotting away in that prison having committed no crime. You've got nothing left to prove to anybody."

"Oliver's right, brother. We need you here. I've asked Betty Covington to marry me. We're going to build a house on the hill above the creek. We could sure use your help."

Oliver nodded while Benjamin spoke, anxiously awaiting his turn to jump back into the conversation.

"That's right brother. Slavery is ending sooner or later one way or the other. Between my plantation and father's, we are going to have some big decisions to make and there is going to be a lot of work to be done. We need you. Father needs you. And mother can't stand to see you go away again, especially not after what has just happened to you."

Alfred's eyes did not leave Jim's face. He watched as Jim waited patiently for his brothers to plead their case. Jim caught Alfred's eye and winked at him. The General looked down at the table.

"Brothers. I appreciate what you are saying. I know there is much to be done at home. Oliver, I think I have come to understand the way you see this war. I am not mad at either of you. I just have to go back. People in that army have saved my life. I owe it to them to return."

"Oh come on, Jim!" Oliver's round face was turning red. "You must see how big of a mistake we have made here. You must see that all of the States should have been able to figure this out without killing each other? You have to understand that if we don't find a peace and we lose this war, we will become second class citizens in our own country. Subjects of Northern rule!"

"That's what you would have us be though, isn't it Oliver! Subjects of Northern rule!" Henry had sat silently throughout the conversation, but had heard enough. "I don't give a rip about slavery, Oliver. I bet Jim doesn't either. I can't wait to go fight because we should be able to do what we want. Like folks say, we had to fight them because they were down here."

"You don't know anything about it, Henry! You want to fight because you haven't seen what it's like. And if it wasn't for slavery there never would have been a war. What do you have to say about it anyway. You're just a kid."

"Shut up Oliver! I'm not going to be lectured to by a coward."

"Enough!"

Alfred slammed both fists onto his precious table. The candles hanging about the room flickered under the vibrations. One across the room went out entirely. The gold-leafed mirrors on each wall hung crooked. Alfred felt a rare heat in his face. A loss of his cool. But a strength welled up inside of him and he seemed to expand to imposing size again.

"I will not have my sons fighting in this way! I will not have happen to us what has happened to others. This kind of debate has destroyed families across the South. Across the North as well. Oliver, Henry … don't talk like this is easy. We all know it is not. I rejected secession, but then voted for it when I felt I had no choice. When the only alternative was to send my sons to fight against South Carolina or Georgia. Oliver you rallied troops all over the county. Now I admire it when a man has the guts to change his mind when he feels it is warranted, but you sir are a living breathing monument to the fact this is not so easy that you can call your brothers fools if they disagree with you. Oliver and Benjamin, when you left, young Alfred stayed. As have your brothers out west. I'm not going to fight you about the justice of this war, or who will win or anything else. You are all men and must make up your own minds. Jim, I don't want you to go. I want you to stay. Become the husband and father and grandfather that God wants you to be. But I don't control you. You are a man now. If you feel you have a duty, I respect it as much as I do the different kind of courage Oliver showed when he started speaking out for peace. This is just what this war has done to us. You do what you have to do. But in this family, we will still love our brothers. No matter how much we may disagree."

The brothers all sat silent at the table. Their father's word was final, at least at his own table in his own home. It was Henry who spoke next.

"Father?"

"Yes, son."

"Does that mean I can go with Jim. That I can make up my own mind."

Alfred reached a hand out to his youngest son and placed it on his shoulder with a smile.

"No, son. I'm sorry. You, I still control."

Slowly, the Dockery boys rose from the table and made their way out of the dining room door towards the foyer. Alfred waited patiently until they had all gone. Then, he walked past the mahogany sideboard to the little door that led to the warming kitchen. He opened it softly, knowing Sally had been eavesdropping all along. She stepped gently towards him and fell sobbing into his arms.

But the table was empty now. Jim had long since returned to war. Henry still quarreled with his parents daily over his desire to join Jim in the field. Sally aged rapidly, sick each day with fear for her boys. Oliver traveled the countryside, advocating for peace as he had once rallied for war. Benjamin, at least, was fully immersed in young love and future plans.

Clouds darkened the sky outside and the candles provided dim light. Alfred squinted his eyes and could see all of them in their chairs. Each child stood out at different ages for their own reasons. Jim was still a blonde-headed child with something special in his eyes. A potential that could not be understood when seen in a young child. A capacity for bravery and a sense of duty his father was only now beginning to see, if not yet understand.

Jim Dockery
Gravel Hill, VA

As fast as Jim and Willy ran, the Yankees seemed to run faster. Many were clearing the field. Disappearing into the trees. The Rebels had no thought of stopping. The grouping around Jim headed for a rise in the rolling field. No one occupied the heights. The only Yankees seen on the other side were in full retreat. The Rebels increased their pace, wanting to catch the Yankees before they all escaped. Their charge rose rapidly over the rise and spilled over to the other side. As they came down the back side of the little hill a massive cloud of smoke erupted in a low line along the ground. Men fell all around Jim. Men who had been triumphant seconds before, now silent forever. The second volley followed immediately. Then the third and fourth. The volleys happened faster than muskets could be reloaded. The guns had to be the repeating carbines carried by certain Union cavalry. The rate of fire was several times that of a traditional musket. They had hidden on the hillside just over the rise and waited for their moment of counterattack. Everyone around Jim fell to the Earth. Even those not hit fell in search of cover.

Jim looked to the left and right. There was no organization to the field. Suddenly some Union cavalry were coming forward, while others still retreated. Some Confederates still advanced on either side of the sudden slaughter, while others began to drop back. The carbines kept firing at an alarming pace. Jim heard the thud of bullets hitting men around him, the cries of pain and despair. He sprang to his feet and encouraged others to follow. It was a mismatch. They had to fall back. Perhaps if they did so successfully they could reform and try to flank the force now before them. Willy was at his side again, holding a shattered musket in his hands, then letting it drop to the ground. This time they ran for survival. The memory of that glorious counter-charge now gone.

Unlike Gettysburg, the blue troops rose and gave chase. Others mounted on horseback joined them. They rode with their carbines in one hand, the reigns in another, positioning themselves to slaughter their retreating enemy. Horses and charging men encircled pods of Confederate soldiers, demanding they drop their weapons. Having started the retreat, Jim and Willy were at the front of the pack. As he sprinted, Jim looked back over his shoulder. Fewer and fewer Yankees gave chase, the others all occupied with new prisoners. The stripe of field before the rise was now covered with Rebel soldiers with muskets laying at their feet, hands in the air. Jim just needed to reach more soldiers in gray so he could turn and fight. Perhaps they could counter and recapture the newly taken prisoners. Just beyond the fields there were entrenchments that would provide the high ground against any attack. The sweep of the blue cavalry from the field having failed, the Southern soldiers made their way back to better ground. Up ahead a small group of soldiers were struggling to haul the captured cannon off the field before the Yankees could reclaim it. Their movement through the green was awkward, but just fast enough to salvage their prize.

Now with no approaching column to join, Jim and Willy had nowhere to run but the earthworks. Looking back over his shoulder again, Jim saw that only one horseman was in close range. Knowing he could not outrun him, Jim stopped, swiveled around and began to raise his musket. Before he could do so the horseman stopped mere feet away, looking down at Jim over the barrel of the carbine. To Jim's left, Willy was standing with his arms raised.

"Drop your musket, Johnny Reb. You can be my prisoner or you can die right here. Choice is yours."

Jim looked around and saw no help on the way. He laid his weapon at his feet.

"I am your prisoner, Billy Yank. But I beg of you sir. My little brother here. Let him go. I have been in one of your prisons and I know he will not survive. As you can see he has no weapon. He's a drummer boy. Only reason he is with me right now is because the other fellows he was with were killed by a shell. I told him to stick with me, which was just fine until you boys surprised us over there."

The child was red-faced and panting from exhaustion. Despite much time to grow into it, his uniform still had to be rolled up in the arms and legs to keep from flapping when he ran. He was still months away from his first shave. He looked at Jim in bewilderment, saying nothing.

"I've seen younger men kill before. The only way I know for sure he won't kill any of us is to send him to prison."

The man's words were harsh, but Jim sensed something in his eyes.

"Listen here, Billy Yank. You can believe me or not. That's up to you. But here's how this is going to go. You're in a dangerous spot here because you're farther forward than your boys back there. You don't need to chase us any farther. If I let you take him prisoner, he's as good as dead. So that isn't going to happen. No sir. I'll let you shoot him before I let you starve him. My brother here and I are both going to run. You will drop me with that carbine, I suppose, and then you have to decide whether to kill him in cold blood. To shoot him in the back. A child with no weapon, who had no weapon when you first saw him. Willy, you ready?"

Jim placed both hands on the child's shoulders, grasping him firmly.

"Better to die quick by the bullet than slow in one of those prisons. Trust me. Ready? On the count of three. One … two …

"Wait!" The cavalryman gritted his teeth and shifted uneasily in the saddle. "Kid, get out of here. Sergeant, you are my prisoner."

The child hesitated for a moment, looking up at Jim as he once did at the bailiff. More cavalry was coming up from behind. The child turned and ran as fast as his legs would carry him across the bloodied field toward the entrenchments beyond. Jim walked with his hands raised into the approaching column of blue.

Twelve

Jim Dockery
August, 1864
Near Sohola, PA

Jim was one of the lucky ones, as far as prisoners went. They were packed in tight, but he was pressed to the outside against a small window where he could watch the Pennsylvania countryside thunder past. It was pretty country. Rolling mountains covered over with big hardwoods. The tracks followed along the Delaware River for quite a ways. Nice wide river. Clear water. Jim thought about fishing for a while, as he did most any time he was near water. It was a nice thing to think about. He'd seen far worse than he had ever imagined, and knew well where he was headed. It was nice to think about anything but present reality. His eyes drifted up from the water and to the rolling green hills. He wondered how they might look in fall, all colored up in red and orange.

It was rocky country and at some time in history a mass of men had blasted and bashed through the rocks to create railroad cuts so the steel wheels of commerce would not be impeded. He thought of the words to a hymn often sang at Cartledge Creek Baptist Church. "On Christ the solid rock I stand, All other ground is sinking sand."

Jim thought about how hard it must've been to dig those cuts. He thought of how much he'd like to be done with this Godforsaken war, and be out there in that heat digging and blasting away. And getting paid for it. No one trying to kill him. Just working and getting money and taking care of his family and being alive another day and thankful to have it. Not worried about being some kind of great man. Not the master of a massive plantation. Not glory or bravery or honor. *To hell with all of it. Just working and living and breathing and being free and alive. That's honorable enough, isn't it?*

The train raced into one of the cuts. It sliced through rock and curved along the riverbank. Jim was thinking the thoughts of a free man. Enjoying the absence of the fear that a musket ball would strike him down any second. They picked up steam through the cut. The blasted and hammered-down rocks were whipping by so fast they made a gray smear across his field of vision. He tried unsuccessfully to slow them down with his eyes.

There was a Union guard pushing his way down the middle of the train car. Another bright-eyed child of war. Blue-eyed, blonde-haired type. He had a neat curly-q mustache and didn't seem to have a care in the world. The Confederate boys were behaving, so all he had to do was walk around and pretend he was keeping order. He looked Jim right in the eyes and smiled. They were looking right at each other when it happened. One second the young guard was beside Jim and the next his body was flying back-first toward the front of the car like he was being snatched up for the rapture. Jim tried to watch but something smashed into his face and he spilled over onto the floor, head toward the back of the car. He felt himself sliding toward the front feet-first like whatever had gotten hold of the guard was getting hold of him too. His eyes opened and he saw boys rolling and crashing and pitching all over the place. One flew completely out of a window, cut deeply by the shattered glass as he went by. Movement was everywhere, in every direction. The guard was folded over at the front of the car. Then everything came rushing back at Jim from the front. The door on the end of the train car was bashed sideways and came slicing back through the car like it was floating a couple of feet above the ground. It sliced the young guard in two at the waist, and the upper half of him rode the door as it came racing towards Jim. He looked in the guard's eyes as he had before, but there was nothing there anymore. Jim had seen the lifeless eyes of thousands of dead boys before, but never one rushing at him. It was like being chased by a ghost. He stumbled his way backwards in retreat. The door-turned-guillotine sliced after him with the severed guard on top. With a desperate dive, Jim flung himself backwards onto the floor and made himself as flat as he could, hoping the door would pass over.

When the movement stopped the door was right above him, wedged in tight about half a foot from his nose. His left side was screaming with pain. He couldn't remember anything hitting him, but something seemed wrong. With his free right arm he banged at the door, but it wouldn't budge. He tried to pull his left arm over to use both of them but it wouldn't come. Something was pushing on his head from the right, so he couldn't look that way, but his head and neck were somewhat free to the left side. He turned and saw that some sort of debris was pushing down on his shoulder. He couldn't see beyond his shoulder to where his arm should be. Just above him, at the outer edge of his vision, lay a neatly severed arm in a gray sleeve. Jim's mind slowed down and assessed. *If that is my arm, and I believe it is, I am bleeding badly. I can't reach the wound to stop the bleeding. So it is only a matter of time.*

The pool of blood around Jim was spreading in all directions. He couldn't tell if it was his own. Something was dripping into his eyes from above and causing them to sting. He tried to wipe it away but the right arm was blocked. A liquid ran around his eyes and down to his nose where he could smell it and realized it was more blood. It was dripping down from the door. Little streams ran around the edges of the door and clung to the bottom for a moment before dripping down onto his face. He began to notice just how many little streams there were. A couple on his face. Others dripping onto his neck and chest. He figured it must be from the top half of the guard up above him. *Damned Yankee blood.* He tried to spit out however much of it trickled into his mouth.

His mind tried to go somewhere else. Anywhere. Fishing. An honest day's work in the sun. A walk with a girl in the cool valley behind the Brick House. But there was nowhere good to go. Sounds were everywhere. The deep wrenching of metal giving way and the crackling of wood as the broken train settled. Jim thought maybe the whole mess would collapse and put him out of his misery. There was moaning all about. One boy seemed to be dying on top of the door. He was mumbling something about Jesus. Jim tried to listen but there were few actual words. There was a "God" or a "Jesus" or a "Mama" in there, but most was nonsense. Perhaps the boy thought he was saying something he really wasn't. Jim envisioned the scene on top of the door. A young soldier suffering from some mortal wound. Unable to help himself, or to move. Trapped on the door with the upper half of the dead Yankee guard. Perhaps able to see carnage of all sorts strewn about what remained of the train car. After a while the voice faded to a whimper. Then labored breathing. Then nothing.

But there was no silence to be had. Jim could not bleed to death in peace. Different moans in different voices were all over the car. Some cried for help. Others just made noise. One of the voices was familiar. Jim couldn't place it, but he knew it from somewhere. He tried to occupy his mind by listening to the voice and trying to identify it. The accent sounded like Tennessee, maybe, or perhaps even North Carolina. It was hard to tell. More of a cry than a voice. Jim had seen some familiar faces when they were boarded on the train. Perhaps it was one of them. Whoever the boy was, he was saying the same thing over and over again. Jim listened for what seemed like an hour before he could make out the words. "I wanna die. I wanna die. I wanna die." Finally it came to him. He did know the voice ... it was his own. Everything went black.

He woke with a start and was unsure where he was, and why. When he jolted awake those parts of him that could move moved, and those parts that were wedged in somewhere got wedged tighter. His head bounced up enough to smack the door inches from his face. The entire memory flooded back. The wreck, the door, the blood. Jim had never been one for tight spots. Now, half-dazed, having lost blood, the tight quarters began to get the best of him. His heart fluttered and he could see his breath on the door right above him. He began squirming and fighting desperately to no avail. But then as his mind woke out of the haze he figured that a fast beating heart was no good for a bleeding man. He forced himself to calm down against his every instinct.

He had no idea how long he had been out cold. It was still light outside. A couple of trickles of sunlight snuck between the unseen heap of wreckage above. There was a strange tight feeling on the skin on his face, and a sour smell. The moans continued, but they all blended together and Jim couldn't make out any one voice above the others. He shouted his name just to hear his voice and to make sure the moaning he was hearing wasn't him. Behind the moans now he could hear more voices outside the train. Uninjured voices yelling real words, though he couldn't make out many of them. *A rescue party?* That thought brought Jim around a bit and he wondered if he might actually get out of the train alive.

He looked over where the arm was supposed to be. For a moment all he could think of was reaching the loose arm that was laying a couple of feet away. Not that any doctor on Earth could reattach it, but if it was his arm, he wanted it. He couldn't bear the thought of being pulled off the train and his arm being tossed out in the woods somewhere or worse still buried with someone else's body. He banged furiously at the door above him with the right arm, and tried to twist himself in any direction he could to get to the other arm. None of it did a thing. Unable to grab it, Jim stared at it real hard as if he could move it with his eyes. It just sat there, and for the first time since he left Cartledge Creek, Jim Dockery began to cry.

There was shouting outside the train car, just on the other side of the wreckage. Then there was an awful wrenching sound. Jim's tears began to dry and he regained focus. He looked over at that arm one more time and saw something he had missed before. The bars on the sleeve. It was a lieutenant's uniform. It wasn't his arm at all. With a few tears still sliding over the dried blood on his face, Jim began to laugh. *Wouldn't that've been a damn sight, me being hauled off in a stretcher cradling some other fella's arm?*

The world started moving. The train car rocked back and forth and the voices got louder. The door itself started to wiggle in front of Jim's eyes. It made a sound like a saw blade working. He heard himself calling out "I'm under here, I'm under here." The door popped up from his face and a flood of light poured in, blinding him momentarily. He had never been so happy to see the enemy. With another heave the boys in blue pulled a slab of wood up from Jim's left shoulder. There, still attached, was his own arm. It was bashed and bloodied, but it was still there. He opened and closed his fingers to make sure they still worked.

They lowered Jim off the train through a big hole in the wall and got him onto a stretcher. When his eyes adjusted to the light, what he saw was worse than he'd seen on any battlefield. He had been in the third passenger car. It was now nothing more than a tangle of twisted steel and splintered wood. The massive, straight iron rods that drove the wheels were twisted into knots, and there wasn't one wooden board not torn to pieces. The two cars ahead were even worse. Jim's car had pushed almost all the way up to the front of the second car and opened it up like a zipper. The front of the car was compressed to a fraction of its former size, and the rest opened up like a big "Y." The floor was gone. Men crawled around on all fours trying to pull bodies out from under the car. It had no roof either, and the boys on board had been scattered all about the ground around the tracks for a hundred feet or more.

The front passenger car was so thoroughly smashed that what remained was no more than six or eight feet long. Before the wreck it had held forty or more passengers. Jim stared at the car in awe. He envisioned the demolished remains of the passengers all mashed together, and could not imagine how anyone would ever separate them or tell one from the other. Along the ground was a metal rod ten or twelve feet long. There was a prisoner laying there dead with about half the rod on one side of his belly and the other half sticking out his back.

Three local townspeople were standing around staring at the body scratching their chins, working on the problem of how to remove it.

Up in front of the passenger cars was the tender, which was jacked up on end above what was left of the engine. The axles were broken and scattered about, and the floorboards were snapped like twigs. Up on top was a Yankee guard sitting upright with a rifle in his lap. At first Jim figured him for a sentry, keeping watch to make sure none of the boys that weren't hurt didn't cross the river and disappear. He soon realized this was not the case. The sentry's head was leaned down into his chin and his eyes were wide open. Somehow he had been flung on top of the tender and landed dead in that position. Jim marveled at how the sentry could have ended up like that. He kept watch all day, because no one could climb up to retrieve him.

Yankee soldiers finally set Jim down near dozens of other boys on stretchers. Again there was a chorus of moans. Locals and blue-clad soldiers were scurrying about, offering assistance. Others stood guard over the injured, as if any of them could get up and run. Down the tracks was a long line of boys in gray standing with a crowd of guards all around them. Somehow there were boys who could still stand.

A soldier with a neat beard and patch over one eye was tending to Jim. He went about his business quietly until the bandages were in place, then stepped back to admire his work. Only then did he look Jim in one eye with a smirk.

"Have you any idea what has just happened to you, Johnny Reb?"

"Don't suppose I do, Billy Yank."

"A drunk on the switchboard at the Erie Railroad sent two trains head-on into each other. I wish the other train would have been full of you Rebels too, but sadly that is not the case. So once again you boys are more trouble than you're worth. We should've just killed you all in the field."

"Perhaps you boys up North should mind who you let run your switchboard."

"Perhaps you should shut your mouth before I shut it for you. Enjoy your stay in Elmira. If you live that long, you Rebel bastard."

Jim let the argument die. It was neither here nor there. The eye-patched soldier moved on to bandage the next man in line. Jim tried not to listen, but a few moments later heard, "Have you any idea what has just happened to you, Johnny Reb?" He tuned out the rest.

A mass of humanity was engaged in the burial effort. At the edge of the woods soldiers and civilians stood shoulder to shoulder digging with every kind of shovel, spade or anything else that could break ground. Between Jim and the digging crew was a long line of Confederate dead. Near them was a short, neat row of bodies wrapped in blankets that he figured for dead Yankee guards. Beside them were Northerners hammering at whatever wood could be found, making coffins. Some were crude things made out of raw tree lumber. Others were made from timbers pulled off the wrecked train cars. Jim watched as they boxed up boys by the dozen. Those covered in the blankets each got their own coffin. The Confederates were four to a box. With a great deal of effort, four Southern boys were heaped into a box made from the side boards of a train car. One of them carried a great deal of excess girth, so the soldier making the box had to lean hard on it so another soldier could nail it shut. The box didn't have any corners because each board had been left jagged on the edge either by the wreck or where someone had ripped it off the train. On the side of the box was the word "'Erie," part of the name of the Erie Railroad.

"I'm in no hurry to be put in any box at all," Jim muttered to himself, "but I sure as hell don't want to be buried in one bearing the name of the sorry bastards that have just killed me."

Thirteen

Jim Dockery
August, 1864
Elmira Prison Camp
Elmira, NY

The guards barked at the men, who lined up in ranks for the Mess Hall. Each line had 300 or more men, holding buckets, carved wooden bowls or sawed-off canteens. Whatever would hold their rations. They shuffled at a brisk walk from the barracks and tents down the hill toward the pond. They passed close by two men wearing large barrels. The bottoms were knocked out to make room for the legs, and holes were cut in the tops just wide enough for the heads to stick out. Both men moved forward in choppy steps as their knees banged audibly against the barrels' insides. A group of guards kept them moving by jolting the backs of the barrels with bayonets. Words were crudely painted on crosses nailed to the barrels. One said "Ration Thief." The other, "Dog Eater." As they passed Jim saw men spitting on the ration thief and heckling him. The dog eater escaped their scorn.

Down the hill there was an opening between the tents and the pond. Several fellows were standing behind barrels or old boxes turned on end. Handmade trinkets sat on top of some. Carved from wood or bone. On others were piles of dead rats of all sizes. Prisoners held up rats by their tails and inspected them as they might once have watched their mothers inspect fresh fruits in markets back home, poking or thumping at them to check their freshness. When satisfied, they handed over coins or tobacco to complete their purchases. Within steps were makeshift fires on which rats were being roasted or fried in metal bowls or buckets. Some men emerged from the Mess unsatisfied and made their way straight for the makeshift market, looking to make up for what their prescribed meal had lacked.

The Mess Halls were long and low buildings on the north banks of Foster's Pond, a slender puddle of backwashed water from the Chemung River that made its way into camp under a fence line near the southeast corner of the stockade. Before entering the doors, Jim looked to each side of the Mess. On the left men waded in the water to bathe or wash their clothes. On the right they squatted to shit in the same water. In the August heat, the stench from the pond was suffocating.

In the Mess the ranks were split by long chest-high tables where the men stood to eat. Guards shouted "fifteen minutes" while the various receptacles were filled with the evening meal. Soon Jim looked into his pail and saw a thin piece of light bread topped by a paper-thin sliver of salt pork no more than three inches long. A watery broth was poured over it all, so weak he could see the bottom of the pail. He paused and looked at the man beside him. The fellow had already consumed the pork and was drinking the broth. Suddenly aware of Jim's stare, he grinned a toothless grin and spoke.

"Welcome to Helmira. Eat up, boy. Rumor is we're going on bread and water next week."

Around him the men were greedily slopping down their meal, as if eating faster would somehow cure their starvation. The man across from Jim had one end of the pork between his fingers and the other between his teeth, vigorously trying to tear off a piece to swallow.

Others blew on the broth to cool it enough so they could slurp it down. The table itself had been hammered together rapidly from green lumber like everything else in the stockade. It bowed up noticeably at each end. Deep cracks followed the grain of the wood from one end to the other. The wood itself was caked in a sticky film of spilled broth and the grime of starving prisoners who planted their elbows on the table by the thousands each day. The flies that frequented Foster's Pond entered the Mess in droves and hopped curiously from the grime to the prisoners to their bowls. Throughout the meal there were usually at least two or three flies in Jim's bowl.

The guards were barking again. "Time's up! Move out!" It seemed to Jim he had just arrived. He slurped his soup rapidly and tucked the pork into his cheek because it wouldn't break apart. The men shuffled out the other end of the Mess and into the light by Foster's Pond. Behind him Jim could hear the guards barking at the next mass of men being marched into the Mess. There was a constant flow of starving men herded through the Mess to receive almost enough food to keep them alive another day.

Repulsed by the pond, Jim turned and headed back up the hill. There was a commotion up at the main gate. The gate Jim had entered for the first time the night before. The massive wooden doors were opening and a crowd of bored men gathered to pass the moment with fleeting novelty.

A plain wagon pulled by two mules entered. Behind the wagon, a curious little mutt of a dog scooted in just before the gates shut. His countenance the closest a dog can get to smiling. He didn't just run, he pranced, with an air of great accomplishment for having broken into prison. He ran quickly and eagerly down the path toward the Mess. To the unsatisfied boys just finishing their meal, he must have looked like a steak with legs.

The dog stopped his mad sprint, perhaps realizing the world inside the walls was less glamorous than he had imagined. He bounced eagerly back toward the wagon. Having no other source of entertainment, the men watched. The wagon driver stood and shooed the dog with his arm, shouting, "Get outta here, you sorry cur."

With that the hunt was on. If there was no one to claim him, he was no more than a rat. Though eating another man's dog was an offense, eating a stray was a matter of survival.

Three or four of the boys eased up on the dog as if to pet him. He turned and cocked his head to one side. Self-preservation prevailed. He was on to them.

Suddenly he darted right between the men and scampered back down the path toward the Mess. Two of them fell down trying to spin around and give chase. Another fellow who was ambling along the path lunged at the animal and fell flat in the dirt. Two boys came at a hobble trot from amongst the tents carrying a large wooden box, which presumably they would have thrown on top of the dog had they ever been able to get within range. The whole scene took on the appearance of a mouse scurrying about a room full of old women. The hungry boys lurched and grabbed and often fell whenever the mutt dashed by them, but on account of their pathetic physical condition, none could lay a finger on him. One fellow gave up chase and resorted to tossing rocks at the dog whenever he passed by. Others saw the genius in his method and started to follow suit. Soon every rock in the yard was being tossed at the mutt, but still he escaped.

Two big strong fellows emerged from the Mess and surveyed the silly scene unfolding before them. One of them was half a foot taller than most of the other men, with a thick head of sandy hair and a boxer's jaw. His forehead was wide, giving his head a large, square appearance. Jim imagined this fellow was more dangerous with a clubbed rifle than a dozen men loaded to fire.

A circle had formed around the dog. Without a word to plan, the boys had started to do as a group what they couldn't do alone. They surrounded the animal and inched toward him step by step, each man likely forming his own plan of how he'd rob the meat from the others once they'd helped him catch it. The surrounded prey ran in every direction searching for a path to freedom. Finding none, he began to whimper and wail. Rocks were still flying, and some were beginning to find their mark.

The big fellow approached the circle. Without pausing, he passed between two of the men and walked straight up to the dog. Not another rock was thrown. Everyone was quiet. The dog didn't move and didn't make a sound. The fellow reached down and picked up the dog. He held the mutt up to his chest and stroked its mangy hair.

"This is my dog. His name is … Mac. If anyone eats him, he'll have hell to pay."

As he left the circle, the men parted to let him pass. There he was joined by the other fellow, a slightly shorter but even stouter man that favored him in the face. Together the two of them quietly walked away from the circle toward the barracks.

* * *

In the evening the men were left to their own devices until the order to bed down was given. Like any large group of men, the prison developed its own social order. Many were based on home State, brigade or even division. Some were based on the world outside the walls, others solely upon what happened inside them.

There were the oath takers, Southern soldiers who early on swore allegiance to Union. Their barracks were a little less crowded, their meals a little less lean. They were given jobs within the stockade and were treated with lenience by the guards. But they were detested by the prisoners of the cause.

Officer rank amongst the prisoners still held some sway. The men all envisioned themselves returning to battle, and thus respected military hierarchy. Throughout the war prisoners had been exchanged and returned to battle. New arrivals at Elmira openly expected the same.

Some men became instant outlaws within the prison walls. Or perhaps they were before. Stealing rations. Fighting for the sake of the fight. They were cast aside by their fellow prisoners, most of whom tried to treat each other with empathy.

But of all the social lines and pecking orders, strength was king. On some subconscious level the men must have known that all social order amongst the condemned was illusory. As weeks and months passed with no paroles, they were no longer a part of the war outside. As men grew thin and ill and died, the return to an unfortunate state of nature revealed itself. A man that could whip you had power over you. Even if he did not abuse the power, such a man could rob you of food and health, could steal a few days from your limited lifespan in order to add them to his own. Jim had seen this when the entire circle of starving men watched in silence as that one big fellow strode into the middle of them and took their potential meal as his pet. There were no bars on his shoulders or that of his companion. Yet no one dared to challenge them.

Little cliques and groupings found each other in the evenings and dotted the landscape of the prison yard with tiny campfires made from scraps, splinters or whatever combustible material was available. The different groups claimed their own geographic territory, again like animals in the wild. There they would spend the long hours that stretched out before them.

Jim had no group. He walked the yard alone. The six men in his tent had barely spoken to him upon his arrival. He was another unwelcome body in their tiny home. Another mouth to feed. He paced up and back along the main path that ran between the main gate on one end and Foster's Pond on the other.

"Hey, you! Come over here."

The voice came from one of the campfires just off the main path. Jim looked over but did not respond.

"Yeah, you. The fellow pacing up and down the road."

Jim walked toward the fire. It was growing dark but he could make out the shapes of three men sitting on logs turned on end around the tiny fire. There was a fourth makeshift stool that sat unoccupied. The firelight competed with the shadows and revealed the men in momentary detail. He recognized the two large men that had rescued the mutt from the starving hunters. In the taller man's lap was the mutt, looking quite content.

"Didn't we see you earlier today?" The tall man with the dog was doing the talking. "During the great dog hunt?"

"Yes. I was there."

"Didn't throw a single rock, though, did you?"

"No."

134

"Why not?"

"I can't imagine I would do anything to hurt a little ol' dog like that."

The thicker fellow from earlier in the day spoke next.

"Yeah, well, let's see how hungry you get. I bet a few years ago you never imagined you'd kill a man. Much less a whole bunch of them."

"That's fair. A whole lot of things are happening I never imagined. I sure never thought I would be in a prison."

"Have a seat there, fellow. It turns out we have an empty stool." The taller man was talking again. "And besides, any man who could be there by that scene and not go to throwing rocks is somebody we might want around. Even if you do talk a little too pretty like a lawyer or something."

The tall man smiled and his two companions laughed. Jim took his position on the empty stump.

"What's your name, fella?"

"Jim. Jim Dockery."

"Where you from, Jim?"

"North Carolina."

"Reckon you must be one of those plantations owners that got us into this war, hunh?"

"Something like that."

"Well, Master Jim, we're all from Northern Virginia. I reckon North Carolina's alright."

"We're better than alright. There are more soldiers wearing gray from North Carolina than from any other state."

"Maybe so, but we have all the generals."

"Ha! First you poke fun at me for talking too pretty, then you act proud to have all those West Point gentlemen instead of fighting men. They can point at maps give orders all they want, but somebody has to do the shooting and dying. You should make up your mind what kind of soldier you like best."

"Wooo, big brother! I think he may have you there. What do you think, Robert?"

The third fellow had not yet spoken. He had red, ruddy cheeks and a bit of a belly, especially for a soldier. He had been smiling quietly throughout the conversation.

"I like him already, Hig. Can't hurt to have another smart fellow around. Especially a strong, smart fellow."

The tall man stood and reached out his hand to Jim.

"I like you, too, fella. Name's Cap. This here's my brother Hig. Short for Higginbotham. Don't call him that, though, or he's liable to throw you head-first into that lovely pond we got down there. Other fellow there is Robert. He grew up with us."

"Pleasure to meet you all. What did you fellows do to land yourselves in jail?"

"Horse stealin."

"Took a dollar from the offering plate at church."

"Got caught kissing the sheriff's daughter."

All four men laughed. Jim was surprised how well they seemed to have adapted to their new surroundings. He knew instantly he had found his place within the prison. Here, with these men, around this fire. At what they called simply, "the spot."

"Seriously, how did you get here?"

"We've all been caught twice," Cap answered. "All three together at that. Pickett's Charge the first time. Gettysburg. We were with General Armistead. Within arm's reach of him when he got shot. After they beat us back, we headed back across the field. Our friends were laying all over. Yankees sent little groups out to round bunches of us up. You wouldn't have believed that charge, Jim. Never been anything like it in the whole world."

"Oh, I believe it … I was there."

"Now I like you even better. Where'd they get you?"

"My second time too. Place called Deep Bottom near Richmond. First time was in Haggerstown. I got out of Gettysburg, but I had this hole in my leg from the charge. Lost a lot of blood and dropped in the middle of the road once I got to Maryland. Yankees picked me up at the hospital a couple of days later."

"You marched from Gettysburg to Haggerstown with a hole in your leg?" Robert asked. "That's pretty tough stuff. In the middle of the summer too."

"I was just doing what I was told."

"Us too. Charging across an open field into the entire Union Army wasn't exactly a plan we made up for ourselves."

"You ain't lying, big brother. The fact that you and Robert and me all survived is a miracle. Means something. Has to. Must be something we're meant to do. At least one of us, anyway."

The four soldiers sat silently for a while. The fire crackled quietly and began to dim. Voices of fellow prisoners drifted to them from similar campfires across the stockade. Outside the walls music was playing. In the still evening Jim could hear unconstrained laughter, both male and female, intermixed with the sound of glasses clinking together. There were lanterns lit at the corners of two tall towers just outside the prison walls. Two male voices came from tall shadowy figures in taller hats beneath the lantern on the left-hand side of the taller tower. The voices were muffled, but the word "cheers" drifted down to Jim more than once, followed by glasses clinking again. Their bodies tottered about in the lantern light as if not fully under control. Their motions were jerky and haphazard like those of a stringed puppet in the hands of a rookie puppeteer.

Suddenly a different figure appeared beside them. The silhouette was of a long-haired lady in a full formal dress. Something in her dress caught the faint light of the moon and gave off a pale glow contrasted to the dark male shapes across from her. She drifted to the lantern opposite the men, and the yellow light flickered across her face. He could not see the face in detail, but she seemed to look down from the perch right at him. Though he could have been nothing but a dark lump in a firelight to her distant eyes, he felt seen. Very much seen. As if she saw no one but him, and at that saw through him. The sounds from the stockade faded away, even the voices right beside him. In the prevailing silence she sent words down in a whisper, falling on no ears but his own. In a moment she was gone, and no one stood atop the tower except the two loud, gesturing men.

"Gentlemen, what is the story on the tower?"

Cap smiled at the newcomer.

"They pay a nickel to go up there and look at us and talk about how pathetic we are. To them we're a bunch of animals in a big zoo. There's a bar between the two towers and it's become quite the hot spot for the locals. On a nice day it's full up there all day long. Getting a look at those pathetic, slave-holding rascals that must be wiped out by the hand of God."

"I thought God was supposed to be on our side, Cap?"

"Well, Robert, that's the trick. I've never yet met a fella in a war that thought God was against him?"

"Good point. Can you imagine that? 'Ladies and Gentlemen, I know the Lord wants to preserve the Union, but I sure as hell don't want any part of it.' "

"Right. I'm sure that's what my granddaddy said when he fought with George Washington. 'The Good Book tells us obey the laws of our government. Right now that's the British. But I'm gonna shoot dead everyone one of them taxing sons of bitches whether it sends me to hell or not.' "

"Sure, Hig. But you know granddaddy never said a 'hell' or a 'son of a bitch' in his life."

"Reckon not, Cap. Never went to prison either. How about you, Jim? The Lord with you or against you in this war? Jim … ?"

He was still looking up at the tower. Even the two loud Yankee men had descended. Jim was focused on the space below the lanterns where she had stood.

"She's not still standing there, Jim," Cap reminded him. "Besides, you can't fall in love with a shadow. Dark as it's getting you couldn't even tell what color her dress was."

"Yellow."

"Or her hair."

"Brown."

"Fine then. Her eyes."

"Green."

"Did she talk you too, Jim?"

"Sure did."

"And what, I dare ask, did she say?"

"Home is waiting, and death can wait."

They all looked at Jim curiously for a moment, then Cap continued.

"Boys, it looks like we've got ourselves an eagle-eyed, rabbit-eared Romeo over here."

"Don't discourage it, Cap" said Hig. "Boy, you need your imagination in here. Some days it's all you got. And we're gonna be here a while. Anyway, I wasn't looking at the girl. I was looking at those two drunk Yankee boys and wondering how in the hell they're up there instead of in a field somewhere with a musket. Probably up there toasting how proud they are about how *they* whipped the Rebs at Gettysburg, when *they* hadn't done a damn thing."

"Don't get too gloomy on us little brother. You need your imagination in here but you need some humor too. That black ass gloom will get you nowhere in a place like this."

"Wouldn't bother me if they were real fighting men up there. But those silly drunks? I know what it is too. There's too damn many of them. They have more people than us. That's why we're here. That's why there's an army of freed slaves in here every day hammering together those sorry barracks buildings."

Finally Jim's trance was broken.

"What are you talking about, Hig? What's all this talk about how long we're gonna be here. I've been in one of these prisons before down at Point Lookout in Maryland. The Yankees turned me out of there after a little while because they wanted some of their own men back. We won't be here long."

"Don't count on it, Jim. We need to plan on being here for a while. Boys are showing up here by the hundreds every day and nobody is leaving. Meanwhile they're building barracks as fast as they can. Cap and Robert and me only been here a couple of weeks and already this place is stuffed to the gills. They done figured it out. They stockpile us in this yard instead of trading prisoners, South'll run out of men a far sight faster than the North will. Only so many of us. Might as well let us die in here instead of shooting at us out there where we can make a fair fight of it. Look around at these boys hobbling around like they're a hundred years old. Only reason we can walk around here like we own this place right now is because we're still strong. Hadn't been starved yet. Won't always be that way. A lot of fellas are gonna die in here. We got to stick together and make sure we ain't some of them. Might not matter anyway. This could be it for us, boys."

"It's fine little brother. Calm down a bit, now. Hig, look at me, brother. No sense in getting all worked up, now. OK?"

"Alright, Cap. Alright."

Hig's broad chest and shoulders rose and fell deliberately. He took two or three deep breaths and calmed himself. Jim saw that this exchange was one that had been repeated between the brothers for years.

"You know fellas, Hig is probably right. Even though he gets all riled up. I haven't even heard a rumor about a prisoner exchange in two weeks. We had better all stick together. Jim, I been knowing these boys all of their lives. The three of us got nowhere to go but to stick together. We could use another fella with us. So what do you say, Jim, you with us?"

"From what I've seen so far in here, I couldn't imagine a better unit to join."

Jim stood up from the stump and walked the semi-circle around the fire. He shook each man's hand formally. As he shook Cap's hand, the little mutt dog Mac whined slightly from his new owner's lap. Jim reached his hand down and Mac reached up and placed one paw in his fingertips.

* * *

The smell in the tent that night was worse than the death smell Jim had experienced after battle. Chronic diarrhea had been common in war camps, but here at Elmira it was an epidemic. The flimsy blanket beneath him did little to soften the uneven ground beneath the tent that twisted his back as he tried to sleep. The smell would slowly dissipate, but then would spread through the little tent again. The type of intake provided in the prison could not support the output of chronic diarrhea. An inconvenience at home, here it was a death sentence. There was a very soft whimper from one of the men in the tent. Jim assumed it was the one afflicted with this most unfortunate condition. It sounded like the whimper of a small child, which is probably what it was. The young soldier turned himself and more of the smell escaped into the tent. Now the whimper came to Jim's ears muffled as if the boy's face was pressed down into a blanket below.

"Mother. I shouldn't have run away. Mother. I'm sorry. Please come get me. Lord, please come get me."

Jim plugged his ears. To block the voice. To block new thoughts from his mind. He thought of the goodness and strength of the men he had met that day. How fortunate he was to find them. But his mind turned over and again to the words Hig had spoken. They would not be paroled. They would not be sent home. There was a fine line between Jim and the poor boy dying in the tent with him. Between Jim and whomever had preceded him on that fourth stump by the fire. Between the bold strength of Cap and Hig, and those withering and starving all around them that may have been just as bold and strong a few moments ago. Since he left home Jim had feared a death violent and swift. Now he feared a creeping insidious death whose horror spread over weeks or months. A death advancing no cause at all. He would prefer a death for any cause, no matter how violent the death, how imperfect the cause.

Fourteen

Benjamin Dockery
Early September, 1864
Rockingham, NC

Cartledge Creek flowed gently around a bend. Near the middle, its current was split by a single large rock. The water hugged the rock around each side, then spiraled off in each direction, collapsing back on itself in an eye-shaped eddy. It slowed for a moment just past the rock, inching toward the end of the eye and then darting off quickly. The water up against the back of the rock seemed still, but underneath it swirled gently, catching bugs and worms and suspending them a moment outside the main current. The lurking fish swayed gently, using less energy than out in the current, finding their meals hovering in the shelter of the rock.

To the right the water ran down in a shallow riff that tumbled easily over the sand, gravel and flattened oval rocks. On the far side it kicked out to the right before being stopped and redirected by a steep cut bank. There it remained deeper and swirled in massive slow loops that bounced along the bank until the creek narrowed and its pace increased again. Over the years the water had burrowed into the muddy bank, cutting below the surface so that the bank hung well out over the creek. This created another great hiding spot for fish, which hovered under the lip of the bank, out of the reach of raccoons or kingfishers. Some morsels of food floated right under the cut of the bank and could be taken safely. Others required the fish to dart out quickly before returning to their safe havens.

Benjamin Dockery could see little of this, but knew it all very well. He approached from the shallow side, nearest the road. The sun was just beginning to rise and the trees on the far side of the hole blocked what little light was in the air. It was a bit too cold for fishing, but he had his reasons to try. He exhaled into the air just to see his breath in the cold.

Benjamin held a cane pole about nine feet in length. Attached to the narrow end was a horse hair fishing line strung together to be the same length as the pole itself. On the end was a single hook, which he baited with one of the wriggling red worms he had dug up earlier that morning. Standing at the very edge of the creek, he held the hook in his left hand and the bottom of the pole in his right. He extended the pole high above him, still holding the hook. Thrusting both hands forward, left and then right, he pushed the worm forward in an arc and extended the pole tip forward and down. Just as the hook swung low over the water, he flipped the pole tip up again. The force of the thrusting pole rippled down the line all the way to the hook, which swung back upwards until the line straightened and fell. With both pole and line fully extended, the hook and worm entered the water a full eighteen feet away from where Benjamin stood.

Though his eyes were uncertain where the worm had entered the creek, he could feel that it was well short of its target. He held the tip of the pole up slightly, keeping any slack from forming between the tip and hook. Not so tight as to drag the worm through the water backwards and send the fish darting in all directions. Just enough to feel what was happening to the hook below the surface. He closed his eyes tightly to shut out the rest of the world. The line dribbled to the left with the current. There was a slow drag that his experience told him was sand, followed by the slight tick of the hook scraping over the gravel. The worm was in the flattened out part of the creek on the near side of the big rock. Dead water, other than the occasional cruising fish that grew bored of patrolling the more productive spots.

"Nobody home, there. I'll leave it for a second just in case."

Benjamin talked to himself, or to the fish, only when he fished alone. He could not remember when he first started it, but believed it to have been born from the sheer joy of catching a big fish. "Oh goodness, look at that one!" Over time, it was no longer confined just to admiring his catch.

"Alright, let's try this again."

Same cast, with a little more push put into the last pop of the rod tip. Same result. He looked down at his feet and realized the water was a foot higher than normal. It had rained two days prior and the runoff was yet to work its way downstream.

"Well, if that's the only way to do it, I guess I'll have to do it then."

He stepped gingerly into the creek. The cold water crept in over his shoe tops and spread its way through his shoes. The cold climbed right up his bones and into his spine. He stopped momentarily with both feet in the water. He stared at his feet and thought of the water splashing into his shoes and onto his pants as he charged blindly at Mechanicsville. Of the wails and cries he heard down by that creek the next morning.

"Some soldier I was. War still raging on and here I stand at home fishing."

But there was something else he did not say. Even when a man speaks to himself alone in a river, there are things he dares not say aloud. His shame at his early return home was only so deep. There was something deeper. This talk of battle and courage and the cause was all well and good until she came into the picture. When he was with her, none of it mattered. And at war, he would never be with her. Not once had he seen judgment in her eyes. Never did she make him feel she wanted a hero. What she wanted, it seemed, was him. Not some story about how she once loved a man who died valiantly facing his enemy in a glorious field of fire, giving his life for some cause. What she wanted was him. She wanted his life for hers. For the family they would raise. She would rather him be here and blind, than away at battle guided by eagle eyes.

So it seemed. And so he hoped. His only fear was that some part of her was ashamed of him. Only her opinion mattered. If she felt that way, she had never shown it. But he wished to know for sure. Though even deeper, he knew. Nothing else mattered but her.

He smirked to himself, and let out a brief, audible laugh. He took a few more steps into the creek and felt the cool current circling his ankles. When he pitched the line again he felt a tiny thud instead of a splash. The worm was on the big rock.

"Here we go. Just gonna ease you off there just a little bit … there we go. OK, fishy, here you are. Dinner bell. Come on, be there."

After the worm slid off the back of the rock and into the eddy below, Benjamin brought the rod tip up high and simulated the suspension of a worm washed into the creek by the rain, floating unattached with the current. It sank down and he felt the line slack as it hit the bottom. He picked it up just off the bottom and let it drift down again. Near the end of the eddy there were two quick jolts of the line in the direction of the cut bank. He flicked his wrist to the right against the current and felt as the fish reacted to the hook and dove deeper, pulling the long, limber pole down toward the surface.

"There you go! Hang on there, fellow. No hurry. Just hold on here. Hold on."

He let the fish play himself out for a moment, then raised the pole tip slowly higher. The fish emerged from the deep pool, trying in vain to dive deeper, his fluttering tail trying to drive his nose straight down. With a steady raise of the rod the fish came out of the pool for good and onto the sandy bank at Benjamin's feet. He slid his left hand over the fish's mouth, tucked his thumb below the belly and slid the other four fingers carefully over the back, folding down the sharp spines of the dorsal fin.

"Look at that! Guess it isn't too cold after all."

145

The fish, a redbreast bream, filled every bit of Benjamin's hand. It was as round as a salad plate and over an inch thick. Below the eye, the gill plate and breast were the orange-red of a sunrise. Between the eye and the mouth were little curvy streaks of greenish blue.

Benjamin tucked the cane pole between his right arm and his side. Still holding the fish in his left hand, he took the shank of the hook in his right. Part of the worm was still attached and was sticking out of the tiny mouth. The fisherman pushed the hook slightly into the mouth until he felt it pop loose, then turned the hook to the side and pulled it from the mouth. He took a length of string from his pocket that had a skinny, six-inch stick tied firmly to one end. He slipped the stick through the fish's gill and out his mouth, then slid him down the string. He tied a knot in the end of the string between the gill and mouth, making the fish the anchor that would keep additional fish from sliding off the string. Benjamin then tied the end with the stick to his shoe laces. The fish skittered around in the water around Benjamin's ankles, wrapping the stringer around his foot, then swimming the other direction and unwrapping it again. Meanwhile another hooked worm was drifting down into the eddy behind the big rock.

Betty Covington

Dogs were barking outside the Brick House. Betty Covington awakened in the northwest bedroom on the second floor. She had visited the previous evening to discuss wedding plans with Sally. Her future mother-in-law offered her a room rather than letting her head home in the cold. The sun was rising behind the house, so little light came through the windows. It was Sunday morning so the dogs meant one thing: Benjamin was back. She knew he had left the house before first light. He had come into her room and revived the fire in the fireplace so she wouldn't be cold when she woke. Her eyes had popped open as he placed logs on the fire and stoked it until a high flame crackled and gave off enough heat to fill the huge room to its twelve-foot ceilings. She knew General Dockery had servants for such things, and that it was improper for Benjamin to be in her room, but she loved him for it. *He truly loves me*, she thought. *He wants to keep me warm and cozy even if I don't know it was him.* She watched him with smiling eyes as he worked silently in the fireplace, then shut her eyes tight to let him believe his sneaking had been successful.

With eyes shut, she heard his footsteps slowly ease toward her. He was trying to be quiet, she realized, but a grown man in heavy shoes on a wooden floor can only be so quiet. Her heart fluttered under the quilts and she fought a smile as he got closer. The footsteps stopped. She could feel him standing just above her. A warmth came over her. She wanted to rise up and pull him back under the covers with her. But even more, she wanted him to have just what he wanted, and that was to take care of her without her knowing. She felt his fingers brush her hair across her forehead. His presence lowered closer to her face until she felt his lips gently kiss the spot he had just cleared of hair. Her pulse quickened again and she clenched her teeth not to smile. The footsteps circled the bed and faded down the narrow servant's staircase to the warming kitchen. As soon as he was down the stairs, she opened her eyes wide, and let out a deep breath. She admired the fire for a moment, turned her pillow to the cooler side and fell back asleep, smiling.

Now, with the sun rising and the dogs barking, Betty slipped out of bed and tiptoed briskly across the room barefoot, her long white nightgown flowing behind her slight frame as she went. On either side of the northwest corner were two tall windows that began low on the wall and finished far above her head. She threw open the wooden shudders on the lower window pane and looked up the sandy lane towards the Cartledge Creek Road. As expected, Benjamin could be seen in the distance with two large dogs jumping and circling him, welcoming him home as if he had been gone again to war. He was still well in front of the house to the left, and would soon pass out of view for a moment before the lane swung back around.

Looking up from the scene below, Betty saw her own translucent reflection in the window in front of her. Her dark eyes stared directly into mirror images of themselves. She had the thoughtful look often employed when someone notices themselves, but then cracked a smile and giggled. With that giggle, her true, joyful eyes appeared. The eyes that made others wonder what she knew that they did not.

Benjamin and the dogs came back into view. The dogs had ceased their jumping and circling. They walked calmly beside Benjamin, one at each side, tongues hanging out of their mouths. He wore light colored trousers and she could see that his pant legs were wet. His overcoat was thick, gray wool, Confederate issue. A black, broad-brimmed hat was pulled down tight, shielding his eyes from the rising sun. His walk was very upright and solid, a man's walk. A stringer of fish hung from his belt. Five or six large redbreast bream dangled about knee-high as he walked. Hanging below them was one broad black tail. As he walked and the fish shuffled with his steps, she could see the gaping mouth and green back of the largemouth bass to which that tail belonged. As he passed directly in front of her, she rapped at the window to grab his attention. The dogs halted and looked keenly towards her. Benjamin removed the hat from his head and held it above him a bit to better block the sun. He looked toward the window and smiled, waving the hat back and forth. She knew he could not see her, but he waved anyway. When the hat came off, there was her man. The firm, rugged facial features of a man that would stand in a cold stream and catch her breakfast, with the softness around his eyes of a man that would kiss her forehead while she slept. Her face lit up, and she saw her own joy in her reflection. There at once she could see both the man she loved, and the way he made her feel.

Fifteen

Jim Dockery
Mid-September, 1864
Elmira, NY

The Elmira Prison Camp was getting low on rats. The threat to restrict prisoners to bread and water had been carried out. Rats and stray dogs were the only meat in camp. What few rats entered the camp now had grown wise. Robert, the master rat hunter, would often sneak down near the southeast corner of the prison where the backwash of the Chemung River poured into the stockade and formed Foster's Pond. The wall spanned low over the water to deter any ambitious prisoners from trying to swim against the current to freedom. Two guards constantly stood watch over the site. Each time Robert crawled down in that direction, he did so with two rifles trained on him at all times. He wasn't crawling to hide from the sentries. He was crawling to hide from the rats.

It was fall and the days were growing shorter. The sun slipped below the wall behind the Dead House on the opposite end of the long, skinny pond each evening. There, the withered bodies of fallen prisoners were carted and processed each day. As the sun lowered itself below the walls of the dreaded little, frame house, silhouettes lurked about in the shadows, hammering together coffins day and night. Dusk coincided with cooking in the Cook House, which sat along the pond banks beside the Mess Halls. As soon as the light began to fade and the smoke began to rise from the Cook House chimneys, enterprising rats would slip into the prison under the wall and swim along the pond edge toward the Cook House.

"The little bastards have gotten smart on us," Robert had told Jim one night. "They love this kind of place. It's full of dead bodies, rotten food and nasty water. It's rat heaven in here. But they've figured out that there's a whole heap of Southern boys that know how to trap and hunt trying to kill them. So they don't live in here anymore. They come in, eat up and get out. Smart little bastards."

Long after most little groupings around camp had given up the hunt, Robert still showed up at the spot some evenings with a sopping wet rat shoved down his pants leg.

Jim had accompanied Robert on his hunts on several occasions. For a stealthy hunter, Robert talked quite a bit. He whispered almost inaudibly to himself in a running commentary on everything he was doing to stay low and invisible. How he had made the slingshot. How he had figured out how to follow the rats and take them out before anyone else could find them. How other hunters would be waiting for the rats up close to the Mess. Back at the spot he smiled and laughed and spoke only when spoken to. He let Jim, Cap and Hig do most of the talking. Then Hig got sick and fell silent. His gums and teeth ached too much to speak more than absolutely necessary. Then the talking was left to Cap and Jim. And talk they did. For hours sometimes. About anything and everything. Telling the same stories, voicing the same opinions, over and over, just to pass the time. No matter how often the same tales were repeated, Robert always sat by with a quiet smile, until it was time to head out for a hunt.

But something had changed. Robert seemed to struggle to pull himself up off the stump at the spot whenever he had to move. His face was gray and his expression rarely changed. After a few evenings with no rat, Jim realized he was the new hunter in the group.

Cap and Jim crawled on their bellies down near the mouth of the pond, leaving Hig and Robert by the fire in their silence. The ground was drenched from recent rain. Both men coated their only clothes in the mud that pooled near the banks of the pond. As they crawled along two muskets were trained on their heads. Cap propped himself up on one elbow and gave an ironic salute to one of the dutiful guards. On cue, a rat came swimming under the fence line, hugging within inches of the near bank. The two friends crawled on their bellies along the bank in order to see where the rat would climb out of the water.

The slight wake that trailed the rat came to a sudden stop. His head peeked up out of the water and over the edge of the bank. Jim was focused on a low spot on the pond bank feet from the rat. He silently pulled Robert's slingshot from his pocket, along with a jagged rock. Cap began to snicker under his breath.

"Shhhh. You'll scare him off."

Cap covered his mouth with a bony hand. The rat slid out of the water at the low spot, right where Jim knew he would. Jim pulled himself up slowly into a kneeling position and leveled the slingshot before him. Cap started snickering again but smothered the sound with his hand. The more serious Jim grew, the harder Cap fought his laughter, until finally the laugh had to go somewhere and snorted out of his nose. As he snorted the rat started to dart away and Jim let go of the strap. Cap stopped laughing instantly. The rat writhed around on the ground, unable to run. Jim jumped to his feet, strode over to the rat and wrung his neck. He pushed the dead rat down into his pants so that no one in camp would see it.

"Hoddamighty, Jim. That was impressive."

"Well thanks, Cap, but why in the world were you laughing at me?"

"I'm sorry, Jim. I couldn't help it. It all just seemed so serious, like we were down in Africa hunting lions or something. But we weren't hunting a lion. We were hunting a damn rat."

With that he started laughing again. Jim finally cracked a smile.

"And then I got to thinking about fancy rich fellows chasing foxes on horseback with fine dogs, bright red jackets and funny black hats. And here I sit with a rich plantation owner shooting rats with a homemade slingshot that just crawled out of a pond people shit in all day."

Finally Jim was laughing with him. The two men, recently kids, then killers, now prisoners, sat on the banks of Foster's Pond half wasted away and laughed out loud. Their only clothes were stained in foul mud. Their faces were sunken and pathetic in a way that didn't seem possible just weeks ago. One of them had a rat stuffed down his pants, and both couldn't wait to eat the rat to stay alive another day. Yet they laughed out loud together.

The two friends walked up from the pond to the spot, keeping off the main path where the bulge near Jim's knee might have been visible. There were too many prisoners hungry enough to steal a meal, or at least to find out the secret to hunting the newly endangered Helmira rat. They were still smiling slightly when they came to the spot. Robert and Hig were staring silently at the fire in the same positions where Cap and Jim had left them. The smiling stopped.

Jim turned his back to the path and skinned the rat as Robert had taught him. Cap sharpened the end of a long stick that would serve as a spit. Hig tried to smile at the prospect of meat for dinner, but Robert never looked up from the fire. Cap dug two long forked sticks into the ground on opposite sides of the fire, while Jim threaded the sharpened stick through the body of the rat. Soon the rat was crackling over the fire. Cap and Jim sat and quietly watched the dark, oily meat cook. In deference to their comrades, neither said a word.

Three prisoners were walking down the main path toward the pond. None of the boys had seen them before. They must have been new arrivals. They looked thin, but not as feeble or frail as the longtime Elmira residents. The one in front, the leader, immediately eyed the rat roasting on the stick above the fire. He drifted slightly in the direction of the fire and sniffed the air. The other two drifted after him.

Mac, who was curled up in Cap's lap, watched the men suspiciously.

As they grew closer he began to growl the growl of a much larger dog from a place somewhere deep in his throat. Cap casually sat Mac down at his feet. He unfolded himself from his stump and towered over the men. The sight of him was far less imposing than a few short weeks ago. When Mac realized his owner shared his suspicion, he began barking wildly at the three approaching men.

Suddenly all three of the strangers sprang into action. One man each jumped at Cap and Jim, while the leader went for the rat. At once Jim felt a blow to his head and the impact with the ground. Whoever had hit him had fallen with him. As they rolled to the ground Jim mustered strength he did not know remained and rolled himself on top of his attacker. Robert's slingshot was in Jim's hand and he belted the man in the forehead with the prongs of the weapon. He looked up toward the fire and saw Cap in action. He had one small man in a head lock against his chest. The man was kicking his legs and clawing at Cap's bony arm with both hands. Cap also had the leader by the foot. With one leg suspended in the air, the rat thief was trying to lunge forward toward the fire. Mac had latched his tiny jaws to the ankle of the free leg that the man was using for leverage to get away from Cap. If he broke free, Jim thought, he may tumble face first into the fire.

Jim wanted to rise and subdue the man himself, but the man beneath him was struggling to escape. The ring leader finally kicked free. He stumbled out of control toward the fire, but then danced on his tip toes around the flames to one side. It was a move a starving man of Elmira could never have made. Jim knew this was a serious adversary. The invader smiled an evil smile and grabbed the stick from the fire. As he did there was a blur from Jim's right. A dark figure flashed between Jim and the lead attacker. The villain's head rocked to the side and a spray of spit and blood shot into the air amongst the smoke and rising particles of flaming ash. The rat stick dropped back onto the two forked branches and settled back into its spot. The leader swung wildly at the head of the blur, which was coming into focus as Hig. Hig grabbed him by the shirt and drove his fist directly between his eyes. The man fell flat onto his back, all four limbs spread out around him. Cap released the small prisoner he had around the neck.

The embarrassed thief held his neck gingerly and moved to assist his leader. Jim carefully got up and let the third crook join his fellows and limp away.

Jim was amazed by the spectacle he had just seen. Hig had barely moved in days. Cap's knees and elbows had creaked audibly during the rat hunt. The sudden burst of strength displayed by both men came from somewhere other than their bodies. Jim knew in that instant that the brothers must have been remarkable soldiers.

For a moment, in the campfire light, both men became larger than life again. The shadows of dusk and the glory of battle concealed the gaunt eyes and frail limbs. They were for a moment the men they had always been.

But the moment passed. Robert was still staring into the fire. He had never moved. Hig turned to head back to his stump and his steps faltered. He stopped by the fire and the light took away the illusion. The arms hung limp in the sleeves. The broad shoulders were caving and had no muscle spanning the distance between them. The eyes were old again. Most alarming, almost half of his lower lip was dangling limply from his mouth. Cap noticed just as Jim did. He walked to his brother, took him by the shoulders and looked into his face."

"Brother? Brother, are you OK.?"

"I'm OK, Cap. I'm fine."

He struggled to annunciate. There was no lip to form the sounds.

"Hig, sit down." Cap led his brother to his stump and eased him down. Cap's eyes cut to Jim's. For the first time there was fear in Cap's eyes. Not just fear. Terror. Hig's eyes lacked focus. He was in shock. The ring leader had not landed any more than a glancing blow. Hig's lip had simply given way.

"I'm fine, Cap! Damn it! I'm fine."

"Hig. Brother. It's time."

"I ain't going over there. I AIN'T going over there!"

"Hig. You've got scurvy. Brother you haven't had a bite of fresh fruit or vegetable in a month. You've got to go."

"You want me to punch you like I did that sonfabitch!"

"Take your shot if that's what it takes, little brother. You know I'm right, Hig, you've got to go."

"I ain't going over there! Everybody that goes to that hospital dies!"

"They got fruit over there, Hig. They got medicine. Over here you die. Across the pond you got a chance."

Hig's slurred voice was loud and angry. Surely he heard himself, and the weakness of the voice must have fed his anger once again. Cap tried to soothe him, tried to calm him like he had done their whole lives. He got down on his knees in front of his brother and spoke so softly Jim could not hear him. Even in his emaciated state, Cap's hands were massive. He cradled Hig's head in his hands and pulled himself within inches of his brother's face. His lips were moving but all Jim heard was the cooking of the rat meat and the voices from fires across the yard.

Hig's face began to soften. His rage passed into sadness. Tears came from both eyes and climbed over Cap's fingers. When he spoke it came out in a slurred whimper.

"But no one ever comes back. When people go over there, no one ever comes back."

"You will, Hig. You will. I know it."

Cap pulled his brother to him and hugged him. His head on Hig's shoulder, he turned slightly to face Jim. Tears were streaming down Cap's face as well.

The two brothers rose slowly and headed into the darkness toward the pond. On the far side was the hospital. What Hig said was true. Most men who went that way never returned. What Cap said was true as well. Hig had no chance on this side of the pond, without medical attention. Perhaps, Jim thought, he had no chance either way. He watched as Cap and Hig headed down to the far end of the pond. They came and went from the glow of campfires along the path. Two tall silhouettes, the taller with his arm around the other. Occasionally he saw a third, tiny silhouette; Mac, prancing along at his savior's feet. In one dim circle of firelight well across the stockade, Jim thought he saw Hig falter, and Cap catch him. He thought they had vanished for good for a moment, but then caught their vague shapes again as they turned the end of the pond near the Dead House. Then finally they merged into darkness.

All along Robert had been gnawing at a leg of the rat. He stood from his stump and turned toward the barracks. He stopped for a moment and turned back to Jim.

"You're a good man, Jim. This here was the finest unit I was ever a part of."

"Thank you, Robert. I couldn't agree more."

He turned back to the barracks and limped away.

"Robert …?"

The great rat hunter did not turn back around. His steps were labored, but soon he disappeared between the long, white barracks buildings that shone in the light of the moon.

Jim was alone.

He sat a good while studying the fire. In the time since his arrival enough men had died that he now lived in the barracks with Robert and the brothers. Or now, it seemed, with Robert and Cap. The evenings were growing cold and still men were arriving in camp faster than barracks could be built. Scurvy, diarrhea, small pox and starvation did their part, but still there were more prisoners than beds. The snow would fall soon and men would freeze to death in the tents. Good, strong men who did nothing but volunteer, in their minds, to protect their homes. Men who survived battles, thin rations, substandard supplies and terrible camp conditions.

Jim looked up at the empty observation towers. He had looked every day for her return. Several times he thought he saw her, only to conclude otherwise. Now no one climbed the towers at all, but for the occasional guard. The war-time entrepreneurs had been shut down. The Union army had made the towers a part of the camp. Still he looked, in hopes she might one day return and look down on him again. It only happened in his dreams.

It was getting cool outside and the prisoners were gradually drifting to bed. Cap and Mac made their way back through the shrinking circles cast by dimming campfires. They moved faster than before. Jim's daydream escaped him, but he was glad real company was on its way.

Cap took his place on the stump next to Jim's. Mac hopped up and took his place in his owner's lap. No one said anything at first. Jim handed Cap part of the rat that he had saved for him. When he did Mac made a hungry little growl. Cap broke off a piece and fed it to the dog, then began slowly eating the rest.

"Most fellows would've eaten the whole thing, Jim. Not saved any for Mac and me."

Cap was trying to smile, but Jim could see it was difficult. He looked as if he'd seen a ghost, or several of them.

"Well, Cap, most folks would have split the last couple of dozen rats three ways instead of four."

They sat for a while without speaking. Almost all of the other fires were out, or reduced to a little smoldering red coal. Jim had no desire to go to bed, and sensed none in Cap. It would be a few more minutes before the guards cleared the yard and forced them to their bunks. He prodded the fire until a single twisting column of flame rose up from the sticks.

"Have you ever been over there, Jim?"

"No. I haven't."

"Don't. It's awful. I mean, just think of all I've seen. The death, the bodies. Field hospitals. Pickett's Charge for goodness sakes. It might be the worst thing I ever seen. All these low cots in the tents. At least half the boys I seen were laying there dead. The smell. Boys shitting themselves until they die from it. People with scurvy sneezing and teeth come out. And the moaning. Like after a battle but different. I know it might not make any sense, but there's different moans. Those strong boys dying in the fields with musket balls in their guts. They moaned like men dying a man's death. But these boys rotting from disease. They sound like old men that's lost their minds. I can't explain it. It's just ... different."

Jim thought for a while about what to say. His whole life he had never had to search for words. They were just there. Even when he chose not to speak them, they were there if he needed them. Not this time. He searched, but the words would not come.

"I ain't got no brother no more, Jim. He ain't never coming back."

"He's got a better chance over there than he does over here. You said it yourself."

"That was before I went over there. There's no hope over there. There's no medicine. That's just a place where sick people go so we don't watch them die."

"Did you think of bringing him back?"

"Tried to, once I saw what it was like. Bastard guard stuck his bayonet up under my chin and told me to get going."

"He'll be back. Hig's the strongest man I've ever seen. And I've seen a few."

"No doubt he's strong. But all of us are just men. All of us. Can't survive everything."

"Not you. You're some other kind of creature. You've got some kind of strength down in you I haven't seen before. Hig too. It's in your blood somehow. I knew it the day you got Mac. The day you took me in. I saw it tonight when you guys found strength none of us should have anymore. No. Not you. You can survive this place. If there was ever a creature that could, Cap, it's you."

"You're putting a lot on me, friend."

"Damn right, I am. You can't give up. You can't die. I need you. You can't die."

Well-fed guards were darting about the camp from fire to blackening fire. As they did, the last remaining prisoners pulled themselves up and headed to bed.

"Jim."

"Yes, Cap."

"There's something I gotta ask you. It might not make any sense. Since I was two I've had a brother. It's who I am. I don't know who or what I am otherwise. You know what I mean."

"Absolutely. Me too. Since the day I was born."

"What I wanted to ask you ... I need a brother, Jim."

"Hig will be back. But no matter what happens, Cap, no matter what life does to either of us, you've got a brother. That I promise. Always."

Sixteen

Sally Dockery
October, 1864
Rockingham, NC

Sally sat alone at the table. The candles in the chandelier had dimmed. All but a few had gone out. Alfred had offered his hand to lead her from the table, despite the fullness of her plate. She politely refused. Miss Anna and her helpers scurried in and out until the table was neat and empty. All except for Sally's full plate. No light shone through the wooden blinds in the windows. There was one pale pool of light on the table. Sally was just beyond its reach. Her plate still illuminated, her small figure just into the shadows.

Two big slices of fresh tomato overlapped one another on the corner of the greenish-blue Brick House china. Bits and pieces of its regal scene were visible amongst the uneaten supper. A stately home sitting above the lush green grounds. Also on the plate was a small mountain of field peas with fresh chopped onions scattered on top.

The light brown juice from the peas ran down around the curvature of the plate and soaked into a wedge of crumbly cornbread, cooked in a black skillet and sliced into wedges like a pie. Two perfectly fried chicken wings sat in the middle of the plate. Sally knew they were perfect without taking a bite. Anna would have seen to that. Not too heavy on the breading. Heavier on the lard, a nice deep bubbling pool. Heat low enough to crisp the outside while leaving the inside juicy.

Sally knew it was a good-hearted ploy. For Miss Anna to cook her favorite meal to try to make her eat. She had not had a full meal in weeks. Knowing Jim had so little, the taste of all food turned her stomach. Anna's ploy had failed.

Her own was a good-natured ploy as well. Chicken wings. They had never really been her favorite, of course, but not a soul on Earth was aware. Alfred was a drumstick man. Some of the children preferred dark meat. Others white. When the basket was passed at a picnic or the buffet picked over at a church covered dish, she noticed the lowly wings always remained. Someone always fussed at her for waiting until everyone else was fed until she would dare take a bite herself. "Miss Sally, go ahead and get yourself something to eat." "The way those boys eat there'll be nothing good left at all." "You've been cooking all day, sit down and let me make you a plate." "There's nothing left but those sorry ol' wings."

Really all she wanted was for everyone else to have their favorite. So she set about convincing the world that she preferred wings. Now even Alfred had forgotten from the years before that she was once as much of a drumstick lady as he was a drumstick man. Miss Anna, who knew Sally's tastes better than anyone, had no idea at all. Hundreds of times over dozens of years, well-meaning souls saved out those "sorry ol' wings" for Miss Sally, so that no one else would get them first. "Miss Sally I grabbed those wings for you before any of those children got them." "I knew you wouldn't get these for yourself, Miss Sally." "Here you go my dear, these are special just for you." She had fooled them one and all.

The thought of her own deceptive genius brought a smile, though a brief one. The last of the candles burned out above her. There in the dark she sat before her "favorite" supper, one she didn't want at all. Her mind drifted north, to Elmira. In a dream she carried a steaming basket right by the starving soldiers and handed it to Jim. He opened it to find two perfectly fried short thighs and a wedge of cornbread, spread with a layer of freshly churned butter.

Jim Dockery
Elmira, NY

Jim sat alone at the spot. It was morning and there was no fire. Hig was dead and Cap was leaving. Robert had grown even more withdrawn and distant. He hadn't managed to eat in three days.

There was no grass to be seen. The ground was gravelly mud. Jim, as always, had slept in his shoes again. The first snowflakes in Elmira arrived before the first leaf turned in Rockingham. He removed his socks some nights to wear as mittens, and slept with frozen feet in stiff shoes. At the spot he pulled off the shoes slowly over scabbed feet, stretched his legs and tried to move his toes. The mud was cold with traces of ice. He returned the socks to his feet, then the shoes, then sat silent.

Months had passed now, and every simple act stretched out in time. He could move more quickly at times if he wanted, but why? Over time he slowed every little activity of life, down to the time it took to remove a sock from his hand and place it on his foot. Just a few more seconds. Just a few more minutes. The longer each task took to complete, the fewer tasks were required to fill a day. The fewer tasks in a day, the faster the day would seem.

It wasn't working.

With each task complete came a moment of loss. *What do I do now?* The one luxury of the difficulties of normal life was that when doing something, anything, he could think of nothing else. Thought had become yet another enemy. Thought led to awareness. Awareness, here, was despair. Robert had started to think, then shortly thereafter started to die. It was done now. He could never turn it around. No one ever did. But Jim would try to turn it around for him. Try to get him extra food. An extra blanket. Something to keep him alive for another day. After all, it was something for Jim to do. Something other than thinking, despairing, dying.

Jim pulled his left pant leg above his knee. The knee was getting that look. The look many men got before they died, that Cap had after a bout with chronic diarrhea. The joint seemed swollen and round, larger than normal. Details of the joint were visible now. His skin was beginning to lay tight on the curvature of his bone, forming angles and divots never before seen where muscle once had been. The measuring stick was in his pocket. He had whittled it down to the width of his thigh a few days after he arrived in camp. Twice that morning he had already done it, but felt he had to do it again. He pulled the stick from his pocket and laid it across his bare thigh. There was an inch and a half on either side. Jim moved it to the far left, then the far right. Turned it over. Moved it every way he could, searching for some mistake. He even held it up to the sun as if to find that someone had snuck into his pocket and added to the stick's length. Of course, they had not. The stick had not changed. But it was now applied to measure a different man. He was officially starving.

Too weak to stand, too scared to think, Jim began to stare at the original observation tower and doze again. His eyes glazed over and fluttered between open and shut. In the space between vision and dream he started to see her again. And hear her. From the top of the tower in her formal yellow gown, brown ringlets dancing across her slight shoulders, speaking in a whisper somehow heard across the distance, the words rolling down the tower and over the wall, across the masses and between the frozen, stoic crowds to his ears as if delivered just for him. "Home is waiting, and death can wait."

Movement on the grounds brought him back to reality. The tower was silent and empty, as it had been for weeks.

The parolees were on the move toward the gate. Guards attempted to impose some order on their ranks, halfheartedly. Only a few civilian home guards exerted much effort. The spectacle was a welcome distraction from Jim's woefully undistracted state. Jim rose slowly like he had seen old men do. He pushed down on the stump with both arms and straightened his legs one at the time. His first few steps forward were hobbled and slow, his feet still rubbing awkwardly against the side of the shoes, the socks providing little buffer. He made his way across the yard to the mass of men being herded together to be sent through the gates, to the depot and onto trains headed for Baltimore where they would be paroled and exchanged.

Only one man had been exchanged in the prison's last three months. Everyone knew why. Hig had been right. It was simple math. Why would the North exchange soldiers with an enemy that was running out of men?

The assemblage loosely arranged before Jim made clear just how right Hig had been. Few of the departing men could ever hope to fight again. Of the 1200 men, 300 could not even walk. It was the largest parade of stretchers Jim had ever seen. Most of the boys looked like they couldn't survive the march to the depot, much less the train ride south in packed cabins with no doctor in sight. Those who could stand were propped up only by their desire to escape the gates to die at home, and their faith in a coming reunion with fallen friends and family. Chief amongst them were the actively sick. Scurvy, dysentery, smallpox, diarrhea. Deadened eyes buried in faces void of expression for months now fought through to show the brightness of hopeful celebration. Voices unheard for days spoke of family, God and girls, but mostly of home. Each hopeful chatter was dotted with coughing, vomiting, shivering. Undeterred, the sick continued to speak and try to smile. Near the front was a healthier group. Some showing no signs of sickness at all, appearing healthier and better fed than those they left behind. A few guards, no doubt, had palms greased by those fortunate enough to be able to grease them. Carpenters, rat sellers, oath takers.

The guards kept a border around the group as a jealous mob formed near them. Jim walked around the perimeter looking for Cap. The clothes, the bodies, the faces of most were so similar. He looked for the tall silhouette, and for Mac. When he got close to one group, a snarly oath taker barked he should back off unless he wanted small pox, that the men nearest to Jim were all infected. He circled back near the back, where he saw three different men crouch down and shit in the middle of their ranks so as not to lose their coveted place in the march to freedom.

Jim spotted him near the outside of the pathetic band of pilgrims. Hunched over slightly, his hair withered and mostly gone. Skin pallid like those around him, tight against the cheekbones of the fleshless face. The eyes appeared blackened and tiny, sunken so far into the skull that little expression could be managed. Those bulging forearms were nothing more than scraps between skin and bone. The broad, strong forehead was sunken, giving Cap the look of an old man confused about who and where he was. Cradled in his arms, peeking out from a ragged blanket was the mutt, Mac, looking no better than his owner.

"Long road ahead, Cap."

"You'll be behind me soon, Jim."

"Never could have made it in this place without you."

"You can now."

"I'll try. You think of me when they throw that feast for you the day you get home."

"Yours is coming too, Jim. Home's awaitin', right?"

Jim tried to smile and began to walk away. He did not want to watch Cap disappear through the gates.

"Jim?"

"Yes, Cap."

He held out the little bundle in his outstretched arms.

"He'll never make the trip. I doubt we'll eat until Baltimore. The boys will eat him for sure. I need you to take him, Jim."

"He's your traveling companion, isn't he?"

"Not this time. He's gotten me through this place, maybe he'll do the same for you."

Jim took Mac from his friend, nodded his head and continued to circle the mob.

The stretchers were carried by other prisoners headed home. They laid down the stretchers and waited for the word to march out of the Elmira gates for good. Jim noticed two boys crouched beside the stretcher they were charged with carrying, seeming to inspect the poor boy on top. One of them laid his head on the boy's chest while the other felt about his wrist. A guard came over to them and both prisoners stood to address him. When they did, the boy's arm fell awkwardly to the side. The elbow was wedged in the ground with the forearm sticking up. The wrist rolled limply over and the hand unfolded with one finger extending out, pointing at the prison gates. The guard barked something to the men that Jim couldn't hear. He moved on stiffly through the assemblage, shouting this or that at the men.

The two departing prisoners lifted the stretcher and headed away from the gates. Both strained to bear the weight of the dead body. His arm was now hanging off the side of the stretcher as if reaching for the gate. Below his arm on the stretcher was a large, dried blood stain. They walked clumsily over the uneven ground around the right of Foster's Pond, bogging slightly in the mud. Pausing to rest, they lay the stretcher in the mud and eased down onto swollen knees. Up again, they passed the pond, turned right and disappeared into the Dead House.

The call came out that the gates were opening. The band of ghosts near the gate began to clamor. Those near the front crowded the gate. Those behind them shuffle-stepped as close to the front as they could. The whole mob condensed itself as the men in front could move forward no more and the men in back could no longer stand to be still.

From the Dead House, the two stretcher bearers emerged empty-handed. Having heard the call, they moved frantically and painfully back by the pond and through the mud. The shorter man fell twice, the second time face first into the foulness where the pond had expanded during the rain. *If he was not sick before*, Jim thought, *he will be now*. The taller prisoner waited, though the jumpiness of his fleshless legs revealed his impatience.

"Come on, Johnny. Gotta go. I'll clean you up on the train. Come on now. Keep moving."

Johnny pulled himself slowly from the mud and followed. Near the gate men were already exiting the camp. Guards maintained the perimeter and turned back prisoners who tried to sneak amongst the departing. The stout guard who had sent the two men to the Dead House came near the rear, barking now for them to hurry, that the train would wait for no man. The taller man was walking slowly, getting closer to the moving crowd. The other was on the ground again. He gathered himself and looked up the hill to the group disappearing through the gates. He gritted his teeth and did something Jim had not seen a prisoner do in weeks. He ran. His legs wobbled as if the ground was giving beneath him, but still he ran, gaining on the men ahead of him. When he reached the taller gentleman — now at the back of the line and still waiting for his comrade — he collapsed face first to the ground once more. His tall friend rolled him over and cradled his head in both hands. The larger man pulled his downed friend close in, looking directly eye to eye, noses touching. He was saying something, repeating it over and gain. Searching for a response. Then dropped his head onto the smaller man's chest and wrapped his arms around his motionless body. He pulled back and was sobbing. Screaming. His voice was so broken and debilitated Jim could only make out one word. "Brother."

The stout guard grabbed him by the shoulder and pulled him to his feet. The guard said something with a cold face and pushed slightly in the man's back. Still sobbing and screaming, looking always backwards, the tall man limped toward the gate. He grabbed his hair in both hands and pulled down hard until his head was bent into his chest. Screaming. Sounds only. No words. But kept moving, toward the gate, the train, and home. He was the last prisoner out of the gate, and as the doors closed behind him Jim could still hear his awful yell.

The jealous men left behind began slowly to disperse. Two prisoners bearing an empty stretcher came from the Dead House. They walked toward the gate against the tide of prisoners headed back across the yard. Jim stood and watched them as they lifted Johnny from the ground and laid him on the stretcher. Along the side of the stretcher near his arm was the same dried blood stain Jim had seen moments earlier. They lifted Johnny with effort from the ground and carried him around the pond, through the mud and into the Dead House.

Jim felt sicker and closer to death than he had in all his months since he left Cartledge Creek. Mac was still wrapped in the blanket under Jim's left arm. Not making a sound. His fur was mangy and matted, and his little face was drawn and sad like the prisoners themselves.

Jim looked at him and the dog looked back at him with expectant eyes as if he knew what Cap had asked of him. Jim stared into his eyes and thought of Hig and Cap, of Robert back in the barracks and of how long the stick seemed when he measured his leg. He thought of home and Sunday mornings, of sermons at the meeting house about right and wrong. Well-meant orders about moral choices that seemed so momentous to him as a boy as he had just been, but so luxurious and frivolous to him now as a man. As Jim walked slowly back to the spot, he pulled the blanket gently over Mac's head. He adjusted the dog softly so that its head fit neatly into the crux between Jim's elbow and his side. Still walking, still appearing just as the other men in camp, he pressed his elbow to his side as firmly as his weakened body would allow. Mac struggled for but a moment. Kicking and squirming under the blanket. Jim held firm as he walked. He grabbed Mac's mouth through the blanket to prevent any noise the other prisoners might hear. His mind left him. It perched on the observatory and looked down upon him with all the disgust and bewilderment of the men in tall hats who tipped glasses there weeks before. In a moment the dog was still. Tears were streaming down Jim's face and over his lips, leaving trails through the grime. He kept the dog concealed and headed to the spot. Half would be for Robert, but he would never tell him what it was.

Seventeen

Ben Covington
January, 1865
Fort Fisher, NC

Ben Covington sat down to rest in his latest temporary home. His unit had marched all the way from Georgia and gone straight to work setting up the guns along the parapet. His sweat turned cold in the ocean breeze as soon as the work was done. Amos and another slave that had made the march helped Ben and his gun mates pull the guns through the thick sand and up to their positions. When they were finished, armed guards led the slaves down to their camp in the back of the fort, well within range of the Yankee guns that were expected to appear any day. Ben crouched down in the corner of the gun chamber and crossed the arms of his gray wool coat to keep warm.

There was a pleasant feel to the salt air. The ocean breeze carried away the battle smells from just a few days prior. *This would be a fine spot if nobody was gonna shoot at me.* His back was against the wide wooden planks that gave shape to the gun chamber at the top of a massive sand mound known as Shepherd's Battery. Behind him was Fort Fisher's land face, the shorter wall of the "L" shaped fort. He and his comrades had just positioned their gun at a little crook in the wall beside the fort's main gate. On the other side of the tall wooden gate was a palisade fence of high, wooden stakes that ran to the Cape Fear River at the fort's rear. Along the beach beyond the land face, was a similar fence, designed to slow a charging enemy and give the defenders time to aim and fire. Running unseen below the fence line underneath the projected battlefield were buried torpedo tubes, waiting to blast an unsuspecting enemy from below.

The beach behind him ran for miles of flat sand curving slightly left towards Wilmington, the last remaining viable port of the Confederacy. The long beach was little more than a strip of sand, dividing the surging Cape Fear on the left with the raging Atlantic on the right. The land face was a row of giant sand heaps topped with gun chambers, spanning the distance from the river to the sea. Along the beach was the sea face, constructed in the same manner as the land face, but over twice as long. Far at the end of the long sea face was the Mound Battery, a tremendous mountain of sand where river and ocean met, with big guns that could occupy blockade ships while the low, fast blockade runners slipped quickly into the river mouth, turned right and escaped to Wilmington with whatever they had been able to trade for cotton, hopefully musket rounds and shells.

Fort Fisher was a veteran to tiny battles fought to skirt the blockade and maintain some economy for the struggling South. A blockade runner would come steaming through the inlet full speed with lights off, its captain an old salt of the shifting shoals literally running blind over treacherous ground. Behind were capable Union captains with slower ships but bigger guns, sending shells splashing around the Confederate pirates. The big guns from the Mound Battery would open up on the blockade ships, rarely with the luxury of aim or daylight. More times than not, the distraction worked and the goods slipped through. Then, as the runner slipped past the back of the fort in the Cape Fear River, the shoals master would blow his whistle and take in the cheers of the fort's defenders, celebrating their own little contribution to the cause. Meanwhile the bulky blockade ships would ease unmolested back to their posts, perhaps firing a few rounds at the fort for good measure.

Other times the pirates were not so lucky. Racing from oncoming shells, the hull of a speeding blockade runner would push its way deeply and irretrievably into the accepting sand of the hidden bars and shoals of the inlet. The blockade ships would steady themselves, taking time to train their guns carefully. The cannons from the Fort would take aim as well, and the battle was on. Captains and their crews, knowing they were sitting ducks, were prepared to abandon a grounded ship and detonate it on the shoals, rather than let the Yankees capture their cargo. The fort defenders became rescuers, retrieving the crew and whatever cargo could be salvaged while shells splashed the water high above their lifeboats in the dark.

Ben was happy to be alone for the moment. At home in Cartledge Creek, he had taken long walks in the woods, or worked alone for hours in quiet. Now, in the artillery, there was always company and always noise. Never a moment alone. Little groups of men were scattered about the grounds inside the fort. Some chatted amongst themselves. Others played music that scattered in the wind before it traveled to Ben's ears so that he saw the odd sight of men picking at instruments, dancing and opening their mouths wide, all in silence. A few campfires were burning but their smells were likewise carried away before they reached him. Amongst the men were piles of debris from the first bombardment of the fort. Much of it consisted of the splintered remains of guns much like the one Ben would man when the Yankee fleet made its anticipated return. Most prominent within the grounds were the charred remains of the barracks. That was one smell the wind could not carry away fully. The smell of green lumber freshly burned. Most of the men's coats and blankets had burned as well.

From the outside, the fort did not appear to be a fort at all. It was simply a series of high dunes clumped together between ocean and river. From the inside however, Ben could see the substantial substructure that made a fort behind the piles of sand. The gun chambers carved out neatly along and between the mounds. The bombproofs, cavernous hideaways tucked below the heaping earthworks, held up by tremendous timbers that must have been carried a great distance from the mainland. There a gunner could hide in relative safety while the shells battered the gun chambers, darting out at chosen moments to return fire. There was no more Charleston. No more Savannah. No New Orleans. Only Wilmington. No other ports where the blockade runners could distribute their goods and prop up the failing war effort. The once invincible boys in gray had begun losing battles they would once have won, often with nothing to load in their rifles. In anticipation of the expected second assault of Fort Fisher, Ben and the other artillery men had been ordered not to fire their guns at will as the Yankee attackers would, but to fire only once per half hour unless more shells could be obtained. The bombproofs, it seemed, would host the gunners for the majority of the battle. The Confederacy hung by a thin thread of sand, occupied by barely two thousand men, many with empty guns.

Ben rested his head against the planks behind him and closed his eyes. His mind eased and slowed. He did not feel sleep coming but felt something he once took for granted ... peace. There was a gentle, rhythmic roll of the waves breaking upon the shore. Though it was cold, the sun warmed his face as he leaned his head back and smiled. When the wind picked up, thousands of grains of sand lifted and flew low across the dunes, whistling as they skimmed little ridges and bumps until they landed to await being lifted again. There was a pleasantness in God's creation, he thought, interrupted only when its chief inhabitants couldn't get along with themselves. *Maybe man was God's only mistake. What a world this would be without us!* He smiled at this thought and concentrated on the sun and the sounds and the refreshing feel of the salty air.

Just as he began to nod off, something crossed his feet. Ben opened one eye and saw a ghost crab looking back at him. His little dark eyes rose above his paper-thin, white shell in Ben's direction. All eight legs tiptoed with invisible speed as the crab dashed first to the left, then right, back to where he started near Ben's feet. The crab crouched low into a footprint in the sand and almost completely disappeared.

Suddenly a black brogan shoe stomped down into the footprint, squashing the crab where he hid. A grotesque nasally laugh followed. Ben was so focused on the crab he had not seen the other fellow approach. Now he looked up, shielding his eyes from the sun to get a look at his sudden visitor.

"Little bastard didn't see that coming, I bet."

"Why did you have to go and do that?"

"What? That sand roach? He your pet or something there, rookie?" The crab-squasher seemed rather proud of everything he said. Almost always letting out a false laugh at the end of each sentence.

"Naw. I was just watching him skitter about. Shame you killed him for nothing."

"You for real, rookie? I done hurt your feelings? For a little killing? Reckon you're in the wrong business then."

Ben contemplated a retort but lost interest. The crab-squasher was kicking sand over the top of the killed crab. He was young to be calling anybody "rookie." His face wore many days of insignificant beard growth. The hairs were long and even, showing they'd been care for, but there weren't many of them. The result was a very thin beard of very few long hairs. It gave the appearance of a large house that had been painted with one can of paint. His hair was longish across the front, and brushed heavily to one side, giving it a floppy appearance. The skin visible through the scattered beard was delicate but red, and appeared to have been scrubbed vigorously each and every morning. His uniform was as plain as the rest of them, but with buttons polished to a high shine. The buttons were finer and larger than most. Ben immediately suspected he had brought them from home with a box of polish and sewed them onto the uniform himself. In all he gave the appearance of someone who might have played a soldier in a high school play, and even at that been given few scenes of significance.

"I saw you boys march in here and set up earlier. Reckon you're pretty happy you weren't here back on Christmas like I was?"

"Well, friend, Savannah this Christmas was no picnic either. That Sherman aims to kill us all, I think."

"Savannah, hell. You guys didn't see more than a little squabble down there. Nothing like what we saw right here."

"I suppose you're right."

"Bet your ass, I'm right. That's how come I know you're a rookie. Can't be more than about eighteen, I bet. You look like a month ago you were probably sitting with your mama in the church pew, checking out the pretty girls in the choir and figuring out how to get one of them down to the creek with you or something."

"I wish I was sitting in that church today. Feels like a few days and feels like years all at the same time."

"Yeah, I'll have my eyes on you boy when the shells start flying again. You ain't seen shit."

"I suppose I've seen a little, but not so much as you have I am sure, friend."

"I bet you've been sitting here by yourself trying to figure out where to run to when the shit kicks in. Haven't you?"

Ben gave up shielding the sun to keep a look at the crab-squasher. He leaned his head back against the planks and rested his eyes once again.

"I said, haven't you there rookie, been thinking about where to run to? Hunh?

No response from Ben.

"Well I don't know if you got it figured out yet or not but there ain't nowhere to run to. When they start coming at us you can drown in two directions or get shot in two others. So pick your poison, rookie."

Ben sat silent for what seemed like five minutes. He heard no footsteps and felt the presence of the crab-squasher still standing there. When Ben finally spoke, he didn't open his eyes.

"I bet you were happy to have those bombproofs when the shells started exploding. If it wasn't for those I don't know that anybody could have survived that beating you guys took. I heard they thought they had blown you all up, and you boys climbed back out of those bombproofs ready to fight and scared them half to death."

"Damn right we was ready. Damn right they was scared. But not me. I manned my gun the whole battle. No bombproofs for me. I'd rather die up here than cower down there under the ground. You won't see me down there with you and them other yaller bastards."

"I meant no offense, friend. Just saying this is a fine fort to make a defense. Couple of thousand boys to defend a fort against the whole Yankee navy and the army landed out there on the beach. That's a fine fort."

"Kiss my white ass, rookie! It ain't the fort it's the man. And there ain't never been no Dickinson go crawling in the ground like a damn earthworm. Not from my Dickinsons anyway."

"I bet not, fella, I bet not. Sounds like you come from good stock."

"Bet your ass I do."

"I guess when things get hot I should be glad to have you around."

"That's right. You get in trouble, I'll be right there two pits over. I'll be the one giving those Yankee boys more hell than anyone else on this here wall."

"I can honestly say, Dickinson, I do truly look forward to seeing you in action."

Ben finally opened his eyes, shielded the sun with his hat and re-established eye contact with Dickinson, who smiled a broad, childish smile of great self-satisfaction.

"One more thing, Dickinson. Mind if I pray for you?"

"You can tell Jesus he can kiss my white ass too."

Ben leaned back against the planks and rested his eyes again.

"Well, friend, I'll put in a good word for you, but I suppose I'll let you tell him that last part yourself."

Eighteen

Leonidas Jackson
January, 1865
Elmira, NY

Leonidas Jackson's mind was blank. He had shut it down. Forced out every coherent thought. Compressed it down to a tiny compartment in his skull it took little to fill. So small it became occupied by the rhythm of simple repetitive sounds. Eight hooves rising and falling. Plodding. The barely audible crunch of the frozen mud or snow as they landed, always in perfect rhythm. The clack of that one repaired section of wagon wheel, the remnant of a forgotten crash. Always the same sound at the same moment in each identical revolution.

It was a trick he learned in long days of work in sunbaked Southern fields. When the feet were blistered and swollen. When the sweat covered from head to toe, and streams ran into the eyes and mouth faster than blistered hands could wipe them away. When hours of stooping took their toll on the neck and back, which throbbed constantly and shot pains down an arm or leg as the sun crossed the center of the sky and started down the other side. When the muscles required to repeat the same tasks over and again began to lock and refuse to move. When the vision blurred all around save for a tiny circle appearing straight away between Jackson and the next menial task in an unending chain of menial tasks. Hundreds of physical events beyond what he thought was the last he could manage. Reduce every task to a rhythm. A rhythm with a sound or a feel. Somehow more easily reproduced than a choppy disconnected series of unrelated actions. The only way to run a hundred miles, he had thought in those days, was in a million identical steps. Each step its own end, with no thoughts of the hill to climb.

When the rhythm takes over, the mind can rest. No thoughts of misery. No thoughts of the endlessness of the task. Just repetition. One bend, one reach, one step, one hoof landing at a time. It had worked in the oppressive heat of Southern summers. Why not in the oppressive cold of a New York winter? Let the mind go. Otherwise it will think. And it can only think of cold. And when thinking of cold, one grows colder.

The sun was just rising outside the camp. A ring of orange spread low across the horizon against the distant hills. Back across the sky a few stars were still faintly visible. The camp was silent save for lonely sounds of the solitary wagon.

Jackson's breath seemed to turn to ice instantly in the air about his face before it could move beyond his nose and mouth. His hands trembled in thick gloves as he held the reigns. He opened his mouth slightly so his teeth would not chatter. It made the lips colder and the throat more exposed, but chattering would ruin the rhythm, which would bring back thought. And there was nothing to think of but cold.

Much of the yard was still covered with tents. At the end of each row of tents, two younger fellows jumped out and peeked inside, one at the time, down the row. When they pulled back the openings, the frozen tents cracked audibly. Most of the time the men peeked in and moved on. Occasionally they climbed inside and returned carrying a body. The bodies were straight, erect and pale. Frozen stiff.

It was then Jackson had to work his hardest not to think. To survive by not feeling. There was no rhythm to the awkward movements of piling a body into the wagon, or of the chatter between the two young fellows that loaded and reloaded new passengers, then rode on top on them in the back of the wagon.

"That there was the coldest dead Johnny Reb I ever saw, Jackson."

"Pratt ain't lying, old Jack. He was lying straight on the ground with just a little blanket on him. His jacket froze solid to the ground."

"That's right. One of the other fellows in there had some sort of stick. Look like a chair leg. We had to pry him up with it."

It was always something of this sort. Observation of tragedy with bemused detachment. Jackson never said a thing. In fact, he usually navigated the wagon through its entire circuit without saying a word. For some reason they persisted in expressing their thoughts to Jackson, despite never receiving a response. Eventually they shrugged at each other and said no more, at least until the next body was collected.

The stiff body placed upon the morning's pile, Jackson flicked the reigns with his frozen hands and began the rhythms again. The stars in the western sky had finally gone. In the east a plain orange disc had replaced the bands of light that had colored the whole horizon. In the cloudless sky there was nothing to capture and reflect the new light. Day was coming, and the darkness gone, but the light was pale and colorless. Even the sun seemed cold.

"Sixteen bodies ol' Jack. Three days in a row."

The smaller of the two smiled broadly at his friend as he spoke.

"That's right, Pratt, sixteen. Pay up. Not more like you said. Sixteen on the mark, again."

The larger fellow dug into his pocket and produced two plugs of tobacco, which he held out in his palm toward the other. Then, before the smaller fellow could take the money, Pratt snapped his hand shut.

"Double or nothing tomorrow. More than sixteen."

"Forget it, Pratt. Pay up now."

Jackson did not turn around. He drove the wagon on the path between the barracks and Mess, approaching the bend around Foster's Pond to the Dead House. Just as he passed the Mess he saw an odd sight. Odd for this early on this cold of a day. It was a prisoner, walking alone, coming up from the pond toward the wagon. He walked without purpose or meaningful direction. His butternut uniform so worn that his pale skin was visible in several places. He stopped and started and changed direction so many times it was clear to Jackson he was in distress.

As usual, Pratt spoke first.

"Where you going, Johnny Reb? You searching for Dixie? Just lay down in the back here with your friends and die."

"That's right Johnny. Bottom rail on top now."

"Hush, boys!" Jackson finally spoke. "Can't you tell this boy can't see. We got to help him."

"Shit. He ain't never helped me."

"He can help himself."

"I said hush, now. You don't have to help him. I will. All you have to do is ride and shut up."

The man was walking with his hands stretched out before him. His path was jagged. He angled this direction and that. His eyes were wide open but revealed little. His steps small. His mouth slightly open. Gradually he made his way to the wagon. One of the horses snorted, and the man turned and approached it, again with his hands feeling through the air before him. Finally his hands located the head of the horse. He stroked the horse's head and mane and whispered in his ear. The horse seemed to calm him.

"Young Reb, can you see?"

"No sir. I could before, a few minutes ago. These spots started showing up. At first I was able to look around them, but they got bigger and bigger until eventually they started forming together into one big black spot."

"What are you doing out here son?"

The soldier stood looking in the direction of the voice. Silent far longer than in normal conversation.

"I can't say really … I went out there to die, I guess … break through the ice and die. There was this lady, though. She was standing on the observatory and she was all alone. A beautiful girl. I've seen her there before. Yellow dress. Always the same yellow dress. She has long curly hair. Beautiful long curly brown hair. It bounces on her shoulders when she walks across that tower."

"Young Reb, I think I need to take you over to the hospital. There's not anybody up there anymore. You know they shut down those towers three or four months ago."

"But I could see her. And she saw me too. She spoke to me. I could hear her. And I know I can make it. I know I can make it because of her. She told me so, sir. She told me so."

"There ain't no such girl, son. At least not here. Maybe she in your head. I best take you over and let the doctor have a look at you."

"Please don't take me over there, sir. No one ever comes back. Just take me back to my barracks, sir. I'll die in that hospital sir. Please."

"OK, son. Calm back down, now. Pick your poison."

The man turned back to the horse and stroked his mane again.

"There you go, son. I see that horse calms you down. You must have known a horse or two back home."

"Yes sir, I do. We had a bunch of them back home. We..."

"You had a bunch of them, did you? I guess so. I bet that's not the only thing you had a bunch of, either."

The man's eyes narrowed, became more alert. His shoulders shrank.

"You are right, sir. We had a bunch of those too."

"Yeah, that's what I thought. You talk too good not to be from one of them families. Well, come on. You want my help, don't you?"

"Yes sir, I do."

Jack helped the man up gently into the wagon. The prisoner looked at Jackson and twitched slightly as if trying to focus his eyes.

"Thank you, sir. And I just wanted to say. There was just ... something I wanted to say."

"You ain't got to say nothing to me, son."

"I just. I've never said it before. Only thought it a lot. Thought it my whole life."

His eyes turned the color of red eyes turn when they cry. His face shuddered and his frail body throbbed as crying men do. But the eyes of his dried-out body could not make tears.

"I just never understood it. I never understood how we could buy a person or sell a person or tell a person what they have to do. I never understood the ones that have fought for that, with that being their reason to fight. I can't see your eyes now sir, but I've looked in men's eyes my whole life and there is something there that says they are a man. Something says they were made a man by God. And I just never understood it."

Jack looked back at him. He looked at the young boy before him, not more than twenty years in age. He looked into his broken eyes and quivering face.

He had looked into such eyes before. On a cotton plantation in Mississippi. It was owned by the Timmons family and had been for some time. Conrad Timmons, the master, was a terrifying red-faced man whose drunken fury was known for miles in all directions. He was known to turn to the whip every day, often for the slightest offense. When presented with his bastard children, the product of regular rapes of young female slaves, he promptly sold them and never mentioned them again. There was an even more vicious master farther down the river. One whose slaves were never heard from again. Who was said to shoot rather than whip any offenders. It was to him that Conrad's bastards were sold, along with whatever slaves Conrad determined had committed unpardonable sins. It was more than rumor, for the villain came to retrieve them himself. His wagon was painted bright red. When it came down the lane, everyone dashed into the cabins or ducked behind trees. The young mothers of bastard children tried to hide them away. The man, Deveraux, was always shoddily clad, with a coiled whip conspicuously on his side and two pistols in his belt. He wore a thin mustache and a pointy beard like a gunslinger. There was a rumor he had suffered an injury as a young man, stealing his manhood and his fertility in a most unfortunate way. Jackson never knew if this was true, only that the man's evil was of a level that must have been acquired from life. No one is born that mean.

Jackson was sold to Timmons as a young boy. Timmons drank daily, and was often unconscious by supper. His wife Elizabeth was a kind, gentle woman, who rarely spoke in her husband's presence. She often appeared with heavy make-up around her eyes, most commonly the day after one of Conrad's whipping rages. When he was passed out or away on business, she permitted their children to play with the slave children. The plantation was immense, and there were no other children near. Conrad and Elizabeth only had three, two girls and one boy. When the baby, Conrad, Jr., was born, Elizabeth had almost died in childbirth. After that, there were no more.

Conrad, Jr. and Jackson were inseparable as children. Everyone referred to them as Connie and Lenny. As small children they jumped every fence, chased every rabbit and fished every creek on the twelve-thousand-acre plantation. Though the circumstances that brought them together were well known to all, there was no evidence either saw the other as anything less than equal. Elizabeth tried to conceal their brotherhood from her husband for years, though ultimately he became aware. He never protested openly, at least not such that Jackson knew. Whenever they encountered him, though, they darted instinctively from his disapproving glare.

One winter afternoon as Conrad approached, they ran side by side behind the horse barn and ducked into the woods. The cold winter air numbed their faces and bit their ears as they let their legs fall faster and faster down the hill through the trees. They sliced between the large hardwoods and leapt downed logs that once stood high above the forest. As the hill steepened they stumbled and rolled through the leaves to the creek bank, laughing and breathing the cold air deep into their lungs. They tiptoed across the old oak tree that served as a bridge over the rocky creek ten feet below. Seated on the middle of the tree and facing one another as they had done so many times before, they continued to giggle while they caught their breath. Connie produced a small pocket knife and made a shallow line on his palm. He squeezed the skin and a few drops of blood emerged along the cut. Instinctively, Lenny held out his hand and allowed Connie to do the same to his palm as well. They pressed their hands firmly palm to palm and locked their fingers together.

"Lenny Jackson," Connie said, "You are my blood brother, forever."

Though never barred from his friendship with Connie, Lenny did seem mysteriously to receive every difficult assignment around the place. Despite Elizabeth's influence, he was never cut any breaks. His days in the fields were longer, more painful and hotter than everyone else's. If that was the price of friendship, he thought, he would happily pay it. He learned to work, keep quiet, and never complain.

During their teenage years the boys began to share ideas. Their relative stations in life were no longer unspoken shadows. They were the topic of frequent discussion. Lenny revealed the pain of bondage hiding behind his faithful appearance. Connie reassured him that things would change. One day this would be his plantation. No drunkenness. No rapes. Free men working for an honest wage.

At this thought Lenny would always smile and nod, and say nothing.

It happened the year both boys turned eighteen. It was late on an October evening. Connie's birthday. A full moon was well into the sky. The day had been hot but the fall air was cool when the sun fell. There was no wind. Lenny's thin cotton clothes had clung to him in the heat of the day, then stuck when the evening came and the sweat dried. There was dust and cotton on his clothes, face, hair and hands. As he approached the cabin, the smells of sweat and dirt and cotton were replaced by something pungent and unexpected. Each day when he made this walk his nose was overtaken by dinner cooking. He still lived with his mother, though his father was dead and his siblings who knows where. She waited until late evening to cook so his dinner would be hot when he got home. But this night the smell was different. Not the inviting smell he was used to. It was the smell of dinner burning.

When he entered the cabin, his mother was not there. The others who lived with them were gone as well. The only two people in the cabin's one room were Conrad and Connie. The cornbread hanging above the fire in a pan was black and smoldering. The smoke poured through the hole in the roof. Conrad held a dead chicken in one hand, his whip in the other. He looked at Lenny with that same look that had sent the boys scurrying as children. Connie stood beside his father with sunken shoulders, and looked only at the ground. Conrad looked down on his son, then back at Lenny with a sadistic grin.

"Well, if it isn't my nigger step-son. Looking forward to a big plate full of stolen chicken tonight?"

As he had long been conditioned, Lenny Jackson did not speak.

"Talk to me, boy! Proud of yourself for stealing this chicken?"

Lenny felt a heat well up in his face. His pulse throbbed in his neck. The soreness of the muscles across his shoulders and arms reminded him of how his work had hardened and strengthened him. If he could get to the drunkard before his whip flew, he could defeat him. Connie, he thought, would stand by idly and let him do so. He would watch his father beaten and feel joy in his heart.

But Lenny did not move. And he did not speak.

"The red wagon's coming for you boy, if you don't admit you took this chicken!"

Connie continued to look at the ground. Lenny could hear him sobbing. Fearing separation from his friend, Lenny finally spoke.

"No, sir. I did not, sir. I've been in the field all day."

As Lenny spoke, Conrad flicked his wrist and pain wrapped itself instantly around Lenny's head. A red gash opened from his chin across his face under his ear. Pain stretched all the way around the back of his head. He could feel blood begin to run down his face and neck. The back of his head felt suddenly cold as if a swath of hair had vanished. He felt blood running down into the hair below.

He spoke no more. Conrad recoiled the whip, crossed the cabin and grabbed Lenny by his arm. He dragged him out the door and into the clearing amongst the cabins. More of the slaves had come out now and formed a faint circle in the moonlight, outlining the clearing. They knew what came next. There was a single oak in the middle of the clearing. Its bark bore the diagonal gashes of whippings past. Lenny shuffled his feet and kept up with Conrad as he dragged him to the tree. The smell of liquor and stale cigar smoke was strong. Conrad whispered to Lenny as they moved.

"All these years I have put up with you. Well, now you can see why. Today my boy learns how this world works."

Conrad slammed Lenny face first into the tree. It was narrow enough that even a small man could reach around and grab his own wrists on the far side. Conrad yanked Lenny's arms around the tree. He removed his belt and cinched it tight around Lenny's wrists.

"Connie, get your ass over here."

Connie complied. Lenny could not see him, but could hear his steps. All of Lenny's senses were heightened. He felt the blood trickling on his head and each molecule of cold evening air as it dipped down into his lungs. It seemed as though he could smell every drink of liquor, every puff of smoke that his tormentor had partaken to celebrate the adulthood of his only son. He knew the presence of his fellow slaves around, but heard nothing from them.

Father and son circled the tree and looked into Lenny's face, pressed up against the bark of the tree. The moon lit their faces, revealing every detail.

"Son, you look this nigger thief in the eye and you tell him the truth. You tell him, 'Lenny Jackson, you are my nigger, and I will strike you down like the hand of Almighty God.' "

Conrad grabbed his son's face and thrust it to within inches of Lenny's. Lenny looked into his friend's eyes. Connie stared back at him. His face quivered and his eyes were red and glassy. The tracks of tears were visible all over his face.

"No."

Conrad smacked his son violently three times, each harder than the last. The boy's face, already red, turned a deep crimson. His tears stopped, but his face continued to cry.

"You tell him, now!"

As the boy spoke, in barely a whisper, his voice trembled and stammered over every syllable.

"Lenny Jackson. You are my nigger, and I will strike you down like the hand of Almighty God."

Conrad smacked him again with even more force.

"Louder, you little shit! I can't hear you!"

"Lenny Jackson. You are my nigger, and I will strike you down like the hand of Almighty God."

"Louder! Yell it! Let these savages know who you are!"

"Lenny Jackson! You are my nigger, and I will strike you down like the hand of Almighty God!"

"Again!"

"Lenny Jackson! You are my nigger, and I will strike you down like the hand of Almighty God!"

He was screaming now. His father handed him the whip, and the boy backed away, as he had been trained. Conrad ripped Lenny's shirt from his body to expose his back to his blood brother. Instantly the first lash cut Lenny's back and seemed to go right through his body. With each lash the boy screamed as instructed, time and time again. Each time he yelled it was louder. Each time he whipped it was harder. Lenny Jackson again felt his pulse thundering in his neck. He took his entire universe and shrunk it down to that tiny little vein in his neck that pulsed with rapid rhythm. He let his mind leave him, and endured.

On the icy wagon in the Elmira stockade, Jackson stared deep into the reddened eyes of the slaveholder before him. His pulse quickened as his mind took him back somewhere he did not want to go. The red wagon had come the next day and he had never seen Connie again. Or his own mother. No opportunity for reaction was given. Just the whipping, then the hell that existed down river.

Jackson's face softened. He dug deep into his Union blue overcoat. He pulled out something wrapped in a rag. He unwrapped it and stared at it for a moment. A large biscuit with a thick piece of ham in the middle. The man beside him did not look but began to sniff. Jackson opened the man's hand and pressed the biscuit into it. The man's hands trembled and he gazed in unfocused disbelief at Jackson. He ate the biscuit ravenously, quickly, desperately.

In the back of the wagon, Pratt and his companion gawked in disbelief. For the first time all morning, they said nothing.

"What barracks, son?"

"Twenty-four, sir."

The rhythms of the wagon returned, as it made its slow way through the snow and frozen mud. As the wagon approached the barracks, the prisoners of barracks twenty-four were lined up single file for the morning roll call. Many stood barefoot in the snow. Some wore only their underwear. Others wore shirts and pants filled with holes and tears. A few had Union blue overcoats, but with the tails chopped awkwardly so that none could impersonate guards in an effort to flee. All of the men were shaking, shivering, dying. As the wagon stopped a guard could be heard yelling as he walked the line.

"I said Dockery, damn it! He's not lying in there dead so he must be here. Where the hell is Dockery?"

The man beside Jackson straightened himself as he swallowed his last bit of biscuit.

"Here, sir! Dockery is right here, sir!"

Nineteen

Ben Covington
January 14, 1865
Fort Fisher, NC

The view from Fort Fisher had changed. Ben Covington stood on top of Shepherd's Battery as he had the day before. One day his wonderment was at the creation of God. The next it was at the creation of man.

There were dozens of Yankee warships just offshore from the fort, at least sixty in all. They were arranged in three long lines that arced around the fort, surrounding it as much as geography would allow. In front of the three long lines were the low-lying ironclad monitors with their imposing turret guns. Behind the main lines were two more equally massive lines of ships laying back in reserve. The ships were of every shape, size and type. The war had brought much progress in the means of killing one's former countrymen, and for this attack no ship was too old or too new. Tall-masted wooden ships with rows of cannons along their sides, paddle-wheeled steamers with towering smokestacks, ironclad tall ships like the New Ironsides which had withstood so many Rebel attacks, and the seemingly unassailable monitors that sat so low as to provide little target for Confederate guns. The sun rising behind the fleet gave an odd glow to those ships clad in iron, those most feared by the Southern defenders.

The front line of attackers moved steadily into range of the fort, then dropped anchor and prepared for battle. Along the tops of the mounds were many like Ben, manning their guns only until it became necessary to flee to the bombproofs below. Amidst the historical bombardment about to be unleashed by the fleet, the garrison of Fort Fisher would only offer a harassing fire. Much of the work would be left to the fort itself, built from heaps of earth to withstand any bombardment man could offer.

Just as the ships reached anchorage and readied to fire, the giant Columbiad gun roared from one of the mounds down the beach. This signaled the other guns along the sea face to fire. Through the smoke growing along the sea face, Ben saw the New Ironsides fire the first shot from the fleet. With that, the bombardment had finally begun. Ben looked at his gun, and at his fellow men from his gun crew. He wanted badly to stand his post and fire his gun. In their eyes, the others seemed to want the same. But orders were orders. As the bombardment increased, the men vacated the gun chamber and headed for the bombproof below.

* * *

The entrance to the bombproof was a low door framed with timbers the size of railroad ties. Ben ducked under the door and into the darkness, with other men breathing down his neck to get in behind.

The pale light that entered from the doorway cut a slanted rectangle into the darkness. Two lanterns hung from wooden pegs driven into large timbers that framed the room by pushing back the earthen mound. The lanterns skipped and bounced on their pegs in reaction to the pounding of the shells above. The lantern light swam randomly about the darkness in ghostly shapes, revealing momentarily the details of the room and its terrified inhabitants.

The roaring explosions above shook the entire mound and reverberated into Ben's gut. With each blast sand would rain down from the bombproof ceiling. Occasionally a blast would sound just above, and the sand would fall in clumps, raising doubt the structure would hold. With each blow, Ben convinced himself a shell had exploded directly above them. That it was the worst they would have to endure. Then would come another. Closer. Louder. He found himself holding his breath during the blasts, then gulping air in the moments of silence as if emerging from a youthful dive into Cartledge Creek.

Soon there were no such moments of silence. No singular blasts that could be separated one from the other. The shells exploded so fast that their effects became constant. The blasts became one uninterrupted roar. The shuddering of the Earth became an ongoing quake. The incremental collapse of the sandy mound of protection was a steady rain of sand and earth. Still at times it worsened, until Ben was sure he and his fellow defenders were soon to be buried alive. But that moment did not come.

There was movement in the darkness across the bombproof. A spotlight of roving lantern light held for a second on the face of a regal officer with a long black beard. He motioned with his hands and shapes began to move in the shadows. *Their thirty-minute wait is over*, Ben thought. *It is time for them to go fire their gun at the fleet.* The officer and five men awkwardly made their way across the room into the rectangle of light, then disappeared into the violence.

In their absence conditions underground remained the same. Ben closed his eyes and tried to imagine the reality of the bombardment outside. *How will those men ever reach their gun? How will they manage to aim and fire?* In his mind there was one constant, massive explosion that roamed the fort destroying everything in its path. Nothing could escape or survive. There were no individual shells, but one all-knowing destructive force. Striking wherever the most damage could be done. As if the attack was directed by the hand of an invisible god.

He thought again of those poor boys out there trying to fire their weapon. He said a prayer for them aloud with his eyes open, looking to the door and hoping to see them appear. Time passed without their return. Too much time. Ben began to conclude the worst, but continued looking at the door. Hoping. There was nothing else to do.

Suddenly someone was there. A lean silhouette against the slanted rectangular light. He was covered in sand from head to toe. There was a smear of blood across his forehead. His hat was gone. There was a long, disheveled beard matted with sand. It was the officer from moments before. Yelling at the top of his lungs. His forehead creased and reddened. His eyes grew more desperate as the destruction behind and above him drowned out his words. Ben tried and failed to read his lips. The man took another step into the bombproof and let out an even more desperate yell. Unable to convey his message, he threw up his right arm in disgust. The left arm did not move. It was gone. As he gestured wildly with his right arm, there was strange, pathetic movement about his left shoulder. Something hanging from the socket flopped about in the tattered remains of a shirt sleeve, attempting a gesture to match that of the healthy right arm.

None of the other men from his gun crew had returned. Now here stood their leader shouting into oblivion, receiving no assistance. Ben knew the hospital bombproof was over fifty yards away, a long way to run under heavy fire, especially with an injured man to carry. He measured the odds but for a moment, then rose and moved toward the desperate officer. Another figure emerged suddenly from the darkness and pushed his way past Ben. He grabbed the officer and led him back out the door as Ben stood frozen, wondering what had just happened and why. Had he been too slow to offer assistance? Had another man seen him rise and jumped up to cut him off? To steal his moment of bravery? Or even to save him from a near certain fate?

Ben crouched in the doorway. The light from the outside blinded him momentarily. When his focus returned, he could see only what lay directly before him. A young private in a clean uniform, boosting the shattered officer onto his shoulders. Before heading down the land face in the direction of the hospital bombproof, the young soldier looked back to the doorway, to safety, and to Ben. It was Dickinson, the crab-squasher. His face was stern and determined, until he saw Ben. He smiled for but a moment, winked at Ben, then grew serious again. As he took his first step, a shell exploded in front of him. The blast knocked Ben away from the door. Shell fragments buzzed by his face and lodged in the earthworks. He opened his eyes to find his legs completely buried in sand. Out in the light a massive crater now held the remains of Dickinson and the bearded officer. Parts of both men were interspersed throughout the crater. Ben could not tell where one man started and the other stopped. Amidst the carnage was a single polished brass button.

As Ben dug out his legs, faces appeared around him. Familiar faces. His gun crew. The time to go fire his gun had come. Regardless of the carnage before them, and the likelihood it foretold their immediate fate, the men dutifully began their climb up the sand to their gun.

The ladder to the top of the battery had been shattered by a Yankee shell. A butternut soldier lay twisted and intertwined with the splintered planks. Ben and the others scrambled around him, up the sand toward the top of the mound. The constant roar heard below ground was much louder above. Everywhere sand erupted to the sky as if underground mines were being detonated by invisible soldiers. Shells exploded mid-air in a never-ending chain, no second passing without a direct hit on the fort. Chunks of metal rained down from all directions. The roar and the eruptions seemed oddly disconnected. Amidst the constant sound, each explosion seemed to produce no sound at all, as if the roar had some other all-powerful source, and the pitiful sound of exploding shells was drowned out altogether. An odd, hot thickness hung in the air, even in the heart of winter. Ben felt himself swimming through a substance halfway between air and water, born of lead and fire, smoke and death.

Old thoughts from school raced through Ben's mind. Pompeii. The eruption of Vesuvius. The great mountain exploded into fire and smoke. Floods of liquid fire poured down onto the citizens below. The great teacher Pliny was nearby in a boat, at what he thought was a safe distance. But more than ash fell from the sky. A storm of volcanic rock rained down, pelting Pliny's boat until both vessel and passengers were lost. The citizens scurried about in futile efforts to flee, shouting from smoke-filled lungs, "The gods are punishing us!"

Some higher power certainly seemed to be punishing the garrison of Fort Fisher. To be punishing the South. Ben knew the only two such powers were God and the devil. For the first time in the war — in his life — he wasn't sure which was for him and which was against him.

Amid the destruction, Ben refocused on the task at hand. There was no safe place above ground. *Get to the gun, fire, get back. The less time out here the better.* Mentally, he ran through the motions of readying the gun for a meaningful shot, visualizing each step, imagining each more efficient than ever before.

There at the top of the mound was the gun. His feet stopped their churning in the deep sand. He stood before the gun as his fellow gunmen arrived. The large metal barrel of the gun lay helplessly half-buried in the sand. One of the large wagon-like wheels was flat to the ground beside it. The other had rolled away from the wreckage and toppled out of the gun pit altogether. They had no gun to fire.

On top of the mound, Ben could see the view of the entire L shape of the fort. The constant explosions ripped both the land face and sea face, and much of the land in the angle between. Everywhere were bodies, shattered cannons, shell fragments and craters. Out to sea was an immense wall of smoke, created by the Northern fleet and now screening it from view. Where Ben had earlier seen the fleet, now he saw only its handiwork.

He felt a tug at his collar as his fellows abandoned the useless gun chamber and fled back to the bombproof beneath. As he turned he saw something out of the corner of his eye. A small boat emerged slowly from the dense smoke that concealed the fleet, angling away from the mass of smoke and down the beach from the fort. Others were close behind. The land troops were being brought to shore. Even without their gun, Ben and his comrades would have a fight on their hands.

January 15, 1865

The hours passed slowly back in the darkness of the bombproof. The roar continued. The Earth still shook. Sand still rained down from above. Gun crews still departed to fire their guns every half-hour. Minutes later, some would return. Others would not. Ben still anticipated the moment the ceiling would collapse and his grave would come to find him. But that moment still did not arrive. Time passed, and nothing changed. Until finally, there was a new sound.

The roar was suddenly joined by a scream. As the scream increased, the roar faded away. Dozens of steam whistles sounded from their ships behind the veil of smoke. The shriek was deafening, but anything was welcome compared to the roar of the bombardment. The Earth stopped moving. After what seemed like days, the roar was completely gone. Soon the steam whistles faded also. At last, there was silence. From his bunker underground, Ben thought he heard crashing waves for the first time since the battle had begun.

From the momentary silence a new roar began to build. First individual bursts, then many in rapid succession, then once again one constant sound. This roar was not right overhead. The shaking of the ground was diminished. The bombardment of the land face had ceased, and the bombardment of the sea face had begun again. This could only mean it was time for the Yankee Army to advance on the land face. Their navy would occupy the few remaining guns on the sea face, without threatening to kill its own countrymen attacking by land.

"Get your guns ready boys. On my signal get up and out of here as fast as you can. We want to show them something when they come across that beach. No shot wasted. Pick off the officers first."

The young officer speaking was in the doorway of the bombproof. Ben could not see his face. But the voice sounded young. Younger than Ben himself. He backed himself out of the doorway, looking up toward the top of the battery. His shoulders raised and lowered themselves slowly, then he jumped back in the doorway.

"Take to the wall men!"

Ben and the others grabbed muskets and rushed to the doorway. Even through the narrow passage they poured out efficiently and rushed up the sandy mound. The smoke was lifting along the land face as it thickened along the sea face. Ben looked to his right toward the sea and watched the Northern Navy as they charged up the beach. They were a mass of blue moving over the sand towards the fort. The sunlight that pierced the smoke above the beach caught their drawn swords that waved erratically over their heads. Pistols in one hand, swords in the other, the men in blue had no weapons that would serve them until they reached the walls of the fort.

Ben could see the flash of sharpshooter fire here and there from the gun pits near the target of the charge. Some of the sword-wielding attackers dropped amongst their comrades, then were swallowed up as the men charged over and past them. More often than not, the men who fell appeared to be officers. The sharpshooters were seeking to rob the attacking force of its organization. Cannons from the sea face fired directly into the advancing federals. Even more deadly were the blasts from the big gun atop the Mound Battery at the far end of the fort. As the cannons found the range, they opened huge gaps in the charging mass of blue. But for every Union sailor down, two more seemed to appear. The gaps were filled instantly as the men blended back together into a solid blue advance.

Even in the din of the bombardment, a Rebel yell rang out from the men near the corner of the "L". They poured from the tiny doors of bombproofs and swarmed the walls of the fort assuming battle positions, impatiently awaiting the order to open fire. When the order was given there was a ripple of fire and smoke along the wall. The entire mass of men in blue went down as if a wave of death washed across them. To Ben it seemed as if each piece of lead from the Confederate volley had traveled through one man, and then another and another, until all of them had fallen. Soon though, all but those in front rose and recommenced their charge, swords glistening in the sun once again. By the time they rose to their feet the Confederates along the wall had reloaded and trained their weapons again. A second volley rang out and again a wave flattened the entire federal advance. The front row of defenders traded their discharged weapons for new ones loaded by a row of men behind them. From then on there were no volleys, but the men in butternut and gray fired as rapidly as possible, the second row always loading while the front aimed and fired.

The mass of blue thinned as it advanced. Now as men fell there were no others to replace them. Behind them Ben could see waves that rolled in, broke down, then spread out thinly across the sand before sliding backwards into the sea from whence they had come. Behind the thinning charge was a trail of the dead and wounded. When the charge reached the palisade fence, it slowed to a trickle, with sailors fighting through breaches in the barrier. The thinning of the charge continued until one man was left alone in the front. He was of tiny stature, not bigger than a boy. He did not look to the side or behind to see if anyone came with him. Now the sun reflected only off of one saber raised to the sky, as the lone, tiny soldier bound up the wall of the fort through deep sand. Fire and smoke rose from hundreds of muskets all along the wall, yet none of their shots stopped his solitary charge. His path slowed as the wall grew steep and the sand thick. Still he came. Ben felt himself pulling for the little soldier, though his fate seemed sealed from the outset. The solo attacker crested the parapet and stood upon the bags of sand lining one of the gun pits. For the first time, he was within range to make use of his sword or pistol. At that moment his body snapped to a fully erect position as if it had received a jolt of energy. His motion ceased. He froze in that position for what seemed an exaggerated moment. Then, fell lifelessly forward amongst admiring enemies.

The action shifted down the land face. Just as the naval advance was faltering, the army advance was coming straight in Ben's direction. They came in a long, single line, angling toward that section of the land face closest to the Cape Fear River. Ben was positioned on the first gun chamber. Beneath him was the fort's main gate, where the Wilmington Road entered from the direction of the Yankee charge. They approached rapidly, many of them falling to Confederate musket fire the closer they came to the fort. Ben aimed his rifle at officers, as instructed, and fired as often as possible. As the Yankees got closer, Ben anticipated the explosion of the underground torpedoes, the network of explosives designed to erupt from below the charging federals and wipe them out by the hundreds. No such explosion ever came. He looked down the beach toward Wilmington, anticipating the appearance of General Bragg, the commanding general in Wilmington who was expected to arrive with Hoke's Division and ambush the Yankees from behind. No such attack arrived. The defense would be left to the thin garrison scattered about the fort's sandy walls.

Soon the neat blue line came apart, though not due to the Confederate volleys fired down upon them. An icy swamp stood between the advancing enemy and its target. The lone bridge was narrow, and some of its planks had been removed by the defenders before the bombardment began. A bottleneck ensued, and the line became a mob. The Confederate volleys became more effective. More powerful still were the blasts from two cannons positioned at the riverside gate aimed directly in the face of the federal advance. The gun crews fired feverishly, taking out scores of blue soldiers with each blast. Many of the attackers abandoned the bridge and waded through the mud and ice. These slower moving targets often found an unpleasant burial as the defenders took advantage of their adversaries' creeping pace, picking them off from behind the safety of the high, sand-bagged walls. The palisade fence slowed the advance as well, but not for long. Axe men in blue wailed at the gaps torn in the fence by the fleet, and widened them to allow their fellows to pour through. Slowly but surely all these barriers were overcome, and the Yankees kept coming. The beach was littered with hundreds of the dead and wounded, but still they came.

There is plausible deniability when you kill a man across on open field. You aim your weapon at a mass of men approaching you. You train it upon an individual. Maybe because he is an officer. Maybe he became separated from the mob. Maybe something about his uniform caught your eye. Maybe for no reason at all. But you train your weapon on him and squeeze the trigger. Your weapon fires. His head snaps back and he falls to the ground. You know nothing of him. As a son, a brother or a father. Whether he had letters in his pocket written by firelight, to be sent home in the event of his death. You don't know for certain he did not survive. Perhaps all you did was stop his charge and send him home to be nursed by those he loves. So many muskets were firing down upon him that you may not be responsible at all. Perhaps you missed. Perhaps one of your comrades struck him down and your bullet passed harmlessly through the spot from which he had just fallen.

It was not so along the crest of Shepherd's Battery when the Yankee charge arrived. The fighting became hand-to-hand, so when you killed a man, you knew it.

Ben stood above a teenage boy staring up from the ground back at him. His eyes focused on Ben's. The eyes were widened by shock, but tempered by resignation. Many men die in battle without ever knowing what happened to them. This boy knew. Ben pulled at his rifle, but the bayonet would not dislodge from the boy's throat. It had gone clean through and the barrel of the rifle was lodged in the neck. Ben pulled more desperately, to no avail. The eyes still watched. Finally Ben pushed his foot firmly down onto the boy's chest for leverage and gave the rifle a jerk. The machinery in the throat gave way with a snapping jolt and the bloody bayonet came free. The hole in the throat opened widely and dark red oozed out. A single tear slid down from one of the widened eyes. They stayed open but their humanity quickly disappeared. Ben looked up from the boy as more men came over the wall, then immediately thrust his bayonet into the gut of another charging Yankee soldier.

This time the bayonet came out quickly. Ben flipped his musket around in his hand and clubbed the butt of the gun into the face of the man falling down before him. He felt the bones beneath the man's forehead give way under the weight of the gun. He spun it back around and fired into the chest of another man climbing over the parapet. His eyes locked with another Yankee, who began to raise his weapon to fire at Ben. Ben grabbed the musket of the clubbed man and fired it into the face of the aiming solider. The body snapped back and the musket fired harmlessly into the sky as the man crumbled to the ground on top of the others Ben had killed.

Seeing two soldiers standing atop the parapet firing down into the blue mob, Ben resolved to do the same. He loaded his weapon and leapt onto the sandbags lining the gun chamber. Suddenly shells began to fall all around him. He did not know whether they came from the Mound Battery in order to repel the charge, or from the fleet in order to aid it. Just as he aimed down into the charging army an unexploded shell lodged into the sand beneath him. Ben stared down into the depression in the sand where the sizzling metal ball had vanished, then once again readied to fire at the next wave of blue soldiers now climbing up the sandy hill. The shell exploded beneath the ground and the wall at Ben's feet gave way. He toppled from the wall down amongst the bayonets and muskets of those determined to kill him.

Sin

She suspended him in a place between resistance and resignation. The resistance, he resented, but was exquisite. It coaxed him to resign, which he fought, for the moment.

Everything was as his mind had commanded. All different. The view, the feel, the smell, even the taste of the air around him. The darkness and dampness of the room, with but slivers of air and light sliding between the planks in the walls. Everything faded to movement, and touch. His hands moved rapidly, greedily touching her at all the places he couldn't restrain from touching. He willed his hands off of her, grabbing the thin bedding beneath them. Anything to slow the loss of thought, of control, but always movement forced away thought and will, and his hands freed themselves and took in all of her again.

Something changed inside of him. He tried to bury it, take it back, hide it. But she knew, and she changed. The resistance was gone. Her arms and legs closed around him. He tried still to go back but it was futile now. His mind controlled nothing of his body. She controlled everything now. The moment of his control was gone and could not return. He felt it slipping, then charging away, and even as he felt it escaping he tried still to grab or claw or stop it somehow, for just a moment more. When he did his arms closed more tightly around her, his fingers dug into her shoulders, making it worse. There was a moment in which the tiny room spun wildly and his mind finally left him. Conscious thought departed. No guilt. No weakness in the knees and stomach taking those steps to her door, just one more time. Everything was compressed down to that unidentifiable place, that one moment that justified all sin and contradiction.

She did not smile. She did not look at him. She had made no sound, no artificial encouragement or affirmation, though he suspected she knew he wanted to hear it. Looking down, she grabbed the thin cotton dress from beside her on the bed, and pulled it back down over her.

Even as his mind returned and guilt assaulted from a thousand angles, its attack was interrupted momentarily as he mourned the covering of her body. He wanted just a moment more to look at her as she lay there. The length and leanness of her muscles, the darkness of her skin, the wild thickness of her hair, the beads of sweat suspended on her neck and breasts, even the tiny fibers of cotton stuck to her arms and legs. He stood and felt the dirt floor between his toes as he dressed. His senses broadened and he smelled the lingering smell of cornbread and beans cooked in the pot that hung above an open fire. He saw the cracks between the planks of the cabin, just wide enough to allow sight of a few blades of grass on the field beyond, wide enough to make him wonder what could be seen from the outside.

Once clothed, he ran his fingers through his hair and took one last look at her as she lay on the bed. The cotton dress hugged the curves of her figure. She tugged at its sides, pulling them farther down her legs. Still, she looked down, and did not speak.

PART III

Twenty

Amos Covington
January, 1865
Near Fort Fisher, NC

Amos Covington had kept to the woods all day, and now walked the road at night. He held Ben's donkey, Buck, by a short length of rope, climbing on to ride when his feet gave out. Before him lay a fork in the road.

The woods were thick, but low. Low enough that the moon cast a clear light down through the tops of the scrub oaks onto the path below. Thick enough that no light could penetrate down to the floor beneath the thicket. The well-lit sandy path cut a white "Y" through the blackness of the surrounding forest. Amos stopped at the bottom of the "Y" and studied the diverging white paths before him. He stood still a while. The only sound was the rhythm of the frogs calling from the low, wet spots along both sides of the road. Amos knew where the two roads led. Though there was much mystery as to what either journey might bring, there was no mystery as to their intended destinations. One was a road he had traveled before. The other was to a new world. He turned and looked back down the lane behind him. Another strip of white, moonlit sand heading back to the sea. Back there was a ravaged fort occupied by soldiers in blue. Soldiers sent to liberate Amos and those like him.

If them boys is really here to free slaves, I'm glad to have them. But I'm not wearing a blue suit and fighting this war, and I'm not being put on one of those slave ships to be sent north.

After the battle, he had watched the other slaves in camp. Some gleefully approached the Yankees, embracing their newfound freedom on whatever terms it was offered. Their first act of freedom was to take up shovels and dig graves for their liberators. Others were eager to volunteer. There were black soldiers camped outside the fort having taken part in the battle. Amos watched some of his fellow slaves beaming with pride as they approached the black soldiers and offered their services. Still others snuck off into the woods, saying nothing to anyone. *Are they scared of the Yankees,* he had wondered? *Afraid to leave their families behind in bondage?* He did not know. But as for himself, Amos had decided that if he was to travel to freedom, he would do it on his own.

So now he stood in the coastal thicket, looking before him again at his choice of paths. One led west back to Rockingham and slavery. And family. The other north toward freedom. Alone. He felt the chill of the January night, made cooler by a gust of wind. The frogs seemed to increase their rhythm and their volume as he stood. Soon their sound reached the level of a frenzy, coming at him from all directions. There seemed to be thousands of them, cheering in anticipation of his decision. Some seemed to shout left, others right. Buck shook his head sharply back and forth and snorted, reacting to the racket. Amos felt his aging heart pound in his chest, keeping pace with the sound around him. Finally he moved. He took a half step toward one path, then checked himself, then froze. A second later, he started confidently down the opposite path. Buck snorted again and followed behind.

Betty Covington
Rockingham, NC

The butter churn sat by a stool in the kitchen. It was stoneware and came up waste high on Betty Covington. She untied the knot in the clean cloth that had been tied tight around the lid. As she removed it the pungent smell of the clabbered milk poured into the room. She removed the lid and threaded the dasher handle through the hole so she could churn the milk. The work was hard, and repetitive. Each time she pushed the dasher down the milk thickened, making the work harder as she went. She let her mind wander to prevent focus on the strain in her arms and shoulders.

Soon her mind turned where it always did. To Benjamin Dockery, and to their future. She imagined herself churning butter in her own kitchen for her own table. She imagined their own home on land near Cartledge Creek, with a wide front porch where she and Benjamin could rock their children and watch the evening sun sink into the pines across the field. She imagined spending the day with him, and not having to say goodbye at night. She imagined their wedding, with all their kinsmen home from the war, together for the celebration. She pictured in her mind a beautiful dress that she would make herself, though the material would cost most every dollar she had saved from teaching school. A dress just for her that no one had ever worn before. It would be a surprise to Benjamin. He would see it for the first time when she appeared in front of him on their wedding day.

She heard a faint noise drifting in from outside. The echoing of trumpet notes. This was the signal from McKay, the shopkeeper at Dockery's Store just past the church near the Alfred Dockery home. The announcement to the countryside that new mail had arrived. Her father would want to retrieve the mail immediately to see if there was news from her brother Ben off at war. Rarely did she accompany him. The wagon ride was too cold. But on this day, she would. She had dress materials to buy.

Amos

The trees grew taller the farther Amos traveled. Low scrub oaks gave way to towering long leaf pine. The path turned from sand to gravel to clay as the terrain changed around him. Less light filtered through the forest. There were no more white paths through short trees. Everything was gray and black and cold. The ground along the road was black and dry. There were no frogs calling. For long periods he heard no sound but his own growling stomach.

Traveling by night was a constant battle against the eyes and the imagination. His eyes found every slight patch of darkness in the distance that stood out against the paler darkness in which it swam. Each dark spot was another potential enemy. An opportunist hunting for fugitive slaves to be sold to uncouth owners looking for a bargain. Keeping him not only in bondage, but far away from his family. He fought to focus his eyes on every suspicious object. Each seemed to move, even to stalk him in the night, actively concealing its dangerous nature. To breathe in and out as he approached, only to prove to be a stump or a bush. Every owl was a band of criminals hiding in the woods, conspiring. Every gust of wind a ghost of the death he had just witnessed, that lurked all over the war-torn country. In the darkness, the mind rarely imagines the harmless. A docile stray dog. A lonely traveler like Amos himself. A conductor on the Underground Railroad. Less often still is the wind just the wind, or a rock just a rock.

His eyes had cried wolf one too many times, and his mind caught on. He relaxed as much as he could, and continued forward with his mind more at ease.

"Where the hell you runnin' to, nigger?"

Amos halted. His airway tightened. His pulse pounded up into his throat.

"I said where the hell you runnin' to, nigger?"

The voice came from a low, dark spot at the edge of the woods to Amos's right. He saw no definition to the object. Just a dark patch at the base of the trees. It seemed one of the rocks was finally speaking.

The figure rose up slowly from the ground and moved awkwardly toward Amos. As it approached it became a man, then an injured man, then a Confederate soldier. The man hobbled himself to within inches of Amos, then leaned heavily on the crutch beneath his right shoulder. He was a tall, lean man with a wide, flat face. His head appeared as a large egg turned on its side. It was a broad, asymmetrical oval, with a grotesque gaping mouth full of blackened teeth. A grimy face with the beginnings of a long, oily beard. On top of the head was a worn, gray kepi with long curls of hair popping out from all sides. The soldier leaned in for a close look at Amos, who noticed that the left eye was badly blackened.

"I don't aim for no trouble, sir."

"Yeah, I reckon you don't. Man that's walking a trail at night doesn't need no more trouble than he's already got, now does he?"

Amos stood stiffly in the middle of the road and said nothing.

"Reckon somebody learned you not to talk back. Ain't that right, field hand?"

Amos gave no response. He kept his head down. He did not look into the man's eyes.

"It's alright, nigger. I already know what you thinking. Go one. Say it. Say what you thinking."

Nothing.

"Alright. I'll say it for you then. If the only folks on the road these days in the middle of the night got troubles, then you must have troubles too, you white sonofabitch!'

The soldier exploded into loud, cackling laughter, clearly proud of himself.

"Wooooeeee! Hell, you right too. I got about more trouble than anybody. More'n you even, I bet. Hell, reckon you been a slave all your life about to be free, and me I been free all my life and about to be a slave. If'n they don't kill me first."

Amos raised his head slowly and looked the soldier in the eye.

"There you go, nigger. You getting it now. That's right. I ain't gonna turn you over to nobody. Hell, if I do they'll get ahold of me. Don't just arrest deserters around here, they hang'em. And that's only if they don't shoot'em on sight. Word is they're deputizing any sonofabitch they can find and paying by the head, dead or alive. 'Cept for runaway slaves. Got to bring them in alive and still get less money than for a dead white man."

The soldier adjusted himself as he spoke. He shifted all his weight to the right foot, the healthy one, and stood a moment with the left dangling just above the ground. When he lowered it Amos heard a sound like the squishing of feet in wet socks and shoes. When he heard it, Amos's eyes turned down toward the foot.

"That's right. If I woulda stayed they'd have cut it off. So I got me the hell out of there. Helluva deal, ain't it. You stay, they cut off your foot. You leave, they track you down and shoot you or hang you. I ain't no goddamn coward if that's what you're thinking. Been in six engagements and right in the thick of every damn one of them."

Amos stood looking at the man for a few moments. He looked weak. He must have lost a lot of blood. But he talked too loud for a man on the run. Amos longed for the quiet that was his only moments before.

"Good evening, sir. I wish you luck in your travels."

He gave a slight tug to the rope and began to walk away with Buck right behind.

"Hold on a goddamn minute, nigger. You think I stopped you just to chat? I got a proposition for you."

Amos stopped and looked back.

"I had a donkey about like that one. A few hours ago, some fellows jumped me. Right about dusk. Three of them. Young as shit, too. Took my donkey, my pistol, everything but my canteen and a few days hard tack. Would of taken that too, but one of them told the other two they ort not to kill me or leave me for dead. I been settin' right there where they jumped me 'til you came up.

"So here's the deal. I can't get nowhere on this foot. I'm only going about a day's march from here. In another mile or so I know how to get off this road and get where I'm going on deer trails. Won't nobody see us. You been traveling jest by night, ain't you? This way you can move along faster. I can show you how to get back on the road once you drop me off. And we can share the hardtack too. And all you got to do is let me up on that donkey for a while."

"Just until you take a notion to kill me, I figure."

"Shit. Look at you and look at me. You'd whip my ass going and coming with me on one foot like this…come on, what do you say?"

Amos stood silently in the road for a minute. Then he pulled the rope firmly with his right hand, and braced the left on Buck's neck so the deserter could climb onto the animal's back.

* * *

The deserter was snoring loudly. His army blanket had been over him, but now his long legs stuck out at odd angles. There was a low glimmer from the fire, which needed tending. The day had broken somewhere nearby, but the sun was not yet above the trees. To the east the forest glowed and a pale light joined with the fire to allow Amos to study his traveling companion. He had taken off his brogans before he went to sleep, and they were sitting just outside the little ring they had cleared for the fire. His thick, gray wool socks were threadbare at the heels. There was dried blood caked on the left sock, starting from the top of the foot and wrapping around the heel. It spread across the bottom of the foot where it must have pooled as the deserter walked. Even above the sweet smells of the fading fire, Amos could smell the infection in the deserter's wound.

Amos got up and moved over to the rock where he had sat by the fire a few hours before. The two men had traveled well into the night, mostly along deer trails where they frequently pulled spider webs and tree limbs from their faces. Still, the deserter had talked the entire way.

There was a good bed of red coal simmering underneath the one black log that refused to catch the night before. Amos added a few thinner sticks and tossed in some twigs and leaves. He stoked the coals and smoke from the burning leaves poured out of the fire. A slight breeze directed the smoke toward Amos, who shut his eyes too late. Turning his face from the fire, he opened his eyes widely and held them open to let the smoke sting pass more quickly. As the leaves burned away and the wood began to catch, the smoke thinned and the fire gave off heat in its place.

There was a little satchel on the ground beside the brogans. Amos reached in and pulled out a tin cup and a piece of hardtack. The hardtack was about three inches square, though the edges were crude and irregular. It was too hard to bite. He would need to find a way to soften it. Amos walked through the woods to a tiny creek that trickled nearby. They had used it to fill their canteens when they arrived. The creek bed was stiff sand, with a few fist-size rocks jutting up through the water. At most spots the water was no more than two or three inches deep, but there was one pool about two feet in length where the water reached a depth of ten inches or more. Amos rolled up his right sleeve and reached down into the cold water. He picked up the largest rock in the pool. It was a flat, oval rock the size of a dinner plate. One end was sunk down into the sand, while the other lay gently on the bottom. He removed the rock and tossed it onto the bank. Sand and debris kicked up from the bottom and clouded the pool. As he watched, the slight current grabbed the grains of sand and carried them slowly toward the other end of the pool. As they settled or drifted away, the pool cleared again. Something began to take shape on the sand at the bottom. When the water was finally clear, there was a decent sized crawdad sitting stunned at the loss of his cover.

Amos positioned his hand at the surface behind the tail of the little creature. He eased the hand slowly into the water and lowered it gently toward the bottom. Then with a jolt he snatched the crawdad from the bottom before it could dart away. He pinched it between his thumb and index finger right behind the claws and held it up for a closer look. It was a dark, reddish brown, and held its claws stiffly out to each side, unable to reach back and pinch Amos. He brought his two fingers together quickly. The claws lowered and the head dangled. He thumped the head off with his thumb and tossed the rest of the creature into his mouth.

He grabbed another stone from the bottom of the pool, but found no crawdad. The tin cup was sitting by the river with the hardtack inside. Amos laid the hardtack on the long, flat rock that had hidden the crawdad, and pounded it into pieces with the second rock. He gathered up all of the small pieces and dropped them into the tin cup. Cupping his hands together, he scooped water into the cup, then stirred it with a skinny stick. He returned to the fire and sat the cup along the edge of the red coals. As the gruel warmed, he stirred it periodically with the stick until his breakfast was ready.

The deserter was still asleep, though he tossed about often. He was badly tangled in his army blanket, which by now covered little of him. He mumbled a bit in his sleep, and then blurted out a few words.

"Tell you what. Shit. Uh-huh. Wooeee!"

Amos stirred the gruel and shook his head. He smiled for the first time in days.

"Fucking niggers! Don't need their ass!"

The deserter smacked his lips loudly, then grinned a wide grin, revealing his scattered, black teeth. He rolled back onto his back and began snoring again.

Betty

Dockery's Store was a small, unpainted structure that had the appearance of a modest house. It looked much like the Covington home, but smaller. When the door opened, the heat rushed out into Betty's face. She stepped in briskly and her father, John Covington, quickly closed the door behind her. There was a fire in the fireplace in the corner. Basic plank shelves hung from floor to ceiling, covered with all order of containers of household and farm supplies. Betty loved the smell of woodsmoke and the feeling of being in a place of important business. In one corner was a handsome mahogany chest with four wide drawers. This lone piece of furniture was itself the post office, housed conveniently in the store. Beside it on the ground was a rough box stamped with the words "Black Jack Township." The box was padlocked and had a narrow slit in the top. The township voting poll. The top drawer of the post office dresser was equipped with a metal lock for safekeeping of important items. Just below the keyhole, however, was an open hole through the wood. Somewhere along the way the postmaster had lost the key. When someone important came for their mail — probably General Dockery from the mansion just across the street — a hole was carved into the drawer so that it could be unlocked. It had never been repaired.

Behind a dusty counter sorting mail was McKay. An old, dented trumpet lay on the counter before him. He was wearing a bright white shirt and shiny red suspenders. The shirt was buttoned to the very top button at the base of his neck. His moustache was curled in perfect loops at each end. His spectacles were round and sat low on his nose. His mouth was curled slightly in a clever smirk. He cut his eyes quickly at Betty and an extra spark entered his already shining eyes.

"Ms. Covington, ma'am." He bowed to Betty and nodded to John as if seeking permission to proceed. John smiled and the postmaster continued.

"I do have news for your little project. I am told that a blockade runner was brought into Wilmington port. I am told there are lovely fabrics on board. Silk, lace, everything a lady in your position would need. I will be in Cheraw next week to see the goods and would be happy to purchase the best they have."

Betty glowed. She handed an envelope to McKay.

"This should cover it. The best they have!"

"Indeed, young lady. Your wish is my command."

Amos

"I ain't never owned no slaves. Ain't never had no money. Don't get me wrong, I'd like to have a few. I'd buy your ass if I had some money. Tell you the truth, I ain't never give a shit about niggers either way. Reckon we shoulda just left your asses in the jungle. Maybe then we wouldn't have had to fight this here war. Maybe that's what they'll do when this is over with. Maybe they'll just ship your asses back to wherever the hell it was you came from. Be rid of you. Free ones too. All of you. Ya'll ain't been worth the trouble. Sorry as shit, most of you. But you talk about sorry. Ain't no nigger ever born sorrier than this brother of mine we're fixin to go meet. He's the dumbest, sorriest bastard alive.

"I ain't seen him in going on nine years now. Way back before the war started. I quit him on account of him asking for money all the time. Every time I saw him anyway. When you meet him, don't be afraid of him. Wouldn't hurt a fly. Growing up we used to take turns throwing rocks at him and he never done a thing. We'd throw rocks and try to hit this mark he's got on his face, yelling, 'ring that horseshoe!' That was his nickname, Horseshoe, on account of … well, I'll let you figure it out. But don't be afraid of him none. He's just strange, that's all. I mean, you know what I mean. He ain't right."

Amos walked along with the little piece of rope in his hand. The deserter was up on Buck's back. He was leaned all the way forward with his head resting on the donkey's neck. He had his face turned toward Amos and talked right at him with his head turned sideways.

"Don't you want to know what's strange about him?"

Amos kept walking.

"Well, he can't think right or something. He had an accident when we were little and he ain't never been right since. But don't worry about that. Good news is he won't yell at you or call you a good-for-nothing nigger or anything like that. I never heard him say a cross word to nobody. You know why?"

No response.

"'Cause the dumb sonofabitch can't talk! Wooooeee! Hell, that's the best part of him. He's so stupid I reckon anything he would have to say wouldn't be too damn smart to begin with, so the world ain't missing much, know what I mean?"

"So how did he ask for money?"

"Say what now?"

"You said he was always asking for money. If he can't talk, how did he ask you for money?"

"He'd reach down in his pockets and pull 'em inside out to show they was empty. That's how he done it. But you'll see here in about one minute. There's his house right there."

There was a small clearing to the right of the trail. In the middle sat what used to be a house. It was two stories of unpainted wood. There were two windows up and two down, but no sign that there had ever been shutters. The roof had been split down the middle by a tremendous tree. One of its ends stuck out of the shattered roof about three feet out over the porch. The exposed wood was two feet wide and thoroughly rotten. Near the base of the porch were long sections of rotten wood that seemed to match that suspended above. They lay broken in piles all over the red clay yard. Most of the left half of the second story was collapsed. Through the window Amos could see wooden planks extending down from above at odd angles. The four legs of a chair stuck straight up into the air. What appeared to be a bed post poked through one of the panes of glass, which spider webbed out in all directions. The front porch sloped sharply to the left until it fell away from the house altogether, making it impossible to access the front door.

Bricks were scattered in the yard to the left of the house, near the base of a collapsed chimney that now rose only a few feet from the ground. On the far side of the house there was a working chimney, though one with several bricks loose or missing. Smoke was rising slowly from the top. Amos scanned the grounds and did not see a woodpile. There were several stumps of chopped trees around the place. One, just to the right of the house, had a series of logs in decreasing width lined up almost end to end headed away from the stump. To either side were piles of branches cut from the trunk.

"Horseshoe! Horseshoe, you dumb sonofabitch! It's your oldest brother. Let us in."

The window on the right-hand side of the front porch creaked open. The deserter climbed onto the porch gingerly from the far right and headed for the window. He looked back at Amos.

"Come on there, field hand. He don't give a shit."

Hesitantly, Amos followed his traveling companion onto the porch and through the open window. A rich smell of rot met him as he ducked through the window. The room they entered was once a dining room. Trash was gathered in piles along the edge of the room, with animal bones amongst the rags of old table cloths and clothes. Toward the inside wall was a cupboard that was turned on end and smashed. Broken dishes fanned outward from the scene of the collapse. In the corner next to the cupboard was a chamber pot that reeked of human waste. It was full, and green flies landed, hopped about and took off again.

The men passed through the dining room and entered a plain square room with a round, pine table in the middle. The room was curiously free of clutter. Sitting at the table was Horseshoe. His face was gaunt and his chin very long. He had black hair that was cut irregularly as if he had done the job himself. The upper lip extended well beyond the lower so that the two black teeth remaining showed outside of the mouth like a saber tooth tiger. But that wasn't what was most exceptional about him. Above the left eye was the perfect imprint of a horseshoe. It sunk into his head at least a half inch. The left eye itself was perpetually turned upwards, as if he was forever trying to look at his wound.

The deformed man turned toward the two men before him. Not only did he say nothing, his face said nothing. He wore no expression at all. The deserter sat down across the table from his brother and motioned for Amos to do the same.

"Horseshoe. I run away from the army. My foot is squashed and if I didn't leave they were gonna cut it off. I need you to let me stay with you for a while. They'll have the law after me. Reckon I'd rather be dead than hobbling ass around on one foot. I ain't no goddamn cripple. I'd rather be dead or a nigger than a goddamn cripple like you, Horseshoe." He exploded into cackling again, this time turning to Amos with his eyebrows raised as if to share the joke.

While the deserter was cackling at himself, his brother casually produced a revolver from under the table, leveled it carefully, and shot his brother between the eyes.

The deserter snapped backwards, overturning the chair and spilling onto the floor dead. Amos looked across the table at Horseshoe. His heart was racing and the palms of his hands were flat on the table. Horseshoe laid the gun gently on the table. Smoke slid from the barrel and rose in rings toward the ceiling. Horseshoe reached into his shirt pocket and tossed a tin star onto the middle of the table. For the first time his face bore an expression. Amos took it for a laugh but it was a gurgling, heaving sound that came from deep in the throat. As Horseshoe laughed he began to cough and was soon in a full-blown coughing fit. The next thing Amos knew he found himself flying out the dining room window across the yard and into the woods.

Betty

Betty sat in a rocking chair with her work spread out on her lap. Two orange cats were curled up on the far side of the porch. The smaller of the two stretched herself out lazily, reaching far out in both directions until she was nearly twice as long as the big cat sleeping next to her. A small, round black and white cat was crouched along the right runner of the rocking chair looking up at Betty with eyes asking permission to hop up into her lap.

"Now you know I can't let you up here when I'm working." She reached down and scratched the cat on the back of the head. The cat turned her head slightly and snuggled her head up tighter into the palm of Betty's hand.

In her lap was the roughest, cheapest cotton calico she had ever seen, purchased at the highest price. The strands of cotton fabric were woven together crudely. She could see plainly the thick crisscross pattern the loom had made. It was about the cheapest way cotton could be made to stick together to make any clothing at all. Scattered through the grid of raw fabric were strands of husk that had never been separated from the cotton.

The day it came in she had been out in the yard and heard the faint trumpet call. She imagined fine silk trimmed in exotic lace. A wedding dress fit for the best of times, made during the worst of times. A dress that would have his heart racing through the service, dying for the moment he could get his hands on her. He should remember his bride as beautiful on their wedding day, not just as beautiful as could be expected under the circumstances.

Then, at the store, holding the calico in her hands, she saw in McKay's eyes that he was as heartbroken as she was.

"McKay. I thank you very much for getting this for me."

His face reddened instantly. She felt guilty for opening it in front of him.

"I tried Miss Betty. I tried. Nothing good is getting through anymore. It was all they had. I am so sorry."

She had fought the emotion welling up inside her. Kept her face straight.

"No, sir. I thank you very much. It *will* be beautiful."

McKay had again busied himself, and did not look up again. As Betty and John walked out the door, he spoke through muted tears.

"Miss Betty, *you* will be beautiful."

Now, back on the porch, the dress was taking shape in her blistered hands. She sewed tuck after tuck into the rough fabric, shaping it more finely than it was ever meant to be. She created a design of tucked rows across the top, and gave shape to the long, full sleeves. Down the dress she made long rows of tucks which flowed out toward the ground, and sewed little buttons between the rows. She was spinning calico into silk.

The front door squeaked and John appeared in the big brown coat he wore to go to town. He stepped to the rocking chair and looked down at Betty.

"My dear, I'm headed to the post office. There will be some news of your brother Ben, I hope. Here, I have something for you."

He handed her a fold of paper. She opened it and looked up with amazement at her father.

"It's Irish lace, from better times. It has been wrapped up for years waiting for a proper use."

She sprang into her father's arms, stood hugging him for minutes, not wanting to let go. Her eyes were shut tight, and just a couple of tears formed but did not fall. Finally, she pulled back from him. She blinked her eyes and opened them wide so they could dry and refocus. As she regained her vision, she saw someone approaching slowly up the lane. It was the shadow of a formerly much larger man. His simple clothes were shredded at the ends and hung loosely on his body. His eyes were sunken and saddened. As he came closer, he reminded her of a much older version of someone she once knew. By the time he reached the steps to the porch she realized it was the man himself.

"Amos! My goodness! Amos, is that you?"

"Miss Betty. Mr. John, sir. Mr. Ben went over the wall down at Fort Fisher. The Yankees, they got him. He went over that wall and I didn't never see him again."

Twenty-One

Sally Dockery
February, 1865
Rockingham, NC

Dearest Father:

I hope this letter has found its way to you with speed. Its contents needed to be seen by your eyes first, not by Mother's. So, I mailed it to the Covington's box, and trusted them to deliver it to you. I do apologize for the subterfuge. In this way you could decide how to address the issue with Mother. As you have probably guessed, I write with sad news. In addition to our ongoing military struggles in the western theater, more and more boys are taking ill. More are dying in camp from disease than in the field from battle. I fear that brother John will soon be among them. He took camp fever a few weeks ago, and at first it seemed he had it beat. The weather intervened, and all in camp with this ailment took a turn for the worse, John included. I delayed writing for some time, hoping to tell you of his struggle after the fact, as yet another trial one of your sons had survived. Though we have not given up, I have become afraid that if I wait for the triumph before I write, I might instead write after the tragedy has occurred. I did not think it proper to wait for that.

I have made it my mission to assure that he has the best medical care we can offer. That he is better fed than the mass of men in our starving camp. This has helped, I believe. Many that caught the fever after John have already left us. But the medicine we have does not seem to slow the fever's progression. As I write the situation has become grave indeed.

Please be assured that I will continue to do all I can. Know also that he has fought as valiantly against this fever in camp as he has against the Yankees in battle. It has been an honor to fight with him. A humbling honor to have him in my command. He was well-raised, and is a fine man. You and Mother have much reason to be proud.

I do not envy your responsibility of conveying this to mother. I will never forget holding baby James Turner in my arms, hearing him struggle for breath. Or young Puss, how playful and bright he was. Those losses certainly damaged us all, though doubtless Mother the most. I was at John's bedside moments ago. In his eyes he is still the little boy playing on the farm. As perfect and immortal as every child seems. I must stop now. I am afraid I have written too much.

Your Devoted Son,
Major Thomas C. Dockery

Sally sat in the dim light of Alfred's study. Letters and papers were scattered all over the desk. Many had fallen to the floor. She had rummaged through his correspondence without concern for maintaining order.

It was well into the evening. The flickering candlelight washed over the letter, trembling in Sally's hands. Providing just enough light to allow her to make out the words. She read it again. Had now done so several times. Alfred had told her merely that John was sick. That

Thomas was looking after him. Had not told her the true gravity of the situation. Then he quietly left to tend to business. Perhaps there was a grand plan to his hesitancy. A method to his madness whereby he would ease her gently into the news. But Sally was not one to wait for that.

Her Turner blood kicked in. This was not to happen to her son. To her family. She would not sit at home while her son died in some far away camp. History dictated otherwise.

With a bag furiously packed, she darted out the back door, past the detached kitchen and down the path under the oaks toward the stables. Ever present in the kitchen, Miss Anna came running out into the dark, holding her skirt up so as not to trip over it as she ran.

"Miss Sally! Miss Sally!"

Sally did not stop. She heard Anna behind her. Ignored her. Did not need to hear anyone's reasons why she should not go to help her dying son.

The saddle was all her small frame could lift. As she fought with the weight and readied one of the horses for the ride, Anna appeared in the door behind her. Sally glanced up, then continued as if she had not seen Anna at all.

"Miss Sally? Where in the world are you headed off to this time of night, and with Mr. Dockery not here to accompany you?"

Sally did not look up. She continued to struggle with the saddle and the bag.

"Mississippi."

"Ma'am?"

"Mississippi! John is sick. He needs my help."

She had finally readied the horse, and now used a stool to mount it. At last she looked Anna in the eyes, seeing her servant's bewildered look.

"I'll need you to be getting out of my way now, Anna. It's a long ride and I need to get started."

"But Miss Sally. Mississippi is on the other side of the country. Begging your pardon, ma'am, but you're sixty years old and I haven't seen you ride a horse in years."

"Well, I haven't had a reason to. But now I do."

Miss Anna just stood there. Said nothing else.

"Anna. You know how I feel about you. You are very dear to me. But we are talking about my son. If I have to run you over with this horse to get out of this stable, I am going to do it."

Miss Anna stepped to the side. Her face now showing sadness and fear. Sally walked the horse out of the stall and had him in a trot before she exited the long stable building. She hit the end of the row of stalls and turned sharply left, showing no rust from the years since her last ride. It was Benjamin's horse. Thrower he was called. Both because he was a gift from cousins with that last name, and also because of what he had done to the first three people that tried to ride him. He had become a good horse over the years. The spunk that had landed three slaves on their backs in the dust was channeled into sheer speed. It was for his speed that Sally had chosen him.

As they left the stable and darted under the oak limbs and past the Brick House, Thrower made the most of his newfound freedom. The speed of the cold air rushing across her face was a shock to Sally, who spent most winter days in the Brick House near an open fire. The oaks on either side of the lane reached out for each other over her head. Their silhouettes stood jet-black against a slightly paler sky. Scattered stars rifled in and out of view between the black shadows of branches and leaves above. It was as if every star was shooting, with only the world standing still. Even out on the Cartledge Creek Road, little light reached her path. The longleaf pines rose tall on either side of the road. The beginning of deep stretches of dense woods. Bright pairs of eyes appeared here and there along the edges. Odd, hollow sounds echoed from deeper down into the darkness. The cold wind traveled down between the tunnel of pines and chilled Sally in the saddle. Still she rode on. Determined. Driven by genetics. By history. By the sheer force of motherhood. Despite her fear, her doubt, her age, Sally rode undeterred.

She saw light flickering in the distance. Torches on each side of the road. But why? There had been rumors of the Yankee approach, but General Sherman wasn't finished burning South Carolina yet. It was too soon. Sally decided to ride right past whomever she found. No good could come from stopping. There was movement ahead as she approached. Two horsemen came gradually into view. Men. Large men. Her heart quickened and she pushed Thrower harder. But the horses ahead came nose to nose in the middle of the road, leaving little room to either side. She slowed the horse and looked for a path around. The torchlight flickered across the face of the nearest of the men. She pulled the reigns and stopped Thrower in his tracks.

Her heart still pounded wildly in her chest as she waited. A mountain of a man climbed down from the horse on the left. She looked down and away. Waiting.

"Well, hello there Kerenhappuch Turner. Headed down to Guildford Courthouse, are we?"

Her husband stood before her with a knowing smile. Solomon sat atop the other horse, watching dutifully.

"How did you know what I would do?"

Alfred walked over beside her, looking up at her. No longer smiling.

"I knew you would want to go to him. To save him. It is who you are."

"You can't stop me, you know. Not for good. You stop me tonight I will leave tomorrow."

"Oh, darling you sound like Jim did when you wouldn't let him go to war. I guess we know where he got it. But it's twice as far from here to Mississippi as it was from Virginia to Guilford when your great-grandmother did it. And it is winter. And you are a lovely old woman, married to a broken-down old man."

She was crying now. Softly. Alfred was glassy eyed himself, though she knew he would not openly cry. Somewhere within her she had known it was folly. That there was no way she could have made the ride. But dying on the roadside had seemed preferable to waiting idly for her son to die.

Alfred moved closer. He placed his hand gently on her leg and looked into her eyes as she sat high upon the horse.

"We keep going somehow, Sally. With Puss and James Turner. With this war, and now John. I don't know how. Because we have to,

I guess. For each other. For our children that remain. For God. When all of this is over, I don't know what we'll have left. But we will go on somehow. I promise that we will."

John Dockery
February 11, 1865
Mississippi

The tent flaps rustled in wind. More cold air pushed through. John's broken thoughts tried to consider why fever always felt cold. He slipped in and out of consciousness. In and out of rational thought when awake. Thomas' voice sounded far away now. At once soothing and commanding. A voice he had heard his whole life. From the swimming hole to the battlefield. Even as it barked out instructions over the roar of explosions and musket fire, to John it was still the same laughing voice from his childhood. But now the words were gone. Just the voice in the distance. In a whisper. John could not hear the words but felt the intent. Commanding him to survive, while assuring him it would be fine if he did not.

From even farther away another sound approached. A different sound. More solid than Thomas' whispering voice. Less human. Repeating itself over and again. Louder each time. Familiar for reasons John could not place. He fought to focus. To pull the sound's identity from his memory. A horse. Approaching furiously. At full gallop. Behind tightly closed eyelids he saw it come into view. Down the dirt lane between the tents. Past men in ragged uniforms gathered tightly by fading fires. Coming right for him. A woman with the reins, tears in her eyes. Soon she was beside him. But not in the tent. In a cabin far away. Cool water from the Bloody Run Creek dripped down from above, through the holes punched into the wash bins that now hung over his bed. He did not know her, but still he did somehow. A familiarity he could not place. Again he fought to focus. But then he realized something had changed. The fever was gone. No water dripped from above. He was no longer cold. She reached a hand to him and he rose without trouble. They walked hand in hand to the cabin door, and exited into a glorious light.

Twenty-Two

Jim Dockery
February, 1865
Elmira, NY

It was the middle of a February night, and the fires in barracks twenty-four were out.

The fire man only came twice a day. Once in the morning, once in the evening. He quietly went about his business, not responding to anything the boys might say. He made a fire in each stove, one situated near each end of every long, low barracks building lined up within the stockade. A chalk ring "dead line" was marked on the warped wooden floor around each stove. Any entry into the circle meant punishment fierce and swift. Expanding out across each barracks was a different line, an invisible line. Those bunks closer to the stove's radius of heat were warmer, the men who slept there far more likely to survive. As the heat faded and the invisible circle contracted, death filled the void. Death lurked always at the circle's edge, surrounding the prisoners and closing in stealthily as they slept in their bunks. Only the heat could push it away. But as the night dragged on and the fires blackened and cooled, the heat fell back under the constant pressure of death's silent advance.

A man along the circle's changing edge could feel each night as he was released from one embrace and encompassed by another. A slight warmth from a flickering fire, sliding across the face back toward the stove from which it had come. Immediately behind it a dead chill pushing the heat back to its fading source. The line would inch nightly across each shivering body. Often the men would reach for it, paw at it, as if it could be grabbed and held. They fanned it, hoping to catch the retreating warmth and brush it back onto their faces, even if just for a moment. When it was gone it was gone, until the fire man returned the next day. After another wagon had come and carted off more dead men. After another night of clinging to thin blankets and the cold skin and bone of freezing comrades. After eyes opened throughout the barracks, shocked to have opened one more time, to face one more day in hell.

Jim was awake in his bunk. He was on the very top, the third level. The bunk itself was against the wall. With the stoves near the end of barracks twenty-four, Jim often found himself within the invisible line. When the fires were hot, he could feel the heat rising from the bunks below and filling his space near the top of the building. Some of it escaped, and even more was pushed back. The walls and ceiling had been rapidly knocked together from green lumber, chopped, hewn and assembled by the lowest bidder. The wood had soon warped and curved, leaving gashes in the breastworks meant to defend against the assault of the elements. The relentless cold air exploited every weakness, constantly pushing in from the walls and down from the ceiling.

His old comrades were all gone now. Once the newcomer, he was now the ring leader of a new set of bunkmates. There were two boys from Virginia captured not far from where Jim had been, and a new boy from southern Maryland captured in his first engagement. Jim didn't know the new boy's real name, but the Virginians called him Mason-Dixon. None of them had much to say any more. They communicated primarily with looks. The Maryland boy had been talkative for a day or two, but then took with cold and fell silent. The Virginia boys had somehow survived life outside in the tents until almost Christmas, when the last barracks were completed. There had been eight other men in their tent originally, all of whom died awaiting a spot within the warped barracks walls.

Jim looked down at the stove. It was black. No red gleam at all. Still, seven or eight of the boys gathered around it, withered blankets over their shoulders, drinking in the last tiny remnants of heat before returning to their bunks. One of them was on his knees, across the dead line, his hands almost touching where the fire had just been. He had no blanket on his shoulders.

An Irish sergeant appeared in the doorway beside Jim's bunk. At the sound of the door, the men gathered around the dead line scattered lamely across the floorboards, or climbed awkwardly upward past other prisoners to their bunks. The blanket-less man shuddered as if about to move, then settled back into the space he already occupied.

"Get your sorry Rebel ass away from my fire and return to your bedding this second!"

The man shuddered again and tried to turn his neck to see the sergeant. His lips parted as if he were about to speak, but no sound came. He sunk back to his prior position.

Some of the men began to shout at him. "Get going, buddy. Get going."

The Irishman tromped across the planks rapidly toward the stove.

A gray-headed fellow closest to the stove slipped off his bunk and began to pull at the poor fellow, trying to return him to a bunk, any bunk.

"Come on, let's go. Sarge is coming."

Neither words nor his muscles could move him. The Good Samaritan from the nearby bunk pulled at the man with all his might, but he would not move. The sergeant clubbed the man in the back of his head with the butt of his rifle. Then spun and did the same to the Samaritan. Both were left as twisted clumps on the wooden floor.

Even with eyes well-adjusted to the dark, Jim could not see their injuries. Both men were completely still. He could hear a slight whimper form the Samaritan. From the blanket-less man, he heard nothing.

The sergeant stood silent looking over his handiwork. He turned the blanket-less man over with his foot. The starved boy rolled easily when pushed by the massive, stout leg of the well-fed Irishman. The sergeant stood for another moment, then spoke.

"Next one of you out of your bunk will get the same or worse. Good night, little darlings."

He tromped out as heavily and rapidly as before, then slammed the door behind him.

The commotion had awakened most all of the prisoners sleeping anywhere close to the stove. Jim was glad of that. He had already been awake himself, and had been in the same position too long. Wedged in with three other boys, he was powerless to turn as long as they slept.

The bunks were made from the same cheap lumber as the barracks, and by the same unskilled hands. Beneath the boys was a single worn blanket. Beneath that was the wood. Every knot, rough edge, warped spot and nail pop was felt by the boys every night they spent at Elmira. For a time, the prisoners around camp sought to correct this state of affairs by collecting all the grass or straw they could find in order to make bedding. They returned home from the Mess one evening to find their homemade bedding gone without explanation. Enterprising as always, the men responded by sitting in circles for long afternoons whittling every stick or board they could find. They piled the shavings in the bunks, again hoping to warm and soften their nights of sleep. This was confiscated as well, the guards saying it encouraged vermin. At this the jailed soldiers laughed, having been covered in slithering "gray backs" long before they softened their beds.

Each man in Jim's bunk had one blanket. With one underneath, that left three blankets to cover four men. They were wedged tight, head-to-toe, toe-to-head. The three blankets were spread across the top. Parts of Jim were covered double, parts not at all.

In the wake of the Irishman's visit, Jim heard prisoners calling out turns up and down the barracks. Each bunk was so tight that no turn could be accomplished but in concert.

227

"All turn right," one boy would call.

At that he and his bunkmates would all rotate in the appointed direction.

Jim had been on the outside edge of the bunk, which gave him a front row seat for the incident at the stove. Now he needed to turn, though that would place his nose against the next man's heels.

"All turn left," Jim called out.

He rolled himself away from the sight of the two battered boys on the barrack's floor. As he turned, his nose was clipped by the toes of one of the Virginia boys, turning also in the same direction. Mason-Dixon did not move.

"Mason-Dixon. You need to turn. Didn't you hear Jim say turn?"

One of the Virginian feet in Jim's face tapped Mason-Dixon twice in the nose to encourage him.

There was a knothole in the barracks wall. It was a full moon out and a circular ray of cold, white light shone through the hole onto the face of the Maryland boy. Jim was lying on his left side. His left eye could see only the Virginia boy's shoed heels. His right eye could see just over those heels and into Mason-Dixon's face. He closed the left eye and narrowed the right to get a clearer look. Jim's right eye stared directly into the left eye of Mason-Dixon, illuminated by the single ray of light. The eye stared back at Jim, intently. In the eye was a determination, a focus. Jim did not speak, but wondered why Mason-Dixon did not turn. Perhaps his joints were failing him, or his will. But that's not what the eye was saying. It was saying "There is nothing they can do to me that I cannot handle. I will fight through this frigid night and hope the sun will rise tomorrow. I will take everything these Yankee bastards dish out and show them I'm a better man than the whole lot of them. I will walk back into my father's house one day … one day soon, and I will walk back in a man. Ready to take control of my life. Ready to take a wife and build a house and a family and a life. Once I get through this, I can get through anything the world has in store."

Jim heard a gust of wind howl against the thin barracks wall. A column of frigid air forced its way through the knothole like a rifle shot, tracing the path made by the white cold light before it. He could see Mason-Dixon's hair blow as the wind hit hard against his face. The eye did not blink.

Jim felt the tiny grayback vermin slither onto him as they abandoned Mason-Dixon's cold body.

* * *

That evening Jim and the two Virginia boys made a little fire at the spot. For hours no one said a word. The wind was up and keeping the fire going was a full-time job. An empty stump post sat by the fire, the Dead House looming behind it. It had been Hig's post, then Mason-Dixon's. Jim began to wonder if it was cursed. The wind picked up as the evening crept on. The fire was a lost cause. The sun had disappeared behind the mountains and the full moon was coming back into view. Soon the fire man would light the evening fires. The three men exchanged a knowing glance, then all rose and headed toward the barracks.

"You know, Jim." The younger Virginia boy spoke first. "There was a Richmond boy out there skating on the pond today, says that Lee has split Grant's army in two. Suppose that means the war will be over soon and we'll be headed home."

"Is that right? Isn't that about the fifth time we've heard that one?"

"Well, I guess, but it's got to be true. This boy heard it straight from Richmond."

"He's right, Jim. This boy just arrived on the train today. There was lots of new boys today, hundreds of them. He orta know what's happening out there."

"Boys, we didn't even know what was happening out there half the time when we were out there ourselves. I've heard so many rumors about how this war's ending and we'll be home soon, that I just can't listen to them anymore."

"Since when did you get so gloomy, Jim?"

"Since Gettysburg. Since I realized the South was running out of guns and bullets and men. Since my big brother quit the war and started arguing for peace. Since all the ports started falling. You tell me, how are we going to win this war without a single port where somebody can ship us some bullets and cannon balls?"

"Forget it then, Jim. Forget it."

"Yeah, Jim. Give us a break. Is it so terrible we might want to believe a rumor once in a while? Maybe that's what kept us alive out there in those death tents knee-deep in snow."

"OK boys. OK, I'm sorry. I've been in this place over five months. Most of the buddies I've made in here have died in these walls or been sent home to die. I haven't seen my family in a long, long time. I threw away the stick I used to measure my leg with because I couldn't stand to look at it anymore. My Dad can't send money because he's outside the Yankee lines, and every time he sends food the guards have a feast of it and bring me the crumbs. I've seen enough of this war. I've seen enough of this prison. It's time I realized the plain, simple truth. I'm never going to get home, boys. Maybe none of us are."

"Hold up now, Jim. You're the one that taught us how to live in here."

"That's right. You're the one that said the fastest way to die in here is to believe your gonna die. To get broken. You can't get broken on us, Jim. We need you."

"Sounds like you've got it all figured out. What in the world do you need me for?"

"Because you're our friend, Jim."

Jim stopped walking right in front of the barracks. He looked at the boys with eyes that burned but could not cry. In the wind he felt his knees buckling beneath him. Every joint he had stiffened in the cold as a gust came up from the frozen Foster's Pond and squeezed a frozen grid of icy air down each aisle between the barracks buildings. He felt like an old man about to be exposed for some mortal sin, breaking the hearts of his grandchildren.

"Let me tell you what kind of friend I am. I had a friend. A true friend. Cap taught me how to survive. He and his brother Hig and their buddy Robert. They were the toughest and best men that ever lived in these walls. Hig rotted away in here. Rotted. Robert did too. Died right here where were just sitting. The Yankees sent Cap home in the October exchange because they knew he couldn't live. I'm sure he didn't. So the boys who taught me what I taught you … how to catch rats and stay out of trouble … they're dead. So how good were those lessons, huh boys?

"And the day they sent Cap out of here, he gave me his dog, Mac. He gave me his dog because he knew if he died on that train the other boys would get him and we all know what would happen then. Well, no sooner than the gates shut behind Cap's back, before he could even get to the train station, I was sitting right there at that spot where we just sat, cooking that dog on a fire, buying myself a few weeks of life. Trying to buy Robert a few more days. Because the rumors at the time were … guess what … that this war would be over in a few weeks. So don't tell me I'm your friend. Don't tell me how much you need me. That's what kind of friend I am. And that's what I think of all these Godforsaken rumors and this Godforsaken war."

Jim turned and walked into the barracks. The Virginia boys followed. Inside, the fire man was building the evening fire. Beside him, the Irish sergeant was re-drawing the chalk line over a blood stain on the plank floor.

The boys looked up at their bunk. To their surprise, a frail, bearded boy was sprawled out across the entire bunk, snoring loudly.

"Well. What do we do now?"

"It's warm," Jim replied. "Let's get in the damned bed. We can probably fold that boy up anyway we want and he won't even blink."

* * *

In the middle of the night there was silence, punctuated occasionally by the howl of the winds outside. Jim woke suddenly and felt the chill of the invisible line start with his feet and ease gradually toward his face again. He did not turn to look, but knew the fire was out. The cold gripped him inch by inch. As the line climbed to his chest, a scratch rose in his throat and a pin prick in his nose warned of a coming sneeze. He sneezed loudly three or four times, each sneeze snapping his head and shooting pain down his spine. He cleared his throat and spat onto the floor, but still sneezed again, and again. When he did the Virginia boys both stirred. The toe of the Virginia boy behind him rubbed against the back of his head. He could feel not only the shoe, but the big toe that protruded from the end. Finally, one of the Virginia boys called a turn.

"All turn left."

Jim paused a moment so as to not have his frozen nose brushed by the Virginia boy's toe. Again, like the night before, he turned to find his right eye staring into an open left eye a foot away. The new boy had not turned. In the moonlight through the knothole, Jim studied the face. Though the boy was emaciated, it seemed his face was once full and round. Though young, he had a thick beard. The eye was grotesquely wide and betrayed no life or thought. The eye looked right back at Jim's, but did not focus. The boy did not move. The eye was yellowed and swollen. The lips below were terribly red and chapped. Though the boy had just arrived, he already looked starved.

The wind howled and again found the knothole portal into the boys' bunk. The beard and hair of the new boy fluttered … and the eye finally blinked. When it blinked it seemed to regain focus, then narrowed, as if studying something with curiosity. The boy raised up on his elbow and looked at Jim. Exposed by his starvation, the bones framed a round face, no doubt cheerful when full. The eyes, still yellow, brightened beneath raising eyebrows. The chapped lips cracked into a smile with surprising ease.

Jim sat up and looked the boy full in the face.

"Ben? Ben Covington? Is that you?"

Twenty-Three

Alfred Dockery
March 7, 1865
Rockingham, NC

Much of the town of Rockingham had come out to see the show. The Yankees had let it be known exactly what they were going to do, and exactly when they were going to do it. The officer in command wanted an audience. He wished to make a point.

There were dark rocks along most of the banks of Falling Creek. In spots, though, were tiny, flat sand beaches. One sandbar curved along the middle of the creek as it bent. There the sand was wide and dry enough for folks to stand and children to play. The adults in the group all wore the same expression. Deadened eyes in exhausted faces. Waiting for an inevitable atrocity to occur. Not even the most ardent unionist celebrated what was about to unfold. Not even the most strident Confederate believed he could stop it. They huddled together in small groups, staring upstream and saying little. Waiting.

The local children seemed not to realize the gravity of the occasion. They splashed through the shallow water between the bank and the sandbar, skipped rocks and chased each other to and fro. It was an unexpected treat to play in the creek this early in the year. A couple of the older boys rolled up their pants and waded about, hunting salamanders.

Among the townspeople were dozens of men in blue uniforms. They moved freely and energetically between and around the dark, quiet pods of mourners, some the same locals they had robbed of food and valuables since their arrival. Theirs was a mood of celebration. The anticipation of a grand event.

The sun dipped slowly below the trees. Had it set to the south instead of the west, no one in Rockingham would have seen it. The black smoke from Sherman's march through South Carolina still cast an impenetrable shadow over the southern sky. But to the west the orange light slithered between the branches, reached out over the creek and reflected against the towering brick walls of the Richmond Manufacturing Company. It rose sharply from the creek below and towered over the entire scene. Many of the spectators had helped to build it. Brick by brick, from the dirt to the sky, providing good jobs to the eager workers of Rockingham. The massive water wheel turned steadily along its shaft, scooping the water of Falling Creek and creating the energy needed to run the machinery inside. That machinery spun locally grown cotton into weavable strands, and wove those strands into fabric. Before it left those walls, that local cotton was sewn into uniforms of butternut and gray, ready to be shipped all over the South and worn by brave young men whose Rebel yells chilled blood and gave birth to legends. Until this day.

General Dockery stood alone. He was close to the mill, but stayed higher up the bank and looked down on the scene below. He focused on a family standing on a large rock that jutted out over a deep pool. The black water entered the pool from a shallow riff above. It shot through rocks of various sizes, turned white at the bottom and collected momentarily below the large rock. There it slowed and swirled in a regular counterclockwise pattern. The pattern accelerated near the bottom of the pool, then spun open, fanned out and rolled down another riff on its way downstream.

The couple on the rock was young. Their clothes rough and worn. The man had removed his coat and draped it over his wife's shoulders. There was power in his shoulders, though he was hunched slightly as if accustomed to stooping. In his left hand, strangely, was a fiddle. He wore no hat, and his hair was sandy and matted down to his head. Clinging to his arm was his young wife, slight and pale-skinned with curly red hair, mirrored by that of the little girl beside her. In front of the father was a short, thick boy, maybe 9 or 10 years old. He wore over-sized pants and a white, long sleeved shirt. He locked his thumbs in the waist of his pants as the older men often did. The man had his hands on the boy's shoulders. The hands were short and thick and powerful. *Like "these ol' yaller hands"* the General thought to himself, and looked at his own, thick, well-creased palms. The hunched-over man's children did not play with the others. Their eyes shared the look of the adults.

Thick, worn hands. Children understanding this solemn occasion. I see. This man works here. He is about to lose his job. Doesn't matter much what he thinks of this war. He won't be able to feed his family tomorrow.

A few feet away at the base of the great mill was a man who seemed to be in charge. He wore a crisp and clean blue uniform dotted with shiny gold accents, fit for a gala of West Point royalty. There was no doubt he had dressed for the occasion, but his uniform did little to conceal that he was generally a sorry looking fellow. Indeed, the uniform was at least two sizes too big, and seemed more to accentuate rather than hide the uncouth nature of the man. He held his hat in his hand, exposing damp, matted hair pulled thinly across his head in an apparent effort to conceal patches of exposed scalp. His long nose pointed down and out over his mouth, which didn't smile, but seemed like it was just about to, and to do so in as sinister of a fashion as possible. In contrast to the matted hair on his scalp, his sideburns were bushy and wild, extending nearly a foot below his oversized ears. Each sideburn gave the appearance of a grotesquely fat caterpillar curling up off the side of his face, looking about trying to decide where to crawl next.

With him was a woman of striking appearance, and she seemed very much with him. She did smile, in as sinister of a fashion as one might expect from her companion. Sinister or not, she was beautiful. And knew it. Her face was pale and round, with impossibly smooth skin, framed by a thick head of long wheat-colored hair that fell around her shoulders and captured the fading light of the setting sun. She wore a long black dress, tighter and less demure than Southern decorum allowed. She had the kind of beauty that angered other women. There was a knowledge in her hazel eyes of things a well-brought-up girl her age was not meant to know. It gave her eyes a look that sent men straight past admiration and directly into lust, a fact other women seemed to recognize. By looks the couple was mismatched. By something intangible in both of them, maybe not.

When he was done studying her, the General turned his eyes back to the Yankee officer. To his surprise, the man was looking right back at him. When their eyes met, the foul Yankee's lips curled into a sneering smirk. He tilted his head slightly toward the woman, then nodded at the General and smiled a bit more broadly. He turned his attention to a young officer nearby and whispered something to him. The young man in blue then darted through the mob, speaking to every other man in blue with a stripe on his arm.

The army sprang to action with great excitement. They fashioned torches from branches wrapped in cloth no doubt pilfered from the mill. They dipped them into buckets of tar and lit them on fire. The light above was growing dim, but dozens of torches now dotted the landscape from the mill down to the creek bend by the sandbar. Mothers clamored to pull their children closer. The General watched as one of the torches launched from the far side of the river and drifted in a high arc over the creek to the opposite bank. Another solider gathered it up and tossed it back across. Soon dozens of flaming torches were sailing back and forth across the creek. Streaks of yellow and orange light rolled across the rippled surface of the creek below, crossing one another as the torches sailed above. The light caught the faces of jubilant Yankees as they scampered about, launching one projectile, then grabbing for another. Other torches illuminated the clumps of defeated citizens, who

236

continued to huddle together in motionless silence. There was much cheering and shouting amongst the Northern troops. The vile officer finally smiled in full, let out an ironic imitation Rebel yell and squeezed his arm around the drawn-tight waist of his traveling companion. She watched the fiery arcs cross the creek and laughed out loud, pure joy in her eyes. As the torches flew they grew closer and closer to the mill. Each made its way upstream in a series of agonizingly slow zigzags, prolonging the citizens' dread and the soldiers' celebration. Finally, the Yankee soldiers waved the torches near the base of the mill itself, awaiting the order to torch the city's grandest structure.

One of the young men in the head officer's entourage strolled over to the hunched over man and his family. He jerked the fiddle from the man's hand, put it to his chin and drew the bow. Hopping about like a court jester, he played a loud, jerky version of Pop Goes the Weasel. When he finished, he tossed the fiddle high in the air. It came down at its owner's feet, shattering on the giant, jutting rock. Pieces of the fiddle fell into the creek, where they swirled in the current momentarily, then sped up and disappeared down the riff below. The man in sideburns gave a signal and his men busted out the nearest windows of the mill and tossed in the torches. There was a shudder of movement among the townspeople as the first torch went in. The General watched as the flame appeared in each window of the long building one by one, the fabric meant for the backs of Southern soldiers now serving as fuel for Yankee fire. In seconds the awful light could be seen along the entire length of the building. Flames jumped from the windows and licked at the brick walls above. There was an awful sound from within the building, after which the orange light began to appear in the windows above. It began in the middle of the second floor, then spread rapidly in both directions.

The Yankees watched in joy as the mill burned. They cheered each new sight of spreading flame. Each destructive sound. The townspeople dispersed. They climbed slowly up the banks and the hillside toward town. Some turned and gave one sorrowful glance into the orange light before turning into the dark and disappearing over the hillside. The fiddler and his family lingered longer than most. As did the General.

Finally they turned and headed upward towards Dockery.

"Young man."

"Yessir."

"Do you know who I am young man?"

"Reckon I do, sir."

"I know you have matters to attend to, son, but if you could, I suggest you come out to see me Monday or Tuesday. I have a lot of things that need doing, and I expect you could do some of them."

"Sir? You talking about a job, sir?"

"I am."

The man titled his head up slightly and looked the General in the eye. Something in his eyes changed, though slightly. There was still pain. Still despair. Still lost pride. Even outright fear. But there was a tiny change, even with the flames just behind him. Even with the crackling of the burning mill and the shouts of Yankee celebration close at hand. A tiny little change in a portion of his eyes. Something new appearing. Something the General had put there. Hope.

The General saw it, and a power welled up inside of him to know such a thing was still possible.

"Thank you, sir."

"Of course."

The man squeezed his son's shoulder and headed up the hill. He stopped and turned back to the General, who was once again facing the fire.

"I will see you Monday, sir."

With that he hobbled up the hill with his family and disappeared with the others. Now no one was left except General Dockery, the men in blue, and the Irish girl with the bedroom eyes.

Twenty-Four

Ben Covington
March, 1865
Elmira, NY

Ben joined Jim and the Virginians by the fire, taking over the stump vacated by Mason-Dixon, and by Hig before him. Once the fire was lit and the boys were settled in, they all looked at Ben in anticipation.

"What are y'all looking at me for?"

"Didn't Jim tell you? You're the evening's entertainment."

"Jim, what in the world are they talking about?"

"Ben, I know you're not much for being the center of attention, but you're the only one that has anything to say that we haven't already heard. The rest of us are all talked out. And besides, I want to know how in the world you ended up here."

Ben rested his elbows on his knees, cradling his head in his hands, not wanting to relive the journey that had brought him to Elmira. He closed his eyes and was there again.

* * *

He stood huddled with a band of ragged and bloodied men amongst the carnage that lay inside the mounds of Fort Fisher. Men in blue moved all about the fort. Piling debris in heaps to burn, dragging bodies or body parts into long lines in the sand. Some spit in Southern faces or prodded Southern backs with bayonets. Others were more gracious, even kind.

Ben noticed one chubby gentleman with a long white beard, a lieutenant. He was making his way down the line of beaten Rebel faces, offering water and assessing wounds.

"Shit, boys," said one of the men standing near Ben, "reckon we didn't have a chance in hell of defending this fort against jolly ol' Saint Nick himself."

A few of the men snickered. Most were in no mood. The bearded man walked over to Ben.

"Are you OK, young fellow?"

"Yessir."

"No ammunition on you? They already took it?"

"Wasn't any to take."

"That seems to be the way of it. So few of you, so few bullets and cannon balls. How did you ever expect to defend this fort?"

"I thank you for your kindness, sir, and I mean no offense, but we defended her once, and almost did again."

Santa Claus put his hand on Ben's shoulder.

"I suppose you did, son. I suppose you did. Here, take a sip of water."

"Thank you, sir."

He moved on to a little grouping of officers Ben figured was trying to decide what to do with a thousand stubborn, unarmed Rebels. Heads were shaking, shoulders shrugging. The blackened wood of the burned-down barracks offered no solution. One sharp-nosed officer did most of the talking and kept pointing down the beach.

Ben looked over the fort. The Yankees were everywhere. There were so many of them. Some were scavenging the place, climbing in and out of every tunnel or passageway they could find, coming out with all kinds of loot. Some carried torches in and out of the tunnels, which Ben knew was a perilous business. Any second one could walk into a magazine with a flaming torch and blow the whole fort sky high. One pack of boys was sitting atop one of the mounds along the sea face passing a bottle of brown liquor they had found underneath. Behind them was the rolling ocean, dotted with dozens of Yankee warships. Landing boats lined the shallows. The drinkers sat on the sandy mound within feet of dead bodies. Southern sand. Southern bodies. Southern liquor. Southern wind flapping a Yankee flag and blowing through Yankee hair. Ben didn't hate them. He figured they felt just as strongly about the war as he did. So he couldn't hate them. He just hated being conquered.

Finally, the men with all the stripes on their shoulders decided what to do with the Fort Fisher garrison. They herded them like cattle and marched them across the destroyed interior, through the gates and out onto the beach. Each man was forced to step over the strewn remains of the once proud fort. Cannons and guns broken to pieces. Splintered timbers of unknown origin. Bodies, broken and torn. Burned up flags with shattered poles. Scraps of metal from exploded shells, some smeared with human remains. Big gaping holes and scars in the ground where thousands of shells exploded. All that stood were the earthworks the Confederates had thought would make Fort Fisher invincible.

Ben felt an ache in his chest as he walked through the gate. He had always thought that when he marched out of that gate he would be going home. Right above the gate was the spot where he had made his stand. Where a section of the wall had come down with him on top of it. Littered with broken cannons rendered unable to slow the Yankee assault. As he passed through the gate, he could see it all from the outside. The men he had killed were still there, covered in blood and sand. Yankee soldiers and black men were lining up bodies. Ben looked for Amos but didn't see him. Though he knew his family needed Amos, Ben hoped he was free by now.

He couldn't tear his eyes from that collapsed wall. It may have failed him in the end, but it had saved him from a thousand bullets.

Allowed him to kill more men than he was able to count. *Many of them knew they would get it,* he thought. *They didn't know who I was but they knew somebody would get them. Yet they came anyway. Same as we've been doing over and over again on battlefields across the country. Maybe they aren't that much different than we are after all.*

The Yankee officers marched their prisoners onto the beach, where they stayed all day and through the night. It was dead cold and the wind whipped in unimpeded from the ocean. No sand walls to block the wind. No bed rolls or blankets to keep the men warm.

The wind blew bitter that night. Countless specs of sand picked up and blew low and swift across the beach, biting the men in their faces, eyes and ears. Ben couldn't sleep but kept his eyes closed just to fend off the sand. They were camped within the high tide line, so the sand was rock hard and damp. Ben's clothes soaked water up from the sand as he lie on the ground. His tail bone throbbed under his weight, but when he turned on either side his hips would ache within minutes. With nothing under his head, his neck lay awkwardly on the ground and tightened into a knot.

Ben thought of the oddity of suffering from a crick in his neck. Here he had just been invaded and defeated by his enemy, had numerous bullets stopped from killing him just by a plank or two of wood and a pile of sand. Bayonets were thrust into the ground all around him when they might just have well gone through him. But that same night he was bent out of shape about having nothing to use as a pillow.

His body cried out for sleep but there was none to be had. It was as if someone waited for him to nod off and then shouted in his ear. The clouds were low and fast in the wind, and there were no stars. In the damp and cold, with the whipping sand, Ben prayed a bit and wished he could see the heavens above. Yet the clouds would not clear. Unable to sleep, he crawled around looking for someone to help. One young soldier lay bleeding through a bandage where his hand used to be. He was so frail and tiny. "Not a hundred pounds soaking wet," as the General used to say.

"What's your name, friend?"

"Clanton, sir. Robert Clanton."

"Are you a praying man, Clanton?"

"Yessir."

"Lord, this here is Robert Clanton. Where you from, Clanton?"

"South Carolina."

"From South Carolina. I don't know what your will is for him, Lord, but I offer him up to you. He's hurt pretty bad, Lord, but he's one tough little fellow. I don't know if you'll take him tonight, Lord, but I bet he'd be of a great deal of service to you down here. He'd do your work, I'm sure of it. Raise a fine family. Do you have a girl, Clanton?"

"Yessir. JoAnn, sir."

"If it be your will Lord, take him off this beach and back to JoAnn down in South Carolina. All praise to your name, Lord. Amen."

Clanton echoed Ben's "Amen" and never spoke again. Ben fell asleep sitting upright, with the young man's head cradled in his lap.

* * *

The entire world erupted. The jolt that opened Ben's eyes was beyond any blast from the previous day's bombardment. It was as if all the shells that had fallen on the fort were merged into one. He woke up sitting upright, with his eyes already looking back down the beach to the fort. The sun was rising out to sea, casting a pale purple light across the fort. Rising from the corner closest to the waking prisoners was a massive plume of smoke, dust and debris. It rose straight up into the air half a mile, expanding in every direction. Objects lifted with the plume, then fell out at random. Planks of wood, wagon wheels, men. Ben knew immediately that some drunken fool had located the main magazine with a flaming torch in hand. He heard later that some of the Yankees tried to blame the boys on the beach. When they found the buried torpedo lines that ran from the fort out onto the beach, they assumed the Rebels had sent in some kind of charge from their place of confinement. Of course they were designed to work the other way around. Charges were to be sent beneath the feet of the unsuspecting, charging enemy, sending entire companies blasting into the air. But that never happened. Nor did anyone send charges in the opposite direction. Ben knew exactly what the truth was.

The blast killed 200 Yankees. Probably some of those same boys he had seen sitting on top of the mound, sipping brown liquor with the ocean breeze in their hair. *I hope they don't tell their mamas how it happened,* Ben thought. *Every mama that loses a boy in a war has the right to assume it happened in some big act of bravery. Carrying a flag over the wall of a fort or something like that. Not sitting up on a beach drinking liquor and getting blowed up by a numbskull drunk who took a flaming torch inside a powder magazine while looking to steal something.*

People scurried about all around the edge of the fort. Some running towards that big cloud looking to help. Others running away, perhaps figuring it might come down on top of them. It was at least half an hour before the debris settled back to Earth. The purples and oranges from the rising sun cast an eerie glow on the melting cloud. When it finally settled one of the grand mounds of the fort was simply gone.

After that the Yankees wasted no time shipping out their prisoners. Likely they knew their own men had caused the explosion, but they weren't taking any chances. They loaded the Confederates into the same transport boats that had brought the invaders to shore and carried them out to ships moored beyond the breakers. It was Ben's first time at sea.

The captors loaded their prisoners onto ships and led them to dark chambers below decks. Ben followed the shouting of the guards and the steps of the men before him, laying down in his designated patch of floor. In the darkness, he could feel the touch of flesh all over him. Against each arm was another man's arm. Against his head were feet. His own feet pressed into another man's hair.

The ocean was beyond view, but made its anger felt as it tossed the ship from side to side. The aged timbers popped and cracked as if the entire ship would come to pieces. As it rolled, the men were constantly smashed together, one direction and then the other. The elbows of the men flanking Ben always digging into his sides. He tried to squirm to ease the assault, but was wedged in too tight. After a while he just lie there and took it.

The darkness was complete. The kind your eyes don't get used to. Ben could have been within feet of longtime friends and never known it. He kept his eyes open for a long time, waiting in vain for the darkness to clear. He tried blinking his eyes 10 times as his mother told him as a child, but that failed as well.

The sense of smell more than compensated for the loss of sight. Time passed in a vacuum. One long, sleepless night. However long it may have been, men had to relieve themselves. An obese soldier lay next to Ben, twitching and bouncing his legs and mumbling to himself. Ben figured he had to go and was trying desperately to hold it. Finally, the portly fellow muttered "Aw, t'hell with it," and took a deep breath. Ben smelled the urine and then felt it running up under him when the boat pitched to the left. The big fellow whimpered a bit and Ben spoke to him.

"Don't worry about it, big man. Not your fault."

"Speak for yourself you dimwit, that jackass just peed in my hair!"

It was still early on. The men had no idea how bad it would get. By the time the boat reached New York, every man had relieved himself in both ways a man can. Many of the malnourished boys had developed longstanding cases of diarrhea. Even worse, many got sea sick and vomited, which was the worst smell of all. The ceiling was only a few feet above, and the cabin was sealed tight. The stench was tightly confined, and the men swam in it.

Ben tried to pass the time thinking. He tried to think about anything except where he was and where he was going. Or what he had just seen. But those were the only places his mind would go. He tried everything. He thought about home. He thought about God. He thought about Heaven. He even thought about pretty girls, figuring if nothing else could hold his mind maybe that would. He tried to count sheep like when he was little. For a moment, he thought about the boat rolling all the way over and drifting down slowly to the bottom. Nothing worked. The dark and the rocking and the smell and the pain wouldn't let him think about anything else for long. He tried to break them up and think of them one by one. When he thought about the dark it made him scared. When he thought about the rocking it made him dizzy. When he thought about the smell it made him sick. When he thought about the pain it made him want to die.

* * *

"So there you go boys. You wanted a new story. There's a story for you. Happy?"

Jim and the Virginia boys stared blank-faced at Ben. No one spoke for a while.

"How did you make it through, cousin?"

"I finally decided to just let it go. I pretty much let my mind turn to mush. I just let the awfulness of that boat spread over me all at once and sort of went into a trance. Maybe time went faster when I did that. I don't know.

"But I have thought about it since then. You fellas know how it is. There's nothing to do in here but think. I got no idea how long it takes to pitch and sway your way from North Carolina up North in a boat like that. It was a long way and it seemed like a long time. Only to be dragged some place where you're confined in a prison, piled up four to a bunk in little ramshackle sheds that weren't built right. Told when you can eat and when you can sleep. But me and those other boys, we weren't the first folks to be packed into a boat like that and carried some place we didn't want to go. And there's some folks been put on a boat like that for a lot longer than us."

Twenty-Five

Jim Dockery
March, 1865
Elmira, NY

Rain fell. The ice was breaking. Everywhere were sneezes and coughs as bodies suddenly freed from the dry freeze struggled to adjust to the relative warmth and total damp of rain and melting snow. Small trickles of water swelled to creeks that ran down the gravelly ground to Foster's Pond from all directions, all other points being higher in elevation. Even when the rains stopped, the little rivers ran. Piles of snow pushed to the side over the frozen months had accumulated every available particle of dirt and soot the camp had offered. Having long lost their white purity, they stood as hardened, gray mounds that represented cold, but not beauty. With each new snowfall, the freed slaves that worked the camp shoveled and piled more snow onto the mounds. They always increased in size. New snow would cover their gray filth, but only for a day or two. Then they became just as filthy and unsightly as before, only wider and taller. Under the warming rain and rising temperatures, the piles finally began to diminish. The hardened mounds turned to mush, and seemed to sink into the ground. At the base of each began a tiny rivulet of gray water.

The first melted drops sunk into the ground around the piles. Then as more and more broke free from the icy mounds, they no longer disappeared into the saturated ground. The first trickles weaved their way along seemingly random paths between ruts and scars in the ground, around rocks and between the gravel, always pulled by gravity to the path of least resistance. At the front of each the water swelled in a tiny circle with a defined edge that curved down to the ground. They pooled at spots, until they filled whatever crevice might have hindered their progress, then spilled over at the lowest point and continued the perfect charge toward Foster's Pond.

Jim watched from the spot as a newly forming trickle came slowly by. In battle he had seen well-trained geniuses of combat squabble and falter about their path of choice. Where to go and why. How to get most efficiently from point A to point B. With all their intelligence, education and experience, there was always resistance, as the military reached around its collective ass to reach its elbow. But here were molecules of water, finally freed from their frozen prison, anxiously and perfectly headed to their rightful home. Without any will or ability to complicate the obvious, they simply went where they were supposed to go.

As they traveled down the slight slope toward the pond, they joined others formed by the fall of rain, the melting of ice, or both. They converged here and there, doubling their speed and momentum at each miniature confluence, joining together into more formidable forces. Gathering speed as they neared the banks of the pond, they rifled into the swelling body of water sending little riffles and bubbles across the recently thawed surface. Around the pond were dozens of points of entry. Water poured in from outside the gates as well. The river outside swelled beyond its banks and a rapid flow poured in under the wall toward the pond. Days earlier men had stood on the surface of the pond with no fear of breaking through. Now the ice on the surface was mostly gone, though a few broken chunks still bobbed about, themselves melting directly into the pond, contributing to its rise.

The mountains outside the walls were dim and blurred in the darkened, misty skies, but Jim could see that the white caps were turning to gray. Foster's was already well beyond its solid, winter banks and rising visibly. Along the bank a bald-headed prisoner in a withered butternut uniform shoved a skinny stick into the mud at the water's edge. He stood and watched it without movement. Jim and Ben sat at the spot and watched the old man as he eyed the stick. Minutes later the water was more than a foot beyond the stick. The old man stepped cautiously into the water, which lapped at the top of his brogans. He pulled the stick from the mud and replaced it at the new high-water mark, stepped back and continued to watch. Jim and Ben kept their eyes fixed on him, as the rain began to fall around them again.

Alfred Dockery
Rockingham, NC

General Dockery's study had become a mess. His war-related correspondence had grown to fill all available space. General Wheeler had passed through with General Kilpatrick's Union cavalry hot on his trail. When Wheeler sent word of his acceptance of Dockery's invitation to use his home as temporary headquarters, Dockery's papers were hurriedly stashed into wooden boxes, and pushed to one side. During his occupation, General Wheeler and staff lacked for paper and made their plans and letters on the backs of whatever papers they cared to grab from the boxes. General Dockery did not know what he still had and what he didn't.

A fire burned in the fireplace behind him as he sorted the papers by candlelight, and pondered yet another attempt to deliver food or clothing to Jim.

First, he had sought to ship food and clothing directly to Jim at Elmira. Each shipment, he had later learned, was rejected because shipped from within Confederate lines. Later, he had corresponded with the Noah Walker & Co. clothiers from Baltimore, ordering clothing to be shipped to Jim. Walker had informed the Northern authorities of massive orders from all over the South, none of which he was ever allowed to fill. The General then corresponded with several relief efforts, North and South, all intent on shipping clothing to the freezing prisoners. Most notably, he corresponded with John J. Van Allen of Watkins, New York, only a few miles from Elmira. Van Allen had been appointed by a relief organization in Baltimore, hoping he could use his local contacts to persuade the prison to open its gates to donations of free clothing for the men. Predictably, the War Department delayed, then laid out an impenetrable bureaucratic process for providing any clothing to prisoners. Recognizing the fool's errand laid before him, Van Allen abandoned the endeavor. Finally, Dockery even wrote the tall, rowdy gentleman in the top hat he met in a tavern in Washington. Abraham Lincoln, the sworn enemy of Dockery's own sons, had written him a letter of just one line right after North Carolina seceded. Perhaps, the General thought, he would allow a father to send food and clothing to his dying on. No response ever came.

But now, the General predicted, all of Richmond County would be under federal control within days. Thus, perhaps one more attempt to help his son survive Elmira was warranted.

General Sherman had made it known he would not burn North Carolina to the ground as he had Georgia and South Carolina, hoping to fan the growing flames of discontent with the war. As seen plainly at the Richmond Manufacturing Company, cavalry General Judson Kilpatrick failed to fully digest the message. Most every turpentine mill along the Pee Dee River had been burned just so Kilpatrick's raiders could marvel at the flames. The Richmond Manufacturing Company and the Shortridge Mill were in ashes, having been dubbed targets of military significance because they made Confederate uniforms. Unfortunately for the Confederates, they couldn't load Richmond County fabrics into guns or cannons. Fewer houses were burned than in nearby Cheraw, South Carolina, but the notion that no houses would be burned was one Sherman may have uttered but Kilpatrick declined to hear. Though few were burned, fewer still were fully intact. The houses stood, but the barns, the cupboards and jewelry boxes were left empty. Sherman had a large army to feed, the men themselves had salaries they wished to supplement, and Kilpatrick had a French chef to pay and a lovely Irish woman from South Carolina to keep confined to his bed. His looks made it all the more necessary to lure her with luxury.

Although the Brick House was undisturbed, there was a constant reminder of the ongoing occupation. In the otherwise silent evening was one woeful, recurring sound. As the charred remains of the Richmond Manufacturing Company smoldered and smoked, its water wheel continued to turn. It dipped into Falling Creek, scooped up the cool water and continued its effort to produce energy for a mill that no longer existed. Its cause of dressing Confederate soldiers for battle was now lost, but this was a fact the wheel refused to acknowledge. Once in motion it continued in motion. It knew no other way.

As the wheel turned, its shaft grated against a damaged babbitt, the power of the wheel producing an awesome shriek with each rotation, a noise like nothing a man would make, unless from the kind of horror that robbed him of self-control. As it spread for miles in all directions its waves broadened and took on the quality of a massive rumble. Miles from Falling Creek, the General heard the sound anew every few seconds at regular intervals, unable ever to forget the state of affairs in Richmond County. His powers of concentration were tested repeatedly as the rumble sounded again and again. It sounded as though a sorrowful god channeled all his pain into slow, rhythmic strikes at a giant, hidden drum.

Jim

The smallpox hospital consisted of a few rows of tents on the far side of Foster's Pond. It was a holding cell for the Dead House. Even as the final barracks were finished, the men with smallpox remained exiled to flimsy tents. With nothing but time on his hands, Jim had watched for hours and never seen a doctor enter the tents. The only traffic was food going in, and bodies coming out. For hours each day, no one came or went at all. Even the location of the tents, apart from the main hospital and separated from camp by the pond, showed a priority not of saving the men afflicted with the disease, but of keeping them quarantined. Perhaps that's why the doctors never came. Activity at the smallpox hospital was slight. At the Dead House, it was furious.

The water that had run down the gentle slopes to the pond had combined with that pouring in from a thousand hillsides beyond the gates, and was now climbing back up the slope. The far side of the pond was low, and filled fast. The water spread itself across the low flat land like the remnants of a broken wave.

Now, suddenly, as the water lapped at their posts, the long-forsaken smallpox tents became the sight of frantic activity. The men strong enough to stand attempted to walk away. The water forced them to walk around by the Dead House so they could circle around the pond and head for higher ground. In an instant the water seemed to rise faster. Jim and Ben watched as the coming flood transformed from passing curiosity to genuine emergency. Its rise became audible. The tents grew shorter, rapidly. An immobile man on a tent floor would soon be drowned.

A pathetic figure emerged from the tent farthest to the left, safety being to the right. He stood in front of the tent, grasping a tent post firm with both hands. He was naked and bald and wore a long beard. His frame was so slight he gave a skeletal appearance from across the pond. The water was near his knees and rising. Repeatedly he released the tent post slowly with one hand, hesitated, then hugged tight to it again. He seemed to doubt his first step like a small child who has climbed a tree and holds on tight, fearing his father below will fail to catch him when he jumps. Paralyzed, he held one hand flat above his eyes like a ship's captain trying to see into the distance. He looked back across the rising water toward the Dead House. In the direction of his stare, small flat boats and rafts approached, piloted by guards or freed slaves. They paddled from tent to tent, attempting to transport those who could not transport themselves. Apparently the man was near blind. He looked directly at the boats, but did not appear to see them. When he finally made his leap of faith, letting go of the post, he began walking away from the Dead House, farther from safety. His steps were labored, and he reached his hands out for supports that were not there. Though his pace was slow, he got farther and farther from the approaching boats.

Once filled, the boats raced back to the far side of the pond, where the smallpox patients were being gathered. Other boats shuttled bodies from the Dead House. Some in coffins, some not. In all, dozens of men had joined the effort, none seeming to hesitate for fear of catching disease from the men they sought to save. The very men who left them in the tents to die had sprung into action to avoid their drowning. Somehow there must have been some perceived moral difference, whether conscious or not. As they rushed back and forth, the blind man wandered farther still in the wrong direction. The water reached his waist. Above him on the wall was a guard, waving his arms frantically and yelling something at the blind man below. Another, taller guard left his post and stood beside his comrade, but said and did nothing. He crossed his arms and watched in silence. The blind man continued wobbling, arms outstretched. Jim wondered how long it had been since the man had stood, or walked. How much will to live it must have taken for him to rise from his expected deathbed. To take that first step, and then so many more. Had he thought he had taken his last step? Had he accepted his fate? Was drowning somehow different to him as well? Somehow worse than what he had come to accept? Or had his mind left him before the flood came, his body carried forward in the wrong direction by a misdirected instinct of self-preservation?

Finally, his movement stopped. He stood sill for a moment, then raised his hands straight above his head. As if held at the back and leaned down for baptism, he slowly eased backward into the water. There were ripples but for a second. The water closed. There was no monument or shrine to his point of disappearance.

Seconds passed. He did not resurface. The guard from above leapt down from the wall and splashed into the water below. Near chest deep, he struggled about in irregular circles. He dove under at random spots and resurfaced feet away. Giving up his search, the guard stood still in the rising water. It had reached his chin, and he seemed to bounce up and down. Jim envisioned him springing off of his tip toes repeatedly, as he himself had done as a child in Cartledge Creek when his brothers had dared him to follow them into the deep water. Just before the guard went under, a raft piloted by a freed slave pulled him from the water and paddled him around the growing pond. The guard lay face down on the raft with his hands on the back of his head.

The current of the rising water pushed the raft up against the prison wall. Up above, the tall guard stood upon the wall, arms crossed, staring blankly at the water below.

Alfred

Between the rumbles of the distant drum, the General heard a horse approaching. He walked to the front door, where he found Anna waiting, candle in one hand and Bible in the other. Soon in the doorway was a rather large, but very young horseman. He was at least six-and-a-half feet tall and broad of beam, no more than fifteen or sixteen years old. The General knew him to be Nathaniel McCassick, the over-anxious son of a blacksmith in town with well-known anti-war beliefs. Nathaniel had gone the other way, perhaps more stridently due to his father's persistent pull in the opposite direction. His clothes seemed to be his father's, most notably because of the faint smell of smoke given off as the large boy sweated in them. He looked silly, both because the clothes were too formal for his age and too small for his bulk. In the flickering candlelight, the General could see the boy was red-faced and flustered. He was breathing hard as if the horse had been riding him, instead of the other way around. There was a look of conflict in his eyes. He desired to speak, it seemed, but decorum commanded he allow the General speak first.

"Nathaniel, son, what is it?"

"General, si ... sir. The blue ... the Yanks, sir. Yanks. Coming this way, sir."

"Nathaniel, calm down a moment, son. How do you know they are coming here?"

"There was talk. They was talking. A lot of talking, sir, General, sir, in town. He was, Kilpatrick, sir, Judson Kilpatrick, was doing lots of talking in town about how he wanted to tour the town's mansions. Big, bragging talk. Sarcastic, sir. So I followed him about all day at a distance, sir, and he was coming up this way."

"Thank you, son. Thank you. Now tell me, which road."

"The one along the creek."

"How far behind you?"

"I got out ahead of him once I saw where he was headed. I knew it would be for you, sir, on account of your house and all."

"Nathaniel, calm down son and listen to me. How far behind you?"

"He's probably headed up the big hill right now, General sir."

"That's five minutes, or less even."

"Yes, sir, that's why I'm like this, sir. How can I be of service? Take your horses into the woods? Pull a wagon of your things down the road? Shoot the sonofabitch? What can I do?"

The General reached out and grabbed the boy by the shoulders. He locked his deep-set, pale brown eyes with the terrified eyes of the young boy. Nathaniel stood nearly half a foot taller than the General and outweighed him easily. Even still, the General soothed and calmed the scared boy.

"No, son. You have done more than should ever have been asked of you. You get out of here now son, as fast as you can. They find you here they will hang you, do you understand? Ride your horse straight behind the house. There is a path. It leads down to the creek. This horse of yours can clear it easy. Lead her back up the hill 'til you find a wider path at the top. Turn right and ride 'til you find the other road to town. You know the one?"

"Yes, sir."

"Good. Don't go anywhere near the Cartledge Creek Road. If they see you, they will assume you are up to no good. Now, go."

The General shut the door and watched the boy wheel the horse around the house as he was told.

"Miss Anna, go wake Solomon and get the livestock." He turned to look at her but she was gone. He ran down the hall to the back door of the house. Solomon and several of the other slaves were already leading the livestock into the courtyard formed by the back wings of the Brick House. He nodded with approval as he moved between the black figures in the dark courtyard, all working with quiet efficiency. He exited the courtyard and ran on aging knees under the oak trees toward the stables. The ground below was solid black. He bounded over the knots and twists of oak roots that rose up from the ground here and

SAM MCGEE

there. He could not see them, but felt them with his feet as he hastened to the barn. He pitchforked hay into a large cart, and with no animal to pull it, pulled it himself back across the uneven ground, a shot of pain radiating down his back each time a wheel rolled unwillingly over a root. Soon several animals and enough hay to keep them occupied were hidden in the courtyard. The General let the cart drop with all its weight the second he cleared the gate. He pulled the high, dark doors of the courtyard behind him and latched them shut. Everyone else in town was hiding horses in the woods. If his men could keep the livestock quiet, the Yankees might walk right by them. Sweating and sore, he re-entered through the back door and headed back to the foyer. His uninvited guests would be there any second.

Jim

Water was everywhere. While Jim and Ben focused on the spectacle in the low land south of the pond, the water had begun climbing up the hill to the north as well. First it had filled the Mess Halls and the Cook House, then the first row of barracks. They sat and watched as long as they could. Trickles and streams still entered from above. The real push, though, came from below. The old, bald prisoner eased back step by step, ever faithful to his self-appointed task of recording the high-water mark. When finally he stood in the walkway directly in front of the spot, Jim and Ben rose and headed for their barracks.

Inside the men were crammed tight around the tiny windows. The view was only of the next barracks, and the scared, sunken faces of other boys looking back at them. Water passed under and around the adjacent building. The space between the buildings filled rapidly. Every few moments a prisoner or guard would pass between the buildings, the men in the windows marking the depth on their legs as they passed. Splashes around brogans, followed by wakes trailing behind ankles, then knees, then no more men passed by at all. Silently each man picked a landmark of some type on the wall of the opposite building. The edge of a plank, a scar or smudge on the wall, anything that could benchmark the rising tide. Jim focused on a deep, diagonal scar a foot long in one of the planks. Within minutes half of it was concealed, then all of it, then Jim struggled to remember what it had looked like. He chose another benchmark higher, then another, inching toward the high window full of familiar faces.

Startled voices began again in the building. Ben grabbed Jim's shoulder and pointed toward the door. Water was rifling white and bubbling under the door and into the barracks. A flat sheet of brown water rolled across the floor in tiny waves. The men on the bunks turned their eyes from the window and picked new benchmarks inside the barracks walls. Jim looked back over his shoulder to the window on the other side. No faces looked back.

Alfred

The saber of the lead horse clanged rhythmically against a canteen as it came down the lane between the oaks. The cavalry approached single file, spreading its horsemen over a longer distance, increasing its apparent size. The lead horse rode right to the front step of the Brick House porch. The horses behind bent their course alternatively, one left, one right, and so on until a long line of horsemen stood shoulder to shoulder across the front yard.

A nervous young officer with a carefully manicured beard, positioned himself to left of the lead horse, a torch held above in his right hand. Beside him, the lead horsemen leaned over and spat on the ground. The officer from the incident at Falling Creek. The one that had smirked viciously at Alfred before the mill went up in flames. He had the same mealy appearance as before, only worse for having spent the intervening hours around the smoke and soot of his handiwork.

"General Kilpatrick, sir."

"Yes. *General* Dockery."

"You know of me, sir?"

"Indeed, I do."

"Then how may I be of service, sir? Do your men or horses need anything?"

"How may you be of service? Well, let me think about that. How may *you* be of service to *me*?" He smirked his now familiar smirk and looked from left to right, searching for the approval of his men. "You can exit your home. Unless of course you choose to burn in it."

"General, sir. If you know of me, you must know that I opposed this war from the start. That I opposed secession in the General Assembly. That even to this day my son Oliver and I have advocated for peace."

"You speak of the Confederate Colonel Dockery as a reason your house should be spared?"

"This is my home, sir. It is of no military significance. Take what you must, but spare us our home."

"General Wheeler was here, was he not?"

"He was."

"He had his headquarters here?"

"He did."

"From here he staged a raid and killed a couple of dozen of our boys over by town."

"I believe that to be true."

"You've had six sons fighting for the South."

"One dead. Two returned home. One prisoner. Two remain in the field."

"In this house you quarter Rebel troops who stage raids on my cavalry. The plans for this raid were likely made upon your table. In this house you raise Rebels who invade the North." He was speechifying now. Raising his hands to his men for emphasis, gesturing sarcastically at the fine home. "This house, General, is most certainly a place of military significance."

He pulled back on the reins and his horse reared its feet high in the air and neighed desperately as its rider raised his hat above his head.

"Set fire to the house!"

A cheer sounded out from the backs of two dozen horses. The men dismounted and began forming torches as General Dockery had seen them do at Falling Creek. By now they were experienced and efficient arsonists. Within moments torches were burning on the front lawn. Flashes of the light from the scattered flames being carried to and fro caught the smirking face of Kilpatrick, whose joy was in no manner constrained.

Alfred turned to Sally and Miss Anna, who were watching from the shadows. His face was stern but calm, at least when they could see it.

"Exit quickly through the warming kitchen. Warn the men to move the animals back away from the house. They will not harm us. If I can find it there is something that may stop them."

He walked briskly behind them down the hallway. As they turned left through the warming kitchen, he upped his pace and darted into the study. He crawled over the pine floor, rifling through the wooden boxes in search of the letter. He was proud of the letter, had always kept it close at hand, but was afraid of what would have become of it in the hands of the General Wheeler. As he searched the third and final box, he heard glass shatter. Grabbing the last papers in the box he jumped to his feet and burst through the door between the study and the parlor. Through the windows flames swirled and wild voices shouted. On the floor was a smoldering torch burning amongst the shards of glass.

Jim

All of the men in Barracks twenty-four were crammed onto the top bunks. The bottom two levels were completely submerged. Twelve men were wedged onto the bunk where Jim and Ben normally slept alongside the Virginia boys. Each man was folded up tight, sharp knees and elbows pressed up to one another. Jim was pressed against the wall by the knothole. There was little talk. Boys seated in windows reported anything significant they could see that the others could not. A boat or raft passing by. The extent of the rain. Any breaks in the gray sky. Others mumbled prayers to themselves. No one moved. They were packed too tight.

The distance between the top bunk and the ceiling had never seemed so small. For the first time since the previous summer, Jim was hot. It seemed like only hours ago he awaited a frozen death. Then, instantly, he was suffocating on the hot recycled air trapped in the shrinking space between the water below and the wood above.

The rain finally stopped. Though this gave the men great hope, the water continued to rise. All that had been dropped into the river and onto the camp had yet to finish entering the stockade, climbing the hill and slithering into the barracks.

Jim twisted awkwardly and looked out the knothole behind him. Two freed slaves were struggling to keep a raft tight against the adjacent barracks. The glass of the nearest window was pulsing outward as if being hit from within. Suddenly a broken piece of wood busted through the glass. The end of the broken timber swung violently back and forth clearing shards of glass from the window. One of the freed slaves threw one end of a rope into the window. It lay slack on the water for a second, then pulled tight. The raft now firm against the barracks wall, men began climbing out. The first two men boarded without incident, but the third slid off the side and into the water. He held tight to the side until the others could pull him back on board. Once four prisoners were atop the raft, it began to lay low in the water. The men on board said something to those inside, then shouted. The rope remained tight, and more men tried to board the sinking raft. A tug of war ensued until one of the freed slaves produced a knife and cut the rope, sending the raft drifting rapidly away. One desperate prisoner slid out of the window and gave chase momentarily, but soon gave up. He paddled himself back to the barracks, where he pulled his feet onto the bottom of the open window and tried to climb on top of the building. He struggled to find a handhold, sliding back down on his belly into the water below.

Jim turned to face Ben. Ben's bony, round face was bright red. Beads of sweat lined his forehead and dripped from his long beard.

"What do you see out there, cousin?"

"It doesn't look good. They're starting to crack up out there. There's a fellow trying to get on top of the building. Doesn't look like he can make it."

"This ain't how it's gonna happen, cousin. I've been bombed for days by a hundred ships, stood for hours with nothing between me and the whole Yankee army but a few wooden poles and a pile of sand, seen my entire fort explode a mile high, suffered for days on a slave ship and survived a New York winter with no food and clothes. The Lord didn't get me through all of that just to drown me."

Alfred

General Dockery grabbed the torch from the floor before it caught the rug on fire. He fanned out the few pieces of correspondence on the floor with a shaking right hand. A voice poured in from the broken window.

"Get the hell out of there, Dockery. This house is burning with you or without you."

Another window shattered and the General looked up to see another torch bouncing across the floor in his direction. He stood and threw the torch in his hand back out of the window. Then turned and grabbed the other torch from the floor. The rug was catching and he stomped at it quickly. As he did he spotted the letter amongst the other correspondence on the rug. He grabbed it and bounded out the door into the frenzied Yankees, letter in one hand, torch in the other.

"General Kilpatrick! Stop!" The Yankee cavalry stopped and looked at General Dockery with laughing eyes. "If you don't look at this letter you'll be stripped of your commission long before you get to Richmond."

Kilpatrick stared at Dockery for a brief moment. The hesitation was but momentary. He turned and yelled to his men, "What the hell are you looking at? Follow my goddamned order!"

As the men recommenced their action, General Dockery grabbed the reins of the young, bearded officer's horse. The officer drew his pistol and aimed it squarely between General Dockery's eyes. Dockery firmed up his feet shoulder-width, and raised his head slightly to improve the pistol's intended path. The officer's child-like face quivered behind the pistol in his outstretched hand.

"Son. Read the damn letter or you'll be court-martialed with him."

The General heard another window break behind him. His instincts begged him to turn in the direction of the noise, but his eyes never left those of the young man before him. He calmly held out the letter and tried to still his shaking hand. The man sheathed his pistol and snatched the letter from Dockery. A thud sounded at the General's feet. Startled, he looked down to see yet another torch in the grass a few feet away. He turned back to the house and saw Solomon standing in the broken window, face calm as stone. Three other slave men stood behind him.

"General Kilpatrick, sir," one of the men called, torch in hand as he stood by the shattered windows. "There are slaves guarding the house. What do you want us to do with them?"

"Shoot the bastards! At least in death they'll be free."

"Wait!" It was the bearded officer. He rode to Kilpatrick, arm outstretched, holding the letter.

"What the hell is this nonsense? Give me that!" He snatched the letter angrily and held it open as the young officer tilted his torch above to give him light. Dockery's heart pounded in his chest. The rest of him was frozen. His eyes fixed on the flames of the young officer's torch. A charred piece of rag dangled loosely, decorated by red lines that ate at the fabric in all directions. The red lines approached one another near the thin thread that prevented the clump of burning fabric from falling upon the letter as Kilpatrick read aloud.

"This man is my friend. Do his house no harm. Yours sincerely and respectfully, Abraham Lincoln."

The handwriting was unmistakable, as was the look on Kilpatrick's face.

Jim

Jim eased himself down from the third bunk onto the muddied floor of the barracks. A fat carp lay dying on a second level bunk. The bloated, brown fish puffed its gills open and shut, but no water passed through them. Its oversized scales began to get a sticky, dry look. The round eye of the fish rolled slightly in Jim's direction.

He stared blankly at the fish that stared back at him. He relived the scene hours earlier as the water had lapped at the base of the third bunk, high enough he could feel water seeping through the boards below.

"Water's falling, boys! Water's falling!"

It had been one of the boys on another bunk pushed up against a window. Other boys in windows began to answer him.

"I can see that knothole I lost sight of a bit a go."

"It's back to halfway down the plank that got covered up last!'

Jim had looked back out of the knothole. The water trickled out of the broken window again, down onto the water outside just an inch below. Indeed, the water was finally falling.

Now, hours later, standing safe and staring at the dying fish, Jim heard Ben climb down, and knew his cousin was at his side. Ben stepped over the bunk, scooped up the struggling carp and headed for the door. The cousins stepped out of the door into the water. Six inches of water still stood around Barracks twenty-four, but with the mud below each man bogged up mid-calve. Unable to stand another moment trapped in the barracks, men from all over the camp ventured out to survey the damage.

As they walked the water deepened. Muddy prisoners and guards walked slowly throughout the camp. Several freed slaves led by a well-dressed townsman hustled down the hill toward the pond, carrying several long pieces of lumber with them. Jim pulled his foot heavily from the mud below to make another step in his walk to nowhere in particular. When he put it back down it landed awkwardly on something firmer than the mud and shaped strangely. He immediately knew what it was. Nearby were three black gentlemen. Two were pushing wheel barrows. In each was a muddied body. The third gentlemen was older, quieter. Jim motioned to him and the man walked over toward him.

"I think there's one below my foot."

The black gentleman waded over to Jim, who kept his foot still. The other man stood shoulder to shoulder with Jim, picked his foot up and put it beside Jim's.

"Yessir. You found one alright. Pratt! Got one over here."

A large man with a wheelbarrow turned and made his way in their direction.

The older man put one hand on Jim's shoulder and looked him in the eye. "Thank you, Mr. Dockery, sir. And I am glad to see you looking better than the last time I seen you."

Jim looked back at him. Confused.

A few feet away Ben was on his knees in a deep puddle of water that seemed to connect to all of the other puddles and channels that covered the grounds. He held the fish by the tail with his right hand, and cradled its belly with the left. The fish turned slowly onto its side, then jerked its head desperately. It began to sway slowly back and forth, righting itself slightly. Ben worked the fish forward and backward, passing water through its flaring gills. The fish straightened and began to twist with more purpose. Ben patiently held it in place, watching its strength return. At last, the fish kicked its way from the bony hand and moved several feet away. It slowed and appeared to turn on its side again, then gave a fierce kick and darted below, sending tube shaped patterns spiraling through the water in either direction.

Then Jim remembered. That morning. When he was blind and hungry. The closest he had come to death within these walls. He turned quickly toward the three black men, speaking as he turned, "Thank you for the …" But the men had already disappeared between the barracks.

Huge stagnant puddles lay at low spots here and there. Little streams crisscrossed one another in seemingly random directions that eventually converged and headed back down to Foster's Pond. Near the path in the middle of camp, a current steadily drew water downward toward the pond under the wall and back into the river concealed on the other side. There were ripples in the currents created by invisible features of the ground below. The same scars and ruts that channeled the cold melting ice slowly downward in their weaving search for lower ground, now altered the flow and appearance of the faster, warmer water engaged in the same search.

Jim wondered at the hypothetical path of a single drop. Drifting weightless through the white sky, well above and outside the prison walls below, guided without care by wind and gravity before lighting gently on the Earth below. Becoming part of a fresh, white pile, momentarily covering the ugliness of its unfortunate landing spot. Being shoved roughly to a heap along the path, then freezing tight and heavy into a graying dirty pile. Covered over and again with white with each falling snow, only to turn gray and hard again under pressure of unrelenting winter. Releasing itself from the pack as the ice broke, sliding eagerly down the gray pyramid and gliding across the ground, combining with other drops making the same journey. Trickling roughly over and between the uneven features of land to the pond, then rising brown and warmer back up the hill through a doorjamb and into the prisoners' quarters, resting on their hard bunks, until feeling the pull, always the pull of a billion more drops bound to act together. Letting go and squeezing back through the door, twirling and spinning through a dozen currents back to the path, passing the point where it had lain on a mound, then back down to the pond again. The pull coaxing it backwards though the pond, under the wall of the stockade and into the river. Catching the current of the mighty river and charging away from the prison walls never to enter them again. One day to feel the pull of the sun, to rise again to its home in the clouds.

Alfred

The young boy on horseback appeared at the doorstep again.

"General, sir. I am happy to see your home standing, sir."

"And I am happy to see you alive, Nathaniel. Is there something I can do for you?"

"No, sir." He hesitated momentarily, and shuddered as if he was about to turn and look at his canteens. The hesitation left his face and he straightened his back. "No, sir. I'm quite well, sir. I just came to tell you of Kilpatrick's movement toward Fayetteville, sir."

The General nodded his head at Miss Anna, who as always stayed by the door when any guest was near. She smiled and proceeded to take down the boy's canteens and disappeared to go fill them.

"Thank you, sir. I really didn't mean to trouble you, sir."

"Don't worry about that young man. We may have little else left, but water we have. Now come down off of there and rest for a moment and tell me what you have to say."

"Much obliged, sir. I won't be long. I just thought you might want to hear about ol' Kilpatrick's shirttail skedaddle down near Monroe's Crossroads."

"His what?"

The General motioned toward two rocking chairs along the porch. Beneath the windows busted out by torches days earlier. Despite his intentional formality, the young man broke into a childish grin, and began.

"When they headed out of here, I knew there wouldn't be no more action in these parts. I, well several of us from the local militia decided to ride with Wade Hampton's cavalry. Just wanting a little more of a taste of the war while it was still happening. Hoping to give back to Kilpatrick some of what he give to us.

"It was early one morning, just before the dawn. The early risers were stirring about a bit, but most of the Yankees was still sound asleep. It looked like a few cooks had something going early. By now we knew they was headed toward Fayetteville or thereabouts, so they'd want to cover about as much ground as they could. There was this thick fog laying around their camp, and we stayed back in the trees. No way they could see us that shade of morning and not even really awake at that.

"Hampton had us at the ready, waiting for the right moment. Well, I seen this tiny fellow walking to a sort of high spot there in the camp all alone. I wondered what he was doing, 'til I saw the little bit of light there was glint against something shiny in his hands. A bugle. Hampton must've seen it too, because right about the moment that little fellow pulled his horn up to his lips to play the reveille, our bugler started blasting out the charge. We let out a Rebel yell so loud I bet not a soul heard that little fellow bugling himself half to death.

"You should've seen them flying out of those tents and mounting horses, riding this way and that, as long as it was away from us. Balls started flying pretty crazy in all directions. We were halfway around them in a half-circle firing from different sides, and they was riding in a dozen directions and firing in a dozen more.

"We rode down past this house where some horses were tied up. A few balls must've hit that house and scared the fella inside because he let out of there like his hind end was on fire. He flew out the front door like he done been shot out of a cannon. He was a scrawny little nothing too. He went sprinting down the little slope there in front of the house and was just about the most pathetic sight I ever did see. His stringy little head of hair was bouncing up and down over his bald scalp as he ran. He wasn't wearing a thing but his drawers and nightshirt more fit for a little girl than a man. It wasn't 'til he turned to the side and I saw those sideburns that looked like pinecones fastened to the side of his jaws that I realized it was General Kil-Cavalry himself. We never did catch him, but I do say we got a great deal of satisfaction watching his scrawny little chicken legs sticking out of that girly nightshirt, making like a bat out of hell.

"If that wasn't enough, he had run so fast he forgot to take his woman with him. Marie Boozer was her name, from down about Columbia, South Carolina. They say she was the most beautiful girl from South Carolina, and I don't doubt it. Recall if you ever saw her, General?"

"Indeed I did, son. I doubt any man with blood in him has ever laid eyes on Miss Boozer and managed to forget it. Carry on."

"Well, sir, I reckon she would have been safe up there in that little house, but she didn't think so. Once Kilpatrick got away, the balls were flying pretty good, so some of us hunkered down in this little ditch there. We could see her leaning out of the window of that house talking to one of our boys on horseback. He waved her back in the house and she disappeared back into the window. I guess all those balls rattling against the rooftop got the better of her, though, because the next thing we know she busted out the front door just like her man had done and was running right for us in her unmentionables. I prayed with my eyes open in that instant, because I couldn't stand to lose sight of her with my eyes closed. What I prayed for was for that fog to lift so I could get a better look. There was more of her there to see than I've seen of anything anywhere. The Lord must've been listening because she ended up hunkered down in that ditch right next to me. She was all folded up right there so close I could've have reached out and touched her if I dared. There wasn't half a yard of fabric on her, and what was there was all lace and straps and seemed to point things out more than to cover them up. I got right dizzy for a minute and sort of forgot there was a battle going on.

"I never saw such garments in my life, sir, nor did I know such things even existed. And if you beg my pardon for saying so, sir, the fact that such a thing exists gives me great hope about what my future may hold for me in my adulthood."

Twenty-Six

Ben Covington
April 9, 1865
Elmira, NY

The rumors had been rampant for days. But then again, they always had been. Some days the South was about to win. Other days the North. But lately it had seemed different. Knowledge of the inevitable had set in. Not from any one rumor, or one seemingly credible source from the front lines. It was more intangible. More gradual. The prisoners of the cause slowly came to know that it was lost.

Jim and Ben sat alone again. Silent. Nothing left to say. No energy to say it. Then something changed. An explosion outside the prison gates. Then another. A flash of light. All across the camp the prisoners froze in place and looked to the sky. The sounds brought Ben's mind back to the bombproofs of Fort Fisher. The shelling he endured. The death he narrowly escaped. But his mind didn't stay there for long. The sound was different somehow. Less ominous. His thoughts returned gradually to the present.

Beyond the observation towers fireworks appeared. Great bursts of light, followed shortly by blasts of sound. Then came more. Between the bursts were the yelps of Yankee guards and townspeople. Shouts of unbridled celebration.

So it must be true. Lee really has surrendered. The war is finally over.

He looked at Jim, whose face showed neither smile nor frown. Just the same expression he had worn for days. But the eyes were different. Tried to say something to Ben. A flicker of life flashed through them for just a moment. Something appeared that had been forgotten a long time ago.

That's right, Jim. That's right. We may well die, but we won't die in here. There is hope for us yet.

Alfred Dockery
April, 1865
Rockingham, NC

General Dockery stood at the top of the steep hill on the Cartledge Creek Road. Just across from the spot where Solomon and Anna sat to hold hands on full moon nights. It commanded the same view. The road sweeping down into the valley, with the fork to the right that headed north into the trees. Back to the south, a vast field spread out on the plateau. Yet another field to be planted with no slaves to plant it. By no means his best field, but by no means his worst. Several eager black faces looked up at him, waiting.

"Any one of you that wants to stay is welcome to stay. You will be treated as free men, which is what you are. However many of you stay, I'll divide this land up amongst you. Give you a mule and a plow. It will be your own land. You can keep what you farm here, but I'll need you to work on the other fields as well. I will …"

He stopped abruptly. A wagon was coming along the road. Alfred walked through the crowd before him and waited by the roadside. Solomon was at the reins once more. Dressed again in formal attire. Smiling broadly in the spring sun. Anna sat beside him. Her hair was released from its perpetual bun and hung in braids well below her shoulders. The wrinkles about her eyes were diminished somehow.

"Solomon. Anna. Please stay. I meant everything I said. I need you. Miss Sally needs you. We can build you a house on a prime spot."

"No, sir. We have to be going. There's just things we've got to do."

"Miss Anna, can you not convince him to reconsider?"

"No, sir. Can't do that. But we thank you again for the wagon, sir, and may God bless your family."

Solomon worked the reins and the wagon eased forward. Alfred stood and watched as they headed steadily down the back side of the hill toward the valley below. The General was oblivious now to the audience behind him awaiting the details of his plan for their future. The wagon picked up speed down the steep hill, but suddenly slowed to a stop in the middle of the valley. It sat still for what seemed a long time. Hope crept in. Perhaps they had reconsidered his offer. But then the wagon turned to the north onto the untraveled fork, and disappeared into the forest forever.

Benjamin Dockery

It had rained two days earlier. The ground was dry but the creek still ran hard and high. There was a rare violence to its movement and sound as it passed by.

Benjamin Dockery and Betty Covington lie on a quilt a few feet away. Off to the side was a basket holding their half-eaten lunch. Two pairs of shoes and Benjamin's hat were scattered around the basket. Benjamin was fully reclined on his back with another quilt balled up for a pillow under his head. Betty clung to him from the side, her head snuggled into his chest. Just enough sun came down through the tall pines, lighting the pale green of the saplings and bringing out the color of the wildflowers along the creek bank. He felt the sun on his face, and studied again the delicate line of her neck and shoulders where they rose from her dress. There was no other place on Earth. No other person on Earth. No trouble on Earth.

"Tell me about the dress."

"Tell you about the dress! You know I can't do that."

"Oh, come on. Just tell me a little."

"You'll see it when I come down the aisle. You'll absolutely love it."

Benjamin said nothing, but his bride-to-be could read his smirk.

"I see that look on your face. You'll love the dress and then you won't be able to wait to get me out of it."

"Can't dispute any of that. But can't you just tell me a little more."

"OK, fine. Just a little. McKay got the fabric from a blockade runner. Daddy gave me some Irish lace 'from better days' as he put it. And I have been working on it ever since. You'll have to help me get up the stairs of the Brick House in it, because I plan to toss my bouquet off the balcony and watch all the girls clamor for it."

Benjamin turned his head and kissed her on the cheek. He loved to see her face light up when she talked about the wedding. Loved the thought that he – despite all his failings – could make her that happy.

"And what happens then, Betty? After the wedding is over and the bouquet is thrown. What happens then?"

She propped herself up on her elbow and looked down at him playfully.

"Just listen at you. If your mother could hear the way you talk, Benjamin Dockery. Anyway, I'm quite certain you can figure that part out when the time comes."

She leaned in and kissed him again, then snuggled her head back into his chest. Benjamin lie there listening to the creek rush by, feeling Betty's warmth against him, and dreaming about days to come.

Henry Dockery
and Thomas Dockery

Young Henry Dockery sat alone in the woods. He told his father he was going hunting. The General had just nodded and said nothing. Truthfully Henry didn't even bring ammunition. He just sat on a stump in the dark of the valley along the dry run creek bed with the unloaded rifle in his lap. He had been the youngest to play war in the woods behind the Brick House. Always fought the hardest to prove he belonged. The most extreme in his pursuit of imagined enemies. By the time he was big enough to participate meaningfully, some of the older boys had moved on to real world pursuits. The games were never the same without them. Then they all went to war and left him behind. Now the war was over and he was never to join them. For decades to come he would be asked if he had fought. What would he say now?

Meanwhile in the western theater, Henry's oldest brother Thomas sat alone as well. Dreading a hero's reception any time in his future. Whether from colleagues in business who kept starched collars and clean hands throughout the war, deacons in the church who would ask him to lend his supposedly heroic leadership to the Lord, or broken men in bars offering to buy a round for a valiant, wounded warrior. The war was lost. Any heroism was not enough. His brother John was dead. And for what? If there was any job he had as a leader of men, it was to protect his younger brother, to see him through to the end of the war.

This war has been a failure, and I have let my mother down.

Jim Dockery
June 12, 1865
Elmira, NY

There was a large group gathered by the prison's main gate. It was June and most of the men were already gone. Many had taken the oath and left for home. Others refused, or were too sick to go. The death toll had not slowed in the weeks since the war had ended. Those too sick to travel would continue to die prisoner's deaths long after their release dates had come and gone.

It was Jim and Ben's day. They stood in a pathetic group facing a row of officers. Each prisoner raised his right hand, and swore what each had refused to swear upon arrival at Elmira. "To henceforth faithfully support and defend the Constitution of the United States …"

A short fellow mumbled the oath next to Jim. Tears streamed down his face as he talked. There was a film over his right eye, as if disease had taken its sight. The blind right eye wept even harder than the left.

" … so help me God."

With those final words, the oath was completed. The half-blind fellow collapsed to his knees and sobbed.

"So help me God. Yes, help me God. Forgive me, God! Forgive me, ol' Virginia!"

The large gates slowly creaked open and the men began to crowd forward anxiously. Jim and Ben each took one of the man's shoulders and lifted him to his feet. He leaned in close and looked up at Jim, who tried not to focus on the grotesque sight of the useless eye. It looked back at him. It moved as if it could see, but there was no focus.

"I lied, boys. I lied to God. Spit on their damned Constitution, boys! Spit on it! Shit on it for all I care!"

Ben put an arm around the man's shoulder and looked into the good eye.

"Don't worry, my friend. The Lord knows the fix you're in. He doesn't want you to die in here. He wants you home with your family."

"The Lord don't stand for no lying, boys. Piss on their Yankee flag."

"He don't stand for no dying over words when you got a family that needs you either, friend. You hold your head up high."

"Piss on you too then. I rebuke you in the name of Jesus Christ."

With that he hobbled quickly through the moving crowd, bumping into half of the men trying to make their way out the gates. Holding his head close up to many of them, trying to see them. To measure their piety with his one good eye.

"Jim, did you ever think we'd really say those words? I mean, not just say them, but swear to God that we meant them?"

"Right now, I'd swear I was headed home to marry a goat if it would get me out of this place."

"Well, me too, I reckon. But I guess I never imagined I would really do that."

"Ben, there isn't much I've seen in the last couple of years that I ever imagined. And I don't care to see much of it again, either. But I am imagining some things. I am imagining a table full of supper with food for miles and family members all around. Laying down in Cartledge Creek and letting the clean water wash over me. I imagine riding a horse with a girl on the back and riding so far I might not be able to find my way home. I'm imagining home, and I'm imagining being free. And I bet a lot of other folks are imagining the same thing."

"Well ... let's get going then."

The group slowly moved through the gate. Each man took baby steps, pushing up as far as he could into the creeping mob ahead. Jim felt a great weight with each step as he neared the gate, like wading through deep water. As if some invisible force was prolonging his stay. He stopped directly in the massive wooden gateway. Stood still for a moment. Focusing on the ground ahead. Then stepped forward, never looking back.

Twenty-Seven

Jim Dockery
June, 1865
Somewhere South of Mason/Dixon

"I'm so sorry, Jim. I'd walk more if I could. You know that don't you?
That I'd walk more if I could?"

Ben Covington was sitting on the ground in the pine straw along
the road. Jim stood on the road, looking down at his cousin. What
little muscle remained in his legs twitched with spasms somewhere
beneath his loose-hanging pants.

"I'm tired too, Ben. But if I sat down I don't think I could get back
up again. I think my legs would just seize up on me."

Ben looked up and smiled a desperate smile. Jim smiled back, then
looked up to the treetops. The pine trees were tall on either side of the
road. The sun was high in the sky and cut down between the gap in the
trees to the road. Jim stood sweating by the road listening to the sound
of the locusts as it opened and shut. It was strange to be hot again after

freezing for months. In Elmira it seemed heat would never again be a problem.

"Just hang in there, Ben. There's a house just off the road up here a ways. Maybe if we're lucky we can get a meal, maybe even a place to sleep."

"How you know there's a house?"

"I saw smoke over the tree tops a few minutes ago. I can't see it now because we're too close. Trees are blocking me. But I saw it. I figure somebody must be cooking up their dinner. Thought I smelled it too, but there's no wind at all to bring it this way."

Ben twisted himself around on the ground until he was up on his knees. He pushed his walking stick firm into the ground and held a bent arm up towards his cousin. Jim grabbed the arm at the elbow and stabilized Ben as he pushed himself up onto his feet.

"If there's a full stewpot up around that next bend, I'd rather get a spoon in it sooner than later."

The two men, each barely twenty years of age, hobbled through the dust with their walking sticks toward the distant smell of smoke.

* * *

The little, white house sat in a clearing amongst the pines. It was one-story and there were two windows on the front, each framed by dark green shutters. A swing hung down from the ceiling of the front porch. Two rockers sat on the opposite side. A large yellow dog emerged from under the porch and dutifully barked at the two strangers. His official duties completed, he then trotted straight up to them and rubbed against Ben's withered legs. He panted heavily in the summer heat and raised a paw for Ben to grab.

There was a huge stump sawed off smooth in the yard to the right of the house. A tall, powerful man was splitting logs with great force and precision. Beside the stump were two piles. On one side were freshly cut, round sections of tree trunk. On the other were wedges of cleanly quartered logs. The man placed a log up on the stump and drove the axe head well into the wood. He raised the axe again, the entire log coming with it, then drove the axe and the log down onto the stump, sending an even half of log tumbling in either direction. In seconds he stood up each half and split them with one powerful, swing. He tossed the log quarters into the pile and turned to face his unexpected guests.

Ben was sitting on the ground again, the large, golden mutt licking him in the face.

"Some guard dog I got there, ain't it?"

He was a large man. His gray hair was a bit long, but neat. A broad chest and shoulders rose from his comparably narrower waist. The power in the shoulders defied the age shown by his hands and eyes. His face was red and cheerful, but showed signs of age and long days at work in the sun.

Ben was too busy laughing and playing with the dog to answer. Jim nodded at his host, and smiled back at him.

"Well, sir, he certainly makes for a fine welcoming committee."

For a moment no one spoke. Jim looked down at his traveling companion, unsure of what to say next.

"I bet you boys could use a good meal and a place to lay your head for the night."

"Yes, sir. I … I was trying to figure out how to ask, sir."

"I understand, son. You ain't no beggar. I can see that. I can hear it in the way you talk. But times are what they are. The missus was just about to call me in any minute. I'd be happy to share what we've got with you. It ain't much, but you're welcome to it."

"I am very grateful, Mr. …"

"Vance. My name is Carter Vance. Call me Carter. We're not too formal around here."

"I'm Jim, sir, and this is my cousin Ben. We're on our way home from the war."

Ben pushed himself up to his feet again. As he did, the dog began to whine slightly. Ben reached one hand out to shake with Carter, still petting the dog with the other.

"Nice to meet you, sir. We are much obliged to you." There was a weakness in his voice. Both men were exhausted and starved, but Ben gave the appearance of a man on his last leg.

"Least I could do for two fellas been up there fighting for ol'

Virginia. Come on in."

The three men stepped into the front door and gathered around a table in the room on the right-hand side of the house. The table was pine and rough around the edges. There were 8 chairs and a buffet made from matching wood. Three places were already set.

Carter's wife came into the room with a large pot of stew and ladled generous portions into the bowls before the three men. She too was tall and striking. Her long, gray hair hung straight down past her shoulders halfway down her back. It was not pulled up in any proper fashion of the day. Her eyes themselves seemed almost silver, mirroring the color of her hair. Though her skin wore the toughness of a pioneer's life, the lines of her face were smooth. There were almost no wrinkles in her face, save for the crow's feet that appeared momentarily around her eyes when she smiled politely at her company. Despite her age, Jim found her very beautiful. She was like a Greek Goddess exiled from Olympus and left to a hard, self-reliant life.

"Esther, would you make sure none of our daughters are around. Looks to me like Jim here may be hungry for more than food."

Jim blushed, as did Esther. Jim looked at Carter and was happy to see his good-natured smile. Even Ben looked up from his stew long enough to smile and laugh. Esther shook her head as she left the room.

"Don't worry about it, young Jim. A man with a pretty wife sees the look in other men's eyes. When you're young, you want to crack the jaw of every young buck that makes eyes at your girl. Older you get the more you learn to get flattered instead of mad. Besides, I'm guessing you boys ain't seen many ladies wherever you been."

"No sir. We haven't. And I do apologize … and you are right to be flattered."

"Not true though?"

"What do you mean, Ben?"

Ben looked up from his stew. His eyes showed a gleam they hadn't for days. The warm meal was making him giddy.

"You see, Carter sir, I didn't see any ladies at the prison, but Jim here did."

"Oh is that right, is he the ladies' man of this outfit?'

"Yessir, I suppose he is. Comes from a family of them. One of his brothers has probably married my big sister by now."

"Well, how 'bout you, Ben? Are you a ladies' man, too?"

"Oh, no sir. I always just worked and prayed and fished. They never paid me much mind. But Jim here, they even come to him in his dreams. Outside the prison walls they built these towers. Town folks could give a nickel and look down on us from their perch wearing their fancy clothes and sipping on drinks."

Jim felt his face warm up and knew he was blushing again. Esther re-entered the room from the door behind Jim, and stood beside him with a pensive look on her face. Ben smiled as he told his story, but Esther and Carter listened with great seriousness.

"They shut down the towers long before I got there. But Jim here, he still saw this one pretty girl up there all the time. He'd get wore out, or cold or starving and sit there by the campfire at the spot looking up at that tower. When he'd fade a bit she would appear to him from the tower."

Carter nodded at Esther. She disappeared back through the door.

"She would have on a formal yellow dress and long, curly brown hair. She would look down at him across all those other boys in the yard and whisper words just to him. And he could hear it too, even though she was way up there on top of that tower. What was it she would say to you Jim?"

Jim looked down at the ground and said nothing. A voice came from behind him at the door.

"Home is waiting, and death can wait."

In one motion Jim sprung from the chair and turned to the door behind him. There in the doorway was Cap.

* * *

The three soldiers sat in the moonlight on the front porch. A dark blue, starless sky faded into the tops of the tall pines that framed the clearing where the house stood. The smell of pipe smoke lingered on the porch. No wind came along to blow it away.

Cap and Jim sat on the front steps of the house, talking. Ben sat silently behind them, puffing casually on one of Carter's pipes. The big yellow mutt was lying on his feet. Cap towered over Jim, not just because of his height. Months at home had restored him to his former self. It was almost unbelievable to Jim. His powerful arms and legs had come back to him. His sandy hair, once withered, had returned. The broad forehead and rugged jawbone. All of it. The strength, the power, the confidence. He was even bigger and stronger than the day he saved Mac from the dog hunt. But his eyes were different. Though the confidence seemed to have returned, there was pain that lingered. The face and body were young again, but the eyes betrayed the sorrowful wisdom of age. Even still he was not defeated. And as they spoke Jim looked beyond an inevitable soldier's death to a life that had slowly escaped him.

"You haven't asked me about Mac."

"Don't have to."

"I feel like I have to tell you. It's laid there on my heart all these months. Like a sin. A betrayal, really. I betrayed my best friend. My brother."

"I said you don't have to. I told you that day that he might help you survive that place."

"But you couldn't have meant ..."

"Naw, I suppose I didn't. But somewhere down in there I knew. Once I got home and the months passed and my head cleared, I knew it for sure. I told Robert's mom about it. The day she got the letter he had died. I told her what you did to try to save her only son."

"But how did you know? I could have kept him all for myself."

"Not you. I know you better than that. My brother was dead. You probably figured me for dead same as the Yankees did when they sent me out of there. I knew you would try to save my childhood friend."

"I tried everything I could. The rats were long gone, you knew that. I gave him part of my rations for weeks. If he hadn't have died when he did ..."

"I know. Let's not talk about it anymore. Of course, I have noticed that my new dog warmed up to your cousin there instead of you."

With that, Cap flashed an unlikely smile. Jim's face softened, but he did not smile back. He knew what Cap was doing. Somehow Jim was still unsatisfied. Still haunted by what he had done. But the victim of his crime was releasing him, and all he could do was to accept it, and change the subject.

"Mighty fine stew your mama made us tonight."

"You have no idea what meat was in it, do you?"

"Not a clue."

Ben started laughing. He had been so quiet Jim had almost forgotten he was there. A pale bit of color had come back to his face since they arrived. Jim didn't know if it was more on account of the stew or the affection of the mutt. For the first time since dinner, Ben spoke.

"You'll have to forgive my rich cousin. He's probably never eaten coon before."

"Well, he's gonna be eating more of it. Mama is fixing you up a basket with some bread and meat. There might even be a few grapes and blackberries. The berries are good but it's way early for the grapes. They'll be sour as hell."

"We'll be happy with whatever we can get."

"Robert taught me to trap coons when we were boys. Sometimes it's about the only meat you can get around here. Speaking of Robert, it's time we get going to bed. I'm sleeping over at his house tonight so you fellas can have a place to sleep. Jim, you take my bed, and Ben, you and your new best friend take Hig's. It's still a long way to Rockingham and you boys need a good night's rest."

* * *

Breakfast was scrambled eggs and biscuits with blackberry jam. When the biscuits came out they were so hot Jim had to bounce his from hand to hand for a few seconds until it cooled. He was so hungry again it never occurred to him to drop it onto his plate. He opened it up and spread a large pat of butter on the bottom half. It instantly melted and spread down through the flaky biscuit. He spread a generous portion of the jam on the biscuit as well. There were large chunks of fresh blackberries covered with the syrupy base of the jam. It was the first time he had tasted sugar or butter in over a year. The flavors took him back to a time when food was a pleasure, not just a necessity. He broke off chunks of biscuit and let them linger in his mouth, mourning the moment each bite came to an end.

Esther came into the room with a basket stuffed with food. Jim watched her every move despite an effort not to. She smiled and shook her head before disappearing back through the door. Carter, Ben and Cap were all seated around the table quietly eating. The yellow dog was lying at Ben's feet again. Carter leaned back in his chair and tilted his head to look under the table. He smiled at the dog, then grew serious.

"Ben, I wish I could give you some shoes. I can see the ones you've got there are about plumb gone. Truth is we just gave away the only spares we had to some boys like y'all that passed through a couple of weeks ago. I'm afraid a couple of day's food is about all we can spare."

"Don't worry about that, sir. You've been awful good to us. I'm just happy to be alive, with a full belly and a good night's sleep. Before we came up on this place I thought I was about done for."

"Well son, you might feel that way again before you get home, but you just remember how little it took to get you back on your feet."

"Don't worry about them, pop. After what they've seen, if there was any quit in them they'd a been dead by now. Ain't nothing gonna stop these two. I'm not sure they're even men. They're some other kind of creature."

Cap and Jim traded a knowing smile. The men finished their breakfast and headed out onto the porch. The sun was barely up but it was already hot.

At the edge of the woods was a woman. She was short and round, with a chubby, red face and terribly shy eyes. Her head was wrapped in a rag and she held a small basket in her hands. Cap took a few paces ahead of the group to speak with her. Jim and Ben followed behind. Carter stayed at the base of the front steps. The mutt leaned slightly against Ben's legs as they walked, looking up with sad eyes.

"Jim, I've got somebody here that wants to meet you."

The woman stepped forward with hesitation. Her lips moved twice as if about to speak, but no words came. Jim could see she suffered from a disabling shyness. She looked down at the dog at Ben's feet and fidgeted with the handle of the basket. Cap placed his hand on her shoulder and she smiled and finally began to speak. She looked directly into Jim's eyes as she spoke. Her voice, though high-pitched and stuttering, still held conviction.

"Cap told me what you done for my boy, Robert. Giving him your food. Eating … things you didn't want to eat. He told me you almost died trying to save Robert."

Her voice shook more as she spoke. The eyes grew glassy but no tears fell.

"I don't have nothing to give you except for this pie I made from the blackberries. I bet you ain't had no pie in a while. I … I don't know what else to say to you but God Bless you."

She half-stepped toward Jim, then paused and looked at Cap. He nodded, and took the basket from her hands. Suddenly she fell forward against Jim's chest and squeezed her arms around him tightly. His spindly legs nearly gave way, but he shuffled his feet to remain standing. She lingered there for some time. Cap took a step back and turned his head down and to the side. Robert's mother released Jim, and looked at him one more time with her tiny back eyes.

"God Bless you."

She turned and skittered off without another word. Cap shook hands with Ben. As he turned to Jim, Ben knelt down and whispered in the dog's ear. Cap reached out to shake hands with Jim, his enormous hand engulfing Jim's. He squeezed the hand firmly for a few seconds without speaking, then handed Jim the basket.

"I don't want you boys to go, but you've got to, so you might as well go on."

Jim looked around the modest but well-kept place.

"This is the kind of place you can get used to. Nice place. Fine family."

"It's home. It's what matters most. That's what I've learned. But you've got a home, too. So get the hell out of here. Homes awaitin' and you can't wait no longer to get there."

Twenty-Eight

Ben Covington
July, 1865
Virginia

Ben felt the pebble in the bottom of his shoe. It would take too much energy to stop, remove the shoe, dump the rock and put the shoe back on again. He walked on, hoping the tiny rock would nestle into some spot within the shoe where it wouldn't hurt him anymore. He kept walking. Still felt it. Twisted his foot about in the shoe to help the rock find a more harmless hiding place. Nothing worked. The pebble seemed to change shape and size. Then it felt as if there were more than one. Perhaps several. And now in both shoes. With each step there was new pain, new annoyance. He stopped and sat in the road to look at his feet. The bottoms of the shoes were almost completely gone. Much of the bottoms of his feet were landing unprotected on the road with each step. He was not feeling one pebble. He was feeling thousands.

The bottoms of his feet were wrecked. Thick yellow corns that ached with each step. Blisters. Dried blood. He sat by the road with a foot in his hand, staring in amazement. Jim's voice was beside him. The words were unclear. They seemed distant and muffled. He looked up to see Jim. All he saw was the sun. He became aware of the heat. The glare bore down on him and he felt himself melting in his clothes. He turned his eyes down away from the glare. Jim's feet were in the road beside Ben, but above was only the heat and the sun and the distant, muffled voice.

Ben was up and walking again. There was no shade. No water. The muffled voice and a vague presence at his left. From the road rose wavy lines of heat. Tiny patches of blurred air where the sky itself seemed to melt. The lines rose from hot spots in and around the road. They expanded and spread and came together and enveloped him as he walked. He felt them rise over him and surround him. Soon there were no trees, no road, no presence, no awareness. Just the haze that was left when heat took all else. But still he walked. Blindly into the haze.

Then something felt different. There was no road. No resistance. No steps to take. It seemed he was no longer touching the ground. Suspended in air. Falling.

Suddenly he was surrounded again. Not the haze this time. Not the heat. A cold rush. No breath. Falling still but now with resistance. Drifting into darkness. A darkness everywhere except for one fading glow. A light up above and out of reach. There was an impact beside him. A tingling rush against his face. Invisible arms embraced him. The light came closer. Awareness began to return. The eyes began to focus. The light exploded into view. A deep gasp of air into his lungs. Jim had him around the chest. Dragging him to a grassy bank. Above was a bridge along the hot and dusty road. Below a deep, slow-moving creek.

Jim

Jim walked back down to the black water creek. Already soaked, he waded right back out into the water without hesitation. He stepped gingerly until he found steady ground between the slippery rocks. Spread his legs shoulder-width and turned his feet from side to side, digging them down into the gravel and sand below. The legs quivered in the current, but he was dug in and remained standing.

The cool of the water soothed his sunburned skin and aching legs. A slow steady current brought new water always brushing against him, relaxing his tense muscles. *Why in the world have I not jumped in every creek we've seen? I'm almost glad the poor sonofabitch fell in.*

With the relief, the current brought memories. Brothers and cousins splashing in Cartledge Creek back home. Swinging from vines and letting go. The fear of the rocks below buried by the fear of teasing brothers. Falling safely into the deep pool where the fish hid in the summertime. Emerging from the pool refreshed and relieved. Taking a deep breath and daring another boy to take the plunge. Sitting along the banks with Ben Covington, dreaming of glorious days soon to come on heroic fields of fire. A picnic on a quilt along the bank with a bright-eyed girl from church. The desire to move in closer to her, to pull her to him, trembling and uncertain, with the sounds of singing birds and the rolling creek behind them.

Thoughts of the creek back home turned his eyes to the cut bank on the deeper side of the river. The water was a foot short of its high-water banks, marked by the red clay that cut up under the bases of small trees that grew from ledges that hung out over the water. It was summer and the catfish would be bedding. They burrowed holes much as hermit-like land mammals, laying their eggs in well-hidden beds safe from rush of the river and the appetites of predators. Back home Jim had learned to fish grab, reaching his arms blindly into holes and under rocks or ledges, as likely to find a snake or snapping turtle as dinner.

He tiptoed along the deeper side of the creek, bouncing to keep his head above water and feeling the clay bank for a catfish hole. He turned and looked back to Ben, sitting on the shallow bank with his feet in the water, cupping his hands and drinking from the creek. He still looked dazed, but was making slow progress toward reality. Water would help. But he needed food. The baskets had been empty for days, and had been left on the steps of a house where no one answered the door.

About knee-high Jim's hand found a round hole a foot in diameter. He took a deep breath and lowered his head down near the opening. His hands braced against rocks on the bottom to keep him still in the rolling current. His legs rose behind him, trailing downstream. With a kick he righted himself and kept his ear near the hole. Just as his air was giving out, he heard it. A thump. More like a distant bass drum. The telltale sound of a mama catfish flopping her wide tail in her hidden bed. He rose to the surface, but kept his hand at the opening. In the current and under the black water, he could have lost it easily and struggled to find it again.

Taking another deep breath, Jim lowered himself back down to the hole. He eased his right arm through the opening. The tail drummed again, this time with urgency. Jim pressed as much of his body as he could against the hole, trying to prevent any route of escape. If there was more than one exit, there would be nothing he could do. Even with only one, he had seen fat catfish slide right through his arms, even up into the air to avoid capture. When trapped, however, they would fight.

There was a stillness in the hole. Was she gone? Was she studying the curious invader? Jim worked his fingers like a pianist. Something brushed against them. A whisker dragged across his index finger. He worked the fingers again. Nothing. His lungs were giving out. He knew if he rose the fish would seize the opportunity and dart from the hole. He snorted out from his nose. No air came. A helpless emptiness filled him. He had to rise. Soon. Then a pain ripped across his fingers. The fish clamped down mid-way across the entire hand. Jim bent fingers down into the soft tissue of the fish's mouth. Tucked in beneath the hard, semi-circle of the gaping mouth, they held firmly. His thumb — his only free finger — was buried into the same soft tissue from the outside. The catfish worked its tremendous tail and pulled backwards deeper into the hole. Jim pulled back with his little remaining strength. His feet found rocks beneath him to serve as anchors for leverage. Still the fish would not come. He pulled his right foot from the rocks below and braced it against the clay wall beneath the surface. With one final push he shot himself off the clay wall and the fish followed.

He kicked himself to the surface and gasped for breath, then sunk back into the deep pool into which Ben had fallen from the bridge. The fish flailed beneath the surface. It seemed to move its body in all directions at once. Before it could wrench itself free, Jim blindly felt for the mouth with the left hand, then forced all but his thumb in for a better grip. At the same time, he was kicking himself across the creek and into shallower water. Soon his feet found the creek bottom and dug into the gravel below. He stood in water almost chest deep. Eight fingers lined the inside bottom lip of the fish, with both thumbs tucked tightly under the outside. The fish hung in the water below working its tail gently in the current. Resting. Jim knew what came next. He backed himself toward the bank gingerly. As he got to a depth where the fish would rise above the surface, he dug his fingers in deeper. In one motion, he swung the monster catfish out of the water. She rested no longer. The tail whipped about wildly, smacking Jim on both sides. The whipping action of the fish loosened his grip, which threatened to give way. Jim stumbled backwards rapidly falling onto his back on the bank. As he fell the catfish came loose and for a moment appeared headed back into the creek for good. He threw out his hands in futility as he fell backwards away from the fish. She kicked her tail as she flew through the air, then landed heavily right in Ben's lap. Ben instinctively grabbed her by both pectoral spines before she could roll and bury one into him. There sat Ben on the riverbank, soaking wet with a catfish in his lap as long as his leg. He looked bewildered at Jim, who was lying on his back on the bank, laughing.

"Well, cousin," Jim said, "Dinner is served."

Twenty-Nine

Jim Dockery
July, 1865
North Carolina

Jim and Ben camped in the grass along the road. They had made no fire. It was hot even in the night and there was nothing to cook. They didn't scout off the road for a hidden campsite. Just lay down right by the road itself. The woods were black dark with short, scrubby trees. Above them a sky showing layers of stars rarely seen. Jim's favorite kind of night. When he felt closest to God. A feeling elusive to him.

He was too excited to sleep. The air was familiar. The humidity, and scent of pine. The sandiness of the ground. The long leaf pines that went on for miles. The color of the creeks where they drank and splashed water on their faces when their legs couldn't move anymore. The embrace of familiarity, the intangible feeling of proximity to those things that mattered most, a feeling ever so faint on the battlefields of Virginia and Pennsylvania, completely absent in the Elmira prison camp of upstate New York. A feeling growing now with every step. They were almost home.

He knew life would not be the same. The plantation would be different. The family's level of wealth. Of importance. The transition from war to peace would not be easy. The North would not allow it. There would be a price to be paid. Somehow, though, it would all be fine. With his father. With Oliver. Somehow they would lead the charge, regain prominence in the new unknown world that lie ahead.

However it went, however difficult, it would still be home. The Brick House would be there to greet him, its walls of solid brick a fortress impenetrable by the troubles outside. It had survived the war. It still stood, and waited for him. And his father would be there. His mother Sally with quiet love and comfort. The General with his undeniable strength. For the first time Jim thought his father would see his strength reflected back in his son, who had fought so hard and survived so much. There would still be dinners at the long table in the dining room, candlelight reflected in the mirrors hung on each wall. Even if there was less on the table, his family would still be around it. There would always be honest work to do, horses to ride, walks to take through the dark woods leading to the swimming hole, cool grass to lie in and stare up at the stars as he was doing now. Perhaps some of the servants would stay, though free. Solomon. Miss Anna. They would be sorely missed if they went. But to Jim, if not all of the others, a shadow would be gone. A weight he had carried, knowing the splendor of his young life had been built in large part upon injustice to others. He thought of the freed slave Leonidas Jackson, driving the wagon, picking up the dead bodies within the Elmira stockade. Guiding Jim home. Giving him food. Granting him compassion, even life, despite who and what Jim was. He thought of what he had said to the old gentleman about slavery. It was the only time in his life he had ever said it aloud. He had thought it often, but pushed it down. Was even ashamed of it as a youngster, fearing he was somehow casting judgment on his own family. Jackson's simple of act of compassion had brought it out of him. An honesty possible only when stripped bare.

Perhaps his father would give him land of his own. A place to start for himself. Always nearby, always within reach of family, but still his own man. There would still be Sundays at Cartledge Creek Baptist, dinners on the grounds with pretty girls ready to treat him as a returning hero, fishing and hunting trips with his brothers, all within a short walk.

And no war. No constant threat of sudden death. No starvation. No need to measure his dwindling frame, to fight strangers for the meat of rats, or to fear every growl of the stomach or headache as the approach of deadly disease. No frigid air filling his lungs as the night's fire failed, no painful and exhausting travel with no place to sleep each night. But home. Not as a distant dream he no longer believed would be, but as a true and present reality. Never to venture far again. Home.

He debated whether to tell Ben how close they were. Whether his cousin would be better or worse off knowing that tomorrow was the day they would see home and family again. Should he preserve the surprise? What a moment it would be to see the flicker of recognition in Ben's eyes. The eyes that had been dead for days. Recognizing nothing. Seeing nothing. Revealing no feeling. Getting Ben home was as important as Jim getting home himself. Ben's arrival in Elmira had saved him. He owed him his life, and on this walk he had been dedicated to repay the debt.

Or would the knowledge that home was so close provide Ben with strength for the final leg of the trip? Would it lift his spirits, fuel his legs and awaken his eyes? Perhaps. But the flood of emotion that would come, to someone as weakened as Ben, could stop him in his tracks, so close to home. Could backfire. What an awful failure that would be. One Jim himself might not survive.

Jim's eyelids grew heavy. The day's walk. The lack of food. Even the act of thinking exhausted him. He fought the eyelids for a moment. Still deciding whether to tell Ben. Sleep came quickly. The decision would wait until morning.

Ben

Ben inhaled a shallow breath, slowly. His dried lips were stuck together, but a narrow stream of breath forced its way between them. He sat silent. Motionless. Something seemed wrong again. A strange fullness in his chest. His face felt wide and warm, then began to tingle. The stars blurred in the night sky. Suddenly his mouth snapped open, gasping in a deep breath as if emerging from the river again. The empty feeling returned. The coolness. Smallness. The stars returned to focus. His body was forgetting to breathe on its own. Functions were shutting down. Had been for some time. He had known it. Only didn't know when it would be over. Had thought on so many occasions his body was finished. This time seemed different. Felt different. He was surprised it had taken this long.

He lay beside Jim, focusing on his breath. Inhaling and exhaling voluntarily. Ben had things he wanted to think about. Several minutes passed and his breath seemed fine. He let his body take over and tried to focus. Wanted to reflect. To pray. To make his peace with God. As soon as he tried to think his eyelids grew heavy. Long days of walking in the hot sun. Restless sleep on an empty stomach. He clinched his teeth and fought to keep his eyes open. Even tried to hold them open with his fingers. A losing battle. Soon he was asleep.

Then another gasp. Another deep breath. For a moment he was confused. The face was tingling again. But he was awake, for the moment. Very much awake. Now he feared sleep. The body had forgotten to breathe, at least until the last possible second. Perhaps it would not always remember. Perhaps in sleep even the gasping, life-saving breath would be forgotten. Perhaps the body knew it was time to let go. It was not death he feared. It was death without a final prayer, a sort of self-imposed last rites. Despite these last months, he wanted to give thanks. For his home and family, for God's grace. He wanted to pray for the family that he would leave behind, that would be left to struggle with the prolonged and inhumane manner of his death. He wanted to pray for safe passage for Jim. Finally, he wanted to ask for God's guidance: Should he tell Jim? His cousin knew he was weak. Certainly, he knew Ben might not make it, but just as certainly he did not know that Ben already knew. That this was the night. That he had taken his last step toward Rockingham, and tonight would take the final step to his true home. That this was his last day on Earth.

Ben worked it all through in his mind, punctuating his thoughts with reminders to his body to breathe. His thoughts were broken, disorganized, but with effort he got through each prayer. In the end he decided not to tell Jim. After all they had survived, he knew his cousin would try to save him. That he would fight to keep him alive another day. Giving him his food. Carrying him if he could. Jim's acts of heroism would be to his own detriment. No, it was better for Jim that he not know in advance. He would wake up in the morning and find Ben lying cold beside him. He would mourn him. Find a good spot along the road somewhere to bury him perhaps. It would be but a momentary distraction from his journey. Jim would be smart enough to know that he had no time to waste, that his own body might give out if he gave it time. He got lost on the tangent of the burial. *What type of spot will Jim choose? Near the water maybe? Doesn't matter really. I know where my true home is. But I like the idea of a nice place anyway. A peaceful place.* Then it occurred to him. He had no idea where he was. What state even. Hadn't known for some time now. Jim still spoke to him a lot on the trail. Ben heard little. Understood less. Said almost nothing. Every once in a while he muttered some nonsense just to see if he could still speak. But he had little left to say. Just placed one foot in front of the other. A million times over. He had no sense of their course. Trusted Jim for that. At least as long as he thought it possible that he might get all the way home. Then came a point where it didn't really matter anymore. When he walked just to walk. To be with Jim. To play out the script until the end.

The eyelids grew heavy, the breaths shallow. He stopped his intentional breathing a couple of times to see what would happen. Nothing. The heat in the face came back. The wideness. The tingling. He gasped intentionally, not trusting his body would do so in time. *Not much time now. Need to do this. Final prayer. Don't need to speak it. Just think it. He can hear you.*

Dear Lord. Thank you for this life. It was short, some of it hard, but it was more than I deserved. A lot seems undone. My heart hurts a bit for that. I'm sorry for feeling that way. Forgive me for feeling cheated. I know you have given me so much. But every man wants to live his dreams. Thank you for the days I have had. Help me focus on those, not the ones I didn't get to live. Thank you for everything. Fish in the creek, sun on my back, food on the table. Strong family. Friends. Help my family get over losing me. Bless my sister Betty and Benjamin Dockery. A fine man. A good pair. Help Jim find what they have. He's stronger than anyone I've ever known or seen. Seen so much. Survived so much. So tough. Thanks for your grace. Your guidance. For helping me understand not to tell Jim. Guide him home, Lord. Forgive me the sins still in my heart. Take me in even if I am sinning in my final thoughts. I am so sorry, God. I am so sorry I am crying. I am so sorry I am sad. I know you understand. I can't wait to walk with You. But it is so hard to go. There is so much beauty here. In spite of everything. So much to live for. So much beauty. I want to stay, Lord. I am so sorry but I want to stay. What? Yes. That's right. That's right isn't it. Jesus wept. In the garden. Yes, before they killed him. Jesus wept too. Yes, thank you for that, Dear Lord.

The breathing stopped again. No more air against chapped lips. The raw sting of the lips went away. The aching of the joints was gone. The emptiness of the stomach. The clouds that cloaked clear thoughts. Even the tingle that came when breath failed. All the worldly pains lifted like a fog giving way to the day. Ben was motionless, thoughtless. He did not move, but was elsewhere. Walking freely and happily across an open field, toward a creek running clear below a sprawling oak.

Thirty

Jim
The Next Morning

Jim woke up alongside Ben. Got up quietly so as not to wake him. Knew he would need the extra sleep. It was going to be a big day.

The sun was already up and it was hot. His ragged clothes were soaked with sweat. He pulled himself up onto a rock and pulled on his brogans. Ben's head was turned away but Jim could see his mouth hanging open. There was no sound. No movement.

A jack rabbit came hopping through the roadside camp in a hurry. Taking long leaps. Panicked. He blew right between Jim and Ben, crossed the path rapidly then disappeared into the thicket on the other side.

In a few seconds an old hound came through. Sniffing the ground and zigzagging along the path of the jack rabbit up ahead of him. The hound didn't look up until it got directly between Jim and Ben. It raised its head and cowered down, startled to see the two men. Had been so intent on the hunt that he hadn't noticed them at all.

The hound looked sad-eyed at Jim. Seemed to forget the rabbit. Had found something else to hold his interest. The tail began to wag. He stepped over to Ben and studied him. Then flopped down on the ground beside him and laid his head on Ben's belly. Snuggled in tight with him. Eyes open, still looking at Jim. Ben did not move.

After a moment the dog snuggled up farther onto Ben's chest, stretched his neck out and licked Ben right in the face. Gave an expectant whine, and licked him again. Ben still didn't move. Jim studied the round, bearded face more carefully. The gaping mouth. The hound looked curiously at Ben as well, seeming perplexed that he did not move. Man and dog looked at Ben for a long while. Waiting for something, anything, to happen.

Not now, cousin. Not this close to home.

Ben's arm reached up feebly and hugged the dog. Patted him on the head. Suddenly his body jolted a bit, and he sat up sharply. The dog didn't startle, but curled up into Ben's lap. Ben looked over at Jim. Wild-eyed. Pale. Seemed in shock. Jim took him for having been awakened from a strange dream. Lost for a moment, finding himself another morning in a strange location.

"Anything wrong there, cousin?"

Ben stared back for a few seconds. Still shaking off the cobwebs.

"No, Jim. I'm alright, I guess. Surprised to be alive, maybe."

"Yeah, I know what you mean. I feel the same way about every morning."

There was a rustle in the thicket across the road. The hound snapped to attention, licked Ben on the face one more time for good measure, then tore off in the direction of the sound.

Jim was on his feet now and anxious to go. There was no breakfast to be had. No clean water nearby. But he knew home was on the horizon. He paced around the camp, waiting impatiently.

"What do you say there, Ben? Feel like taking a little walk this morning?"

Ben smiled.

"Can't imagine anything I'd rather do, cousin."

Ben

Ben was truly shocked to be alive. After everything, he had truly resigned himself to death. Believed his time had come. Closed his eyes and never expected to open them. To see this world again. Mourned the loss of this life, but wondered what the next would bring. What the experience of heaven would hold in store. How it would compare to his dreams.

But here he was. His eyes had opened to another day. His thoughts were still muddled. Disorganized. Jim's voice still blended with the outdoor sounds around them as background noise. He still struggled to observe what they passed along the road. The scenery as it changed. The road as it should have grown familiar. Yet there was more energy in his steps. More motivation to continue. To get home. To live. *Thank you, Lord, for another day.*

Again he found a rhythm that made forward progress possible. Just one step after the other. No matter the pain. The road grew hilly. There was a massive climb under the hot sun. Each step seemed to travel straight up, his arms pushing off on his knees with each stride to find the energy to climb one more foot. Doubt crept into this heart. Doubt that he could summit the hill. Still he pressed onward, as he had so many times before. *I can do all things through Christ who strengthens me.*

The hill finally leveled and his strength returned. The steps came more easily. The pain numbed. His speed increased. He felt wind at his back and lengthened his strides. But something seemed different. Missing. Jim's voice was gone. No longer beside him.

Ben stopped, and turned around. Jim had stopped along the road, and was looking at his cousin. Seemed to be speaking to him. Calling his name. Ben looked at his own feet. The brogans reduced to small leather flaps partially covering the tops of his feet. Nothing underneath to protect him from the road. He looked at Jim and struggled to hear his words. *Does Jim need help? Have I missed a turn in the road? I cannot give back steps. Cannot walk backwards from where I have come.* He tried to focus. Could see Jim standing under oak limbs, the world around him lost in a blur in the tunnel that remained of Ben's vision.

Against his every instinct that told him to keep moving forward, he turned toward Jim and retraced his steps. As he grew closer he saw that his cousin was smiling. Not the slight, wry smile he often wore when he found something ironic or funny. A smile of pure joy. Ben stopped and looked around. The sandy soil. The longleaf pines. The path to Jim's right, flanked on each side by towering oaks. The slight dip in the path, before it rose and circled a massive brick house. He looked back at Jim, who was smiling even bigger than before.

"Home?"

"Yes, Ben. We've made it. We're home."

Ben stared at his cousin in disbelief. Tried to think of the right thing to say. Some way to express his gratitude. For helping him through their time at Elmira. Being his guide on the long walk home. Saving him from drowning when he fell in the river. Scavenging for food when starvation was imminent. Instead, it was Jim who spoke first.

"Thank you, Ben. I never would have made it without you. That day you arrived I was hanging by a thread. If you didn't show up that day ... well, thank you, Ben."

"*You* ... are thanking *me*?"

"Of course I am."

"No, Jim. No. That's not right. It is *I* who should be thanking *you*."

"Nonsense, Ben. I couldn't have ever helped you if you hadn't saved me first. So don't thank me, thank yourself. And thank everybody else that saved me along the way. A little child soldier named Willy. A beautiful nurse who made me feel human again. Cap, Hig and Robert. Cap's mom and dad. Even an old freed slave who gave me a biscuit when I was freezing and blind and lost my way."

Ben stood before Jim. Trying again to search for the words. But they would not come.

"I'll see you at the swimming hole, Jim."

"See you at the swimming hole, Ben."

Ben turned back away. Began walking again. His awareness of his surroundings was sharper now. The fork in the road that would take him behind the church, across the creek and up one last hill to his home. Just a few more moments of focus on the road ahead.

It was strange to walk alone. Even for a short distance. He missed the murmur of Jim's voice that had become the background for his travels. Even when his mind had left him and he could not comprehend the words. A call came from behind. He couldn't make it out at first. But there was a call, and the call was meant for him. He stopped and listened. Someone was calling his name.

Jim

Jim had known where he was all day. Every stone seemed familiar. Every blade of grass. This was his territory. Where he had hiked and hunted and ridden his entire life. A few more steps and he was home.

He watched as Ben hobbled away, then turned to walk down the path to the Brick House. His legs stalled. They quivered beneath him and he felt as though he would fall to the ground. He leaned against a tree and looked at the spindly legs as they shook under the rags of his torn pants. Waited for the tremor to pass. Unable to move one step farther. The journey was fighting back, resisting its own end. He looked at the big front door of the Brick House. Gritted his teeth and began to walk toward it again.

The door flew open and two women raced out into the sun. They sprinted across the grass and down the path between the oaks. Each clutched their formal gowns where they bloused out at the waist to keep from tripping over them as they ran. One wore pale blue, the other pink. Both dresses flowing over furious legs. They ran with a purpose Jim had rarely seen. Like the child soldier Willy Crane rushing to gather troops for a charge. Like the ill-fated prisoner running on failing legs from the Dead House, desperately seeking to exit the Helmira gate with his brother. Dust rose behind them in a trailing plume as when Jim and his brothers rode the countryside recruiting soldiers for the Brave Richmond Boys. Two men appeared in the doorway behind them. They shielded their eyes from the sun with their hands, giving the appearance of a soldier's salute. The larger, older man grabbed the younger by the shoulders, shook him, and seemed to tell him something. Then both men joined the charge down the path in Jim's direction.

Jim stepped into the middle of the path and stopped. Watching and waiting as they approached. In the front was his mother, Sally. Dust had collected around the bottom of the long, blue dress. Her hair had pulled down from its careful bun and hung wildly about her shoulders. Her face was flush red. Both tears and beads of sweat ran down her cheeks. She embraced her son in the shade of the oak above. His frail legs gave away and mother and child fell to the sandy ground.

"My son is home! Praise God, my son is home!"

Jim lie on the ground in his mother's arms. He looked up over her shoulder and saw the smiling faces of his father, Alfred, and his brother, Benjamin. Both sweating in the summer heat. Both with reddened eyes. Looking down at Jim in disbelief. Betty Covington appeared from behind the men in her pink dress. Looking as beautiful as she always had, despite the frantic run across the field and through the dirt. She crouched down beside Jim and looked him in the eyes. Her eyes lacked the joy of those around her. Instead there was panic.

"Where is brother Ben? Did he come with you, Jim? Is he alive, Jim?"

"Miss Betty, he has just left me. There, by the fork in the road."

Betty Covington

Betty jumped to her feet and ran toward the fork. Feeling the roughness of the road beneath her bare feet. The heat of the summer day on her shoulders. Screaming her brother's name at the top of her lungs.

"Ben! Ben!"

There he was in the distance. The broken picture of an old man, limping with a cane along the sunbaked path in clothes that swallowed his diminished frame. Continuing forward, ever so slowly, not turning to acknowledge her voice.

"Ben! Ben!"

Finally he stopped. Stood frozen for a moment, then turned with aching difficulty. And there he was. The round, cherubic face burned badly with the sun. His long beard hanging stiff in the stagnant air. He was barely recognizable, but she knew in there somewhere was her brother Ben.

His brow furled, and his eyes looked at her as if he had seen a ghost. Then the face relaxed, and something of a smile came across the cracked lips. The cane fell from his side and he stepped forward toward her. The legs faltered, and he fell to his knees. Ben sat beside the roadside, seemingly unable to move, smiling and reaching his arms out toward his sister.

Soon she stood above him. Saw the bloodied bare feet beneath the ragged remains of shoes. The swollen knees protruding from torn pants. The unimaginable thinness of his arms, legs and face. She cried both from shock and joy. Knelt beside him and leaned gently into his outstretched arms.

Jim Dockery
August, 1865

It was a wagon wheel sound. Rhythmic. Plodding. Like the slow rolling wagon of Leonidas Jackson, collecting bodies for the Dead House every morning. Jim felt the stiffness in his limbs. Tried to move them. Could not. Heard voices above him on the wagon. Sounds from outside as well. The buzz of activity. Hammers coming down on wood and sending little echoes bouncing off unseen structures. He didn't know where he was or where he was going. Tried to retreat into the dream of home that had been his just moments ago. Then it occurred to him. This was Jackson's wagon after all. The walk, the arrival home, had all been the conjured imaginings of a broken mind. It was his day to be taken to the Dead House. Boxed up and taken to some out-of-the-way cemetery reserved for unheralded Rebels. But he was thinking ... so he was not dead. He tried to call out, but could no more shout than move. The wagon jolted to a stop. Something crashed down beside him from above. *Another body? No, something else.* He pushed the heavy object to the side. It was a sack of grain.

He sat up and looked around. The wagon was stuffed full of enough supplies to start a new town. He looked at his arms and legs. The clothes on them were new. He was still skinny but some meat had begun to return to his bones. Slowly sleep's fog lifted and it all came back to him.

The feast on the day of his arrival had been immense. All of his

North Carolina siblings had attended, their families in tow. Ben was propped up in a chair in the shade, his sister Betty feeding him bites of pumpkin pie while freedmen played music in the background. Sally stuck tight to Jim's side for hours, constantly pushing him to eat more and more. One more plate of pork and green beans. One more fried chicken thigh. Just another bite of cornbread. His brothers came to him one by one, congratulating him on his service, and his survival. Oliver and Benjamin told him that he was the true war hero of the Dockery family. Henry sat by his side and asked questions by the dozen, wanting to hear every detail of Jim's war experience. Young Alfred had only beat Jim home by a few weeks. Having been Oliver's constant shadow for years, Young Alfred now stuck close to Jim, his brother-in-arms, who had stuck with the cause long after Oliver and Benjamin had come home. General Dockery traveled from group to group, ever the gracious host. Making all feel welcome. When he looked at Jim, though, something seemed to trouble him. It was only in the cool of the evening, after the crowd had thinned and Sally busied herself with the cleanup, that he revealed what was on his mind.

Alfred came and sat beside Jim at the long table that had been set up in the backyard for the occasion. Pulled a chair up close to him and looked soberly into his eyes.

"Jim. I am afraid I have failed you. There is not much left for you here, son. I will do everything I can, but the plantation is gone. We don't have the hands to farm all of this land, and the prices are so poor for what we grow that it cannot support us all."

Alfred's normally booming voice quivered. As he spoke a single tear escaped from his left eye and ran down his face. He did not wipe it away. It was the first time Jim had ever seen his father cry.

"Your brother Thomas is doing well in Mississippi. We cannot just be farmers anymore. It is the traders that make all the profit. I have a wagon train headed to Mississippi tomorrow morning, son, and I suggest you be on it. I wish you could stay here, son. And I wish I could wait to send you. But I don't know when we will send such a train again that can give you safe passage."

The wagons had been lined up down the path between the oaks at four o'clock the next morning. Sally was inconsolable. She had fallen to the ground after hugging Jim goodbye, and refused Alfred when he offered her a hand. As the wagons pulled down the lane and turned onto the road, she was still in the dirt, sobbing.

The other travelers treated Jim well. An older black lady was assigned as his personal nurse. Tended to his bloodied feet. Fed him double portions of meals three times each day. As he had seen with Cap in Virginia, he saw himself returning to the man he once was.

He crawled across the wagon floor and peeked outside. The oppressive Deep South heat met his face and poured into the wagon. He lowered himself slowly from the wagon and studied the frontier town around him. Heat and dust rose from the streets. A yellow cloud hung low in the air, kicked up by the constant activity in the town square. Young boys climbed across the roof of a new building, hammers in their hands. There was a massive wooden platform with a stack of cotton to the sky. Smartly dressed men studied the cotton, and scribbled in little ledgers in their hands. Leather-faced characters drifted in and out of the drinking establishments clustered together in the growing town. Most were unpainted structures knocked together from wood that hadn't yet lost its color. The men moving about the place had pistols in their belts.

Someone was walking straight for Jim. He was tall with a hard but kind face, and a long beard. His clothes were simple, but seemed new. As he drew closer Jim could see his smile. It was his eldest brother, Major Thomas Dockery. Thomas was laughing by the time he reached Jim. He threw his arms around his younger brother and squeezed him. Jim felt that one arm squeezed him tight, while the other had little power to squeeze. The injury leading a doomed charge from the beginning of the war would never fully heal.

"Welcome to Mississippi, brother."

"I'm so glad to see you, Thomas. I have truly missed you."

Still being squeezed by his brother, Jim noticed something across the square. Something very much out of place. Amongst the cotton traders, the builders and the roughnecks, under the ever-present dust cloud above, were three ladies in formal dresses. The mother was in a long white dress with thin black stripes. She was lecturing one of her daughters, somewhat sternly it seemed. The two girls each wore pastels so as not to wither under the relentless heat. The first, the apparent object of her mother's scorn, wore pale green, with a matching parasol held over her head of jet-black hair. There was no denying she was beautiful, but it was her sister that caught Jim's eye.

Her dress was long, yellow, drawn tight to the waist and then allowed to flow to the ground below. The beautiful brown hair did not wilt under the sun, but hung in perfect ringlets between her shoulder blades. There was a life in her eyes that cut through the dust and traveled across the square to Jim. She wore a slight smile, despite her mother's apparent excitement, and held one delicate hand on the shoulder of her sister, as if to protect her from the reprimand she was being made to suffer. She became distracted for a moment, and turned in Jim's direction. He caught her eye, and her smile expanded, ever so slightly.

"So, brother, how was the wagon ride?"

"Thomas, pardon me for just one moment."

Jim slapped his brother on the back, and walked directly toward the woman in yellow.

Judgment

He sat in a chair and watched all the black faces move around him. All were scrubbed clean for the occasion, dressed in their finest homemade clothes. Big plates weighed down heavy with fried chicken, chicken and dumplings, mashed potatoes and gravy. Slices of pies and cakes piled on the side of the same plates. A few folks sat under the shade on the front stoop of the new church. Most were scattered about the grounds in the heat. Long swallows of cold, ice tea fighting off the heat bearing down from above.

It was the first dinner on the grounds of Holly Grove Missionary Baptist Church, the new black church just across the creek and up the hill from the white church. It was strange to sit amongst them on such a day. To see their looks. To wonder what they thought when they saw him. All but the youngest children had once been owned by him. Bound to him. Subject to his rule. Had he been a good master? Could such a thing be?

Did they hate him? But many had stayed. Had accepted the land and a mule offered with their freedom. Did any of them appreciate him? After all, their new church had been built at his direction, and his expense. Did he do this because he cared for them? Did he do it from guilt?

He had become an old man since the war. Had turned frail. His hair thinned and flat. Command of every room was no longer his. His former slaves moved around him now as if he was not even there.

He saw her in the sparse shade cast by the new church sign. Sitting on a quilt he recognized. It was one his main house servant had made sitting in the house one winter during the war. Her face was still striking, but older. The features still sharp, the hair still cut close to her perfectly shaped head. As always, she wore a dress. She knelt on the quilt and ate, the dress climbing up her thighs slightly. They were larger now, less muscular than in days past. But still they called to him. She reached out with a napkin and wiped the mouth of a teenaged boy, who instantly frowned and wiped the mouth himself. He was a large boy, thick through the shoulders. His skin lacked the jet-black tone of his mother's. His hair was light brown, and brushed back over each ear. The boy looked directly back at the old man. His eyes were deep-set and pensive. The man smiled slightly at the child, who did not smile back. He just continued looking back at the old man with purpose.

The man thought back to the boy's mother picking cotton in the field. The allure of her cabin he had been powerless to resist. The tiny inlets of light that shone between the cracks in the cabin wall on afternoons when he would come to her there. Alfred Dockery turned his eyes from his bastard son, looked to the ground, and wept.

About the Author

Sam McGee is an author, trial lawyer and fisherman from North Carolina. His first book, *Sidelines and Bloodlines*, is a college football memoir written with his referee father and sportswriter brother.

Cartledge Creek is his debut novel, and is inspired by his family's true Civil War story. As a teenager, Sam used to tell everyone who would listen that he would one day buy the old family homeplace back into the family.

He and his wife Marci did so in 2006. That house is the site of much of what happens in *Cartledge Creek*. Sam and Marci live in North Carolina with children Hannah Cole and Brooks, and cats Scout and Calpurnia.

Other Books by Fireship Press

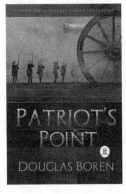

Patriot's Point
Alexander Family Chronicles, Book I
Douglas Boren

1780: At the Battle of Waxhaw, NC, the British Legion massacres the unresisting soldiers of the Virginia Regiment instead of accepting their surrender. In the aftermath, colonists—ordinary men and women, farmers, shopkeepers, and back woodsmen—come together in secret at an abandoned Spanish mission, renaming it Patriot's Point. There they organize themselves into a fighting force, vowing to contain the British advance at all cost until the Continental Army can retaliate. Fewer than two hundred men stand in defiance of over five thousand British soldiers: two hundred patriots, who understand that freedom is not free.

"Patriot's Point takes the reader from the innocence of desire through the blood of need in this fast-paced historic masterpiece." — Dinah Roseberry, author of The Ghosts of Valley Forge and Phoenixville

Beyond the Horizons
Alexander Family Chronicles, Book II
Douglas Boren

In the early days of the Civil War, when things were going mostly for the South, the Confederacy planned to extend its empire to California, taking advantage of the Pacific ports and vast goldfields. But first, they had to secure the New Mexico Territory.

For Mace Alexander and his friends, the Civil War was just the beginning. Through the crucible of war, they would become brothers... though not all would survive. In the broiling heat of the desert and across sun-swept mountains, they would become frontiersmen.

But the deadliest, most ruthless enemy of all awaited them... the Apache Snake Dancers! Their ferocity threatened to drive out the struggling white man forever. In the inevitable clash, there could only be one victor, one survivor. Only one to see... beyond the horizons.

For the Finest in Nautical and Historical Fiction and Non-Fiction
www.FireshipPress.com

Interesting • Informative • Authoritative

All Fireship Press books are available through leading bookstores and wholesalers worldwide.